Skylife

Skylife

*Space Habitats
in Story
and Science*

EDITED, WITH
AN INTRODUCTION
AND NOTES, BY
**Gregory
Benford**
AND
**George
Zebrowski**

HARCOURT, INC.
New York   San Diego   London

Requests for permission to make copies of any part of the work
should be mailed to the following address: Permissions Department,
Harcourt, Inc., 6277 Sea Harbor Drive, Orlando, Florida 32887-6777.

"Open Loops" copyright © 2000 by Stephen Baxter.
"Reef" copyright © 2000 by Paul J. McAuley.

Library of Congress Cataloging-in-Publication Data
Skylife: space habitats in story and science/edited,
with an introduction and notes by Gregory Benford and
George Zebrowski. — 1st ed.
p.   cm.
ISBN 0-15-100292-4
1. Science fiction, American.   2. Science fiction, English.
3. Space colonies — Fiction.   I. Benford, Gregory, 1941–
II. Zebrowski, George, 1945–
PS648.S3 S47   2000
813'.0876208 21 — dc21   99-045540

Text set in Electra
Designed by Kaelin Chappell
Printed in the United States of America
First edition
H G F E D C B A

Permissions acknowledgments appear on pages 353–55,
which constitute a continuation of the copyright page.

TO THE VISIONARIES:

Konstantin Tsiolkovsky

Robert H. Goddard

Hermann Oberth

J. D. Bernal

Olaf Stapledon

Dandridge M. Cole

Arthur C. Clarke

Freeman Dyson

Carl Sagan

who always knew what we
repeatedly forget — that before
anything can be done, it must
first be imagined, and that
guarding every door to our
possible futures stand a
thousand guardians of the past.

Contents

In my personal view of the human situation, the exploration of space appears as the most hopeful feature of a dark landscape.

—Freeman Dyson

In another generation it will seem incredible that intelligent men ever questioned the value of the space program.

—Arthur C. Clarke

Skylife

Introduction:
We All Live in the Sky

GREGORY BENFORD

GEORGE ZEBROWSKI

First there was a flying island.

Then there was a brick moon.

The inventors, Jonathan Swift (*Gulliver's Travels*, 1726) and Edward Everett Hale, were not entirely serious, but the significance of their visions reached well beyond the engineering inventions of the eighteenth and nineteenth centuries. In Hale's alternative to living on Earth, "The Brick Moon" (1869), and its sequel, "Life on the Brick Moon" (1870), people set up housekeeping inside Earth's first artificial satellite and did quite well. Hale's artificial satellite, the first known presentation of the idea, called attention to a technological innovation implicit in our observations of the Earth-Moon system and that of the other planets that possess moons. What nature could do, we might also do. For Hale, the artificial satellite represented not only a technological feat but also the expansion of human possibilities, a vision of social experimentation beyond the confines of Earth. Space exploration has ever since carried the hope of a social and cultural renaissance resulting from the continuation of human life beyond the planetary cradle.

Such visions increased toward the end of the nineteenth century and throughout the twentieth, as if humanity were trying on one after another. They make an impressive library of both fiction and nonfiction. Their foresight in the development of space travel and other technological advances is well known to generations of scientists and engineers for whom works of imagination provided the inspiration and pioneering discussions from which to make practical what seemed fanciful. This anthology highlights some key works of the past, together with fresh visions, and provides a context in which to grasp their immediate and long-term significance. If humankind survives and is not hobbled by setbacks, the attempts to realize these and other visions may exceed all past accomplishments and may redefine our ideas of what are and are not practical expectations.

It does not seem strange in hindsight that the idea of space colonies should have become so prominent in the United States, a nation that has itself been described as a science-fictional experiment. The American attempt at a dynamic utopian vision — based on a constitutional separation of powers and the intended, orderly struggle of those powers with one another as a way to deal with a quarrelsome human nature — is still in progress. But it is also held back by the limits of planetary life.

The first major twentieth-century vision of humanity in space was set down in all seriousness, and with extraordinary thoroughness, by the deaf Russian schoolteacher Konstantin Tsiolkovsky (1857–1935). He did not try to match Jules Verne and H. G. Wells as a writer of stories, but his fiction and nonfiction set out with great imagination and technical lucidity the scientific and engineering principles to be applied in leaving Earth, and presented nearly all the reasons, cultural and economic, why human capabilities should be expanded beyond Earth. He saw that the entire sunspace was rich in resources and energy and could be occupied. Every step from space capsule to moonship was itself a small habitat, a way of taking a bit of our home world, its air and food, with us into the cosmos.

From its earliest beginnings, the concept of space travel is already heavy with possibilities, developing from small vessels to large space stations orbiting Earth, the Moon, or the Sun, and onto the surfaces of planets and their satellites, to the sweeping visions of skylife. It is a large achievement in imagination, and even larger in the doing, to go from these small exploratory steps to the idea of seriously planning permanent new homes for humanity—ones capable of growing, reproducing, and proliferating throughout our sunspace, and beyond.

It was not long before science fiction writers, scientists, and engineers started exploring, in both dramatic and engineering exercises, the myriad possibilities in the idea of space travel. For many years the concept of space habitats lived in science fiction stories about space stations and large ships, and in a number of novels featuring the "generation ship." Olaf Stapledon's *Star Maker* (1937) described the use of whole worlds, natural and artificial, for interstellar travel and warfare. Edward E. "Doc" Smith, today called the father of the *Star Wars* movie saga, used planets similarly in his Skylark and Lensman series of the 1920s, 1930s, and 1940s. Isaac Asimov, in his Foundation stories of the 1940s, showed us Trantor, an artificial city-planet that rules the galaxy.

In general, writers of the golden age of modern science fiction (roughly the late 1930s to the late 1940s) made great advances beyond the idea of the simple spaceship and space station. Don Wilcox's "The Voyage That Lasted Six Hundred Years" (1940) introduced the idea of the generation starship as a means of reaching the stars, in the form that was to be often imitated, one year before Robert A. Heinlein's more famous stories, "Universe" and "Common Sense"—gritty realistic dramas of travelers aboard a space ark who learn, in the manner of a Copernican-Galilean revolution, that their world is a ship.

The understated lines that close "Universe," after the major characters have learned the truth about their world's nature and purpose, are memorable in their implications: "I'm going to show him the stars, prove to him that the Ship moves... We've got to do it, you know" (42).

The uneasy familiarity of generation starship stories springs from our seeing the Earth as a ship, the stars as other suns. Many people either know this fact or are dimly aware of it; but the realization can still startle us in the midst of practical daily life, which tends to push larger truths from our minds. In generation starship stories we see something of how our view of the universe changed in the last thousand years, and how we have come to know our place in it. Any grasp of space habitats must start by our understanding that Earth is a giant biological ark circling its sun.

As in Heinlein's "Universe," the dispelling of illusion and misconception lays the groundwork for surprising hopes and the expansion of human horizons.

Behind the science fiction stories stood visionary nonfiction such as J. D. Bernal's 1929 *The World, the Flesh, and the Devil*, which pictures an urban ring of worlds around the Earth. In the 1950s, Arthur C. Clarke and Wernher von Braun envisioned space stations as giant wheels spinning to maintain centrifugal "gravity." Such stations would orbit the Earth to observe weather, refuel interplanetary spaceships, and train astronauts who would later set up bases on the Moon and Mars. These were conservative proposals that even today are far from realization.

The engineer Dandridge Cole, in his bold and comprehensive visions in the early 1960s, called space settlements "Macro-Life." These might be new habitats constructed from advanced materials, or nestled inside captured asteroids, which would be hollowed out by mining their metals. Asimov described the same concept as "multiorganismic life" and coined his own term, *spome*, for space home. Cole envisioned Macro-Life as the ultimate human society, because of its open-ended adaptability, and delved into its sociology. Asimov proposed the scattering of spomes as insurance for the survival of humankind. Both thinkers saw space settlements as a natural step, as significant as life's emergence from the sea. Cole wrote:

> Taking man as representative of multicelled life, we can say that man is the mean proportional between Macro-Life and the cell. Macro-Life is a new life form of gigantic size which has for its cells individual human beings, plants, animals, and machines.... Society can be said to be pregnant with a mutant creature which will be at the same time an extraterrestrial colony of human beings and a new large-scale life form. (44, 46)

He defined his habitats as a life-form because they would think with their component minds, human and artificial; move; respond to stimuli; and reproduce.

Residing in space's immensities offered a unique extension of the human community, an innovation as fundamental as the development of urban civilization in the enlightened Greek city-state. Yet living in the rest of the space around our sun also re-created some desirable aspects of rural life, since habitats would have to be self-contained and ecologically sophisticated, with the attentiveness to environment that comes from knowing that problems cannot be passed on to future generations.

The arguments that have been presented for such a long-term undertaking are economic, social, and cultural. Few would deny that the solar system offers an immense industrial base of energy and materials, enough to deal with all the problems facing humanity. We live under a sky full of wealth, but our technological nets are too small to catch what we need from the cornucopia above our heads.

Hard Science, High Dreams

While science fiction writers used the idea of space habitats for dramatic stories, engineers and scientists brought to it an increasingly revealing verisimilitude. Fundamentals of physics and economics came into play, and revealed the realities behind what seemed to be merely pleasing speculations. It is not necessary to understand every technical or mathematical detail to see that, in the past century, reality has taken over from imagination's impetus—as the following brief review shows.

Space colonies have some advantages over our natural satellite, the Moon. A rocket needs to achieve a velocity change of 6 km/sec to go from low Earth orbit to the lunar surface. That same rocket can go to Mars with only about 4.5 km/sec investment, if it uses a shell to brake in the upper Martian atmosphere. Also, any deep-space operations could be much better managed from an orbit out beyond the particle fluxes of our magnetic Van Allen Belt, a fraction of the way to the Moon.

Lunar resources are principally rocks that have about half their mass in oxygen. But the Moon has nothing we can unite with that oxygen to burn, such as hydrogen or methane. Since oxygen is a big fraction of chemical fuel mass, usually about three-quarters, the Moon's oxygen would be valuable if it did not cost so much to lift into orbit. (We would also need very high temperature techniques to bake the oxygen out of hard rock.)

Early on, many noted that in energy expended, once one has lifted a mass from Earth to the orbit of the Moon, one is halfway to the asteroid belt—indeed, to most of the rest of the solar system. This is because the planets have considerable gravity wells, but the difference in gravitational energy between the orbit of the Earth and, say, an orbit as far away as Mars is not great. A typical asteroid, gliding in its ellipse between Mars and Jupiter, moves at about 24 km/sec. Earth moves about the Sun at about 30 km/sec. That difference of 6 km/sec is what a spacecraft must provide to move between those two regions. Many asteroids do not orbit the Sun in precisely the same plane as Earth (the plane of the ecliptic); changing that inclination costs about a km/sec for each two degrees of alteration. To reach most interesting asteroids requires changes of about four degrees, so the total cost in "delta V" is 10 km/sec. Going from Earth's surface to the Moon's orbit requires 11.4 km/sec, about the same energy cost.

To someone contemplating a livable satellite in roughly lunar orbit, then, getting raw materials from the asteroids is equivalent in energy expenditure to lifting resources from Earth. Even though the asteroids are, in total flight distance, a thousand times farther away, they have advantages. Maneuvering in deep space is a matter of slow and steady, not flashy and dramatic. High-thrust takeoffs from Earth are expensive, and payloads have to be protected against the heat of rapid passage through the atmosphere.

A tugboat spaceship operating in the asteroid belt could load up long chains of barges and slowly boost them to the needed 10 km/sec, taking perhaps months to do so. Powered by lightweight photovoltaic cells, the tugboat would get the energy for this from sunlight, and perhaps from an additional onboard small nuclear reactor. It would sling mass out the back at high speed, using an electromagnetic accelerator as a kind of electrodynamic rocket. The mass would come from the asteroids themselves, which are rich in iron. Once the barges were set on their long, silent, sloping trajectory toward the inner solar system, the tug and crew would cast off. They would return to the asteroid mining community, to start hooking up to the next line of barges.

At the end of their eight-month flight to Earth the barges would be pulled into rendezvous with a factory that would break down the metals they carry. The cheapest method of using these resources would be to manufacture finished goods in orbit, taking advantage of the ease of handling provided by low or zero gravity. Otherwise, the costly shipping of raw materials down to Earth's surface becomes necessary.

But such shipping assumes that Earth will forever be the final market. It would cost perhaps $10,000 per pound to move metals from the asteroids to near-lunar orbit, a cost far higher than that of supertanker transport on our oceans. And the manufactured product would still need to be moved to the market for it on Earth. Clearly a better way would be the construction of colonies and factories in orbit themselves.

The logical end of this argument is simply to move an asteroid into near-Earth orbit. This demands the setting up of electromagnetic accelerators on a metallic asteroid and slinging mined packets of iron-rich mass aft to accelerate the whole body. The tugboat becomes the cargo. Studies show that at the optimum exhaust velocity of the slung pellets, about a quarter of the asteroid's mass would have to be pitched away at about 50 km/sec to get the asteroid into near-Earth orbit.

In moving the asteroid, one shapes it, hollowing it out for the mass to sling overboard, and applying spin to produce centrifugal gravity on the inner surface. We know a good deal about what asteroids contain, from studying their reflected light. Even today, prospectors can know more about the composition of an asteroid a hundred million miles away than they can find out, without drilling, about what lies a mile below their feet.

Asteroids should be good sources of the metals hardest to find in Earth's crust. They should also have the structural integrity to sustain a moderate centrifugal gravity on the inside, once a cylindrical space has been bored into them. A simple equation demonstrates the relation between spin and radius: $A = S^2 R/1000$. Here A is the centrifugal acceleration in units of Earth's gravitational acceleration, so $A = 1$ is Earth-normal. S is the spin of the cylindrical space in units of a revolution per minute. R is the radius of the hollowed-out cylinder in meters. For example, consider a cylinder of 100 meters radius and spinning about three times per minute; then A is near Earth-normal. The importance of this equation is that one can select high R (for a big colony on the inner surface of the cylindrical space) and spin it slowly, or high spin (large S) and a small colony, low R. NASA experiments of the 1960s showed that people in small containers could take spins up to 6 revolutions per minute without disorienting effects.

The asteroid's massive outer layer would easily protect against background radiation, especially cosmic rays. These "heavy primaries" flooding our solar system are nuclei of helium, carbon, iron, and higher elements. They smash through matter, leaving a train of ionized atoms that can kill a living cell. The Apollo astronauts noticed these energetic events as bright flashes in their eyes every few minutes, even in total darkness. Venturing outside Earth's atmosphere and, more important, its magnetic field, which serves as the main shield against cosmic rays, the astronauts incurred some nerve and cell damage, though it was insignificant. James Gunn, in his novel *Station in Space* (1958), presented this as a disquieting detail, calling our attention to human frailty outside its usual environment.

Living constantly in such conditions demands heavy shielding, about two meters of dirt or rock. This sets a huge requirement for the built-from-scratch O'Neill colony that was to come in the 1970s. The O'Neill design had to carry this mass in its outer rim and support the "weight" of centrifugal acceleration with steel struts—a huge fabrication-and-construction job, even using raw materials from the Moon. By comparison, a cored asteroid is much safer.

The hope behind this ambitious plan was that opening the solar system to industrial development would provide two important resources—sunlight and metals—right from the start. Early visions considered dropping metal-rich rocks directly onto Earth, making iron mountains to mine. Imagine having to write the environmental impact report for that today!—and having to calculate risks, get insurance, and so on.

The second development stage would come atop the first: direct manufacture in space, using the advantages of zero gravity and vacuum.

Chemicals and nutrients mix much more thoroughly in zero gravity, since they do not settle out by weight. Making "foamsteels" with tiny bubbles evenly distributed throughout seems possible, greatly reducing mass while losing little strength. Growing enormous carbon filaments for superstrong fibers seems straightforward. Similar methods, as spelled out in G. Harry Stine's *The Third Industrial Revolution*, sparked the optimism of the 1970s.

Generally, the more scientists learned of space as a real environment, the more hemmed in the writers became. But while the "hard" science fiction authors used these stubborn facts to fashion clever and insightful stories, the visionary intuitions behind the central idea remained plausible, and technical scrutiny supported the high dreams.

A Lofty Frontier

In the 1970s, Gerard O'Neill, a prominent physicist at Princeton University, conducted an advanced engineering feasibility study on space settlements, and reexamined the ideas that Cole and others had developed. O'Neill's group optimistically concluded that the technology already existed. The Moon could be mined as a source of raw materials, and once the first worldlets were built, they would quickly reproduce. The colonies would build solar collectors and beam microwave power back to Earth, as well as export to Earth manufactured goods and the results of research-and-development facilities.

O'Neill asked whether a space settlement of this kind would be viable. A huge requirement for his now classic O'Neill colony was heavy shielding from background radiation, especially cosmic rays, in the form of about two meters of dirt or rock. That design had to carry this mass in its outer rim and support its centrifugal "weight," or spin acceleration, with steel struts—a massive construction job, even with the more easily lofted lunar materials.

There is a crucial difficulty that exists in the use of raw sunlight as a source of energy. The scheme envisions capturing strong sunlight and converting it into microwave energy, then transmitting it by large antennas to Earth, for transformation into electrical power. Later studies showed that unmanned satellites in lower orbits would provide power more cheaply, but these studies led to no projects. As we shall see, the social dimension has loomed large in the plans of even the most detailed technical scenarios.

Direct sunlight is fine and good as a source of electrical power, but growing crops for people in the O'Neill-style colonies is another matter. Plants require considerable power themselves; a square kilometer of prime cropland absorbs a gigawatt of sunlight at high noon, the power output of the largest electrical powerhouses, capable of supporting a city of a million souls. Under less illumination plants still grow, but evolution has finely engineered them; at a tenth of the solar flux, they stagnate. This means that no artificial environment can afford the costs of growing plants beneath electrical lights.

However, the raw sunlight of space is harsh. Earth-adapted plants would wither under the sting of its ultraviolet. There is more solar power available in space, but it is at the high end of the spectrum, which on Earth is filtered out by our ozone layer and atmosphere. Certainly ultraviolet-absorbing canopies can be deployed, but the weather between the worlds has harsher stuff in store. Thin greenhouse shells on O'Neill colonies would not protect against solar flares of such ferocity as occur every few months. Defending people and plants against these fluxes of high-energy particles demands at least five-inch-thick glass, a massive measure. (Indeed, O'Neill colonies have much of their design dedicated to protecting people against solar storms by providing interior shelters. But if people can be moved to shelter for a few hours, crops cannot.)

In the early 1980s O'Neill spoke throughout the United States to drum up support for his ideas and for the National Space Society, which he founded. Already the O'Neill-colony idea (a term he modestly never used, preferring "L-5," the abbreviation for the Lagrangian point that some thought would make the most stable orbit for a colony) was beginning to fade from the public mind. The 1975–85 spike in oil prices was momentary; fossil fuel would within five years plunge to the same cost level (in inflation-adjusted dollars) as 1950. O'Neill's basic assumption, that electrical energy would be hard to generate on the Earth's surface without high costs both economically and environmentally, may yet come true, but market forces and improved technology have taken a lot of steam out of the argument.

Still, O'Neill's salesmanship put the entire agenda forward as no other cultural force had. Economics was central to the movement, blended with social ideas. The cover of the paperback edition of *The High Frontier* (Bantam, 1978) proclaimed; "They're coming! Space colonies — hope for your future." And the back cover sold space colonies as future suburban paradises, with Earth as the city to flee.

Historical parallels abound. The immigrants of the *Mayflower* and the Mormons who moved to Utah came with about two tons per person of investment goods. Freeman Dyson in *Disturbing the Universe* argued that these are better societal models for space colonization than the O'Neill notion of totally planned homes. O'Neill's detailed Island One project would cost about $96 billion in 1979 dollars, and perhaps twice that today. Clearly, such a project would be so massive that only governments could run it. As Dyson remarked, "The government can afford to waste money but it cannot afford to be responsible for a disaster" (125).

O'Neill argued that his colony could build solar collectors and beam microwave power back to Earth to pay its bills. At the energy prices of the late 1970s, he said, the $96 billion could be repaid within 24 years. But a colonist would take 1,500 years to pay off the costs by his own labor, which means the colony would always be a government enterprise, subject to the vagaries of political will of those who lived far away—not a prescription for long-term stability.

Thus Dyson favors asteroid colonization, precisely because it could be done for less and by large families, not large nations. He imagines settlers moving out from early orbital colonies, though not necessarily of the massive O'Neill type. In *Disturbing the Universe* he invokes even scavenging, noting that "there are already today several hundred derelict spacecraft in orbit around the Earth, besides a number on the moon, waiting for our asteroid pioneers to collect and refurbish them" (126). The satellite business would dearly love to see such debris erased from the equatorial orbital belt, since collisions with them loom now as a significant threat to the future of orbital safety.

O'Neill revisited ideas that had been around for most of a century, both in serious speculation and in visionary fiction, but he gave them the plausibility of the latest styles and engineering methods in space exploration. Gary Westfahl's pioneering study, *Islands in the Sky* (1996), documents how others had dreamed these dreams, reminding us that

> Konstantin Tsiolkovsky was boldly predicting in "Changes in Relative Weight" (1894) and *Dreams of Earth and Sky* (1895), that there would be communities in space with millions of inhabitants.... J. M. Walsh's *Vandals of the Void* (1930) and Murray Leinster's "The Power Planet" (1931) both depict space stations which are large and impressive, each housing hundreds of inhabitants, one a space fortress and the other a power station. Jack Williamson's "The Prince of Space" (1931) depicts a perfectly realized space habitat: "They were, Bill saw, at the center of an enormous cylinder. The sides, half a mile away, above and below them were covered with buildings, along neat, tree-bordered streets, scattered with green lawns, tiny gardens, and bits of wooded park.... As they stepped out, it gave Bill a curious dizzy feeling to look up and see busy streets, inverted, a mile above his head. The road before them curved smoothly up on either hand, bordered with beautiful trees, until its end met again above his head."

So much for the claim that O'Neill and his students "literally invented" the idea! Everett C. Smith and R. F. Starzl's "The Metal Moon" (1932) features a similar idea, a huge inhabited globe with an upper half enclosed in crystal with beautiful, Earthlike scenery. A large flying city in space figures in H. Thompson Rich's "The Flying City" (1930). Basil E. Wells's "Factory in the Sky" (1941) is a gigantic sphere in the asteroid belt which is home to over a million people. C. L. Moore's *Judgment Night* (1942) features a massive, artificial "pleasure world" offering a variety of diverse environments. Even in George O. Smith's *Venus Equilateral* stories . . . the solar satellite was actually a functioning community of 500 people, with a broad range of facilities and amenities, described as "so much like a town on Terra." And in the next decade, there are the Space Terminal seen in Robert A. Heinlein's "Space Jockey" (1947), said to resemble an Earth city, the "artificial moon" in Arthur C. Clarke's "The Lion of Comarre" (1949), the twenty-two large resort satellites of Jack Vance's "Abercrombie Station" (1952) . . . (28)

Westfahl raises a point that may be the most significant for the future of space habitats: Why has the extensive science-fictional history of this idea been forgotten?

Westfahl writes that "there are four times during the development of the genre when space stations emerged as important factors—and four times when they faded from view" (29). These were in the late nineteenth century, the 1930s, the 1950s, and the 1970s. Since science fiction has often predicted developments in space travel, this repeated decline of interest in space habitats shows that science fiction is not immune to the waxing and waning interest in ideas as they emerge in serious speculation and in popular culture. The reasons for the decline in project planning may have been human fears, lack of political will, and economic cold feet, with science fiction following suit, often with critical or disappointed treatments of the idea—except in the cases of innovative authors, who in more disillusioned periods might seem out of touch to readers and critics. Construction of the United States *Space Station Freedom* in the late 1990s portends a fresh burgeoning of the idea. In science fiction it has become a staple, used either for utopian or dystopian presentations.

In both fictional worlds and in the possibilities waiting in the real world, to confront space habitats seriously means a complete change in our outlook toward the solar system. Many have argued persuasively that the grand project of uplifting the bulk of humanity to the economic level of the advanced nations requires use of the solar system's resources, especially since manufacturing entails a level of pollution that the biosphere cannot abide. (This hard fact makes impossible the more cozy stories of expansive industrial futures.) To use the resources of our sunspace demands treating it as a genuine "new frontier," not just as a place to go and come back from. But the fundamental changes needed to create a sunspace society are simply too radical for many people, who see such changes as either frightening or infinitely risky. Perhaps it is right for social systems to leave innovation to the visionaries and pioneers; either they will succeed or fail, thus alerting the culture about which way to grow.

Unfortunately, the culture's sometimes useful critical resistance may also destroy valuable developments, leaving them to emerge at a later time or to die.

The style of discussion and pictorial presentation of skylife changed by the 1970s, but the substance was the same. Once again it dawned on researchers—scientists and engineers as well as writers of science fiction—that the planet of our origin may not necessarily be the best place to carry on the business of civilization; that this inadequacy, born of limits that have threatened to choke off the possibilities made plain by our increasing knowledge and technology, might hold for all natural planets; and that sooner or later, we might have no choice but to build the city of man elsewhere.

For a time in the 1970s and early 1980s the popular press, as well as various scientific and technological publications, carried many articles and pictorial visions of space colonies. Bernal Spheres, O'Neill Cylinders, and hollowed-out asteroids showed us parklike and urban environments floating in space, offering secular heavens to the masses of the dying Earth. If it came to a choice between a finite planet, zero population growth, restrictive social regimentation, and rationing of ever dwindling natural resources on the one hand and the openness of free space on the other, then the idea of space settlement seemed about to take on the classic proportions of an idea whose time had come. There would be problems, but at least they would not be our current problems.

Many thinkers argued that here was an economic high ground worthy of culture and technology, that when taken would lead to a permanent, mature civilization. Space settlements were that high ground, the visionaries insisted; but we would have to build them before we could be certain of success, which in human affairs was never guaranteed. Waiting for the right time might mean waiting forever, risking a decline from which humanity might never recover. History was a consistent record of the good happening alongside the bad; to hesitate might be disastrous, hurling us into the irreversible decline of Arnold Toynbee's two dozen failed civilizations, with no new ground upon which to begin again. Such was the argument against the "prioritizers." Asimov wrote to the skeptics:

> I have received a number of letters concerning my article "Colonizing the Heavens."
>
> Some call it fiction. (Real nonsense, I suppose, like reaching the Moon.)
>
> Some say I am trying to subvert the doctrine of Zero Population Growth. (As though it weren't possible to try to colonize space and stop the population growth, too. They are not mutually exclusive.)
>
> Some say it is too expensive. (Not if the world stops supporting military machines.)
>
> Some say that nobody wants an engineered environment. (Nobody? How many people are living in caves these days?)
>
> Some say that nobody would ever want to cross space in three days to live in a space colony. (This from people whose ancestors two or three generations back probably crossed the Atlantic in steerage, or crossed the western desert in covered wagons.)
>
> Some say that Third World people would never go. (Sure. Only aristocrats fled to the New World. All the tired, the poor, the huddled masses yearning to breathe free never came, did they?)
>
> Some say let's solve our problems on Earth before we try to colonize space. (Someone said that to the Pilgrims. Come on, they said, let's solve our problems right here in Europe.) (*The Beginning and the End*, 214)

For Asimov, colonies were not primarily technological feats. He echoed the prevailing historical sense of this age: that frontiers have shaped our world by unleashing new ideas with the European explosion outward. These ideas might have died except for the unrestricted ground of the frontier, where the old cultures could not kill them with preemptive criticism and outright suppression. Space was to be a ground for change, not just suburbs in vacuum. The advocates for skylife were seeking to build castles not in the airless but on the firmest of economic foundations — the great wealth of our sunspace.

Social Spaces

From the beginning, space colonies were advanced not only with the assertion that they were possible, but also out of a concern for the future welfare and survival of humanity. Tsiolkovsky wrote in 1912:

> To step out onto the soil of asteroids, to lift with your hand a stone on the Moon, to set up moving stations in ethereal space, and establish living rings around the Earth, the Moon, the Sun, to observe Mars from a distance of several tens of versts, to land on its satellites and even on the surface of Mars — what could be more extravagant! However, it is only with the advent of reactive vehicles that a new and great era in astronomy will begin, the epoch of a careful study of the sky . . . The prime motive of my life is to do something useful for people . . . That is why I have interested myself in things that did not give me bread or strength. But I hope that my studies will if not soon but perhaps in the distant future, yield society mountains of grain and limitless power. (qtd. in Sagan 71)

Some of this deaf Russian schoolteacher's credo has been realized, but much more can be done.

After Tsiolkovsky, arguments over purpose continued to develop: the whole point of space settlements was to build living, self-repairing and self-reproducing, potentially mobile environments. These would follow the model of natural homeostasis, not the model of social prosthetics, as cities are to a large degree. All crude forms of technology are historically just temporary aids. A responsive social organism is not a slap-dash effort to fit nature with peg legs.

Physics has its place in space settlements, but the crucial sciences supporting a civilization in space are the biological and social sciences.

The greatest return will come not in purely technological advances but in the psychosocial benefits of a revitalized humanity. O'Neill wrote in 1976:

> I believe that our children will judge the most important benefits of space colonization to have been not physical or economic, but the opening of new human options, the possibility of a new degree of freedom, not only for the human body, but much more important, for the human spirit and sense of aspiration. (33)

This thought echoed both Clarke's view of space exploration as beginning a new human cultural renaissance and the views of many social thinkers and scientists, who have warned that a society must not be an end in itself. Organization, with social groups as with living organisms, is double-edged: a secure system may simply consume and repeat itself endlessly. When a society has no prophetic dreams, there is no creativity.

One observation that has been made about the foresight of most human beings, including scientists and science fiction writers, is that in hindsight their views of possible future developments have been consistently too conservative. An ambitious effort of the imagination must be made to see what is physically possible, even when that possibility is humanly difficult or seems unlikely.

Picture thousands of space settlements, ranging in size from a few kilometers to a hundred kilometers or more in diameter, orbiting the Sun, catching our star's energy in an urban shell of space habitats. The societies are pluralistic, constantly diverging in design and philosophies. New ones are being born as population increases. Some even leave the solar system to explore other sunspaces.

Now jump even further ahead: space settlements, spomes, or macrolife (whatever they may be called) are the dominant urban civilization in various sectors of our galaxy. Planets are considered the galaxy's countryside. Some habitats are mobile; others stay at home and surround various stars in what has been called a Dyson Sphere (after Dyson), which can be designed as a porous shell of worlds or sections of a solid sphere. If one were to build only the equatorial belt, then we have Larry Niven's Ringworld, first introduced in the novel of the same name. And to dispel finally any misconceptions one may have about space habitats beyond those of the first, limited space stations, one must do a little calculation.

The mobiles need not be cramped spaces and metal corridors, or small, in comparison to planets. As Asimov described in his 1956 story, "Strikebreaker":

> We are not a small world, Dr. Lamorak; you judge us by two-dimensional standards. The surface area of Elsevere is only three-quarters that of the State of New York, but that's irrelevant. Remember, we can occupy, if we wish, the entire interior of Elsevere. A sphere of 50 miles radius has a volume of well over half a million cubic miles. If all of Elsevere were occupied by levels 50 feet apart, the total surface area within the planetoid would be 56,000,000 square miles, and that is equal to the total land area of Earth. And none of these square miles, Doctor, would be unproductive. (268)

The doctor from Earth, who has come to study a humanity that "had burrowed into that miniature world and constructed a society in it" is surprised that "he had never thought of it that way" (268–69). And yet Asimov's conception may still be seen as conservative, when one considers mobiles hundreds of kilometers or more across, with spacious skies and the ability to reproduce.

Surface area depends on the square of a given distance, while volume depends on the cube. This simple fact means that honeycombing an asteroid provides immense livable room. If the chunk of rock has a typical size R, then one can riddle it with levels for habitation, each separated by, say, a typical distance H. Simple geometry says that the living area of such an enormous apartment house would be of order R^3/H. People need head room of about two meters, and a bit extra for structural support and piping in air and fluids. Probably this sets the net spacing of living levels at a number like H = 4 meters.

We can then ask how big an asteroid need be to give us living room equal to the entire area of the Earth, even including the oceans. That is, we set our R^3/H equal to the surface area of the Earth, $4\pi R_e^2$, for a radius R_e = 6,300 kilometers. Plugging these numbers in and solving, one finds R is about a hundred kilometers. This is remarkable, for there are many asteroids of such size; the largest, Ceres, is 380 kilometers. A Dyson Sphere or Ringworld would have the surface area of millions of Earths. A little bit of mathematics changes our outlook qualitatively, enabling us to look further.

The idea of all humanity living inside a rock only about two hundred kilometers in diameter sounds wildly improbable, at first. But the scaling emerges because of the cubic increase of volume with size. Our hidden assumption, of course, is that unlike on the Earth's surface, one could settle people inside and still supply the needed air and light. Sunlight drives our earthly environment's engines; an asteroid colony would need some power supply. At most, the power needed would be comparable to that received by the Earth as sunlight—about 10^{17} watts, an enormous figure compared with the 10^{13} watts the asteroid would receive in sunlight at the same distance from the Sun. But of course the colony would not need all that energy, nor would it be able to shed the waste heat generated from it after use. On Earth a person in an advanced nation uses several kilowatts steadily, so five billion people would require perhaps 10^{13} watts, just about the incoming sunlight. These numbers are crude guesses, but they give some idea of the scales involved.

Most habitat stories feature an obligatory walk around the artifact scene. A common game played down through the decades was the my-artifact's-bigger-than-your-artifact competition, culminating in works such as Larry Niven's *Ringworld* and the Dyson Spheres of novels such as Bob Shaw's *Orbitsville*. Niven's essay in this volume takes such ideas to their ultimate physical limits, and somewhat beyond.

Sheer scale is an easy way to evoke awe. But space habitats can use cold engineering triumphs to evoke dainty beauty. While space is vast, those living in it may inhabit if not cramped then firmly bounded preserves. What would such limits do to the shadowy depths of our psyches? Charles Sheffield, in his story "Transition Team" (1978), argued that the transformation of mentality is total and irreversible.

Using the volumes of all the known asteroids would yield a new equivalent land area of about 3,000 times Earth's total surface. This suggests that material limits are not primary in determining the possibilities open to humanity; social goals set our ends.

A sprawling, sunspace civilization would not be resource-limited, unlike human societies throughout history. It could live for influence and curiosity, for the power to educate and persuade. Knowing and creating would become more important than economics and personal power. Style and novelty would rule within a stable economic container that could support an endlessly developing string of cultures. Karl Marx and Adam Smith would both be subsumed, because economics becomes truly basic—and irrelevant. Thomas Malthus has been circumvented, because there is a Peter with practically infinite pockets who can be robbed to pay Paul. In this seemingly utopian vision that is nevertheless entirely achievable by all that we know of physical reality, poverty is possible only on emerging planets—which must go through their own rites of passage, their own quantum jumps into self-sufficiency—and no one can help them without doing irreparable psychosocial damage. Our human history may very well be at such a critical juncture now, with only our reason and creative imagination to draw us out of the cradle that might become a tomb if we delay.

Perhaps this description holds the answer to Fermi's Paradox, which asks: If the universe is full of intelligent life, then where are they? One answer may be that most cannot visit us because they are held back by the forbidding economics of interstellar travel; and that those who can do not wish to. Another answer contends that the rise of reason leads to catastrophic modifications of the environment, both external and bodily, and the species perishes. Those who reach a subtle stage of rational development without destroying themselves, or are not destroyed by natural disasters, have no interest in contacting lesser species. The advanced ones converse only with those of their level of achievement, if at all, since such dialog may pose dangers. Or perhaps nearly all intelligent cultures in our galaxy are still provincials in space and time, in their sense of history and grasp of technical possibilities. The possible answers to Fermi's Paradox are many.

Our dilemma is clearly posed by human history: intelligence is at first an innovation, then flares into conflict with its environment, then threatens its environment and itself. If it fails to get past this crisis of "first technologies" and does not grow into a more benign relation with its environment, human intelligence will destroy itself, if not through warfare then through some complex mistake. Skylife may be part of a more productive and satisfying environment for human intelligence—a new adaptation, if we can seize it. But humanity is psychologically frail; failure is the basic theme of our literature and politics, which often regard rationality and creative visions with derision and skepticism.

Unending Utopias

People who live on planets think small, so we must remind ourselves what small means. An average household today commands more horsepower than kings once did. To classify possible civilizations by energy use, as the Russian astrophysicist Kadarshev has proposed, yields a striking perspective. Type I civilizations use the available energy of their whole planet. Type II use the output of their whole sun. Type III harness the power of a galaxy.

We are not even Type I. The possibilities for growth are endless, since the space settlement is a container waiting for a variety of social forms, an economic base for ongoing creativity supported by a high-energy, open-ended industrialism that escapes the restrictions faced by planetary cultures. The mobile space habitat cannot easily die. It is the true fulfillment of the aims of space travel, the ultimate consolidation of gains made by exploiting the space around the Sun. The view from even our cramped, fledgling spaceships has led us to see the planet as an ecological ship circling our sun, and to imagine building worlds from scratch. We have been doing so since civilizations began, in the form of towns and cities, but we have not had enough energy and resources to make our surface habitats work as well as they might.

The idea of space settlements has been decried as technocratic hubris. But nay-saying in the face of solidly based economic and technical challenges leads to social and economic impotence. Like the opening of the Americas, space demands long-term thinking. Reflect that a century passed between Columbus and the first true colony in the New World. Here in the opening decades of a similar epoch, we cannot see any intrinsic limits to sunspace's potential, except possibly psychological ones. It may be that an energy-rich Type I or II culture would face extraordinary problems in the use of its powers, but not in having them. One of the problems might lie in a dangerous scarcity of rebels and critics, because everyone will be so comfortable. (Indeed, does this describe present-day Europe?)

There will certainly be new problems from causes we cannot foresee. Yet we can grasp that the future perfection of our world's problematic industrialism is possible only through an expansion of our horizons, not by shrinking from them. The objections of those who fear that the future may differ from the near past stem from the realization that today's network of familial and corporate power structures may come to an end. Human problems may crumble before human ingenuity, which is always at first a small thing of thoughts and words, dreams and mistakes. Even honestly motivated critics of innovation serve only those who fear the loss of their power and influence in economic and political arenas; they put on the brakes by asking for guaranteed cost projections, for assurances that there will be no mistakes (which means there will be nothing to learn from, no feedback). Objections that ask for this kind of warranty make a well-known logical error known as "the counsel of perfection," which does not recognize degrees of success and therefore seeks to ban any consideration or test of an idea. No demand could place a deadlier obstacle before human creativity.

In *Cannibals and Kings: The Origins of Culture* (1977), the anthropologist Marvin Harris described how technical efficiency depletes resources, precipitating either a sudden decline in a culture or a new level of innovation, which then repeats the same process. But he is ambivalent about the overall pattern of entrapment and futility suggested by his model. The historian of science Bernard Cohen answered him in this way:

> Harris assumes that there have been centuries of post-feudal mechanization and scientific engineering. He doesn't recognize that large-scale innovations in engineering and technology based on advances in fundamental science are a recent phenomenon, barely a century old. It is thus an open question whether future societies may not exhibit a really different growth pattern (even with respect to ecological and reproductive pressures) from that of all previous societies since science has revolutionized the mode of making technological innovations. In any event, as Harris observes... evolutionary theory may make us aware of the "determined nature of the past," but it does not provide the basis for the determination of the future. Admitting that the "intensification of the industrial mode of production undoubtedly portends an evolution of new cultural forms," Harris concludes that he does not "know for certain what these will be, nor does anyone else."

Our energy-rich sunspace can be exploited through the extension of planet-bound forms of social organization, in ways we cannot predict. To give up on catching even a glimpse of the possible patterns is to deny the presence of genuine novelty in history — creative synergies that confront societies with new factors. All shall surely increase as human history accelerates. The exchange between Harris and Cohen is typical of many such debates and suggests a real failure of humanistic culture. Consider that Harris and others who continue to speak do so at a time when the models for creative alternatives — space habitats being only one example — are proliferating in a staggering explosion of human creativity; and this explosion of speculation really began only in the 1970s. Some of these ideas, as Carl Sagan suggested, may become productive social paths.

Through disciplined speculations, such as those of "hard" science fiction, we domesticate imaginative visions within ourselves, trying them on for size and testing them against facts. More, our projections acclimate us to wrenching ideas that do not rest on direct precedent. (Sunspace, after all, will not merely be a replay of the New World. Much tragedy may be avoided; space has no native inhabitants that we know of in this solar system.) Yet this kind of dreaming, with one's eyes and mind open, is still in short supply.

The social and political obstacles to space settlements loom large. Economic objections have grown even stronger since the 1970s. It may be that these objections may never be answered in advance to everyone's satisfaction. And if they could be answered, they might be presented too rigidly and become an obstacle in themselves — so the only way to move ahead may very well be the usual messy paths by which large changes have occurred in the past, some combination of business and visionary megalomania. After hearing all the rational reasons for and against space travel, solar system industrialization, interstellar travel, and mobile habitats, there may come a day when a hard-bitten yet romantic human being will say, "Oh, yeah? We'll do it anyway." Reason and the seeming defiance of it are humanity's right and left hands, and our greatest creative asset, the very heart of the inductive method, which has been described as throwing one's hat over the cliff and jumping after it. Let us hope that practical pioneers make the leap before the shortsighted experts and tired politicians gut them of their will and imagination, turning them into overly doubting invalids, cautious and incapable.

Foresight, at its best, sees only the next few steps. The overall pattern of civilization's developments off-planet are not for us to predetermine; but we should at least not go backward, or in circles. We will need the unique perspective of those who live off the Earth. We've had a taste of this perspective in the view of Earth from space brought back by the astronauts, and in their personal testimonies.

Many have argued that the word *utopian* should be used not in the pejorative sense but in the dynamic sense, as H. G. Wells redefined the word to remove its association with the fear of a static, totalitarian perfection. Wells was foremost a critic of progress who hoped and then, after trying to do something about it by educating the world, gave up hope. Asimov, Sagan, and Jacob Bronowski played this same role of educator in more recent times, struggling with the grim spectacle of human failure and incompetence. Wells felt that it was the fate of all so-called utopian visions to be more or less misread—and he urged not static perfection but dynamic, critical methods that would thrive on change and nurture its creative directions. In *A Modern Utopia* (1905) he wrote that "the state is for individuals, the law is for freedoms, the world is for experiment, experience, and change: these are the fundamentals upon which a modern Utopia must go" (91). It is no wonder that the totalitarian Lenin "felt sorry" for Wells during their meeting, since Lenin's view of human nature, and Stalin's after him, was that of a mad dog wearing a muzzle.

There are deeper constraints at work, say the critics of a more imaginative, risk-taking creative reason. The case for optimism is based on the fact that nature is vast and infinitely rich; and once we widen our field of economic operations off the Earth, there will be no limits to growth or the use of energy. The case for pessimism accepts the vision as possible, but states, sometimes very convincingly, that human beings may not be able to make use of the possibilities that wait. Because of our flawed nature, we will cower in our little corner of the universe and be unable to control ourselves sufficiently to reach for the riches around us. Cruel inner realities will stand against our desire for change. Yet it *is* sometimes in our power to follow creative possibilities, to keep before us what we wish to make of ourselves—what we wish to retain of our nature and what we wish to discard. This has been the way of civilization at its best, to retain some things and modify others even as we backslide.

What will actually happen? No one can guarantee any vision of the future; and we should not shackle future generations with our projects. But we can keep insisting, as James Blish once wrote, that X, Y, and Z are not impossible; we can keep visions alive. This has been the business of science fiction writers and futurists in this century, and many of their visions have stimulated scientists and engineers to produce startling advances, have created new hopes, and have called attention to new problems.

It seems nearly impossible to explain today how small a part "the future" or "futures" has played in human history, because we take such concerns so much for granted now. When Wells published his essay "The Discovery of the Future" in 1902, he opened up a field of thought that had been a blank—a vast continent of darkness, where, he suggested, human creativity might commence a new kind of work: inventing viable futures. In later years, Bertrand de Jouvenel in his *The Art of Conjecture* (1967) described such work as having a character equal to any great work of art.

The debate will never end between those who see only problems and those who see the heights—until some specific examples are explored and become part of our experience. What will people feel who live in space? "What's It Like Out There?" Edmund Hamilton asked in the title of his 1952 story.

On one side we have Norman Spinrad's acid comment, "Living in a space colony would be like being at a science fiction convention held aboard a nuclear submarine... forever!" (186). He was talking about the kind of scaled-down space habitats that might be built after the politicians were through cost cutting. The anthropologist and science fiction writer Chad Oliver warned against such dreams turned nightmares in two eloquent stories, "Ghost Town" (1983) and "Meanwhile, Back on the Reservation" (1981). When he learned of the atomic bomb in 1945, Wells said, "I told you so." He had warned the world—and not just about nuclear fission and the bomb made to work on the principle, in *The World Set Free* (1914), but also about the nuclear arms race, which was about to start.

On the other side we have simple, eloquent gestures. In 1997 a thimbleful of O'Neill's ashes was lofted into orbit in the first commercial "burial," though in their low trajectory the ashes will reenter the atmosphere within a few years (a fiery Viking funeral after all?). His ashes flew with those of Timothy Leary, another dreamer. One wonders how history will regard either of their fancies, since history has the power to make their dreams seem either foolish or wise, and neither conclusion can be guaranteed.

But if we conclude that human survival depends on developed forms of space travel and the industrialization of the solar system, even if they only improve life on Earth, then nothing can be more important. The ultimate aim of space travel is exploration and the growth of civilization. Mobile, self-reproducing habitats, developing along multifarious social paths, may provide the means to this destiny. But this destiny is elective, by no means inevitable, and perhaps beyond human capacity to guide.

America has been, in a way, the first utopian space colony; it was the first truly sophisticated, self-aware, fresh beginning in humankind's brief recorded history. And it may yet be fortunate enough to help our species have another go at a new start—through space settlements that will, in Hermann Oberth's words, "make available for life every place where life is possible. To make inhabitable all worlds as yet uninhabitable, and all life purposeful" (113).

The visionary writers and thinkers of the twentieth century have presented us with essays, stories, novels, poems, plays, and even operas, carrying on an often contentious debate about how humanity's emergence from the cradle of Earth will take place. Artists and filmmakers have created wide-screen images of possibilities. Engineers have drawn detailed plans. They have all looked into a mirror of possibility and seen what interests them most about human purpose. Some have issued warnings: when we build our castles in space, we must make sure to leave out the dungeons. But can we? Should we even try? Is it even up to us?

Science Fiction and Foresight

Any review of the justifications for the human use and occupation of the space beyond our sky must also examine our methods and motives. Logical argument has become so sophisticated in the twentieth century that it has also examined itself, demonstrating that argument alone decides very little beyond its own rules. At the same time, rough analogy and deduction, both sound and unsound, from carefully chosen premises and misstated, often incomplete facts are about as far as most people get, rarely examining what it is they do when they argue. Arguing for the exploration of space is not of the order of deciding how much change we have in our pocket; it involves self-fulfilling prophecies—the creative principle by which new things happen. One might say that creativity is given to us by a universe that is capable of novelty and in which we can, through knowledge and its applications, make new things happen. This is a great and often happy power, but one that is still developing and is not yet free of our inner demons.

We can find all the assumptions we need to reach whatever conclusion we wish—in the sense that it follows correctly from those premises; if the conclusion does not follow, then we adjust the steps and, if necessary, enrich the premises. There will be a rabbit in the hat, because the rabbit was put there. But the great innovation of science and its philosophy is that assumptions are constrained by physical law and the reality that stands outside "the freedom of argument."

The reality of our future(s) in space will not be decided by argument. Therefore, we must leave our minds open to complex realities that will outrun all our mental models. Humankind may fail at skylife, and the arguers will justify that after the fact.

Why do we not have space exploration and expansion at the level of past imaginings? Are recent human generations simply too tired and unequal to the task? Perhaps. But most of the answer comes down to money and fear. A true opening of the sky would rearrange the social and political power centers of Earth. The same may be said for permitting more advanced ways of generating energy. Today's centers of power are not in a rush to put themselves out of power. They know enough of what many developments will mean for them, so they fear those innovations and work to neglect them, to delay them until they can be brought in under the right auspices.

Space exploration, like SETI (the search for extraterrestrial intelligence), needs a time scale greater than a human lifetime to show its potential; SETI may require the scale of human history to date, and even that may not be enough. The disappointments of one lifetime are merely noise in the instruments. Only the doing will reveal the reality—and we may still fail, if humanity is not a breakout species.

One irony waiting to happen is that human civilization may be destroyed by an asteroid strike (there was a near miss in 1989) because we failed to develop the spacefaring capacity to prevent it. Space travel leading to skylife is vital to human survival, because the question is not whether our planet will be hit by a fatal asteroid but when. A planetary culture that does not develop spacefaring is courting suicide. All our history, all our social progress and growing insight will be for nothing if we perish. No risk of this kind, however small it might be argued to be, is worth taking, and no cost to prevent it is too great. No level of risk is acceptable when it comes to all or nothing survival. As Larry Niven put it humorously, "The dinosaurs died because they didn't have a space program."

Imaginings must precede all doing, or we risk having nothing to do and will do nothing to ensure our welfare or our very survival. Worse still, the lack of open, visionary minds may bring on the worst failures, the ones from which we cannot recover. This is the most deadening possibility of all. Lack of imagination, by which we grasp possibilities, is a black tide that drowns civilizations.

That science fiction has not done full justice to the difficult task of imagining skylife's vital innovations is not surprising, since that task is all but impossible on epistemological grounds. No one can see the future, literally. But science fiction can cast narrow beams of light into possibility. It is in itself remarkable that we have foresight of any kind, that we live so much of our lives looking forward rather than back. Foresight clearly tells us that we will look even farther ahead as our lifespans increase.

To return for a moment to the limitations of argument and discussion about possible futures: as in the conduct of science, one must make sure that one's instruments are not making noise that will skew the observations; yet this is what happens routinely in nearly all discourse. The endlessness of premise selection that tempts us with "the freedom of argument" prevents the narrowing down of assumptions to those that belong to reality's constraints. Anything goes, and most people believe and imagine what they wish, often simply taking their premise as their conclusion.

As any science, science fiction takes as a given that if it is well anchored at one empirically trustworthy point, it will be able to see its way to others. We rush ahead in our minds even as we build new realities, but we are rooted in the past and present of our human nature and social histories. Science fiction hungers to include, to wrap itself into the process of becoming, to pull even its own uncertain speculations into the great look back of history. And yet science fiction is a wave breaking from the past and through the present, striving to outrun both but caught in the struggle of brute reality with human creativity. Reality is causal; creativity finds ways through the probabilities.

It is this conflict that has created the loop of self-fulfilling prophecy, and this loop is the engine at the heart of science fiction. A century of science fiction devoted to space travel reveals to us how science fiction dates. Stories and novels may already be judged by how well they have come to grips with the human, historical, and technical implications of skylife; how they have succeeded in seeing and failed to see the expansion of humankind into the galaxy. James W. Valentine, a geologist and biologist, wrote in 1985:

> I fearlessly predict that within 2 million years the descendants of *Homo sapiens,* scattered across the Galaxy, will exhibit a diversity of form and adaptation that would astound us residents of today's Earth and that even then our evolutionary potential will hardly have been scratched. (274)

The astronomer Alan Dressler paints a grimmer picture of a humanity splintered by genetic engineering:

> ...we are most likely near the end of what we have known as humanity. Nature's gifts to us have led us to the secret keys of evolution, and we are not likely to long refrain from unlocking the box of treasures and troubles. (332)

The synergy of skylife and genetic engineering threatens — or promises — to be potent. When that combination is realized, the reader might say, the science fiction of the twentieth century will be merely a piece of antiquarian cultural history, if that, and of no interest to our farseeing successors.

But stop and consider that the above paragraphs are themselves scientific speculation and science fiction — proving only that among us there are those who see possibilities without guarantees or the means either to make them happen or to prevent them from happening. Seeing possibilities is still so much bound up with earning a living — individually and collectively — that it puts a brake on vision. Most of us have no time to see past ourselves; yet insights continue to sprout, good, bad, and indifferent. "Science is my territory," writes Dyson, "but science fiction is the landscape of my dreams." (*Imagined Worlds*, 9) We imagine that we can look back on ourselves from decades, centuries, and even millions of years hence, as if we can see in this way, and perhaps sometimes we can. The loop of science fiction, speculative foresight, and the sciences is the way we dig out what is implied by nature and by our human natures. Our creativities attempt to invent, predict, and prevent what may happen, while time unfolds and hurls us forward, and we strive to swim rather than be pulled along by the current.

Works Cited

Asimov, Isaac. *The Beginning and the End.* New York: Doubleday, 1977, p. 214. First published as a letter in *Saturday Review*, Nov. 1975.
———. "Strikebreaker." *Nightfall and Other Stories.* New York: Doubleday, 1969, p. 268. First published in *The Original Science Fiction Stories*, Jan. 1957.

Cohen, Bernard. Review of *Cannibals and Kings*, by Marvin Harris. *New York Times Book Review* October 30, 1977: p. 1.

Cole, Dandridge. "Macro-Life." *Space World* Sept.–Oct. 1961: 44, 46.

Dressler, Alan. *Voyage to the Great Attractor.* New York: Knopf, 1995, p. 332.

Dyson, Freeman. *Disturbing the Universe.* New York: Harper, 1979.
———. *Imagined Worlds.* Cambridge: Harvard UP, 1997.

Heinlein, Robert A. "Universe." *Astounding Science Fiction* May 1941: p. 42.

O'Neill, Gerard. "Space Colonies: The High Frontier." *Futurist* Feb. 1976: p. 37.

Oberth, Hermann. "Autobiography." *The Coming of the Space Age.* Ed. Arthur C. Clarke. New York: Meredith, 1967: p. 113. Originally "Hermann Oberth: From My Life," in *Astronautics*, June 1959. The American Rocket Society, N.Y.

Sagan, Carl. *The Cosmic Connection.* New York: Doubleday, 1973.

Spinrad, Norman. "Dreams of Space." *Asimov's Science Fiction* Oct.
    1987: p. 186.
Valentine, James W. "The Origins of Evolutionary Novelty and
    Galactic Colonization." *Interstellar Migration and the Human
    Experience.* Berkeley: U of California P, 1985: p. 274.
Wells, H. G. *A Modern Utopia.* London: Chapman, 1905: p. 91.
Westfahl, Gary. *Islands in the Sky.* San Bernardino: Borgo, 1996: p. 28.

The End of the Beginning

RAY BRADBURY

Here it comes, the first space station, out there and inside us all. Watch carefully.

He stopped the lawn mower in the middle of the yard, because he felt that the sun at just that moment had gone down and the stars come out. The fresh-cut grass that had showered his face and body died softly away. Yes, the stars were there, faint at first, but brightening in the clear desert sky. He heard the porch screen door tap shut and felt his wife watching him as he watched the night.

"Almost time," she said.

He nodded; he did not have to check his watch. In the passing moments he felt very old, then very young, very cold, then very warm, now this, now that. Suddenly he was miles away. He was his own son talking steadily, moving briskly to cover his pounding heart and the resurgent panics as he felt himself slip into fresh uniform, check food supplies, oxygen flasks, pressure helmet, space-suiting, and turn as every man on Earth tonight turned, to gaze at the swiftly filling sky.

Then, quickly, he was back, once more the father of the son, hands gripped to the lawn-mower handle. His wife called, "Come sit on the porch."

"I've got to keep busy!"

She came down the steps and across the lawn. "Don't worry about Robert; he'll be all right."

"But it's all so new," he heard himself say. "It's never been done before. Think of it—a manned rocket going up tonight to build the first space station. Good Lord, it can't be done, it doesn't exist, there's no rocket, no proving ground, no take-off time, no technicians. For that matter, I don't even have a son named Bob. The whole thing's too much for me!"

"Then what are you doing out here, staring?"

He shook his head. "Well, late this morning, walking to the office, I heard someone laugh out loud. It shocked me, so I froze in the middle of the street. It was *me*, laughing! Why? Because finally I really *knew* what Bob was going to do tonight; at last I *believed* it. 'Holy' is a word I never use, but that's how I felt stranded in all that traffic. Then, middle of the afternoon, I caught myself humming. You know the song. 'A wheel in a wheel. Way in the middle of the air.' I laughed again. The space station, of course, I thought. The big wheel with hollow spokes where Bob'll live six or eight months, then get along to the Moon. Walking home, I remembered more of the song. 'Little wheel run by faith, big wheel run by the grace of God.' I wanted to jump, yell, and flame-out myself!"

His wife touched his arm. "If we stay out here, let's at least be comfortable."

They placed two wicker rockers in the center of the lawn and sat quietly as the stars dissolved out of darkness in pale crushings of rock salt strewn from horizon to horizon.

"Why," said his wife, at last, "it's like waiting for the fireworks at Sisley Field every year."

"Bigger crowd tonight . . ."

"I keep thinking—a billion people watching the sky right now, their mouths all open at the same time."

They waited, feeling the earth move under their chairs.

"What time is it now?"

"Eleven minutes to eight."

"You're always right; there must be a clock in your head."

"I can't be wrong, tonight. I'll be able to tell you one second before they blast off. Look! The ten-minute warning!"

On the western sky they saw four crimson flares open out, float shimmering down the wind above the desert, then sink silently to the extinguishing earth.

In the new darkness the husband and wife did not rock in their chairs.

After a while he said, "Eight minutes." A pause. "Seven minutes." What seemed a much longer pause. "Six..."

His wife, her head back, studied the stars immediately above her and murmured, "Why?" She closed her eyes. "Why the rockets, why tonight? Why all this? I'd like to know."

He examined her face, pale in the vast powdering light of the Milky Way. He felt the stirring of an answer, but let his wife continue.

"I mean it's not that old thing again, is it, when people asked why men climbed Mt. Everest and they said, 'Because it's there'? I never understood. That was no answer to me."

Five minutes, he thought. Time ticking... his wristwatch... a wheel in a wheel... little wheel run by... big wheel run by... way in the middle of... four minutes!... The men snug in the rocket by now, the hive, the control board flickering with light....

His lips moved.

"All I know is it's really the end of the beginning. The Stone Age, Bronze Age, Iron Age; from now on we'll lump all those together under one big name for when we walked on Earth and heard the birds at morning and cried with envy. Maybe we'll call it the Earth Age, or maybe the Age of Gravity. Millions of years we fought gravity. When we were amoebas and fish we struggled to get out of the sea without gravity crushing us. Once safe on the shore we fought to stand upright without gravity breaking our new invention, the spine, tried to walk without stumbling, run without falling. A billion years Gravity kept us home, mocked us with wind and clouds, cabbage moths and locusts. That's what's so God-awful big about tonight... it's the end of old man Gravity and the age we'll remember him by, for once and all. I don't know where they'll divide the ages, at the Persians, who dreamt of flying carpets, or the Chinese, who all unknowing celebrated birthdays and New Years with strung ladyfingers and high skyrockets, or some minute, some incredible second in the next hour. But we're in at the end of a billion years trying, the end of something long and to us humans, anyway, honorable."

Three minutes... two minutes fifty-nine seconds... two minutes fifty-eight seconds...

"But," said his wife, "I still don't know why."

Two minutes, he thought. *Ready? Ready? Ready?* The far radio voice calling. *Ready! Ready! Ready!* The quick, faint replies from the humming rocket. *Check! Check! Check!*

Tonight, he thought, even if we fail with this first, we'll send a second and a third ship and move on out to all the planets and later, all the stars. We'll just keep going until the big words like "immortal" and "forever" take on meaning. Big words, yes, that's what we want. Continuity. Since our tongues first moved in our mouths we've asked, What does it all mean? No other question made sense, with death breathing down our necks. But just let us settle in on ten thousand worlds spinning around ten thousand alien suns and the question will fade away. Man will be endless and infinite, even as space is endless and infinite. Man will go on, as space goes on, forever. Individuals will die as always, but our history will reach as far as we'll ever need to see into the future, and with the knowledge of our survival for all time to come, we'll know security and thus the answer we've always searched for. Gifted with life, the least we can do is preserve and pass on the gift to infinity. That's a goal worth shooting for.

The wicker chairs whispered ever so softly on the grass.

One minute.

"One minute," he said aloud.

"Oh!" His wife moved suddenly to seize his hands. "I hope that Bob..."

"He'll be all right!"

"Oh, God, take care...."

Thirty seconds.

"Watch now."

Fifteen, ten, five...

"Watch!"

Four, three, two, one.

"There! There! Oh, there, there!"

They both cried out. They both stood. The chairs toppled back, fell flat on the lawn. The man and his wife swayed, their hands struggled to find each other, grip, hold. They saw the brightening color in the sky and, ten seconds later, the great uprising comet burn the air, put out the stars, and rush away in fire flight to become another star in the returning profusion of the Milky Way. The man and wife held each other as if they had stumbled on the rim of an incredible cliff that faced an abyss so deep and dark there seemed no end to it. Staring up, they heard themselves sobbing and crying. Only after a long time were they able to speak.

"It got away, it did, *didn't* it?"

"Yes..."

"It's all right, isn't it?"

"Yes... yes..."

"It didn't fall back...?"

"No, no, it's all right, Bob's all right, it's all right."

They stood away from each other at last.

He touched his face with his hand and looked at his wet fingers. "I'll be damned," he said. "I'll be damned."

They waited another five and then ten minutes until the darkness in their heads, the retina, ached with a million specks of fiery salt. Then they had to close their eyes.

"Well," she said, "now let's go in."

He could not move. Only his hand reached a long way out by itself to find the lawn-mower handle. He saw what his hand had done and said, "There's just a little more to do...."

"But you can't see."

"Well enough," he said. "I must finish this. Then we'll sit on the porch awhile before we turn in."

He helped her put the chairs on the porch and sat her down and then walked back out to put his hands on the guide bar of the lawn mower. The lawn mower. A wheel in a wheel. A simple machine which you held in your hands, which you sent on ahead with a rush and a clatter while you walked behind with your quiet philosophy. Racket, followed by warm silence. Whirling wheel, then soft footfall of thought.

I'm a billion years old, he told himself; I'm one minute old. I'm one inch, no, ten thousand *miles*, tall. I look down and can't see my feet they're so far off and gone away below.

He moved the lawn mower. The grass showering up fell softly around him; he relished and savored it and felt that he was all mankind bathing at last in the fresh waters of the fountain of youth.

Thus bathed, he remembered the song again about the wheels and the faith and the grace of God being way up there in the middle of the sky where that single star, among a million motionless stars, dared to move and keep on moving.

Then he finished cutting the grass.

Bigger than Worlds

LARRY NIVEN

Though the first generations of vessels into space will necessarily be small, one striking feature of high vacuum and zero gravity is the architectural freedom that must follow. With only centrifugal acceleration to supply "gravity" as needed, the essential limits on building are set by imagination, not the strength of materials. Here a science fiction writer with a technical background allows his mind to play with possibilities.

Just because you've spent all your life on a planet doesn't mean that everyone always will. Already there are alternatives to worlds. The Russian space station may have killed its inhabitants, and the American Skylab has had its troubles, but the Apollo craft have a good record. They have never killed a man in space.

Alas, they all lack a certain something. Gravity. Permanence. We want something to live on, or in, something superior to a world: safer, or more mobile, or roomier. Otherwise, why move?

It's odd how much there is to say about structures larger than worlds, considering that we cannot yet begin to build any one of them. On the basis of size, the Dyson Sphere — a spherical shell around a sun — comes about in the middle. But let's start small and work our way up.

The Multigeneration Ship

Robert Heinlein's early story "Universe" has been imitated countless times by most of the writers in the business.

The idea was this: Present-day physics poses a limit on the speed of an interstellar vehicle. The ships we send to distant stars will be on one-way journeys, at least at first. They will have to carry a complete ecology: they couldn't carry enough food and oxygen in tanks. Because they will take generations to complete their journeys, they must also carry a viable and complete society.

Clearly we're talking about quite a large ship, with a population in the hundreds at least: high enough to prevent genetic drift. Centrifugal force substitutes for gravity. We're going to be doing a lot of that. We spin the ship on its axis, and put all the things that need full gravity at the outside, along the hull. Plant rooms, exercise rooms, et cetera. Things that don't need gravity, like fuel and guidance instruments, we line along the axis. If our motors thrust through the same axis, we will have to build a lot of the machinery on tracks, because the aft wall will be the floor when the ship is under power.

The "Universe" ship is basic to a discussion of life in space. We'll be talking about much larger structures, but they are designed to do the same things on a larger scale: to provide a place to live, with as much security and variety and pleasure as Earth itself offers — or more.

Gravity

Gravity is basic to our lifestyle. It may or may not be necessary to life itself, but we'll want it if we can get it, whatever we build.

I know of only four methods of generating gravity aboard spacecraft.

Centrifugal force seems to be most likely. There is a drawback: coriolis effects would force us to relearn how to walk, sit down, pour coffee, throw a baseball. But such effects would decrease with increasing

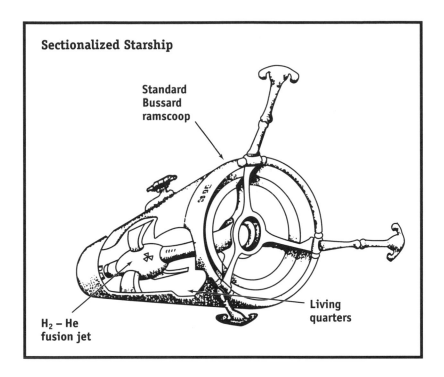

Sectionalized Starship

Standard
Bussard
ramscoop

Living
quarters

H₂ – He
fusion jet

moment arm—that is, with larger structures. On a Ring City, for example, you'd never notice it.

Our second choice is to use actual mass: plate the floor with neutronium, for instance, at a density of fifty quadrillion tons per cubic foot; or build the ship around a quantum black hole, invisibly small and around as massive as, say, Phobos. But this will vastly increase our fuel consumption if we expect the vehicle to go anywhere.

Third choice is to generate gravity waves. This may remain forever beyond our abilities. But it's one of those things that people are going to keep trying to build, forever, because it would be so damn useful. We could put laboratories on the sun, or colonize Jupiter. We could launch ships at a million gravities, and the passengers would feel nothing.

The fourth method is to accelerate all the way, making turnover at the midpoint and decelerating the rest of the way. This works fine. Over interstellar distances it would take an infinite fuel supply—which we may have, in the Bussard ramjet. A Bussard ramjet would use an electromagnetic field to scoop up the interstellar hydrogen ahead of it—with an intake a thousand miles or more in diameter—compress it, and burn it as fuel for a fusion drive. Now the multigeneration ship would become unnecessary as relativity shortens our trip time: four years to the nearest star, twenty-one years to the galactic hub, twenty-eight to Andromeda galaxy—all at one gravity acceleration.

The Bussard ramjet looks unlikely. It's another ultimate, like generated gravity. Is the interstellar medium sufficiently ionized for such finicky control? Maybe not. But it's worth a try.

Meanwhile, our first step to other worlds is the "Universe" ship—huge, spun for gravity, its population in the hundreds, its travel time in generations.

Flying Cities

James Blish used a variant of generated gravity in his tales of the Okie cities.

His "spindizzy" motors used a little-known law of physics (still undiscovered) to create their own gravity and their own motive force. Because the spindizzy motors worked better for higher mass, his vehicles tended to be big. Most of the stories centered around Manhattan Island, which had been bodily uprooted from its present location and flown intact to the stars. Two of the stories involved whole worlds fitted out with spindizzies. They were even harder to land than the flying cities.

But we don't really need spindizzies or generated gravity to build flying cities.

In fact, we don't really need to fill out Heinlein's "Universe" ship. The outer hull is all we need. Visualize a ship like this:

1. Cut a strip of Los Angeles, say, ten miles long by a mile wide.
2. Roll it in a hoop. Buildings and streets face inward.
3. Roof it over with glass or something stronger.
4. Transport it to space. (Actually we'll build it in space.)
5. Put reaction motors, air and water recycling systems, and storage areas in the basement, outward from the street level. Also the fuel tanks. Jettisoning an empty fuel tank is easy. We just cut it loose, and it falls into the universe.

A Flying City

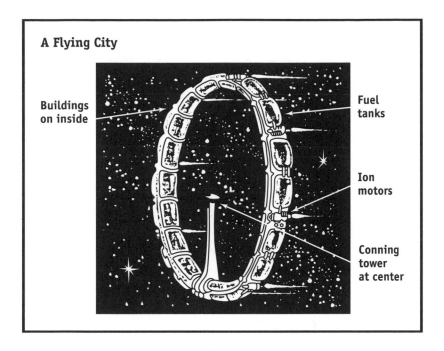

Buildings on inside

Fuel tanks

Ion motors

Conning tower at center

6. Use a low-thrust, high-efficiency drive: ion jets, perhaps. The axis of the city can be kept clear. A smaller ship can rise to the axis for sightings before a course change; or we can set the control bridge atop a slender fin. A ten-mile circumference makes the fin a mile and a half tall if the bridge is at the axis; but the strain on the structure would diminish approaching the axis.

What would it be like aboard the Ring City? One gravity everywhere, except in the bridge. We may want to enlarge the bridge to accommodate a schoolroom; teaching physics would be easier in free fall.

Otherwise it would be a lot like the multigeneration ship. The populace would be less likely to forget their destiny, as Heinlein's people did. They can see the sky from anywhere in the city; and the only fixed stars are Sol and the target star.

It would be like living anywhere, except that great attention must be paid to environmental quality. This can be taken for granted throughout this article. The more thoroughly we control our environment, the more dangerous it is to forget it.

Inside-Outside

The next step up in size is the hollow planetoid. I got my designs from a book of scientific speculation, *Islands in Space,* by Dandridge M. Cole and Donald W. Cox.

Step 1: Construct a giant solar mirror. Formed under zero gravity conditions, it need be nothing more than an echo balloon sprayed with something to harden it, then cut in half and silvered on the inside. It would be fragile as a butterfly, and *huge.*

Step 2: Pick a planetoid. Ideally, we need an elongated chunk of nickel-iron, perhaps one mile in diameter and two miles long.

Step 3: Bore a hole down the long axis.

Step 4: Charge the hole with tanks of water. Plug the openings, and weld the plugs, using the solar mirror.

Step 5: Set the planetoid spinning slowly on its axis. As it spins, bathe the entire mass in the concentrated sunlight from the solar mirror. Gradually the flying iron mountain would be heated to melting all over its surface. Then the heat would creep inward, until the object is almost entirely molten.

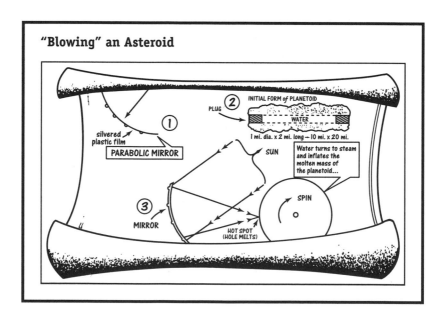

"Blowing" an Asteroid

Step 6: The axis would be the last part to reach melting point. At that point the water tanks explode. The pressure blows the planetoid up into an iron balloon some ten miles in diameter and twenty miles long, if everybody has done his job right.

The hollow world is now ready for tenants. Except that certain things have to be moved in: air, water, soil, living things. It should be possible to set up a closed ecology. Cole and Cox suggested setting up the solar mirror at one end and using it to reflect sunlight back and forth along the long axis. We might prefer to use fusion power, if we've got it.

Naturally we spin the thing for gravity.

Living in such an inside-out world would be odd in some respects. The whole landscape is overhead. Our sky contains farms and houses and so forth. If we came to space to see the stars, we'd have to go down into the basement.

We get our choice of gravity and weather. Weather is easy. We give the asteroid a slight equatorial bulge, to get a circular central lake. We shade the endpoints of the asteroid from the sun, so that it's always raining there, and the water runs downhill to the central lake. If we keep the gravity low enough, we should be able to fly with an appropriate set of muscle-powered wings; and the closer we get to the axis, the easier it becomes. (Of course, if we get too close the wax melts and the wings come apart...)

Macrolife

Let's back up a bit, to the Heinlein "Universe" ship. Why do we want to land it?

If the ship has survived long enough to reach its target star, it could probably survive indefinitely; and so can the nth-generation society it now carries. Why should their descendants live out their lives on a primitive Earthlike world? Perhaps they were born to better things.

Let the "Universe" ship become their universe, then. They can mine new materials from the asteroids of the new system, and use them to enlarge the ship when necessary, or build new ships. They can loosen the population-control laws. Change stars when convenient. Colonize space itself, and let the planets become mere way stations. See the universe!

The concept is called *Macrolife:* large, powered, self-sufficient environments capable of expanding or reproducing. Put a drive on the Inside-Outside asteroid bubble and it becomes a Macrolife vehicle. The ring-shaped flying city can be extended indefinitely from the forward rim. Blish's spindizzy cities were a step away from being Macrolife; but they were too dependent on planet-based society.

A Macrolife vehicle would have to carry its own mining tools and chemical laboratories, and God knows what else. We'd learn what else accidentally, by losing interstellar colony-ships. At best a Macrolife vehicle would never be as safe as a planet, unless it was as big as a planet, and perhaps not then. But there are values other than safety. An airplane isn't as safe as a house, but a house doesn't go anywhere. Neither does a world.

Worlds

The terraforming of worlds is the next logical step up in size. For a variety of reasons, I'm going to skip lightly over it. We know both too much and too little to talk coherently about what makes a world habitable.

But we're learning fast, and will learn faster. Our present pollution problems will end by telling us exactly how to keep a habitable environment habitable, how to keep a stable ecology stable, and how to put it all back together again after it falls apart. As usual, the universe will teach us or kill us. If we live long enough to build ships of the "Universe" type, we will know what to put inside them. We may even know how to terraform a hostile world for the convenience of human colonists, having tried our techniques on Earth itself.

Now take a giant step.

Dyson Spheres

Freeman Dyson's original argument went as follows, approximately.

No industrial society has ever reduced its need for power, except by collapsing. An intelligent optimist will expect his own society's need for power to increase geometrically, and will make his plans accordingly.

Dyson Sphere (all around sun)

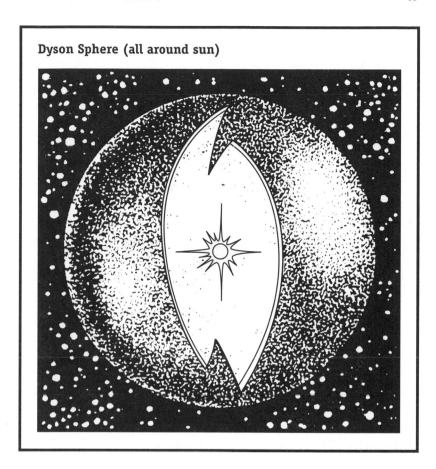

According to Dyson, it will not be an impossibly long time before our own civilization needs all the power generated by our sun. Every last erg of it. We will then have to enclose the sun so as to control all of its output.

What we use to enclose the sun is problematic. Dyson was speaking of shells in the astronomical sense: solid or liquid, continuous or discontinuous, anything to interrupt the sunlight so that it can be turned into power. One move might be to convert the mass of the solar system into as many little ten-by-twenty-mile hollow iron bubbles as will fit. The smaller we subdivide the mass of a planet, the more useful surface area we get. We put all the little asteroid bubbles in circular orbits at distances of about one Earth orbit from the sun, but differing enough that they won't collide. It's a gradual process. We start by converting the existing asteroids. When we run out, we convert Mars, Jupiter, Saturn, Uranus . . . and eventually Earth.

Now, aside from the fact that our need for power increases geometrically, our population also increases geometrically. If we didn't need the power, we'd still need the room in those bubbles. Eventually we've blocked out all of the sunlight. From outside, from another star, such a system would be a great globe radiating enormous energy in the deep infrared.

What some science fiction writers have been calling a Dyson Sphere is something else: a hollow spherical shell, like a Ping-Pong ball with a star in the middle. Mathematically at least, it is possible to build such a shell without leaving the solar system for materials. The planet Jupiter has a mass of 2×10^{30} grams, which is most of the mass of the solar system excluding the sun. Given massive transmutation of elements, we can convert Jupiter into a spherical shell ninety-three million miles in radius and maybe ten to twenty feet thick. If we don't have transmutation, we can still do it, with a thinner shell. There are at least ten Earth-masses of building material in the solar system, once we throw away the useless gases.

The surface area inside a Dyson Sphere is about a billion times that of the Earth. Very few galactic civilizations in science fiction have included as many as a billion worlds. Here you'd have that much territory within walking distance, assuming you were immortal.

Naturally we would have to set up a biosphere on the inner surface. We'd also need gravity generators. The gravitational attraction inside a uniform spherical shell is zero. The net pull would come from the sun, and everything would gradually drift upward into it.

So. We spot gravity generators all over the shell, to hold down the air and the people and the buildings. "Down" is outward, toward the stars.

We can control the temperature of any locality by varying the heat-retaining properties of the shell. In fact, we may want to enlarge the shell, to give us more room or to make the permanent noonday sun look smaller. All we need do is make the shell a better insulator: foam the material, for instance. If it holds heat too well, we may want to add radiator fins to the outside.

Note that life is not necessarily pleasant in a Dyson Sphere. We can't see the stars. It is always noon. We can dig mines or basements. And if one of the gravity generators ever went out, the resulting disaster would make the end of the Earth look trivial by comparison.

But if we need a Dyson Sphere, and if it can be built, we'll probably build it.

Now, Dyson's assumptions (expanding population, expanding need for power) may hold for any industrial society, human or not. If an astronomer were looking for inhabited stellar systems, he would be missing the point if he watched only the visible stars. The galaxy's most advanced civilizations may be spherical shells about the size of the Earth's orbit, radiating as much power as a Sol-type sun, but at about 10μ wavelength — in the deep infrared . . .

. . . assuming that the galaxy's most advanced civilizations are protoplasmic. But beings whose chemistry is based on molten copper, say, would want a hotter environment. They might have evolved faster, in temperatures where chemistry, and biochemistry, would move *far* faster. There might be a lot more of them than of us. And their red-hot Dyson Spheres would look deceptively like red giant or supergiant stars. One wonders.

In *The Wanderer*, novelist Fritz Leiber suggested that most of the visible stars have already been surrounded by shells of worlds. We are watching old light, he suggested, light that was on its way to Earth before the industrial expansion of galactic civilization really hit its stride. Already we see part of the result: the opaque dust clouds astronomers find in the direction of the galactic core are not dust clouds but walls of Dyson Spheres blocking the stars within.

Ringworld

I have come up with an intermediate step between Dyson Spheres and planets. Build a ring ninety-three million miles in radius — one Earth orbit — which would make it six hundred million miles long. If we have the mass of Jupiter to work with, and if we make it a million miles wide, we get a thickness of about a thousand meters. The Ringworld would thus be much sturdier than a Dyson Sphere.

There are other advantages. We can spin it for gravity. A rotation on its axis of 770 miles/second would give the Ringworld one gravity outward.

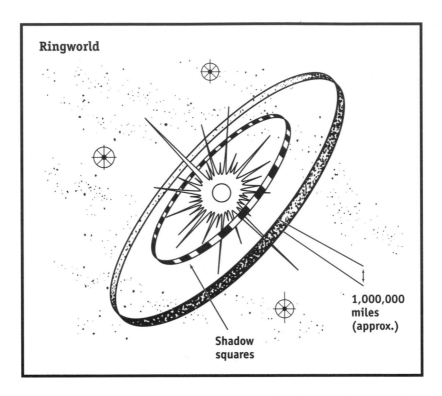

Ringworld

Shadow
squares

1,000,000
miles
(approx.)

We wouldn't even have to roof it over. Put walls a thousand miles high at each rim, aimed inward at the sun, and very little of the air will leak over the edges.

Set up an inner ring of shadow squares — light orbiting structures to block out part of the sunlight — and we can have day-and-night cycles in whatever period we like. And we can see the stars — unlike the inhabitants of a Dyson Sphere.

The thing is roomy enough: three million times the area of the Earth. It will be some time before anyone complains of the crowding.

As with most of these structures, our landscape is optional, a challenge to engineer and artist alike. A look at the outer surface of a Ringworld or Dyson Sphere would be most instructive. Seas would show as bulges, mountains as dents. Riverbeds and river deltas would be sculptured in; there would be no room for erosion on something as thin as a Ringworld or a Dyson Sphere. Seas would be flat-bottomed — as we use only the top of a sea anyway — and small, with convoluted shorelines. Lots of beach-front. Mountains would exist only for scenery and recreation.

Multiple Rings

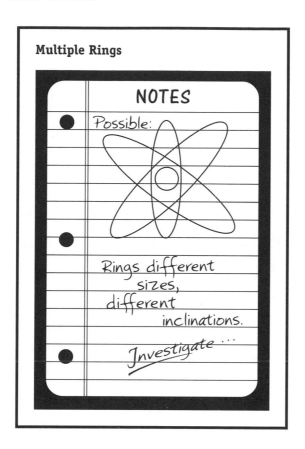

A large meteor would be a disaster on such a structure. A hole in the floor of the Ringworld, if not plugged, would eventually let all the air out, and the pressure differential would cause storms the size of a world, making repairs difficult.

The Ringworld concept is flexible. Consider:

1. More than one Ringworld can circle a sun. Imagine many Ringworlds, noncoplanar, of slightly differing radii—or of widely differing radii—inhabited by very different intelligent races.
2. We'd get seasons by bobbing the sun up and down. Actually the Ring would do the bobbing; the sun would stay put (one Ring to a sun for this trick).
3. To build a Ringworld when all the planets in the system are colonized to the hilt (and, baby, we don't *need* a Ringworld until it's

gotten that bad!) pro tem structures are needed. A structure the size of a world and the shape of a pie plate, with a huge rocket thruster underneath and a biosphere in the dish, might serve to house a planet's population while the planet in question is being disassembled. It circles the sun at 770 miles/second, firing outward to maintain its orbit. The depopulated planet becomes two more pie plates, and we wire them in an equilateral triangle and turn off the thrusters, evacuate more planets and start building the Ringworld.

Dyson Spheres 2

I pointed out earlier that gravity generators look unlikely. We may never be able to build them at all. Do we really need to assume gravity generators on a Dyson Sphere? There are at least two other solutions.

We can spin the Dyson Sphere. It still picks up all the energy of the sun, as planned; but the atmosphere collects around the equator, and the rest is in vacuum. We would do better to reshape the structure like a canister of movie film; it gives us greater structural strength. And we wind up with a closed Ringworld.

Or, we can live with the fact that we can't have gravity. According to the suggestion of Dan Alderson, PhD, we can build two concentric spherical shells, the inner shell transparent, the outer transparent or opaque, at our whim. The biosphere is between the two shells.

It would be fun. We can build anything we like within the free-fall environment. Buildings would be fragile as a butterfly. Left to themselves, they would drift up against the inner shell, but a heavy thread would be enough to tether them against the sun's puny gravity. The only question is, can humanity stand long periods of free fall?

Hold It a Minute

Have you reached the point of vertigo? These structures are hard to hold in your head. They're so flipping *big*. It might help if I tell you that, though we can't *begin* to *build* any of these things, practically anyone can handle them mathematically. Any college freshman can prove that the gravitational attraction inside a spherical shell is zero. The stresses are easy to compute (and generally too strong for anything we can make). The mathematics of a Ringworld are those of a suspension bridge with no endpoints.

OK, go on with whatever you were doing.

The Disc

What's bigger than a Dyson Sphere? Dan Alderson, designer of the Alderson Double Dyson Sphere, now brings you the Alderson Disc. The shape is that of a phonograph record, with a sun situated in the little hole. The radius is about that of the orbit of Mars or Jupiter. Thickness: a few thousand miles.

Gravity is uniformly vertical to the surface (freshman physics again) except for edge effects. Engineers do have to worry about edge effects; so we'll build a thousand-mile wall around the inner well to keep the atmosphere from drifting into the sun. The outer edge will take care of itself.

This thing is massive. It weighs far more than the sun. We ignore problems of structural strength. Please note that we can inhabit *both* sides of the Alderson Disc.

The sun will always be on the horizon—unless we bob it, which we do. (This time it is the sun that does the bobbing.) Now it is always dawn, or dusk, or night.

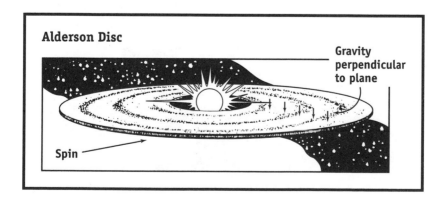

Alderson Disc

Gravity perpendicular to plane

Spin

The Disc would be a wonderful place to stage a Gothic or a sword-and-sorcery novel. The atmosphere is right, and there are real monsters. Consider: we can occupy only a part of the Disc the right distance from the sun. We might as well share the Disc and the cost of its construction with aliens from hotter or colder climes. Mercurians and Venusians nearer the sun, Martians out toward the rim, aliens from other stars living wherever it suits them best. Over the tens of thousands of years, mutations and adaptations would migrate across the sparsely settled borders. If civilization should fall, things could get eerie and interesting.

Cosmic Macaroni

Pat Gunkel has designed a structure analogous to the Ringworld. Imagine a hollow strand of macaroni six hundred million miles long and not particularly thick—say a mile in diameter. Join it in a loop around the sun.

Pat calls it a *topopolis*. He points out that we could rotate the thing as in the illustration—getting gravity through centrifugal force—because of the lack of torsion effects. At six hundred million miles long and a mile wide, the curvature of the tube is negligible. We can set up a biosphere on the inner surface, with a sunlight tube down the axis and photoelectric power sources on the outside. So far, we've got something bigger than a world but smaller than a Ringworld.

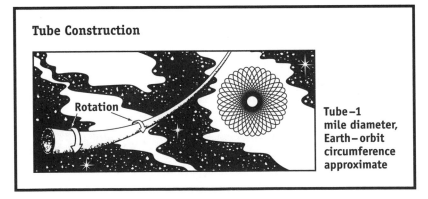

Tube Construction

Rotation

Tube–1 mile diameter, Earth–orbit circumference approximate

But we don't have to be satisfied with one loop! We can go round and round the sun, as often as we like, as long as the strands don't touch. Pat visualizes endless loops of rotating tube, shaped like a hell of a lot of spaghetti patted roughly into a hollow sphere with a star at the center (and now we call it an *aegagropilous topopolis*). As the madhouse civilization that built it continued to expand, the coil would reach to other stars. With the interstellar links using power supplied by the inner coils, the tube city would expand through the galaxy. Eventually our *aegagropilous galactotopopolis* would look like all the stars in the heavens had been embedded in hair.

The Megasphere

Mathematically at least, it is possible to build a really big Dyson Sphere, with the heart of a galaxy at its center. There probably aren't enough planets to supply us with material. We would have to disassemble some

Mega Dyson Sphere

of the stars of the galactic arms. But we'll be able to do it by the time we need to.

We put the biosphere on the outside this time. Surface gravity is minute, but the atmospheric gradient is infinitesimal. Once again, we assume that it is possible for human beings to adapt to free fall. We live in free fall, above a surface area of tens of millions of light-years, within an atmosphere that doesn't thin out for scores of light-years.

Temperature control is easy: we vary the heat conductivity of the sphere to pick up and hold enough of the energy from the stars within. Though the radiating surface is great, the volume to hold heat is much greater. Industrial power would come from photoreceptors inside the shell.

Within this limitless universe of air we can build exceptionally large structures, Ringworld-sized and larger. We could even spin them for gravity. They would remain aloft for many times the life span of any known civilization before the gravity of the core stars pulled them down to contact the surface.

The Megasphere would be a pleasantly poetic place to live. From a flat Earth hanging in space, one could actually reach a nearby Moon via a chariot drawn by swans, and stand a good chance of finding selenites there. There would be none of this nonsense about carrying bottles of air along.

Final Solution

One final step is to join two opposing lifestyles, the Macrolife tourist types and the sedentary types who prefer to restructure their home worlds.

The Ringworld rotates at 770 miles/second. Given appropriate conducting surfaces, this rotation could set up enormous magnetic effects. These could be used to control the burning of the sun, to cause it to fire off a jet of gas along the Ringworld axis of rotation. The sun becomes its own rocket. The Ringworld follows, tethered by gravity.

By the time we run out of sun, the Ring is moving through space at Bussard ramjet velocities. We continue to use the magnetic effect to pinch the interstellar gas into a fusion flame, which now becomes our sun and our motive power.

The Ringworld makes a problematic vehicle. What's it *for*? You can't land the damn thing anywhere. A traveling Ringworld is not useful as a tourist vehicle; anything you want to see, you can put on the Ringworld itself . . . unless it's a lovely multiple star system like Beta Lyrae; but you just can't get that *close* on a flying Ringworld.

A Ringworld in flight would be a bird of ill omen. It could only be fleeing some galaxy-wide disaster.

Now, galaxies do explode. We have pictures of it happening. The probable explanation is a chain reaction of novas in the galactic core. Perhaps we should be maintaining a space watch for fleeing Ringworlds . . . except that we couldn't do anything about it.

We live on a world: small, immobile, vulnerable, and unprotected. But it will not be so forever.

The Other Side of the Sky

ARTHUR C. CLARKE

The sky is everywhere and contains everything, the Earth swimming in the vast sky that is our universe. The sky is literally the limit to our existence.

Clarke's story depicts human activity in near-Earth space just beyond the reality of the Mercury, Gemini, and Apollo projects—steps still well ahead of those taken in the 1960s and 1970s. Clarke wrote this story in the 1950s, yet all the details are right, from weather and communications satellites to the minutiae of life aboard a small space station. These linked vignettes add up to an impressively understated and affecting picture of human life growing away from the Earth as this now alternate twentieth century that might have been is ending.

Special Delivery

I can still remember the excitement, back in 1957, when Russia launched the first artificial satellites and managed to hang a few pounds of instruments up here above the atmosphere. Of course, I was only a kid at the time, but I went out in the evening like everyone else, trying to spot those little magnesium spheres as they zipped through the twilight sky hundreds of miles above my head. It's strange to think that some of them are still there — but that now they're *below* me, and I'd have to look down toward Earth if I wanted to see them....

Yes, a lot has happened in the last forty years, and sometimes I'm afraid that you people down on Earth take the space stations for granted, forgetting the skill and science and courage that went to make them. How often do you stop to think that all your long-distance phone calls, and most of your TV programs, are routed through one or the other of the satellites? And how often do you give any credit to the meteorologists up here for the fact that weather forecasts are no longer the joke they were to our grandfathers, but are dead accurate ninety-nine per cent of the time?

It was a rugged life, back in the seventies, when I went up to work on the outer stations. They were being rushed into operation to open up the millions of new TV and radio circuits which would be available as soon as we had transmitters out in space that could beam programs to any-where on the globe.

The first artificial satellites had been very close to Earth, but the three stations forming the great triangle of the Relay Chain had to be twenty-two thousand miles up, spaced equally around the equator. At this alti-tude — and at no other — they would take exactly a day to go around their orbit, and so would stay poised forever over the same spot on the turning Earth.

In my time I've worked on all three of the stations, but my first tour of duty was aboard Relay Two. That's almost exactly over Entebbe, Uganda, and provides service for Europe, Africa, and most of Asia. Today it's a huge structure hundreds of yards across, beaming thousands of simulta-neous programs down to the hemisphere beneath it as it carries the radio traffic of half the world. But when I saw it for the first time from the port of the ferry rocket that carried me up to orbit, it looked like a junk pile adrift in space. Prefabricated parts were floating around in hopeless con-fusion, and it seemed impossible that any order could ever emerge from this chaos.

Accommodation for the technical staff and assembling crews was primitive, consisting of a few unserviceable ferry rockets that had been stripped of everything except air purifiers. "The Hulks," we christened them; each man had just enough room for himself and a couple of cubic feet of personal belongings. There was a fine irony in the fact that we were living in the midst of infinite space — and hadn't room to swing a cat.

It was a great day when we heard that the first pressurized living quarters were on their way up to us — complete with needle-jet shower baths that would operate even here, where water — like everything else — had no weight. Unless you've lived aboard an overcrowded spaceship, you won't appreciate what that meant. We could throw away our damp sponges and feel really clean at last. . . .

Nor were the showers the only luxury promised us. On the way up from Earth was an inflatable lounge spacious enough to hold no fewer than eight people, a microfilm library, a magnetic billiard table, light-weight chess sets, and similar novelties for bored spacemen. The very thought of all these comforts made our cramped life in the Hulks seem quite unendurable, even though we were being paid about a thousand dollars a week to endure it.

Starting from the Second Refueling Zone, two thousand miles above Earth, the eagerly awaited ferry rocket would take about six hours to climb up to us with its precious cargo. I was off duty at the time, and stationed myself at the telescope where I'd spent most of my scanty leisure. It was impossible to grow tired of exploring the great world hanging there in space beside us; with the highest power of the telescope, one seemed to be only a few miles above the surface. When there were no clouds and the seeing was good, objects the size of a small house were easily visible. I had never been to Africa, but I grew to know it well while I was off duty in Station Two. You may not believe this, but I've often spotted elephants moving across the plains, and the immense herds of zebras and antelopes were easy to see as they flowed back and forth like living tides on the great reservations.

But my favorite spectacle was the dawn coming up over the mountains in the heart of the continent. The line of sunlight would come sweeping across the Indian Ocean, and the new day would extinguish the tiny, twinkling galaxies of the cities shining in the darkness below me. Long before the sun had reached the lowlands around them, the peaks of Kilimanjaro and Mount Kenya would be blazing in the dawn, brilliant stars still surrounded by the night. As the sun rose higher, the day would march swiftly down their slopes and the valleys would fill with light. Earth would then be at its first quarter, waxing toward full.

Twelve hours later, I would see the reverse process as the same mountains caught the last rays of the setting sun. They would blaze for a little while in the narrow belt of twilight; then Earth would spin into darkness, and night would fall upon Africa.

It was not the beauty of the terrestrial globe I was concerned with now. Indeed, I was not even looking at Earth, but at the fierce blue-white star high above the western edge of the planet's disk. The automatic freighter was eclipsed in Earth's shadow; what I was seeing was the incandescent flare of its rockets as they drove it up on its twenty-thousand-mile climb.

I had watched ships ascending to us so often that I knew every stage of their maneuver by heart. So when the rockets didn't wink out, but continued to burn steadily, I knew within seconds that something was wrong. In sick, helpless fury I watched all our longed-for comforts — and, worse still, our mail! — moving faster and faster along the unintended orbit. The freighter's autopilot had jammed; had there been a human pilot aboard, he could have overridden the controls and cut the motor, but now all the fuel that should have driven the ferry on its two-way trip was being burned in one continuous blast of power.

By the time the fuel tanks had emptied, and that distant star had flickered and died in the field of my telescope, the tracking stations had confirmed what I already knew. The freighter was moving far too fast for Earth's gravity to recapture it — indeed, it was heading into the cosmic wilderness beyond Pluto....

It took a long time for morale to recover, and it only made matters worse when someone in the computing section worked out the future history of our errant freighter. You see, nothing is ever really lost in space. Once you've calculated its orbit, you know where it is until the end of eternity. As we watched our lounge, our library, our games, our mail receding to the far horizons of the solar system, we knew that it would all come back one day, in perfect condition. If we have a ship standing by it will be easy to intercept it the second time it comes around the sun — quite early in the spring of the year A.D. 15,862.

Feathered Friend

To the best of my knowledge, there's never been a regulation that forbids one to keep pets in a space station. No one ever thought it was necessary—and even had such a rule existed, I am quite certain that Sven Olsen would have ignored it.

With a name like that, you will picture Sven at once as a six-foot-six Nordic giant, built like a bull and with a voice to match. Had this been so, his chances of getting a job in space would have been very slim; actually he was a wiry little fellow, like most of the early spacers, and managed to qualify easily for the 150-pound bonus that kept so many of us on a reducing diet.

Sven was one of our best construction men, and excelled at the tricky and specialized work of collecting assorted girders as they floated around in free fall, making them do the slow-motion, three-dimensional ballet that would get them into their right positions, and fusing the pieces together when they were precisely dovetailed into the intended pattern. I never tired of watching him and his gang as the station grew under their hands like a giant jigsaw puzzle; it was a skilled and difficult job, for a space suit is not the most convenient of garbs in which to work. However, Sven's team had one great advantage over the construction gangs you see putting up skyscrapers down on Earth. They could step back and admire their handiwork without being abruptly parted from it by gravity. . . .

Don't ask me why Sven wanted a pet, or why he chose the one he did. I'm not a psychologist, but I must admit that his selection was very sensible. Claribel weighed practically nothing, her food requirements were infinitesimal—and she was not worried, as most animals would have been, by the absence of gravity.

I first became aware that Claribel was aboard when I was sitting in the little cubbyhole laughingly called my office, checking through my lists of technical stores to decide what items we'd be running out of next. When I heard the musical whistle beside my ear, I assumed that it had come over the station intercom, and waited for an announcement to follow. It didn't; instead, there was a long and involved pattern of melody that made me look up with such a start that I forgot all about the angle beam just behind my head. When the stars had ceased to explode before my eyes, I had my first view of Claribel.

She was a small yellow canary, hanging in the air as motionless as a hummingbird—and with much less effort, for her wings were quietly folded along her sides. We stared at each other for a minute; then, before I had quite recovered my wits, she did a curious kind of backward loop I'm sure no earthbound canary had ever managed, and departed with a few leisurely flicks. It was quite obvious that she'd already learned how to operate in the absence of gravity, and did not believe in doing unnecessary work.

Sven didn't confess to her ownership for several days, and by that time it no longer mattered, because Claribel was a general pet. He had smuggled her up on the last ferry from Earth, when he came back from leave—partly, he claimed, out of sheer scientific curiosity. He wanted to see just how a bird would operate when it had no weight but could still use its wings.

Claribel thrived and grew fat. On the whole, we had little trouble concealing our unauthorized guest when VIPs from Earth came visiting. A space station has more hiding places than you can count; the only problem was that Claribel got rather noisy when she was upset, and we sometimes had to think fast to explain the curious peeps and whistles that came from ventilating shafts and storage bulkheads. There were a couple of narrow escapes—but then who would dream of looking for a canary in a space station?

We were now on twelve-hour watches, which was not as bad as it sounds, since you need little sleep in space. Though of course there is no "day" and "night" when you are floating in permanent sunlight, it was still convenient to stick to the terms. Certainly when I woke up that "morning" it felt like 6:00 A.M. on Earth. I had a nagging headache, and vague memories of fitful, disturbed dreams. It took me ages to undo my bunk straps, and I was still only half awake when I joined the remainder of the duty crew in the mess. Breakfast was unusually quiet, and there was one seat vacant.

"Where's Sven?" I asked, not very much caring.

"He's looking for Claribel," someone answered. "Says he can't find her anywhere. She usually wakes him up."

Before I could retort that she usually woke me up, too, Sven came in through the doorway, and we could see at once that something was wrong. He slowly opened his hand, and there lay a tiny bundle of yellow feathers, with two clenched claws sticking pathetically up into the air.

"What happened?" we asked, all equally distressed.

"I don't know," said Sven mournfully. "I just found her like this."

"Let's have a look at her," said Jock Duncan, our cook-doctor-dietitian. We all waited in hushed silence while he held Claribel against his ear in an attempt to detect any heartbeat.

Presently he shook his head. "I can't hear anything, but that doesn't prove she's dead. I've never listened to a canary's heart," he added rather apologetically.

"Give her a shot of oxygen," suggested somebody, pointing to the green-banded emergency cylinder in its recess beside the door. Everyone agreed that this was an excellent idea, and Claribel was tucked snugly into a face mask that was large enough to serve as a complete oxygen tent for her.

To our delighted surprise, she revived at once. Beaming broadly, Sven removed the mask, and she hopped onto his finger. She gave her series of "Come to the cookhouse, boys" trills — then promptly keeled over again.

"I don't get it," lamented Sven. "What's wrong with her? She's never done this before."

For the last few minutes, something had been tugging at my memory. My mind seemed to be very sluggish that morning, as if I was still unable to cast off the burden of sleep. I felt that I could do with some of that oxygen — but before I could reach the mask, understanding exploded in my brain. I whirled on the duty engineer and said urgently:

"Jim! There's something wrong with the air! That's why Claribel's passed out. I've just remembered that miners used to carry canaries down to warn them of gas."

"Nonsense!" said Jim. "The alarms would have gone off. We've got duplicate circuits, operating independently."

"Er — the second alarm circuit isn't connected up yet," his assistant reminded him. That shook Jim; he left without a word, while we stood arguing and passing the oxygen bottle around like a pipe of peace.

He came back ten minutes later with a sheepish expression. It was one of those accidents that couldn't possibly happen; we'd had one of our rare eclipses by Earth's shadow that night; part of the air purifier had frozen up, and the single alarm in the circuit had failed to go off. Half a million dollars' worth of chemical and electronic engineering had let us down completely. Without Claribel, we should soon have been slightly dead.

So now, if you visit any space station, don't be surprised if you hear an inexplicable snatch of birdsong. There's no need to be alarmed: on the contrary, in fact. It will mean that you're being doubly safeguarded, at practically no extra expense.

Take a Deep Breath

A long time ago I discovered that people who've never left Earth have certain fixed ideas about conditions in space. Everyone "knows," for example, that a man dies instantly and horribly when exposed to the vacuum that exists beyond the atmosphere. You'll find numerous gory descriptions of exploded space travelers in the popular literature, and I won't spoil your appetite by repeating them here. Many of those tales, indeed, are basically true. I've pulled men back through the air lock who were very poor advertisements for space flight.

Yet, at the same time, there are exceptions to every rule—even this one. I should know, for I learned the hard way.

We were on the last stages of building Communications Satellite Two; all the main units had been joined together, the living quarters had been pressurized, and the station had been given the slow spin around its axis that had restored the unfamiliar sensation of weight. I say "slow," but at its rim our two-hundred-foot-diameter wheel was turning at thirty miles an hour. We had, of course, no sense of motion, but the centrifugal force caused by this spin gave us about half the weight we would have possessed on Earth. That was enough to stop things from drifting around, yet not enough to make us feel uncomfortably sluggish after our weeks with no weight at all.

Four of us were sleeping in the small cylindrical cabin known as Bunkhouse Number 6 on the night that it happened. The bunkhouse was at the very rim of the station; if you imagine a bicycle wheel, with a string of sausages replacing the tire, you have a good idea of the layout. Bunkhouse Number 6 was one of these sausages, and we were slumbering peacefully inside it.

I was awakened by a sudden jolt that was not violent enough to cause me alarm, but which did make me sit up and wonder what had happened. Anything unusual in a space station demands instant attention, so I reached for the intercom switch by my bed. "Hello, Central," I called. "What was that?"

There was no reply; the line was dead.

Now thoroughly alarmed, I jumped out of bed — and had an even bigger shock. *There was no gravity.* I shot up to the ceiling before I was able to grab a stanchion and bring myself to a halt, at the cost of a sprained wrist.

It was impossible for the entire station to have suddenly stopped rotating. There was only one answer; the failure of the intercom and, as I quickly discovered, of the lighting circuit as well forced us to face the appalling truth. We were no longer part of the station; our little cabin had somehow come adrift, and had been slung off into space like a raindrop falling on a spinning flywheel.

There were no windows through which we could look out, but we were not in complete darkness, for the battery-powered emergency lights had come on. All the main air vents had closed automatically when the pressure dropped. For the time being, we could live in our own private atmosphere, even though it was not being renewed. Unfortunately, a steady whistling told us that the air we did have was escaping through a leak somewhere in the cabin.

There was no way of telling what had happened to the rest of the station. For all we knew, the whole structure might have come to pieces, and all our colleagues might be dead or in the same predicament as we — drifting through space in leaking cans of air. Our one slim hope was the possibility that we were the only castaways, that the rest of the station was intact and had been able to send a rescue team to find us. After all, we were receding at no more than thirty miles an hour, and one of the rocket scooters could catch up to us in minutes.

It actually took an hour, though without the evidence of my watch I should never have believed that it was so short a time. We were now gasping for breath, and the gauge on our single emergency oxygen tank had dropped to one division above zero.

The banging on the wall seemed like a signal from another world. We banged back vigorously, and a moment later a muffled voice called to us through the wall. Someone outside was lying with his space-suit helmet pressed against the metal, and his shouted words were reaching us by direct conduction. Not as clear as radio — but it worked.

The oxygen gauge crept slowly down to zero while we had our council of war. We would be dead before we could be towed back to the station; yet the rescue ship was only a few feet away from us, with its air lock already open. Our little problem was to cross that few feet—*without* space suits.

We made our plans carefully, rehearsing our actions in the full knowledge that there could be no repeat performance. Then we each took a deep, final swig of oxygen, flushing out our lungs. When we were all ready, I banged on the wall to give the signal to our friends waiting outside.

There was a series of short, staccato raps as the power tools got to work on the thin hull. We clung tightly to the stanchions, as far away as possible from the point of entry, knowing just what would happen. When it came, it was so sudden that the mind couldn't record the sequence of events. The cabin seemed to explode, and a great wind tugged at me. The last trace of air gushed from my lungs, through my already opened mouth. And then—utter silence, and the stars shining through the gaping hole that led to life.

Believe me, I didn't stop to analyze my sensations. I think—though I can never be sure that it wasn't imagination—that my eyes were smarting and there was a tingling feeling all over my body. And I felt very cold, perhaps because evaporation was already starting from my skin.

The only thing I can be certain of is that uncanny silence. It is never completely quiet in a space station, for there is always the sound of machinery or air pumps. But this was the absolute silence of the empty void, where there is no trace of air to carry sound.

Almost at once we launched ourselves out through the shattered wall, into the full blast of the sun. I was instantly blinded—but that didn't matter, because the men waiting in space suits grabbed me as soon as I emerged and hustled me into the air lock. And there, sound slowly returned as the air rushed in, and we remembered we could breathe again. The entire rescue, they told us later, had lasted just twenty seconds. . . .

Well, we were the founding members of the Vacuum-Breathers' Club. Since then, at least a dozen other men have done the same thing, in similar emergencies. The record time in space is now two minutes; after that, the blood begins to form bubbles as it boils at body temperature, and those bubbles soon get to the heart.

In my case, there was only one aftereffect. For maybe a quarter of a minute I had been exposed to *real* sunlight, not the feeble stuff that filters down through the atmosphere of Earth. Breathing space didn't hurt me at all — but I got the worst dose of sunburn I've ever had in my life.

Freedom of Space

Not many of you, I suppose, can imagine the time before the satellite relays gave us our present world communications system. When I was a boy, it was impossible to send TV programs across the oceans, or even to establish reliable radio contact around the curve of the Earth without picking up a fine assortment of crackles and bangs on the way. Yet now we take interference-free circuits for granted, and think nothing of seeing our friends on the other side of the globe as clearly as if we were standing face to face. Indeed, it's a simple fact that without the satellite relays, the whole structure of world commerce and industry would collapse. Unless we were up here on the space stations to bounce their messages around the globe, how do you think any of the world's big business organizations could keep their widely scattered electronic brains in touch with each other?

But all this was still in the future, back in the late seventies, when we were finishing work on the Relay Chain. I've already told you about some of our problems and near disasters; they were serious enough at the time, but in the end we overcame them all. The three stations spaced around Earth were no longer piles of girders, air cylinders, and plastic pressure chambers. Their assembly had been completed, we had moved aboard, and could now work in comfort, unhampered by space suits. And we had gravity again, now that the stations had been set slowly spinning. Not real gravity, of course; but centrifugal force feels exactly the same when you're out in space. It was pleasant being able to pour drinks and to sit down without drifting away on the first air current.

Once the three stations had been built, there was still a year's solid work to be done installing all the radio and TV equipment that would lift the world's communications networks into space. It was a great day when we established the first TV link between England and Australia. The signal was beamed up to us in Relay Two, as we sat above the center of

Africa, we flashed it across to Three—poised over New Guinea—and they shot it down to Earth again, clear and clean after its ninety-thousand-mile journey.

These, however, were the engineers' private tests. The official opening of the system would be the biggest event in the history of world communication—an elaborate global telecast, in which every nation would take part. It would be a three-hour show, as for the first time the live TV camera roamed around the world, proclaiming to mankind that the last barrier of distance was down.

The program planning, it was cynically believed, had taken as much effort as the building of the space stations in the first place, and of all the problems the planners had to solve, the most difficult was that of choosing a *compère* or master of ceremonies to introduce the items in the elaborate global show that would be watched by half the human race.

Heaven knows how much conniving, blackmail, and downright character assassination went on behind the scenes. All we knew was that a week before the great day, a nonscheduled rocket came up to orbit with Gregory Wendell aboard. This was quite a surprise, since Gregory wasn't as big a TV personality as, say, Jeffers Jackson in the US or Vince Clifford in Britain. However, it seemed that the big boys had canceled each other out, and Gregg had got the coveted job through one of those compromises so well known to politicians.

Gregg had started his career as a disc jockey on a university radio station in the American Midwest, and had worked his way up through the Hollywood and Manhattan nightclub circuits until he had a daily, nationwide program of his own. Apart from his cynical yet relaxed personality, his biggest asset was his deep velvet voice, for which he could probably thank his Negro blood. Even when you flatly disagreed with what he was saying—even, indeed, when he was tearing you to pieces in an interview—it was still a pleasure to listen to him.

We gave him the grand tour of the space station, and even (strictly against regulations) took him out through the air lock in a space suit. He loved it all, but there were two things he liked in particular. "This air you make," he said, "it beats the stuff we have to breathe down in New York. This is the first time my sinus trouble has gone since I went into TV." He also relished the low gravity; at the station's rim, a man had half his normal, Earth weight—and at the axis he had no weight at all.

However, the novelty of his surroundings didn't distract Gregg from his job. He spent hours at Communications Central, polishing his script and getting his cues right, and studying the dozens of monitor screens that would be his windows on the world. I came across him once while he was running through his introduction of Queen Elizabeth, who would be speaking from Buckingham Palace at the very end of the program. He was so intent on his rehearsal that he never even noticed I was standing beside him.

Well, that telecast is now part of history. For the first time a billion human beings watched a single program that came "live" from every corner of the Earth, and was a roll call of the world's greatest citizens. Hundreds of cameras on land and sea and air looked inquiringly at the turning globe; and at the end there was that wonderful shot of the Earth through a zoom lens on the space station, making the whole planet recede until it was lost among the stars....

There were a few hitches, of course. One camera on the bed of the Atlantic wasn't ready on cue, and we had to spend some extra time looking at the Taj Mahal. And owing to a switching error Russian subtitles were superimposed on the South American transmission, while half the USSR found itself trying to read Spanish. But this was nothing to what *might* have happened.

Through the entire three hours, introducing the famous and the unknown with equal ease, came the mellow yet never orotund flow of Gregg's voice. He did a magnificent job; the congratulations came pouring up the beam the moment the broadcast finished. But he didn't hear them; he made one short, private call to his agent, and then went to bed.

Next morning, the Earth-bound ferry was waiting to take him back to any job he cared to accept. But it left without Gregg Wendell, now junior station announcer of Relay Two.

"They'll think I'm crazy," he said, beaming happily, "but why should I go back to that rat race down there? I've all the universe to look at, I can breathe smog-free air, the low gravity makes me feel a Hercules, and my three darling ex-wives can't get at me." He kissed his hand to the departing rocket. "So long, Earth," he called. "I'll be back when I start pining for Broadway traffic jams and bleary penthouse dawns. And if I get homesick, I can look at anywhere on the planet just by turning a switch. Why, I'm more in the middle of things here than

I could ever be on Earth, yet I can cut myself off from the human race whenever I want to."

He was still smiling as he watched the ferry begin the long fall back to Earth, toward the fame and fortune that could have been his. And then, whistling cheerfully, he left the observation lounge in eight-foot strides to read the weather forecast for Lower Patagonia.

Passerby

It's only fair to warn you, right at the start, that this is a story with no ending. But it has a definite beginning, for it was while we were both students at Astrotech that I met Julie. She was in her final year of solar physics when I was graduating, and during our last year at college we saw a good deal of each other. I've still got the woolen tam-o'-shanter she knitted so that I wouldn't bump my head against my space helmet. (No, I never had the nerve to wear it.)

Unfortunately, when I was assigned to Satellite Two, Julie went to the Solar Observatory — at the same distance from Earth, but a couple of degrees eastward along the orbit. So there we were, sitting twenty-two thousand miles above the middle of Africa — but with nine hundred miles of empty, hostile space between us.

At first we were both so busy that the pang of separation was somewhat lessened. But when the novelty of life in space had worn off, our thoughts began to bridge the gulf that divided us. And not only our thoughts, for I'd made friends with the communications people, and we used to have little chats over the interstation TV circuit. In some ways it made matters worse seeing each other face to face and never knowing just how many other people were looking in at the same time. There's not much privacy in a space station....

Sometimes I'd focus one of our telescopes onto the distant, brilliant star of the observatory. In the crystal clarity of space, I could use enormous magnifications, and could see every detail of our neighbors' equipment — the solar telescopes, the pressurized spheres of the living quarters that housed the staff, the slim pencils of visiting ferry rockets that had climbed up from Earth. Very often there would be space-suited figures moving among the maze of apparatus, and I would strain my eyes in a hopeless attempt at identification. It's hard enough to recognize any-one in a space suit when you're only a few feet apart—but that didn't stop me from trying.

We'd resigned ourselves to waiting, with what patience we could muster, until our Earth leave was due in six months' time, when we had an unexpected stroke of luck. Less than half our tour of duty had passed when the head of the transport section suddenly announced that he was going outside with a butterfly net to catch meteors. He didn't become vio-lent, but had to be shipped hastily back to Earth. I took over his job on a temporary basis and now had—in theory at least—the freedom of space.

There were ten of the little low-powered rocket scooters under my proud command, as well as four of the larger interstation shuttles used to ferry stores and personnel from orbit to orbit. I couldn't hope to bor-row one of *those*, but after several weeks of careful organizing I was able to carry out the plan I'd conceived some two microseconds after being told I was now head of transport.

There's no need to tell how I juggled duty lists, cooked logs and fuel registers, and persuaded my colleagues to cover up for me. All that mat-ters is that, about once a week, I would climb into my personal space suit, strap myself to the spidery framework of a Mark III Scooter, and drift away from the station at minimum power. When I was well clear, I'd go over to full throttle, and the tiny rocket motor would hustle me across the nine-hundred-mile gap to the observatory.

The trip took about thirty minutes, and the navigational requirements were elementary. I could see where I was going and where I'd come from, yet I don't mind admitting that I often felt   well, a trifle lonely around the midpoint of the journey. There was no other solid matter within almost five hundred miles—and it looked an awfully long way down to Earth. It was a great help, at such moments, to tune the suit radio to the general service band, and to listen to all the back-chat be-tween ships and stations.

At midflight I'd have to spin the scooter around and start braking, and ten minutes later the observatory would be close enough for its details to be visible to the unaided eye. Very shortly after that I'd drift up to a small, plastic pressure bubble that was in the process of being fitted out as a spectroscopic laboratory—and there would be Julie, waiting on the other side of the air lock. . . .

I won't pretend that we confined our discussions to the latest results in astrophysics, or the progress of the satellite construction schedule. Few things, indeed, were further from our thoughts; and the journey home always seemed to flash by at a quite astonishing speed.

It was around midorbit on one of those homeward trips that the radar started to flash on my little control panel. There was something large at extreme range, and it was coming in fast. A meteor, I told myself—maybe even a small asteroid. Anything giving such a signal should be visible to the eye: I read off the bearings and searched the star fields in the indicated direction. The thought of a collision never even crossed my mind; space is so inconceivably vast that I was thousands of times safer than a man crossing a busy street on Earth.

There it was—a bright and steadily growing star near the foot of Orion. It already outshone Rigel, and seconds later it was not merely a star, but had begun to show a visible disk. Now it was moving as fast as I could turn my head; it grew to a tiny, misshaped moon, then dwindled and shrank with that same silent, inexorable speed.

I suppose I had a clear view of it for perhaps half a second, and that half second has haunted me all my life. The—object—had already vanished by the time I thought of checking the radar again, so I had no way of gauging how close it came, and hence how large it really was. It could have been a small object a hundred feet away—or a very large one, ten miles off. There is no sense of perspective in space, and unless you know what you are looking at, you cannot judge its distance.

Of course, it *could* have been a very large and oddly shaped meteor; I can never be sure that my eyes, straining to grasp the details of so swiftly moving an object, were not hopelessly deceived. I may have imagined that I saw that broken, crumpled prow, and the cluster of dark ports like the sightless sockets of a skull. Of one thing only was I certain, even in that brief and fragmentary vision. If it *was* a ship, it was not one of ours. Its shape was utterly alien, and it was very, very old.

It may be that the greatest discovery of all time slipped from my grasp as I struggled with my thoughts midway between the two space stations. But I had no measurements of speed or direction; whatever it was that I had glimpsed was now lost beyond recapture in the wastes of the solar system.

What should I have done? No one would ever have believed me, for I would have had no proof. Had I made a report, there would have been endless trouble. I should have become the laughingstock of the Space Service, would have been reprimanded for misuse of equipment—and would certainly not have been able to see Julie again. And to me, at that age, nothing else was as important. If you've been in love yourself, you'll understand; if not, then no explanation is any use.

So I said nothing. To some other man (how many centuries hence?) will go the fame for proving that we were not the firstborn of the children of the sun. Whatever it may be that is circling out there on its eternal orbit can wait, as it has waited ages already.

Yet I sometimes wonder. Would I have made a report, after all—had I known that Julie was going to marry someone else?

The Call of the Stars

Down there on Earth the twentieth century is dying. As I look across at the shadowed globe blocking the stars, I can see the lights of a hundred sleepless cities, and there are moments when I wish that I could be among the crowds now surging and singing in the streets of London, Capetown, Rome, Paris, Berlin, Madrid. . . . Yes, I can see them all at a single glance, burning like fireflies against the darkened planet. The line of midnight is now bisecting Europe: in the eastern Mediterranean a tiny, brilliant star is pulsing as some exuberant pleasure ship waves her searchlights to the sky. I think she is deliberately aiming at us; for the past few minutes the flashes have been quite regular and startlingly bright. Presently I'll call the communications center and find out who she is, so that I can radio back our own greetings.

Passing into history now, receding forever down the stream of time, is the most incredible hundred years the world has ever seen. It opened with the conquest of the air, saw at its midpoint the unlocking of the atom—and now ends with the bridging of space.

(For the past five minutes I've been wondering what's happening to Nairobi; now I realize that they are putting on a mammoth fireworks display. Chemically fueled rockets may be obsolete out here—but they're still using lots of them down on Earth tonight.)

The end of a century—and the end of a millennium. What will the hundred years that begin with two and zero bring? The planets, of course; floating there in space, only a mile away, are the ships of the first Martian expedition. For two years I have watched them grow, assembled piece by piece, as the space station itself was built by the men I worked with a generation ago.

Those ten ships are ready now, with all their crews aboard, waiting for the final instrument check and the signal for departure. Before the first day of the new century has passed its noon, they will be tearing free from the reins of Earth, to head out toward the strange world that may one day be man's second home.

As I look at the brave little fleet that is now preparing to challenge infinity, my mind goes back forty years, to the days when the first satellites were launched and the moon still seemed very far away. And I remember — indeed, I have never forgotten — my father's fight to keep me down on Earth.

There were not many weapons he had failed to use. Ridicule had been the first: "Of course they can do it," he had sneered, "but what's the point? Who wants to go out into space while there's so much to be done here on Earth? There's not a single planet in the solar system where men can live. The moon's a burnt-out slag heap, and everywhere else is even worse. *This* is where we were meant to live."

Even then (I must have been eighteen or so at the time) I could tangle him up in points of logic. I can remember answering, "How do you know where we were meant to live, Dad? After all, we were in the sea for about a billion years before we decided to tackle the land. Now we're making the next big jump: I don't know where it will lead — nor did that first fish when it crawled up on the beach, and started to sniff the air."

So when he couldn't outargue me, he had tried subtler pressures. He was always talking about the dangers of space travel, and the short working life of anyone foolish enough to get involved in rocketry. At that time, people were still scared of meteors and cosmic rays; like the "Here Be Dragons" of the old mapmakers, they were the mythical monsters on the still-blank celestial charts. But they didn't worry me; if anything, they added the spice of danger to my dreams.

While I was going through college, Father was comparatively quiet. My training would be valuable whatever profession I took up in later life, so he could not complain — though he occasionally grumbled about the money I wasted buying all the books and magazines on astronautics that I could find. My college record was good, which naturally pleased him; perhaps he did not realize that it would also help me to get my way.

All through my final year I had avoided talking of my plans. I had even given the impression (though I am sorry for that now) that I had abandoned my dream of going into space. Without saying anything to him, I put in my application to Astrotech, and was accepted as soon as I had graduated.

The storm broke when that long blue envelope with the embossed heading "Institute of Astronautical Technology" dropped into the mailbox. I was accused of deceit and ingratitude, and I do not think I ever forgave my father for destroying the pleasure I should have felt at being chosen for the most exclusive — and most glamorous — apprenticeship the world has ever known.

The vacations were an ordeal; had it not been for Mother's sake, I do not think I would have gone home more than once a year, and I always left again as quickly as I could. I had hoped that Father would mellow as my training progressed and as he accepted the inevitable, but he never did.

Then had come that stiff and awkward parting at the spaceport, with the rain streaming down from leaden skies and beating against the smooth walls of the ship that seemed so eagerly waiting to climb into the eternal sunlight beyond the reach of storms. I know now what it cost my father to watch the machine he hated swallow up his only son: for I understand many things today that were hidden from me then.

He knew, even as we parted at the ship, that he would never see me again. Yet his old, stubborn pride kept him from saying the only words that might have held me back. I knew that he was ill, but how ill, he had told no one. That was the only weapon he had not used against me, and I respect him for it.

Would I have stayed had I known? It is even more futile to speculate about the unchangeable past than the unforeseeable future; all I can say now is that I am glad I never had to make the choice. At the end he let me go; he gave up his fight against my ambition, and a little while later his fight with Death.

So I said good-by to Earth, and to the father who loved me but knew no way to say it. He lies down there on the planet I can cover with my hand; how strange it is to think that of the countless billion human beings whose blood runs in my veins, I was the very first to leave his native world....

The new day is breaking over Asia; a hairline of fire is rimming the eastern edge of Earth. Soon it will grow into a burning crescent as the sun comes up out of the Pacific — yet Europe is preparing for sleep, except for those revelers who will stay up to greet the dawn.

And now, over there by the flagship, the ferry rocket is coming back for the last visitors from the station. Here comes the message I have been waiting for: CAPTAIN STEVENS PRESENTS HIS COMPLIMENTS TO THE STATION COMMANDER. BLASTOFF WILL BE IN NINETY MINUTES; HE WILL BE GLAD TO SEE YOU ABOARD NOW.

Well, Father, now I know how you felt: time has gone full circle. Yet I hope that I have learned from the mistakes we both made, long ago. I shall remember you when I go over there to the flagship *Starfire* and say good-by to the grandson you never knew.

Tank Farm

DAVID BRIN

Although this story depicts a dark period of space investment, its pessimism is more hopeful than the era we live in. Possibility, in this story, is kept alive by a simple practicality, just one step beyond the off-the-shelf technology available today. The shuttle's tanks and residual fuel described exist now. The tanks are routinely dumped into the ocean instead of being used. We live in a time of space exploration that has slowed and threatens to stop. For us, today, the window to skylife is open only slightly, and it is closing.

1

"They finally fired Bylinsky."

I was up to my knees in agri-sludge, a frothy brown mess at the bottom of my personal greenhouse tank, when I heard the remark. For a moment I thought I had imagined it.

Your hearing plays tricks when you're wading around in mucky water, barely held to the floor by under a hundredth of a gee. I was groping in the goo, trying to find whatever had gummed up the aspirator. My breath blew up little green and brown droplets that hovered in front of my face for long seconds before slowly settling down again.

"Ralph! Did you hear me? I said Bylinsky's *out!*"

I looked up this time. Don Ishido, our communications and operations chief, hung halfway through the aft hatch of the greenhouse, twenty meters away. He was watching my reaction, maybe in order to report to the others exactly how I took the news. Probably there was money riding on it.

I nodded. "Thanks Don. Bylinsky's days were numbered. We'll miss him, but we'll survive."

Ishido smiled faintly. He must have bet on my poker face. "What do you want me to tell the others, boss?"

I shrugged. "We're still a tank farm. We buy 'em and store 'em, and later we'll all get rich selling 'em back for a profit."

"Even when they cut the water ration?"

"There'll be a way. We're in the future business. Now get out of here and let me finish my recreational farming."

Don smirked at my euphemism, but withheld comment. He ducked out, leaving me alone to my "recreation"... and my worries.

After clearing a clump of gelatinized algae from the input ports, I climbed onto one of the catwalk longerons rimming the pond and turned on the bubbler. The air began to fill with tiny, green, superoxygenated droplets.

I took a leap and sailed across the huge chamber to alight near the exit hatch. There I stowed my waders and looked around the greenhouse to make sure it was ready.

In the ten years I've been living in tanks I doubt I've ever entered or left one without blinking at least once in awe. The hatch was at one end of a metal cylinder as long as a ten-story building is tall, with the diameter of a small house. The walls were stiffened with aluminum baffles which once kept a hundred tons of liquid hydrogen from sloshing under high stress. That ribwork now held my greenhouse ponds.

The former hydrogen tank had a volume of over fifty thousand cubic feet. It, and its brothers, were just about the largest things ever put into space. And this one was all mine—my own huge garden to putter around in during off-duty hours, growing new types of space-adapted algae and yeasts.

I passed through the yard-wide hatch into the intertank area between the two main sections of the External Tank. In the middle the intertank was only four feet across. The hatch closed.

Looking back into the garden tank through a tinted port, I pressed a button to let the sunshine in.

A bright point of light blossomed at the opposite end of the cylinder, mirror-focused sunlight speared through a fused quartz window to strike the cloud of rising bubbles.

I stayed long enough to watch the rainbows form.

The intertank hoop connects the big and little parts of the great External Tanks, or "ETs," as we call them. The smaller cell had once contained 550 cubic meters of liquid oxygen. These days I stored gardening tools in it. Not a day had passed, in the last five years, in which I hadn't wished someone on Earth would recognize the waste, and come and take my toolshed away from me — to be used in some grand and wonderful plan.

Now they were trying to do just that, but not in a way I cared for at all.

"Boss? You still there? There's a telex from J. S. C. coming in."

I grabbed the big steel beam that had once borne the thrust of giant, strap-on solid rocket boosters. Now it served as a convenient place to put the intercom.

"Ishido, this is Rutter. I'm on my way. Don't let them sell us for scrap till I get there. Out."

I put on my hardsuit, carefully double-checking each seal and valve. The lock cycled, and I emerged into vacuum, but not blackness.

Overhead the Earth spanned the sky, a broad velvet blanket of browns and blues and fleecy white clouds. From just five hundred kilometers up, you don't see the Earth as a spinning marble in space. She covers an entire hemisphere, filling almost half the universe.

I drifted, but after a minute my boots touched the metal of the tank again. The same faint microgravity that held my pools inside the garden worked here on the outside.

The tank was the next to last in a row of forty of the great cylinders, nestled side by side. A parallel deck of fifteen huge tanks lay about sixty kilometers overhead, linked to this collection by six strong cables. Twenty meters away from where I stood, one of the half-inch polymer tethers rose from its anchor point, a mirror-bright streak toward the planet overhead.

Sometimes a careful observer could make out B Deck without aid — a tiny rectangle about an eighth the apparent diameter of the moon — against the bright bulk of the Earth. When we crossed the terminator, the tanks in Group B sparkled like gems in Terra's sunset tiara.

Today I hadn't time to look for B Deck. The Feds had finally fired Edgar Bylinsky, the Tank Farm's last big supporter in NASA. If we thought times were hard before, they were going to get worse now.

"Ralph?" It was Ishido's voice again, now coming over my suit radio. "We've got the telex. I think this is the big one."

I pushed off toward the control center. "Okay, what's the news?"

"Uh, they're moving fast. Pacifica's coming in with a couple of official bad news boys."

I could guess what they were coming to tell us. They'd say they were here for "consultations," but actually it would be to say that Uncle Sam wasn't going to sell us any more water.

"Don, when are the bad news boys due?"

"ETA about an hour."

"I'll be right in."

Another hop took me to the entrance of the control tank. It was sheathed in layers of plating cut from dismantled ETs, to protect the crew during solar proton storms.

While waiting for the airlock to cycle, I looked up at the Indian Ocean, where they used to dump our tanks back at the beginning of the shuttle program. That awful waste had been one of the reasons for founding the Tank Farm.

For years ours had been a lonely and expensive gamble. Now we had proved our point. Proved it too well, it seemed.

They let us get a monopoly, and now they want to break us, I thought. And they might succeed, if they cut off our water.

We had safeguarded the Key to Space for them, and expected them to be grateful when they realized its worth. We should have known better.

2

In the beginning there was the space shuttle. Never mind what came earlier. Before the shuttle, space was a place for robots and daredevils.

With tight budgets and all, the Space Transportation System has stayed fundamentally the same. A big, complex, manned orbiter is launched from Canaveral or Vandenburg, strapped to two solid rocket boosters and one huge fuel tank carrying 770 tons of cryogenic propellants for the shuttle main engines. The engines are part of the orbiter, so they can be brought home and reused. The solid boosters drop off minutes after liftoff and are recovered for refurbishment.

But until our group came along, the huge external tanks were simply dumped, after fueling the shuttle to almost orbital velocity.

Once upon a time people thought we were on the verge of colonizing space. But then tight budgets cut the size of the STS fleet, and the cost of a pound sent into orbit remained in four figures. Visions of big O'Neill colonies and grand cities on the moon foundered without the bootstrap mass needed to build the dreams.

The lock passed me through. I stowed my hardsuit in a restorer locker whose nameplate simply read BOSSMAN. While I racked my equipment, I recalled all the times I had explained the Tank Farm to audiences on Earth: to congressmen, housewives, investors — to anyone who would listen.

Back in the early '80s it was shown that the thirty-five-ton External Tank can be carried all the way into orbit *at zero cost* to the orbiter's thirty-ton cargo capacity. Thirty five tons of aluminum and polymers, already shaped into vacuum-tight cylinders, delivered free!

And that wasn't all. On arrival the tanks would contain another five to thirty-five tons of leftover liquid hydrogen and oxygen, usable in upper-stage engines, or to run fuel cells, or to be converted to precious water.

At a time when the grand hopes for space seemed about to fall apart, the ET was like manna from Earth to Heaven. When the government didn't seem eager to seize the opportunity — when they built their cramped, delicate, little "space stations" from expensive modules in the old-fashioned way — the Colombo-Carroll Foundation, a consortium of US and Italian interests, offered to buy the tanks.

We would save them, until the world wised up, then sell them back. Meanwhile, the Tank Farm would provide orbit boosts via the tether-sling effect, saving customers fuel and time and paying our way until other investments matured.

For ten years the Farm had been on course, but it seems we'd neglected a few lines of fine print in our contract. The Feds had to let us buy the tanks at a fixed price, but nothing in the contract said they had to give us the residual hydrogen and oxygen, too.

It never occurred to us they'd not want to give us all the water we needed! Who in the world would have thought they'd ever want to take the Tank Farm away from us?

3

Imagine six very long parallel wires, hanging in space, always aimed toward the surface of the Earth 500 kilometers below.

At both ends the wires are anchored to flat rows of giant cylinders — forty in the upper layer, A Deck; and sixteen in the lower, B Deck. An elevator, consisting of two welded tanks, moves between the two ends, carrying people and supplies both ways.

I've lost count of the number of times I've explained the curious structure to visitors. I've compared it to a double-ended child's swing, or a bolo turning exactly once per orbit, so that one end is always low and the other always high. It's been called a Skyhook, and even a Beanstalk, though the idea's nowhere near as ambitious as the ground-to-geosynchronous space-elevators of science fiction fame.

The main purpose of the design is simply to keep the tanks from falling. The two massive ends of the Farm act like a dipole in the gradient of the Earth's gravitational field, so each deck winds up orbiting edge-forward, like a flat plate skimming. This reduces the drag caused by the upper fringes of the atmosphere, extending our orbital lifetime.

The scheme is simple, neat, and it works. Of course the arrangement doesn't prevent *all* orbital decay. It takes a little thrust from our aluminum engines, from time to time, to make up the difference.

Since our center of mass is traveling in a circular orbit, the lower deck has to move much slower than it "should" to remain at its height. The tethers keep it suspended, as it were.

The upper deck, in turn, is dragged along *faster* than it would normally go, at its height. It would fly away into a high ellipse if the cables ever let go.

That's why we feel a small artificial gravity at each end, directed away from the center of mass. It creates the ponds in my garden, and helps prevent the body decay of pure weightlessness.

When I entered the darkened control chamber, I moved quietly behind the chief flight controller and watched. The controller's main screen showed the interdeck elevator stopped about three klicks above B Deck. The reason for its delay came into view in a few moments: a small delta-wing whose white tiles shone against the starfield. I stood in the shadows and listened as our operators conversed with the shuttle pilot.

"*Pacifica*, this is A for Arnold Deck control. You are cleared for orbit intersection. In a minute we'll transfer you to B for Brown, for final approach. Extend your landing gear now."

"Roger, Arnold Deck. Pacifica, *ready for landing.*"

The orbiter drifted toward B Deck. On the controller's screen I could see *Pacifica's* landing gear deploy in the deep black of space.

The inner face of B Deck was covered with a flat surface of aluminum plates, surrounded by a low fence of soft nylon mesh.

Pacifica was at the highest point of her elliptical orbit. Her velocity would, for a few minutes at apogee, be virtually the same as B Deck's, allowing a gentle approach and contact. (A few purists still refused to call the docking a "landing.") The shuttle gave off small puffs of reaction gas to align her approach.

It was a beautiful technique, and the unargued greatest asset of the Tank Farm. When *Pacifica* was secured to B Deck, she would be carried along in the Farm's unconventional circular orbit until it was time for her to go. Then *Pacifica* would simply be pushed over the edge of B Deck, to fall toward the Earth again, finishing her original ellipse.

I looked at the screen showing the underbelly of B Deck. A great net of nylon hung below the plain of cylinders. Within, like a caterpillar trapped in a web, was *Pacifica's* ET, the External Tank that had powered her into orbit, sent ahead and snagged on a previous pass.

So the bad news boys had brought one of the magic eggs with them. I hoped it was a good omen, though it was probably just a coincidence of scheduling.

Until a year ago most of the orbiters visiting the Farm also delivered their External Tanks, along with several tons of residual hydrogen and oxygen propellants in each. Then a new administration started reneging, stockpiling ETs at the Space Stations instead, and denying us our allotment. The Foundation took them to court, of course, and forced a delivery rate of at least ten ETs a year.

The new administration didn't like losing face. Now they'd found a way to get even. Our contract said they had to sell us the tanks, but it said nothing about the water.

"Um, Dr. Rutter, could I speak with you for a minute?"

I turned to see an earnest-looking, black-haired young woman. She clutched a roll of strip-charts. Emily Testa was a very promising new member of the Farm, sent up by the Italians, the junior partners in Colombo Station.

"This is really a bad time, Emily. Is it important?"

"Well sir..." She caught my warning look. "I mean *Ralph*... Since I arrived, I have been studying the problem of electrical currents in the tether cables, and I think I have learned something interesting."

I nodded as I recalled the project I'd given the young newcomer to get her started. It was a nagging little problem that I'd wanted to have someone look into for some time.

The superpolymer tethers that held the Tank Farm together were sheathed in an aluminum skin to protect them from solar ultraviolet radiation. Unfortunately, this meant there was an electrical conducting path from B Deck to A Deck. As the Farm swept around the Earth in its unconventional orbit, the cables cut through a changing flux from the planet's magnetic field. The resulting electrical potentials had caused some rather disconcerting side effects, especially as the Tank Farm grew larger.

"Go on, Emily," I suggested. But I couldn't help listening with only half my attention. *Pacifica* was coming in, gear extended like a fighter landing on an aircraft carrier. I could hear the controllers talking softly in their singsong dialect.

"Well, sir," Emily said, almost without a trace of accent, "I wasn't able to find a way to prevent the potential buildup. I'm afraid the voltage is unavoidable as the conductive tethers pass through the Earth's magnetic field.

"In fact, if the charge had anywhere to go, we could see some pretty awesome currents: one deck might act as a cathode, emitting electrons into the ionosphere, and the other could be an anode, absorbing electrons from the surrounding plasma. It all depends on whether..."

Pacifica touched down with barely a bump. Her landing gear flexed slightly as she rolled to a stop. The interdeck elevator resumed its descent as the orbiter was tied down by the B Deck crew. Her cargo was removed from the open cargo bay by giant manipulator arms.

Two spacesuited figures drifted down from *Pacifica's* hatch and stood waiting for the elevator. It didn't take a lot of imagination to guess who they were. Our bad news boys.

Emily went on single-mindedly, apparently unaware of my split attention. "... so we could, if we ever really wanted to, *use* this potential difference the tethers generate! We could shunt it through some transformers here on A Deck, and apply as much as twenty thousand volts! I calculate we might pull more power out of the Earth's magnetic field, just by orbiting through it with these long wires, than we would ever need to run lights, heat, utilities, and communications, even if we grew to ten times our present size!"

The boys in the spacesuits got into the elevator. The crew loaded *Pacifica's* cargo after them, encased in blue Department of Defense shrouding.

"Emily." I turned fully to the young woman. "You know there ain't no such thing as a free lunch. Your idea certainly is interesting. I'll grant you could probably draw current from the tethers, maybe even as much as you say. But we'd pay for it in ways we can't afford."

Emily stared for a moment, then she snapped her fingers. "Angular momentum! Of course! By drawing current we would couple with the Earth's magnetic field. We would slow down, and add some of our momentum to the planet's spin, microscopically. Our orbit would decay even faster than it already does!"

I nodded. "Right. Still, it's a good idea. If we were getting all the water we used to receive, so we could run the aluminum engines as before, we might even decide to draw power your way.

"But our solar cells are really more than adequate. We could sell our excess to Earth, if they could only agree on a way to receive it."

She looked a little crestfallen. "Keep at it, though," I said for morale's sake. "Maybe there's a way to turn these electrical phenomena to our advantage. We ought to have a break coming, about now." I tried to sound as if I believed it. Emily brightened a bit.

The elevator started rising, on its way up here to A Deck. I had about an hour to get ready—to shave and shower away the aroma of my garden. It probably wouldn't do any good, but I'd want to look presentable to the bad news boys.

4

We had our meeting in the lounge. Susan Sorbanes, our business manager, took her place to my left, Don Ishido to my right. There were no chairs, but we stood at rest in the feeble gravity, a table made of spun aluminum fibers between us and the federal officials. Our backs were to the giant quartz window.

Across the table, Colonel Robert Bahnz, the new DOD representative, floated impassively. He had said hardly a word, apparently content to leave the talking to Henry Woke, the NASA official who had come up in *Pacifica* with him. Bahnz stood at a slight angle, which had to take a certain amount of work. Was it his way of showing his contempt for the Tank Farm's famous gravity, so unlike the freefall conditions in the government's shiny little Space Stations?

"So you people have decided to hit us on two fronts all at once, Dr. Woke?" Susan spoke softly, but her voice had a cutting edge. "You're going to attack the Farm's man-rating, and you're cutting back on our share of the residual propellants and water."

Woke was a middle-aged bureaucrat who must have convinced himself long ago that space visits were a route to advancement in NASA. I could tell by his faint green pallor that he was doped up against space sickness.

"Now, Dr. Sorbanes," he said. "Safety's been an issue ever since a crewman fell from B Deck two years ago. As a quasi-federal institution, Colombo Station must adhere to man-rating policy. That's all we are interested in."

"We've had a good safety record for ten years, except for that one incident," Susan replied. "And Congress gave us exemptions back in '89, you'll remember."

"Yes, but those exemptions expire this year. And I think you'll find this

Congress less willing to take chances with the safety of its citizens in orbit."

"I don't see why we have to go the gold-plated route NASA and DOD used in the Space Stations," Susan said acidly. "All that approach accomplished was to slow you down by a decade, and almost turn the country off on space for good!"

Woke shook his head. "Perhaps, Dr. Sorbanes. Indeed, it's because NASA has seen the value of the Tank Farm approach that we had last year's unfortunate misunderstanding regarding tank deliveries. Since Stations Two and Three began operating their own propellant recovery units and aluminum smelters, we've found that we need the leftover tanks as much as you do. We're all going to have to share. That's what it comes down to."

Don Ishido shook his head. "That's a load of bull! Our contract only guarantees us a third of the tanks launched, in return for which we use the slingshot effect to boost government and commercial cargoes into higher orbits, and provide shuttles like *Pacifica* with temporary angular momentum loans. That leaves you with two-thirds of the tanks to do with as you wish!

"Let's face it. It's not the tanks that are causing the problem. It's you stealing our water!"

I cleared my throat. It was time to step in, before this broke down completely.

"I think what Mr. Ishido means, Dr. Woke, is that Colombo Station depends on delivery of at least fifty tons of residual propellants a year, for life support, chemistry, and especially to provide oxidizer for our aluminum engines. Without those engines, our orbit will decay, and we'll be forced to use the extremely inefficient method of flinging away tanks to maintain altitude. The Farm will cease accumulating mass, and our value to our investors will disappear . . . this just as we were about to show a real profit for the first time."

Woke shrugged. "Of course we have no intention of cutting off the water and oxygen you need to maintain life support. No one even considered such a thing."

Damn right, I thought. Nothing would alienate the public like that. But trimming our ration, forcing us to spend tanks as fast as we get them — they could pull that off without trouble.

Yeah. We had almost closed a deal with some big Earthside chemical houses to produce large amounts of low-gee biochemicals on B Deck, when NASA Station Two undercut us by $2 million. But the killer had really been the rumors over our water situation. The investors had shied away from the uncertainty.

It hurt like hell. We were just short of making it. We had gobs of solar power, but the Earthsiders couldn't agree on how to receive it. With water and our giant tanks we could run a tremendous chemical plant, but timid companies stopped just short of buying in. We'd planned to set up a space hotel and sell vacations for scores of tourists at a time, but we were stymied by this "man-rating" straw man.

Our ecological recycling system had us ninety-five percent independent of Earth resupply. Our smelter was operational and waiting for customers: we had developed the aluminum engine.

But all anyone wanted to buy was the slingshot effect. We were a glorified switching yard in orbit. And the new government clearly wanted us to stay just that.

Woke kept up his soothing apologia. I had heard it all before. I wasn't the one to fight him, anyway. That was up to our lawyers back in Washington. My job was to come up with miracles. And right now they appeared to be in short supply.

The crewcut DOD man, Bahnz, was staring at something over my shoulder. I shifted a little to look.

Out on A Deck they were readying a Defense cargo for launch. They had peeled away the blue shrouding and set the cylinder near the edge of the deck. At the right moment the package would slip off into the starry field below us, falling away from Earth in a steep ellipse. At apogee a motor would cut in, carrying the spysat the rest of the way to geosynchronous orbit.

Bahnz had a gleam in his eyes as he observed the preparations.

You want my Farm, don't you? I thought. *You peepers fought us in the beginning, but now you see we're the one thing keeping us ahead of the other nations in space. Now you want my Tank Farm for your own.*

Two years ago, they had tried to get us to store "strategic assets" in the A Deck tanks. I threatened to resign, and the Foundation found the guts to refuse. That's when the troubles had started.

Bahnz noticed my look, and smiled a knowing smile.

He thinks he holds all the aces, I thought. *And he might be right.*

There were some old SF stories I read when I was a kid, about space colonies rebelling against Earth bureaucracies. I had a brief fantasy of leading my crew in a "tea party," and kicking these two jerks off of our *sovereign territory.*

Bahnz saw the peaceful smile on my face, and must have wondered what caused it.

Of course the rebellion idea was absurd. It wasn't what any of us wanted, and it wasn't practical. We might be ninety-five percent free of Earth logistical support, but that last few percent would be with us for a hundred years. Anyway, without either water or new tanks every year, Mother Earth's atmosphere would quickly pull us down.

While Don and Susan kept up our side of the charade, I looked out the window, thinking.

Next year would be solar maximum, when the coronal ion wind would come sleeting in from the active sun. The upper atmosphere would heat up and bloat outward, like a high tide dragging at our knees. At solar max we could lose twenty kilometers of altitude in a single year. Maybe much more.

Our investors would be caving in within eighteen months. Even the Italians would soon be begging the US administration to make a deal.

For an instant I saw the Earth not as a broad vague mass overhead, but as a spinning globe of rock, rushing air, and water, of molten core and invisible fields, reaching out to grapple with the tides that filled space. It was eerie. I could almost *feel* the Tank Farm, like a double-ended kite, coursing through those invisible fields, its tethers cutting the lines of force — like the slowly turning bushings of a dynamo.

That was what young Emily Testa had compared it to. A dynamo. We could draw power from our motion if we ever had to — buying electricity and paying for it in orbital momentum. It was a solution in search of a problem, for we already had all the power we needed.

The image wouldn't leave my mind, though. I could almost see the double-ended kite, right there in front of me . . . a dynamo. We didn't *need* a dynamo. What we needed was the opposite. What we needed was . . .

"I think we should recess," I said suddenly, interrupting Dr. Woke in the middle of a sentence. It didn't matter. My job wasn't diplomacy. It was miracle-working.

"Susan, would you show our guests to some rooms? We'll all meet again over supper in my cabin, if that's okay with you gentlemen?"

Woke nodded resignedly. I think he had hoped to go back down right away in *Pacifica*. Colonel Bahnz smiled. "Dr. Rutter, will you be serving Slingshot with dinner?"

"It's traditional," I replied, anxious to get rid of the man.

"Good. It's one of the reasons I came up today." Bahnz's grin seemed friendly enough, but there was an undertone to his voice that I understood only too well.

I waited until they had left, then turned to Ishido. "Don, go fetch Emily Testa and meet me in the power room in five minutes."

"Sure, chief. But what . . . ?"

"There's something I want to try. Now shake a leg!"

I kicked off down the hallway, looking for a computer terminal. I don't think I touched the floor twice in fifty yards.

5

For all of our Spartan lifestyle, there are a few places the crew had tried to make "posh." One is the main lounge. Another is the Captain's Cabin. My digs were given that name when the Foundation first had the idea of setting up a tourist hotel. They figured making a big deal out of dinner in my quarters would give a visit more of the flavor of a Caribbean cruise.

The aluminum walls had been anodized different pastel shades. The gold carpet had been woven from converted tank insulator material. And in wall niches there stood a dozen vacuum-spun aluminum wire sculptures created by Dave Crisuellini, our smelter chief and resident artist.

The Captain's Table was made of oak, brought up at six hundred dollars a pound for one purpose only, to look impressive.

Henry Woke sat to my right as the volunteer stewards served us from steaming casserole dishes. Next to Woke sat Susan Sorbanes. Across from them were Emily Testa, nervously fingering her fork as her eyes darted about the room, and Ishido. Colonel Bahnz sat across from me.

Woke looked considerably less green around the gills. His eyes widened at the soufflé a waiter laid in front of him. "I'm impressed! I'd heard that a hundreth of a gee is enough to enable the inner ear to come to equilibrium, but I hadn't believed. Now, to be able to eat from plates! With forks!" He spoke around a hot mouthful. "This is delicious! What is it?"

"Well, most of our food is prepared from termite flour and caked algae..."

Woke paused chewing. Susan and Ishido shared a look and a smile.

"... however," I went on, "recently we have begun raising our own wheat, and chickens for eggs."

Woke looked uncomfortable for another moment, then apparently decided to accept the ambiguity. "Ingenious," he said, and resumed eating.

"We have a number of ingenious people here," Susan said. "Many of our crew served aboard the Space Stations, and came here when NASA went through cutbacks and furloughed them.

"Others were hired by the Foundation because of their varied talents. Emily here," she said, smiling at young Testa, "is a fine example of the sort of colonist we're looking for."

Emily blushed and looked down at her plate. She was very tired after the last few hours as we had furiously experimented with the Farm's power system.

Colonel Bahnz squeezed an aluminum-foiled beer bottle, his second. "You're right about one thing, Dr. Sorbanes," the DOD man said. "The US Government has subsidized this venture in many hidden ways. Most of your personnel got their training at taxpayer expense."

"Have we ever failed in our gratitude, Colonel?" Susan spoke with pure sincerity. And to Ishido and me, the answer was obviously no. We Tank Farmers think of ourselves as custodians of a trust.

But Bahnz clearly disagreed. "Do you call it *gratitude*, using lawyers' tricks to put restrictions on your country's use of valuable resources when she needs them most?"

"We believe," Susan said, "that need will be greatest in the future. And we plan to be here, with the key to a treasure chest, when the time comes."

"Dreams of glory," Bahnz sneered. "I know all about them. Tell me about lunar mines and space colonies and other fairy tales, Dr. Sorbanes. And I'll tell you about Low Earth Orbit, now filled with garbage and bombs and little cameras from half a hundred bickering, hungry little nuclear powers, all blaming each other for a world economy in a thirty-year skid!

"Have you any idea what would happen if even *one* of these arrogant little 'spacefaring nations' decided to ignite a small enhanced radiation device in that cloud of communications satellites overhead? You know as well as I how dependent we are on orbital datalinks. And you know the only way to defend those links is to put our satellites inside big Faraday cages."

Bahnz struck the nearby aluminum wall. "*This* is what your country needs, Dr. Sorbanes. This tank and others like it! And the propellants for upper-stage launches. And we need this *station*, for the momentum transfer you now almost *give* away to anyone who wants it!"

Susan was gearing up for a major rebuttal. I hurried to interrupt. "People, please! Let's try to relax, if only for a little while. Colonel Bahnz, you seem to like Slingshot. That's your third helping."

Bahnz had plucked another bottle from a passing steward. "Why not," he shrugged. "It costs a hundred bucks a pint on Earth. It's damn fine beer."

"Dr. Ishido is our brewmaster."

Bahnz lifted the bottle to Don and bowed his head in silent tribute. An aficionado of beer need say no more; Ishido nodded at the colonel's compliment.

"Director Rutter," Bahnz said as he turned to me, "Dr. Woke and I will be leaving within two hours. I have held *Pacifica* to please you, but our business here is done. If you have anything more to say, you can speak through your Foundation's Washington office."

Bahnz was obviously the type that got straight to the point, especially when he had had a bit to drink. He showed no trace of that irreverent streak I had known in the officers and officials of the early '90s. Those fellows had been almost like coconspirators, helping nurture the Farm along in a time of tight budgets and dubious senators.

"Two hours, Colonel? Yes. That should be enough time. Just remind *Pacifica*'s crew to check their inertial tracking units before dropoff. There may be a few acceleration anomalies."

Bahnz snorted. "So? You plan to fire up your famous aluminum engines to impress us? Big deal. Go ahead and use up your reserve water,

Rutter. You've got enough oxidizer to run them for maybe two months; then you'll start flinging mass away to keep orbit."

Ishido started to rise. At a sharp look from me he subsided.

"Why Colonel," I said smoothly. "You sound downright happy over our predicament."

The crewcut officer slapped the oak table. "Damned straight! Let's lay it out, Rutter. I think you're a bunch of unpatriotic dreamers who'd do anything other than serve your country. July's court judgment was the last straw.

"We're going to live up to the contract, all right. You'll get your tanks, and enough water to keep from making martyrs of you. But you'll start spending more mass to stay in orbit than you take in. Your profits will disappear. Then see how fast your investors force you out as director!

"Pretty soon, Rutter, *you'll* be buying Slingshot at a hundred clams a pint!" Bahnz emptied the squeeze bottle with a flourish.

I shrugged and turned back to my meal. The second worst thing you could do to a man like Bahnz was to ignore him. I intended to do the very worst thing within an hour and a half.

6

The face on the screen was flushed and angry. In the dimness of Arnold Deck Control Room, I could tell the man was upset.

"What the *hell* do you think you're doing, Rutter?"

I had made *Pacifica* wait for fifteen minutes while the control crew made a show of looking for me, then appeared, to look back at Bahnz with an expression of beatific innocence.

"What seems to be the problem, Colonel?"

"You know damned well what the problem is!" the man shouted. "Colombo Station is under acceleration!"

"So? I told you over dinner to have your crew check their inertial units. You knew that meant we would be maneuvering."

"But you're thrusting at two *microgees*! Your aluminum engines can't push five thousand tons that hard!"

I shrugged.

"And anyway, we can't find your thrust exhaust! We look for a rocket trail, and find nothing but a slight electron cloud spreading from A Deck!"

"Nu?" I shrugged again. "Colonel, you force me to conclude that we are *not* using our aluminum engines. It *is* curious, no?"

Bahnz looked as if he wanted some nails to chew—threepenny, at least. Behind him I could see the crew of *Pacifica*, crouched over their instruments in order to stay out of his way.

"Rutter, I don't know what you're up to, but we can see from here that your entire solar cell array has been turned sunward. You have no use for that kind of power! Are you going to tell me what's going on? Or do I come back up there and make myself insufferable until you do?"

My respect for Bahnz rose two notches. He might be an SOB, but he knew how to get his way. "Oh there won't be any need for that," I laughed.

"You see, Colonel, we need all that solar power to drive our new motor."

"Motor? What motor?"

"The motor that's enabling us to raise our orbit without spending a bit of mass—no oxygen, not even a shred of aluminum. It's the motor that's going to make it possible for us to pull a profit next year, Colonel, even under the terms of the present contract."

Bahnz stared at me. "A *motor*?"

"The biggest motor there is, my dear fellow. It's called the Earth."

He blinked, his mind obviously whirling to figure out what I meant.

"Have a good trip, Colonel," I said. "And any time you're in the neighborhood, do stop by for a Slingshot."

"Rutter!"

I turned away and launched myself toward the window at the far end of the control room.

"RUTTER!"

The voice faded behind me as I drifted up to the crystal port. Outside, the big, ugly Tanks lay like roc eggs in a row, waiting to be hatched. I could almost envision it. They'd someday transform themselves into great birds of space. And our grandchildren would ride their offspring to the stars.

Bright silvery cables seemed to stretch all the way to the huge blue globe overhead. And I know, now, that they did indeed anchor us to the Earth ... an Earth which does not end at a surface of mountain and plain and water, nor with the ocean of air, but continues outward in strong fingers of force, caressing her children still.

Right now those tethers were carrying over a hundred amps of current from B Deck to A. There, electrons were sprayed out into space by an array of small, sharp cathodes.

We could have used the forward process to extract energy from our orbital momentum. I had told Emily Testa earlier today that that would solve nothing. Our problem was to *increase* our momentum.

Current in a wire, passing through a magnetic field ... You could run a dynamo that way, or a *motor*. With more solar power than we'll ever need, we can shove the current through the cables *against* the electromotive force, feeding energy to the Earth, and to our orbit.

A solar-powered motor, turning once per orbit, our Tank Farm rises without shedding an ounce of precious mass. I smiled as I looked out on the fleecy clouds of home and the tanks in a row, like presents waiting to be opened.

I felt Susan come up beside me. "*Pacifica's* gone," she said grinning. "And our acceleration's climbed to three microgees, Ralph."

I nodded. "Have Don ease back a bit for now. We don't want to push the motor too hard on its first day. I'll check in later."

"Where are you going?"

I caught a rung by the hatch. "I'm going to go unwind by spending some time puttering in my garden."

Susan shook her head and muttered "Yuck" under her breath.

I pretended I didn't hear her.

Breakaway, Backdown

JAMES PATRICK KELLY

This story's hard look at human biology in space makes one ask, What will human beings accept? The answer is, Quite a lot. Nearly thirty years after James Gunn's bleak stories about the first space station, published as *Station in Space* (1958), pessimism about the human body in space persists, both in fiction and space medicine. But the problems can be faced and solved, by giving the human body protections similar to those found on Earth. Protections that are not perfect. A long-term solution would involve subtle bioengineering.

You know, in space nobody wears shoes.

Well, new temps wear slippers. They make the soles out of that adhesive polymer, griprite or griptite. Sounds like paper ripping when you lift your feet. Temps who've been up a while wear this glove thing that snugs around the toes. The breakaways, they go barefoot. You can't really walk much in space, so they've reinvented their feet so they can pick up screwdrivers and spoons and stuff. It's hard because you lose fine motor control in micro gee. I had... have this friend, Elena, who could make a krill-and-tomato sandwich with her feet, but she had that operation that changes your big toe into a thumb. I used to kid her that maybe breakaways were climbing down the evolutionary ladder, not jumping off it. Are we people or chimps? She'd scratch her armpits and hoot.

Sure, breakaways have a sense of humor. They're people after all; it's just that they're like no people you know. The thing was, Elena was so limber that she could bite her toenails. So can you fix my shoe?

How long is that going to take? Why not just glue the heel back on?

I know they're Donya Durands, but I've got a party in half an hour, okay?

What, you think I'm going to walk around town barefoot? I'll wait — except what's with all these lights? It's two in the morning and you've got this place bright as noon in Khartoum. How about a little respect for the night?

Thanks. What did you say your name was? I'm Cleo.

You are, are you? Jane, honey, lots of people *think* about going to space but you'd be surprised at how few actually apply — much less break away. So how old are you?

Oh, no, they like them young, just as long as you're over nineteen. No kids in space. So the stats don't scare you?

Not shoe repair, that's for sure. But if you can convince them you're serious, they'll find something for you to do. They trained me and I was nobody, a business major. I temped for almost fifteen months on *Victor Foxtrot* and I never could decide whether I loved or hated it. Still can't, so how could I even think about becoming a breakaway? Everything is loose up there, okay? It makes you come unstuck. The first thing that happens is you get spacesick. For a week your insides are so scrambled that you're trying to digest lunch with your cerebellum and write memos with your large intestine. Meanwhile your face puffs up so that you can't find yourself in the mirror anymore and your sinuses fill with cotton candy and you're fighting a daily hair mutiny. I might've backed down right off if it hadn't been for Elena—you know, the one with the clever toes? Then when you're totally miserable and empty and disoriented, your brain sorts things out again and you realize it's all magic. Some astrofairy has enchanted you. Your body is as light as a whisper, free as air. I'll tell you the most amazing thing about weightlessness. It doesn't go away. You keep falling: down, up, sideways, whatever. You might bump into something once in a while but you never, ever slam into the ground. Extremely sexy, but it does take some getting used to. I kept having dreams about gravity. Down here you have a whole planet hugging you. But in space, it's not only you that's enchanted, it's all your stuff too. For instance, if you put that brush down, it stays. It doesn't decide to drift across the room and out the window and go visit Elena over on B deck. I had this pin that had been my mother's—a silver dove with a diamond eye—and somehow it escaped from a locked jewelry box. Turned up two months later in a dish of butterscotch pudding, almost broke Jack Pitzer's tooth. You get a lot of pudding in space. Oatmeal. Stews. Sticky food is easier to eat and you can't taste much of anything but salt and sweet anyway.

Why, do you think I'm babbling? God, I *am* babbling. It must be the Zentadone. The woman at the persona store said it was just supposed to be an icebreaker with a flirty edge to it, like Panital only more sincere. You wouldn't have any reset, would you?

Hey, spare me the lecture, honey. I know they don't allow personas in space. Anyway, imprinting is just a bunch of pro-brain propaganda. Personas are temporary—*period*. When you stop taking the pills, the personas go away and you're your plain old vanilla self again; there's bushels of studies that say so. I'm just taking a little vacation from Cleo. Maybe I'll go away for a weekend, or a week or a month, but eventually I'll come home. Always have, always will.

I don't care *what* your Jesus puppet says; you can't trust godware, okay? Look, I'm not going to convince you and you're not going to convince me. Truce?

The shoes? Four, five years. Let's see. I bought them in '36. Five years.
I had to store them while I was up.

You get used to walking in spike heels, actually. I mean, I'm not going
to run a marathon or climb the Matterhorn. Elena has all these theories
of why men think spikes are sexy. Okay, they're kind of a short-term body
mod. They stress the leg muscles, which makes you look tense, which
leads most men to assume you could use a serious screwing. And they
push your fanny out like you're making the world an offer. But most important is that, when you're teetering around in heels, it tells a man that
if he chases you, you're not going to get very far. Not only do spike heels
say you're vulnerable, they say you've *chosen* to be vulnerable. Of course,
it's not quite the same in micro gee. She was my mentor, Elena. Assigned
to teach me how to live in space.

I was an ag tech. Worked as a germ wrangler in the edens.

Microorganisms. Okay, you probably think that if you stick a seed in
some dirt, add some water and sunlight and wait a couple of months,
mother nature hands you a head of lettuce. Doesn't work that way, especially not in space. The edens are synergistic, symbiotic ecologies. Your
carbo crops, your protein crops, your vitamin crops—they're all fussy
about the neighborhood germs. If you don't keep your *clostridia* and *rhi-
zobium* in balance, your eden will rot to compost. Stinky, slimy compost.
It's important work—and duller than accounting. It wouldn't have been
so bad if we could've talked on the job, but CO_2 in the edens runs 6%,
which is great for plants but will kill you if you're not wearing a breather.
Elena painted an enormous smile on mine, with about eight hundred
teeth in it. She had lips on hers, puckered so that they looked like she was
ready to be kissed. Alpha Ralpha the chicken man had this plastic beak.
Only sometimes we switched—confused the hell out of the nature lovers.
I'll tell you, the job would've been a lot easier if we could've kept the rest
of the crew out, but the edens are designed for recreation as much as food
production. On *Victor Foxtrot* we had to have sign-ups between 8:00 and
16:00. See, the edens have lots of open space and we keep them eight degrees over crew deck nominal and they're lit twenty hours a day by gro-
lights and solar mirrors and they have big windows. Crew floats around
sucking up the view, soaking up photons, communing with the life force,

shredding foliage and in general getting in our way. Breakaways are the worst; they actually adopt plants like they were pets. Is that crazy or what? I mean, a tomato has a life span of three, maybe four months before it gets too leggy and stops bearing. I've seen grown men cry because Elena pulled up their favorite marigold.

No, all my plants now are silk. When I backed down, I realized that I didn't want anything to do with the day. My family was a bunch of poor nobodies; we moved to the night when I was seven. So nightshifting was like coming home. The fact is, I got too much sun while I was up. The sun is not my friend. Haven't seen real daylight in over a year; I make a point of it. I have a day-night timeshare at Lincoln Street Under. While the sun is shining I'm asleep or safely cocooned. At dusk my roomie comes home and I go out to work and play. Hey, being a mommy to legumes is *not* what I miss about space. How about you? What turned you into an owl?

Well, well, maybe you *are* serious about breaking away. Sure, they prefer recruits who've nightshifted. Shows them you've got circadian discipline.

Elena said something like that once. She said that it's hard to scare someone to death in broad daylight. It isn't just that the daytime is too crowded, it's too tame. The night is edgier, scarier. Sexier. You say and do things that wouldn't occur to you at lunchtime. It's because we don't really belong in the night. In order to survive here we have to fight all the old instincts warning us not to wander around in the dark because we might fall off a cliff or get eaten by a saber-tooth tiger. Living in the night gives you a kind of extra . . . I don't know . . .

Right. And it's the same with space; it's even scarier and sexier. Well, maybe sexy isn't exactly the right word, but you know what I mean. Actually, I think that's what I miss most about it. I was more alive then than I ever was before. Maybe too alive. People live fast up there. They know the stats; they *have* to. You know, you sort of remind me of Elena. Must be the eyes — it sure as hell isn't the body. If you ever get up, give her a shout. You'd like her, even though she doesn't wear shoes anymore.

Almost a year. I wish we could talk more, but it's hard. She transferred to the *Marathon*; they're out surveying Saturn's moons. There's like a three-hour lag; it's impossible to have real-time conversation. She sent a few vids, but it hurt too much to watch them. They were all happy chat, you know? Nothing important in them. I didn't plan on missing her so much. So, you have any college credits?

No real difference between Harvard and a net school, unless you're some kind of snob about bricks.

Now that's a hell of a thing to be asking a perfect stranger. What do I look like, some three-star slut? Don't make assumptions just because I'm wearing spike heels. For all you know, honey, I could be dating a basketball player. Maybe I'm tired of staring at his navel when we dance. If you're going to judge people by appearances, hey, *you're* the one with the machine stigmata. What's that supposed to be, rust or dried blood?

Well, you ought to be. Though actually, that's what everyone wants to know. That, and how do you go to the bathroom. Truth is, Jane, sex is complicated, like everything about space. First of all, forget all that stuff you've heard about doing it while you're floating free. It's dangerous, hard work and no fun. You want to have sex in space, one or both of you have to be tied down. Most hetero temps use some kind of a joystrap. It's this wide circular elastic that fits around you and your partner. Helps you stay coupled, okay? But even with all the gear, sex can be kind of subtle. As in disappointing. You don't realize how erotic weight is until there isn't any. You want to make love to a balloon? Some people do nothing but oral — keeps the vectors down. Of course the breakaways, they've reinvented love, just like everything else. They have this kind of sex where they don't move. If there's penetration they just float in place, staring into one another's eyes or some such until they tell one another that it's time to have an orgasm and then they do. If they're homo, they just touch each other. Elena tried to show me how, once. I don't know why, but it didn't happen for me. Maybe I was too embarrassed because I was the only one naked. She said I'd learn eventually, that it was part of breaking away.

No, I thought I was going to break away, I really did. I stuck it out until the very last possible day. It's hard to explain. I mean, when nobodies on earth look up at night — no offense, Jane, I was one too — what calls them is the romance of it all. The high frontier, okay? Sheena Steele and Captain Kirk, cowboys and asteroids. Kid stuff, except they don't let kids in space because of the cancer. Then you go up and once you're done puking, you realize that it was all propaganda. Space is boring and it's indescribably magic at the same time — how can that be? Sometimes I'd be working in an eden and I'd look out the windows and I'd see earth, blue as a dream, and I'd think of all the people down there, twelve billion ants, looking up into the night and wondering what it was like to be me. I swear I could feel their envy, as sure as I can feel your floor beneath me now. It's part of what holds you up when you're in space. You know you're not an ant; there are fewer than twenty thousand breakaways. You're brave and you're doomed and you're different from everyone else who has ever lived. Only then your shift ends and it's time to go to the gym and spend three hours pumping the ergorack in a squeeze suit to fight muscle loss in case you decide to back down. I'll tell you, being a temp is hell. The rack is hard work; if you're not exhausted afterward, you haven't done it right. And you sweat, *God*. See, the sweat doesn't run off. It pools in the small of your back and the crook of your arm and under your chin and clings there, shivering like an amoeba. And while you're slaving on the rack, Elena is getting work done or reading or sleeping or talking about you with her breakaway pals. They have three more hours in their day, see, and they don't ever have to worry about backing down. Then every nine weeks you have to leave what you're doing and visit one of the wheel habitats and readjust to your weight for a week so that when you come back to *Victor Foxtrot*, you get spacesick all over again. But you tell yourself it's all worth it because it's not only space that you're exploring; it's yourself. How many people can say that? You have to find out who you are so that you decide what to hold on to and what to let go of ... Excuse me, I can't talk about this anymore right now.

No, I'll be all right. Only ... okay, so you don't have any reset. You must have some kind of flash?

That'll have to do. Tell you what, I'll buy the whole liter from you.

Ahh, ethanol with a pedigree. But a real backdown kind of drug, Jane — weighs way too much to bring out of the gravity well. And besides, the flash is about the same as hitting yourself over the head with the bottle. Want a slug?

Come on, it's two-thirty. Time to start the party. You're making me late, you know.

Do me a favor, would you? Pass me those shoes on the shelf there . . . no, no, the blue ones. Yes. Beautiful. Real leather, right? I love leather shoes. They're like faces. I mean, you can polish them, but once they get wrinkles, you're stuck with them. Look at my face, okay? See these wrinkles here, right at the corner of my eyes. Got them working in the edens. Too much sun. How old do you think I am?

Twenty-nine, but that's okay. I was up fifteen months and it only aged me four years. Still, my permanent bone loss is less than eight percent and I've built my muscles back up and I only picked up eighteen rads and I'm not half as crazy as I used to be. Hey, I'm a walking advertisement for backing down. So have I talked you out of it yet? I don't mean to, okay? I'd probably go up again, if they'd have me.

Don't plan on it; the wheel habitats are strictly for tourists. They cost ten times as much to build as a micro gee can and once you're in one you're pretty much stuck to the rim. And you're still getting zapped by cosmic rays and solar X rays and energetic neutrons. If you're going to risk living in space, you might as well enjoy it. Besides, all the important work gets done by breakaways.

See, that's where you're wrong. It's like Elena used to say. We didn't conquer space, it conquered us. Break away and you're giving up forty, maybe fifty years of life, okay? The stats don't lie. Fifty-six is the *average*. That means some breakaways die even younger.

You don't? Well, good for you. Hey, it looks great—better than new. How much?

Does that include the vodka?

Well thanks. Listen, Jane, I'm going to tell you something, a secret they ought to tell everybody before they go up.

No, I'm not. Promise. So anyway, on my breakaway day Elena calls me to her room and tells me that she doesn't think I should do it, that I won't be happy living in space. I'm so stunned that I start crying, which is a very backdown thing to do. I try to argue, but she's been mentoring for years and knows what she's talking about. Only about a third break away — but, of course, you know that. Anyway, it gets strange then. She says to me, "I have something to show you," and then she starts to strip. See, the time she'd made love to me, she wouldn't let me do anything to her. And like I said, she'd kept her clothes on; breakaways have this thing about showing themselves to tcmps. I mean, I'd seen her hands before, her feet. They looked like spiders. And I'd seen her face. Kissed it, even. But now I'm looking at her naked body for the first time. She's fifty-one years old. I think she must've been taller than me once, but it's hard to be sure because she has the deep microgee slouch. Her muscles have atrophied so her papery skin looks as if it's been sprayed onto her bones. She's had both breasts prophylactically removed. "I've got 40% bonerot," she says, "and I mass thirty-eight kilos." She shows the scars from the operations to remove her thyroid and ovaries, the tap on her hip where they take the monthly biopsy to test for leukemia. "Look at me," she says. "What do you see?" I start to tell her that I've read the literature and watched all the vids and I'm prepared for what's going to happen but she shushes me. "Do you think I'm beautiful?" she says. All I can do is stare. "*I* think I am," she says. "So do the others. It's our nature, Cleo. This is how space makes us over. Can you tell me you *want* this to happen to you?" And I couldn't. See, she knew me better than I knew myself. What I wanted was to float forever, to feel I was special, to stay with her. Maybe I was in love with her. I don't know if that's possible. But loving someone isn't a reason to break away, especially if the stats say that someone will be dead in five years. So I told her she was right and thanked her for everything she'd done and got on the shuttle that same day and backed down and became just another nobody. And she gave up mentoring and went to Saturn and now that we've forgotten all about each other we can start living happily ever after.

No, here's the secret, honcy. The heart is a muscle, okay? That means it shrinks in space. All breakaways know it, now you do too. Anyway, it's been nice talking to you.

Sure. Good night.

The Wind from a Burning Woman

GREG BEAR

Science fiction has too often been identified with visionary optimism and called utopian. Yet clearly the history of the genre shows a strong cautionary, dystopian current. As Ray Bradbury reminds us, "It is not only the business of SF to predict the future, but to prevent it." And it can be shown convincingly that science fiction has often tried to vaccinate our culture against the misuse of technologies. H. G. Wells and countless others depicted the consequences of nuclear war; Arthur C. Clarke and others described the militarization of space travel; and recent writers warn about the misuse of biological innovations (Wells was a pioneer here too).

Does humanity distort its visions in their realization? As John W. Campbell once wrote, "Fiction is simply dreams written out. Science fiction consists of the hopes and dreams and fears (for some dreams are nightmares) of a technically based society." We often wrong our best intentions, our grandest dreams, and it is one of the tasks of literature to reflect this fact.

In this story, the threat of an asteroid striking the Earth (a real natural danger in our time) finally becomes a reality. Ironically, the asteroid comes at us with human purpose, as the deadly vestige of a dream. But can we wait for human nature to reform, or to redesign itself to be worthy of its dreams? Waiting for a better humankind to fulfill our dreams has its own costs. A far better answer lies in accepting that the good happens along with the bad, nearly always. And so we should do as much good along the way as possible. This has been the way with our irrepressible species, and the "control of progress" is its own nightmare.

As any good writer will attest, the way of failure, disaster, and misunderstanding makes for better drama than songs of success; this fact is built into our planetary literatures—and it is a tragic fact. Greg Bear writes of measures of right, degrees of responsibility, weighed against one another in reason's shaky but insistent scales. He reminds us of the sad loss that a decline in scientific literacy among politicians might exact from our possible futures.

Five years later the glass bubbles were intact, the wires and pipes were taut, and the city—strung across Psyche's surface like a dewy spider's web wrapped around a thrown rock—was still breathtaking. It was also empty. Hexamon investigators had swept out the final dried husks and bones. The asteroid was clean again. The plague was over.

Giani Turco turned her eyes away from the port and looked at the displays. Satisfied by the approach, she ordered a meal and put her work schedule through the processor for tightening and trimming. She had six tanks of air, enough to last her three days. There was no time to spare. The robot guards in orbit around Psyche hadn't been operating for at least a year and wouldn't offer any resistance, but four small pursuit bugs had been planted in the bubbles. They turned themselves off whenever possible, but her presence would activate them. Time spent in avoiding and finally destroying them: one hour forty minutes, the processor said. The final schedule was projected in front of her by a pen hooked around her ear. She happened to be staring at Psyche when the readout began; the effect—red numerals and letters over gray rock and black space—was pleasingly graphic, like a film in training.

Turco had dropped out of training six weeks early. She had no need for a final certificate, approval from the Hexamon, or any other nicety. Her craft was stolen from Earth orbit, her papers and cards forged, and her intentions entirely opposed to those of the sixteen corporeal desks. On Earth, some hours hence, she would be hated and reviled.

The impulse to sneer was strong—pure theatrics, since she was alone—but she didn't allow it to break her concentration. (Worse than sheep, the seekers-after-security, the cowardly citizens who tacitly supported the forces that had driven her father to suicide and murdered her grandfather; the seekers-after-security who lived by technology but believed in the just influences: Star, Logos, Fate, and Pneuma . . .)

To calm her nerves, she sang a short song while she selected her landing site.

The ship, a small orbital tug, touched the asteroid like a mote settling on a boulder and made itself fast. She stuck her arms and legs into the suit receptacles, and the limb covers automatically hooked themselves to the thorax. The cabin was too cramped to get into a suit any other way. She reached up and brought down the helmet, pushed until all the semifluid seals seized and beeped, and began the evacuation of the cabin's atmosphere. Then the cabin parted down the middle, and she floated slowly, fell more slowly still, to Psyche's surface.

She turned once to watch the cabin clamp together and to see if the propulsion rods behind the tanks had been damaged by the unusually long journey. They'd held up well.

She took hold of a guide wire after a flight of twenty or twenty-five meters and pulled for the nearest glass bubble. Five years before, the milky spheres had been filled with the families of workers setting the charges that would form Psyche's seven internal chambers. Holes had been bored from the Vlasseg and Janacki poles, on the narrow ends of the huge rock, through the center. After the formation of the chambers, materials necessary for atmosphere would have been pumped into Psyche through the boreholes while motors increased her natural spin to create artificial gravity inside.

In twenty years, Psyche's seven chambers would have been green and beautiful, filled with hope — and passengers. But now the control-bubble hatches had been sealed by the last of the investigators. Since Psyche was not easily accessible, even in its lunar orbit, the seals hadn't been applied carefully. Nevertheless it took her an hour to break in. The glass ball towered above her, a hundred feet in diameter, translucent walls mottled by the shadows of rooms and equipment. Psyche rotated once every three hours, and light from the sun was beginning to flush the top of the bubbles in the local cluster. Moonlight illuminated the shadows. She pushed the rubbery cement seals away, watching them float lazily to the pocked ground. Then she examined the airlock to see if it was still functioning.

She wanted to keep the atmosphere inside the bubble, to check it for psychotropic chemicals; she would not leave her suit at any rate.

The locked door opened with a few jerks and closed behind her. She brushed crystals of frost off her faceplate and the inner lock door's port. Then she pushed the button for the inner door, but nothing happened. The external doors were on a different power supply, which was no longer functioning—or, she hoped, had only been turned off.

From her backpack she removed a half-meter pry bar. The break-in took another fifteen minutes. She was now five minutes ahead of schedule.

Across the valley, the fusion power plants that supplied power to the Geshel populations of Tijuana and Chula Vista sat like squat mountains of concrete. By Naderite law, all nuclear facilities were enclosed by multiple domes and pyramids, whether they posed any danger or not. The symbolism was twofold—it showed the distaste of the ruling Naderites for energy sources that were not nature-kinetic, and it carried on the separation of Naderites-Geshels. Farmer Kollert, advisor to the North American Hexamon and ecumentalist to the California corporeal desk, watched the sun set behind the false peak and wondered vaguely if there was any symbolism in the act. Was not fusion the source of power for the sun? He smiled. Such things seldom occurred to him; perhaps it would amuse a Geshel technician.

His team of five Geshel scientists would tour the plants two days from now and make their report to him. He would then pass on *his* report to the desk, acting as interface for the invariably clumsy, elitist language the Geshel scientists used. In this way, through the medium of advisors across the globe, the Naderites oversaw the production of Geshel power. By their grants and control of capital, his people had once plucked the world from technological overkill, and the battle was ongoing still—a war against some of mankind's darker tendencies.

He finished his evening juice and took a package of writing utensils from the drawer in the veranda desk. The reports from last month's energy consumption balancing needed to be edited and revised, based on new estimates—and he enjoyed doing the work himself, rather than giving it to the library computer persona. It relaxed him to do things by hand. He wrote on a positive feedback slate, his scrawly letters adjusting automatically into script, with his tongue between his lips and a pleased frown creasing his brow.

"Excuse me, Farmer." His ur-wife, Gestina, stood in the French doors leading to the veranda. She was as slender as when he had married her, despite fifteen years and two children.

"Yes, *cara*, what is it?" He withdrew his tongue and told the slate to store what he'd written.

"Josef Krupkin."

Kollert stood up quickly, knocking the metal chair over. He hurried past his wife into the dining room, dropped his bulk into a chair, and drew up the crystalline cube on the alabaster tabletop. The cube adjusted its picture to meet the angle of his eyes, and Krupkin appeared.

"Josef! This is unexpected."

"Very," Krupkin said. He was a small man with narrow eyes and curly black hair. Compared to Kollert's bulk, he was dapper — but thirty years behind a desk had given him the usual physique of a Hexamon backroomer. "Have you ever heard of Giani Turco?"

Kollert thought for a moment. "No, I haven't. Wait — Turco. Related to Kimon Turco?"

"Daughter. California should keep better track of its radical Geshels, shouldn't it?"

"Kimon Turco lived on the Moon."

"His daughter lived in your district."

"Yes, fine. What about her?" Kollert was beginning to be perturbed. Krupkin enjoyed roundabouts even in important situations — and to call him at this address, at such a time, something important had happened.

"She's calling for you. She'll only talk to you, none of the rest. She won't even accept President Praetori."

"Yes. Who is she? What has she done?"

"She's managed to start up Psyche. There was enough reaction mass left in the Beckmann motors to alter it into an Earth-intersect orbit." The left side of the cube was flashing bright red, indicating the call was being scrambled.

Kollert sat very still for a few seconds. There was no need acting incredulous. Krupkin was in no position to joke. But the enormity of what

he said — and the impulse to disbelieve, despite the bearer of the news —
froze Kollert for an unusually long time. He ran his hand through lank
blond hair.

"Kollert," Krupkin said. "You look like you've been — "

"Is she telling the truth?"

Krupkin shook his head. "No, Kollert, you don't understand. She
hasn't *claimed* these accomplishments. She hasn't said anything about
them yet. She just wants to speak to you. But our tracking stations say
there's no doubt. I've spoken with the officer who commanded the last
inspection. He says there was enough mass left in the Beckmann drive-
positioning motors to push — "

"This is incredible! No precautions were taken? The mass wasn't
drained, or something?"

"I'm no Geshel, Farmer. My technicians tell me the mass was left on
Psyche because it would have cost several hundred million — "

"That's behind us now. Let the journalists worry about that, if they
ever hear of it." He looked up and saw Gestina still standing in the
French doors. He held up his hand to tell her to stay where she was. She
was going to have to keep to the house, incommunicado, for as long as it
took to straighten this out.

"You're coming?"

"Which center?"

"Does it matter? She's not being discreet. Her message is hitting an
entire hemisphere, and there are hundreds of listening stations to pick it
up. Several aren't under our control. Once anyone pinpoints the source,
the story is going to be clear. For your convenience, go to Baja Station.
Mexico is signatory to all the necessary pacts."

"I'm leaving now," Kollert said. Krupkin nodded, and the cube went
blank.

"What was he talking about?" Gestina asked. "What's *Psyche?*"

"A chunk of rock, dear," he said. Her talents lay in other directions —
she wasn't stupid. Even for a Naderite, however, she was unknowledge-
able about things beyond the Earth.

He started to plan the rules for her movements, then thought better
of it and said nothing. If Krupkin were correct — and he would be — there
was no need. The political considerations, if everything turned out right,

would be enormous. He could run as Governor of the Desk, even President of the Hexamon . . .

And if everything didn't turn out right, it wouldn't matter where anybody was.

Turco sat in the middle of her grandfather's control center and cried. She was tired and sick at heart. Things were moving rapidly now, and she wondered just how sane she was. In a few hours she would be the worst menace the Earth had ever known, and for what cause? Truth, justice? They had murdered her grandfather, discredited her father and driven him to suicide—but all seven billion of them, Geshels and Naderites alike?

She didn't know whether she was bluffing or not. Psyche's fall was still controllable, and she was bargaining it would never hit the Earth. Even if she lost and everything was hopeless, she might divert it, causing a few tidal disruptions, minor earthquakes perhaps, but still passing over four thousand kilometers from the Earth's surface. There was enough reaction mass in the positioning motors to allow a broad margin of safety.

Resting lightly on the table in front of her was a chart that showed the basic plan of the asteroid. The positioning motors surrounded a crater at one end of the egg-shaped chunk of nickel-iron and rock. Catapults loaded with huge barrels of reaction mass had just a few hours earlier launched a salvo to rendezvous above the crater's center. Beckmann drive beams had then surrounded the mass with a halo of energy, releasing its atoms from the bonds of nature's weak force. The blast had bounced off the crater floor, directed by the geometric patterns of heat-resistant slag. At the opposite end, a smaller guidance engine was in position, but it was no longer functional and didn't figure in her plans. The two tunnels that reached from the poles to the center of Psyche opened into seven blast chambers, each containing a fusion charge. She hadn't checked to see if the charges were still armed. There were so many things to do.

She sat with her head bowed, still suited up. Though the bubbles contained enough atmosphere to support her, she had no intention of unsuiting. In one gloved hand she clutched a small ampoule with a nozzle for attachment to air and water systems piping. The Hexamon Nexus's trumped-up excuse of madness caused by near-weightless conditions was now a shattered, horrible lie. Turco didn't know why, but the Psyche project had been deliberately sabotaged, and the psychotropic drugs still lingered.

Her grandfather hadn't gone mad contemplating the stars. The asteroid crew hadn't mutinied out of misguided Geshel zeal and space sickness.

Her anger rose again, and the tears stopped. "You deserve whoever governs you," she said quietly. "Everyone is responsible for the actions of their leaders."

The computer display cross-haired the point of impact. It was ironic — the buildings of the Hexamon Nexus were only sixty kilometers from the zero point. She had no control over such niceties, but nature and fate seemed to be as angry as she was.

"Moving an asteroid is like carving a diamond," the Geshel advisor said. Kollert nodded his head, not very interested. "The charges for initial orbit change — moving it out of the asteroid belt — have to be placed very carefully or the mass will break up and be useless. When the asteroid is close enough to the Earth-Moon system to meet the major crew vessels, the work has only begun. Positioning motors have to be built—"

"Madness," Kollert's secretary said, not pausing from his monitoring of communications between associate committees.

"And charge tunnels drilled. All of this was completed on the asteroid ten years ago."

"Are the charges still in place?" Kollert asked.

"So far as I know," the Geshel said.

"Can they be set off now?"

"I don't know. Whoever oversaw dismantling should have disarmed to protect his crew — but then, the reaction mass should have been jettisoned, too. So who can say? The report hasn't cleared top secrecy yet."

And not likely to, either, Kollert thought. "If they haven't been disarmed, can they be set off now? What would happen if they were?"

"Each charge has a complex communications system. They were designed to be set off by coded signals and could probably be set off now, yes, if we had the codes. Of course, those are top secret, too."

"What would happen?" Kollert was becoming impatient with the Geshel.

"I don't think the charges were ever given a final adjustment. It all depends on how well the initial alignment was performed. If they're out of true, or the final geological studies weren't taken into account, they could blow Psyche to pieces. If they are true, they'll do what they were intended to do—form chambers inside the rock. Each chamber would be about fifteen kilometers long, ten kilometers in diameter—"

"If the asteroid were blown apart, how would that affect our situation?"

"Instead of having one mass hit, we'd have a cloud, with debris twenty to thirty kilometers across and smaller."

"Would that be any better?" Kollert asked.

"Sir?"

"Would it be better to be hit by such a cloud than one chunk?"

"I don't think so. The difference is pretty moot—either way, the surface of the Earth would be radically altered, and few life forms would survive."

Kollert turned to his secretary. "Tell them to put a transmission through to Giani Turco."

The communications were arranged. In the meantime Kollert tried to make some sense out of the Geshel advisor's figures. He was very good at mathematics, but in the past sixty years many physics and chemistry symbols had diverged from those used in biology and psychology. To Kollert, the Geshel mathematics was irritatingly dense and obtuse.

He put the paper aside when Turco appeared on the cube in front of him. A few background beeps and noise were eliminated, and her image cleared. "Ser Turco," he said.

"Ser Farmer Kollert," she replied several seconds later. A beep signaled the end of one side's transmission. She sounded tired.

"You're doing a very foolish thing."

"I have a list of demands," she said.

Kollert laughed. "You sound like the Good Man himself, Ser Turco. The tactic of direct confrontation. Well, it didn't work all the time, even for him."

"I want the public—Geshels and Naderites both—to know why the Psyche project was sabotaged."

"It was not sabotaged," Kollert said calmly. "It was unfortunate proof that humans cannot live in conditions so far removed from the Earth."

"Ask those on the Moon!" Turco said bitterly.

"The Moon has a much stronger gravitational pull than Psyche. But I'm not briefed to discuss all the reasons why the Psyche project failed."

"I have found psychotropic drugs—traces of drugs and containers—in the air and water the crew breathed and drank. That's why I'm maintaining my suit integrity."

"No such traces were found by our investigating teams. But, Ser Turco, neither of us is here to discuss something long past. Speak your demands—your price—and we'll begin negotiations." Kollert knew he was walking a loose rope. Several Hexamon terrorist team officers were listening to everything he said, waiting to splice in a timely splash of static. Conversely, there was no way to stop Turco's words from reaching open stations on the Earth. He was sweating heavily under his arms. Stations on the Moon—the bastards there would probably be sympathetic to her—could pick up his messages and relay them back to the Earth. A drop of perspiration trickled from armpit to sleeve, and he shivered involuntarily.

"That's my only demand," Turco said. "No money, not even amnesty. I want nothing for myself. I simply want the people to know the truth."

"Ser Turco, you have an ideal platform to tell them all you want them to hear."

"The Hexamons control most major reception centers. Everything else—except for a few ham and radio-astronomy amateurs—is cabled and controlled. To reach the most people, the Hexamon Nexus will have to reveal its part in the matter."

Before speaking to her again, Kollert asked if there were any way she could be fooled into believing her requests were being carried out. The answer was ambiguous—a few hundred people were thinking it over.

"I've conferred with my staff, Ser Turco, and I can assure you, so far as the most privy of us can tell, nothing so villainous was ever done to the Psyche project." At a later time, his script suggested, he might indicate that some tests had been overlooked, and that a junior officer had suggested lunar sabotage on Psyche. That might shift the heat. But for the moment, any admission that drugs existed in the asteroid's human environments could backfire.

"I'm not arguing," she said. "There's no question that the Hexamon Nexus had somebody sabotage Psyche."

Kollert held his tongue between his lips and punched key words into his script processor. The desired statements formed over Turco's image. He looked at the camera earnestly. "If we had done anything so heinous, surely we would have protected ourselves against an eventuality like this—drained the reaction mass in the positioning motors—" One of the terrorist team officers was waving at him frantically and scowling. The screen's words showed red where they were being covered by static. There was to be no mention of how Turco had gained control of Psyche. The issue was too sensitive, and blame hadn't been placed yet. Besides, there was still the option of informing the public that Turco had never gained control of Psyche at all. If everything worked out, the issue would have been solved without costly admissions.

"Excuse me," Turco said a few seconds later. The time lag between communications was wearing on her nerves, if Kollert was any judge. "Something was lost there."

"Ser Turco, your grandfather's death on Psyche was accidental, and your actions now are ridiculous. Destroying the Hexamon Nexus"— much better than saying *Earth*—"won't mean a thing." He leaned back in the seat, chewing on the edge of his index finger. The gesture had been approved an hour before the talks began, but it was nearly genuine. His usual elegance of speech seemed to be wearing thin in this encounter. He'd already made several embarrassing misjudgments.

"I'm not doing this for logical reasons," Turco finally said. "I'm doing it out of hatred for you and all the people who support you. What happened on Psyche was purely evil—useless, motivated by the worst intentions, resulting in the death of a beautiful dream, not to mention people I loved. No talk can change my mind about those things."

"Then why talk to me at all? I'm hardly the highest official in the Nexus."

"No, but you're in an ideal position to know who the higher officials involved were. You're a respected politician. And I suspect you had a great deal to do with suggesting the plot. I just want the truth. I'm tired. I'm going to rest for a few hours now."

"Wait a moment," Kollert said sharply. "We haven't discussed the most important things yet."

"I'm signing off. Until later."

The team leader made a cutting motion across his throat that almost made Kollert choke. The young bastard's indiscreet symbol was positively obscene in the current situation. Kollert shook his head and held his fingertips to his temples. "We didn't even have time to begin," he said.

The team leader stood and stretched his arms.

"You're doing quite well so far, Ser Kollert," he said. "It's best to ease into these things."

"I'm Advisor Kollert to you, and I don't see how we have much time to take it easy."

"Yes, sir. Sorry."

She needed the rest, but there was far too much to do. She pushed off from the seat and floated gently for a few moments before drifting down. The relaxation of weightlessness would have been welcome, and Psyche's pull was very weak, but just enough to remind her there was no time for rest.

One of the things she had hoped she could do—checking the charges deep inside the asteroid to see if they were armed—was impossible. The main computer and the systems board indicated the transport system through the bore holes was no longer operative. It would take her days to crawl or float the distance down the shafts, and she wasn't about to take the small tug through a tunnel barely fifty meters wide. She wasn't that well trained a pilot.

So she had a weak spot. The bombs couldn't be disarmed from where she was. They could be set off by a ship positioned along the axis of the tunnels, but so far none had shown up. That would take another twelve hours or so, and by then time would be running out. She hoped that all negotiations would be completed.

The woman desperately wanted out of the suit. The catheters and cups were itching fiercely; she felt like a ball of tacky glue wrapped in wool. Her eyes were stinging from strain and sweat buildup on the lids. If she had a moment of irritation when something crucial was happening, she could be in trouble. One way or another, she had to clean up a bit—and there was no way to do that unless she risked exposure to the residue of drugs. She stood unsteadily for several minutes, vacillating, and finally groaned, slapping her thigh with a gloved palm. "I'm *tired*," she said. "Not thinking straight."

She looked at the computer. There was a solution, but she couldn't see it clearly. "Come on, girl. So simple. But what?"

The drug would probably have a limited life, in case the Nexus wanted to do something with Psyche later. But how limited? Ten years? She chuckled grimly. She had the ampoule and its cryptic chemical label. Would a Physician's Desk Reference be programmed into the computers?

She hooked herself into the console again. "PDR," she said. The screen was blank for a few seconds. Then it said, "Ready."

"Iropentaphonate," she said. "Two-seven diboltene."

The screen printed out the relevant data. She searched through the technical maze for a full minute before finding what she wanted. "Effective shelf life, four months two days from date of manufacture."

She tested the air again — it was stale but breathable — and unhooked her helmet. It was worth any risk. A bare knuckle against her eye felt so good.

The small lounge in the Baja Station was well furnished and comfortable, but suited more for Geshels than Naderites — bright rather than natural colors, abstract paintings of a mechanistic tendency, modernist furniture. To Kollert it was faintly oppressive. The man sitting across from him had been silent for the past five minutes, reading through a sheaf of papers.

"Who authorized this?" the man asked.

"Hexamon Nexus, Mr. President."

"But who proposed it?"

Kollert hesitated. "The advisory committee."

"Who proposed it to the committee?"

"I did."

"Under what authority?"

"It was strictly legal," Kollert said defensively. "Such activities have been covered under the emergency code, classified section fourteen."

The president nodded. "She came to the right man when she asked for you, then. I wonder where she got her information. None of this can be broadcast — why was it done?"

"There were a number of reasons, among them financial —"

"The project was mostly financed by lunar agencies. Earth had perhaps a five percent share, so no controlling interest — and there was no connection with radical Geshel groups, therefore no need to invoke section fourteen on revolutionary deterrence. I read the codes, too, Farmer."

"Yes, sir."

"What were you afraid of? Some irrational desire to pin the butterflies down? Jesus God, Farmer, the Naderite beliefs don't allow anything like this. But you and your committee took it upon yourselves to covertly destroy the biggest project in the history of mankind. You think this follows in the tracks of the Good Man?"

"You're aware of lunar plans to build particle guidance guns. They're canceled now because Psyche is dead. They were to be used to push asteroids like Psyche into deep space, so advanced Beckmann drives could be used."

"I'm not technically minded, Farmer."

"Nor am I. But such particle guns could have been used as weapons—considering lunar sympathies, probably would have been used. They could cook whole cities on Earth. The development of potential weapons *is* a matter of concern for Naderites, sir. And there are many studies showing that human behavior changes in space. It becomes less Earth-centered, less communal. Man can't live in space and remain human. We were trying to preserve humanity's right to a secure future. Even now the Moon is a potent political force, and war has been suggested by our strategists . . . it's a dire possibility. All this because of the separation of a group of humans from the parent body, from wise government and safe creed."

The president shook his head and looked away. "I am ashamed such a thing could happen in my government. Very well, Kollert, this remains your ball game until she asks to speak to someone else. But my advisors are going to go over everything you say. I doubt you'll have the chance to botch anything. We're already acting with the Moon to stop this before it gets any worse. And you can thank God—for your life, not your career, which is already dead—that our Geshels have come up with a way out."

Kollert was outwardly submissive, but inside he was fuming. Not even the President of the Hexamon had the right to treat him like a child or, worse, a criminal. He was an independent advisor, of a separate desk, elected by Naderites of high standing. The ecumentalist creed was apparently much tighter than the president's. "I acted in the best interests of my constituency," he said.

"You no longer have a constituency, you no longer have a career. Nor do any of the people who planned this operation with you, or those who carried it out. Up and down the line. A purge."

Turco woke up before the blinking light and moved her lips in a silent curse. How long had she been asleep? She panicked briefly—a dozen hours would be crucial—but then saw the digital clock. Two hours. The light was demanding her attention to an incoming radio signal.

There was no video image. Kollert's voice returned, less certain, almost cowed. "I'm here," she said, switching off her camera as well. The delay was a fraction shorter than when they'd first started talking.

"Have you made any decisions?" Kollert asked.

"I should be asking that question. My course is fixed. When are you and your people going to admit to sabotage?"

"We'd—I'd almost be willing to admit, just to—" He stopped. She was about to speak when he continued. "We could do that, you know. Broadcast a worldwide admission of guilt. A cheap price to pay for saving all life on Earth. Do you really understand what you're up to? What satisfaction, what revenge, could you possibly get out of this? My God, Turco, you—" There was a burst of static. It sounded suspiciously like the burst she had heard some time ago.

"You're editing him," she said. Her voice was level and calm. "I don't want anyone editing anything between us, whoever you are. Is that understood? One more burst of static like that, and I'll . . ." She had already threatened the ultimate. "I'll be less tractable. Remember—I'm already a fanatic. Want me to be a hardened fanatic? Repeat what you were saying, Ser Kollert."

The digital readout indicated one-way delay time of 1.496 seconds. She would soon be closer to the Earth than the Moon was.

"I was saying," Kollert repeated, something like triumph in his tone, "that you are a very young woman, with very young ideas—like a child leveling a loaded pistol at her parents. You may not be a fanatic. But you aren't seeing things clearly. We have no evidence here on Earth that you've found anything, and we won't have evidence—nothing will be solved—if the asteroid collides with us. That's obvious. But if it veers aside, goes into an Earth orbit perhaps, then an—"

"That's not one of my options," Turco said.

"—investigating team could reexamine the crew quarters," Kollert continued, not to be interrupted for a few seconds, "do a more detailed search. Your charges could be verified."

"I can't go into Earth orbit without turning around, and this is a one-way rock, remember that. My only other option is to swing around the Earth, be deflected a couple of degrees, and go into a solar orbit. By the time any investigating team reached me, I'd be on the other side of the sun, and dead. I'm the daughter of a Geshel, Ser Kollert—don't forget that. I have a good technical education, and my training under Hexamon auspices makes me a competent pilot and spacefarer. Too bad there's so little long-range work for my type—just Earth-Moon runs. But don't try to fool me or kid me. I'm far more expert than you are. Though I'm sure you have Geshel people on your staff." She paused. "Geshels! I can't call you traitors—you in the background—because you might be thinking I'm crazy, out to destroy all of you. But do you understand what these men have done to our hopes and dreams? I've never seen a finished asteroid starship, of course—Psyche was to have been the first. But I've seen good simulations. It would have been like seven Shangri-las inside, hollowed out of solid rock and metal, seven valleys separated by walls four kilometers high, each self-contained, connected with the others by tube trains. The valley floors reach up to the sky, like magic, everything wonderfully topsy-turvy. And quiet—so much insulation, none of the engine sounds reach inside." She was crying again.

"Psyche would consume herself on the way to the stars. By the time she arrived, there'd be little left besides a cylinder thirty kilometers wide and two hundred ninety long. Like the core of an apple, and the passengers would be luxurious worms—star travelers. Now ask why, *why* did these men sabotage such a marvelous thing? Because they are blind unto pure evil—blind, ugly-minded, weak men who hate big ideas..." She paused. "I don't know what you think of all this, but remember, they took something away from you. I know. I've seen the evidence here. Sabotage and murder." She pressed the button and waited wearily for a reply.

"Ser Turco," Kollert said, "you have ten hours to make an effective course correction. We estimate you have enough reaction mass left to extend your orbit and miss the Earth by about four thousand kilometers. There is nothing we can do here but try to convince you—"

She stopped listening, trying to figure out what was happening behind the scenes. Earth wouldn't take such a threat without exploring a large number of alternatives. Kollert's voice droned on as she tried to think of the most likely action, and the most effective.

She picked up her helmet and placed a short message, paying no attention to the transmission from Earth. "I'm going outside for a few minutes."

The acceleration had been steady for two hours, but now the weightlessness was just as oppressive. The large cargo handler was fully loaded with extra fuel and a bulk William Porter was reluctant to think about. With the ship turned around for course correction, he could see the Moon glowing with Earthshine, and a bright crescent so thin it was almost a hair.

He had about half an hour to relax before the real work began, and he was using it to read an excerpt from a novel by Anthony Burgess. He'd been a heavy reader all his memorable life, and now he allowed himself a possible last taste of pleasure.

Like most inhabitants of the Moon, Porter was a Geshel, with a physicist father and a geneticist mother. He'd chosen a career as a pilot rather than a researcher out of romantic predilections established long before he was ten years old. There was something immediately effective and satisfying about piloting, and he'd turned out to be well suited to the work. He'd never expected to take on a mission like this. But then, he'd never paid much attention to politics, either. Even if he had, the disputes between Geshels and Naderites would have been hard to spot—they'd been settled, most experts believed, fifty years before, with the Naderites emerging as a ruling class. Outside of grumbling at restrictions, few Geshels complained. Responsibility had been lifted from their shoulders. Most of the population of both Earth and Moon was now involved in technical and scientific work, yet the mistakes they made would be blamed on Naderite policies—and the disasters would likewise be absorbed by the leadership. It wasn't a hard situation to get used to.

William Porter wasn't so sure, now, that it was the ideal. He had two options to save Earth, and one of them meant he would die.

He'd listened to the Psyche-Earth transmissions during acceleration, trying to make sense out of Turco's position, to form an opinion of her character and sanity, but he was more confused than ever. If she was right—and not a raving lunatic, which didn't seem to fit the facts—then the Hexamon Nexus had a lot of explaining to do and probably wouldn't do it under the gun. The size of Turco's gun was far too imposing to be rational—the destruction of the human race, the wiping of a planet's surface.

He played back the computer diagram of what would happen if Psyche hit the Earth. At the angle it would strike, it would speed the rotation of the Earth's crust and mantle by an appreciable fraction. The asteroid would cut a gouge from Maine to England, several thousand kilometers long and at least a hundred kilometers deep. The impact would vault hundreds of millions of tons of surface material into space, and that would partially counteract the speedup of rotation. The effect would be a monumental jerk, with the energy finally being released as heat. The continents would fracture in several directions, forming new faults, even new plate orientations, which would generate earthquakes on a scale never before seen. The impact basin would be a hell of molten crust and mantle, with water on the perimeter bursting violently into steam, altering weather patterns around the world. It would take decades to cool and achieve some sort of stability.

Turco may not have been raving, but she was coldly suggesting a cataclysm to swat what amounted to a historical fly. That made her a lunatic in anyone's book, Geshel or Naderite. And his life was well worth the effort to thwart her.

That didn't stop him from being angry, though.

Kollert impatiently let the physician check him over and administer a few injections. He talked to his wife briefly, which left him more nervous than before, then listened to the team leader's theories on how Turco's behavior would change in the next few hours. He nodded at only one statement: "She's going to see she'll be dead, too, and that's a major shock for even the most die-hard terrorist."

Then Turco was back on the air, and he was on stage again.

"I've seen your ship," she said. "I went outside and looked around in the direction where I thought it would be. There it was—treachery all around. Goddamned hypocrites! Talk friendly to the little girl, but shiv her in the back! Public face cool, private face snarl! Well, just remember, before he can kill me, I can destroy all controls to the positioning engines. It would take a week to rewire them. You don't have the time!" The beep followed.

"Giani, we have only one option left, and that's to do as you say. We'll admit we played a part in the sabotage of Psyche. It's confession under pressure, but we'll do it." Kollert pressed his button and waited, holding his full chin with one hand.

"No way it's so simple, Kollert. No public admission and then public denial after the danger is over—you'd all come across as heroes. No. There has to be some record keeping, payrolls if nothing else. I want full disclosure of all records, and I want them transmitted around the world—facsimile, authenticated. I want uninvolved government officials to see them and sign that they've seen them. And I want the actual documents put on display where anyone can look at them—memos, plans, letters, whatever. All of it that's still available."

"That would take weeks," Kollert said, "if they existed."

"Not in this age of electronic wizardry. I want you to take a lie-detector test, authenticated by half a dozen experts with their careers on the line—and while you're at it, have the other officials take tests, too."

"That's not only impractical, it won't hold up in a court of law."

"I'm not interested in formal courts. I'm not a vengeful person, no matter what I may seem now. I just want the truth. And if I still see that goddamn ship up there in an hour, I'm going to stop negotiations right now and blow myself to pieces."

Kollert looked at the team leader, but the man's face was blank.

"Let me talk to her, then," Porter suggested. "Direct person-to-person. Let me explain the plans. She really can't change them any, can she? She has no way of making them worse. If she fires her engines or does any positive action, she simply stops the threat. So I'm the one who holds the key to the situation."

"We're not sure that's advisable, Bill," Lunar Guidance said.

"I can transmit to her without permission, you know," he said testily.

"Against direct orders, that's not like you."

"Like me, hell," he said, chuckling. "Listen, just get me permission.

Nobody else seems to be doing anything effective." There was a few minutes' silence, then Lunar Guidance returned.

"Okay, Bill. You have permission. But be very careful what you say. Terrorist team officers on Earth think she's close to the pit."

With that obstacle cleared away, he wondered how wise the idea was in the first place. Still, they were both Geshels — they had something in common compared to the elite Naderites running things on Earth.

Far away, Earth concurred and transmissions were cleared. They couldn't censor his direct signal, so Baja Station was unwillingly cut from the circuit.

"Who's talking to me now?" Turco asked when the link was made.

"This is Lieutenant William Porter, from the Moon. I'm a pilot — not a defense pilot usually, either. I understand you've had pilot's training."

"Just enough to get by." The lag was less than a hundredth of a second, not noticeable.

"You know I'm up here to stop you, one way or another. I've got two options. The one I think more highly of is to get in line-of-sight of your bore holes and relay the proper coded signals to the charges in your interior."

"Killing me won't do you any good."

"That's not the plan. The fore end of your rock is bored with a smaller hole by thirty meters. It'll release the blast wastes more slowly than the aft end. The total explosive force should give the rock enough added velocity to get it clear of the Earth by at least sixty kilometers. The damage would be negligible. Spectacular view from Greenland, too, I understand. But if we've miscalculated, or if one or more charges doesn't go, then I'll have to impact with your aft crater and release the charge in my cargo hold. I'm one floating megaboom now, enough to boost the rock up and out by a few additional kilometers. But that means I'll be dead, and not enough left of me to memorialize or pin a medal on. Not too good, hm?"

"None of my sweat."

"No, I suppose not. But listen, sister — "

"No sister to a lackey."

Porter started to snap a retort, but stopped himself. "Listen, they tell me to be soft on you, but I'm under pressure, too, so please reciprocate. I don't see the sense in all of it. If you get your way, you've set back your cause by God knows how many decades — because once you're out of range and blown your trump, they'll deny it all, say it was manufactured evidence and testimony under pressure — all that sort of thing. And if they decide to hard-line it, force me to do my dirty work, or God forbid let you do yours — we've lost our home world. You've lost Psyche, which can still be salvaged and finished. Everything will be lost, just because a few men may or may not have done a very wicked thing. Come on, honey. That isn't the Geshel creed, and you know it."

"What is our creed? To let men rule our lives who aren't competent to read a thermometer? Under the Naderites, most of the leaders on Earth haven't got the technical expertise to . . . to . . . I don't know what. To tie their goddamn shoes! They're blind, dedicated to some half-wit belief that progress is the most dangerous thing conceived by man. But they can't live without technology, so we provide it for them. And when they won't touch our filthy nuclear energy, we get stuck with it — because otherwise we all have to go back four hundred years, and sacrifice half the population. Is that good planning, sound policy? And if they do what I say, Psyche won't be damaged. All they'll have to do is fetch it back from orbit around the sun."

"I'm not going to argue on their behalf, sister. I'm a Geshel, too, and a Moonman besides. I never have paid attention to Earth politics because it never made much sense to me. But now I'm talking to you one to one, and you're telling me that revenging someone's irrational system is worth wiping away a planet?"

"I'm willing to take that risk."

"I don't think you are. I hope you aren't. I hope it's all bluff, and I won't have to smear myself against your backside."

"I hope you won't, either. I hope they've got enough sense down there to do what I want."

"I don't think they have, sister. I don't put much faith in them, myself. They probably don't even know what would happen if you hit the Earth with your rock. Think about that. You're talking about scientific innocents — flat-Earthers almost, naive. Words fail me. But think on it. They may not even know what's going on."

"They know. And remind them that if they set off the charges, it'll probably break up Psyche and give them a thousand rocks to contend with instead of one. That plan may backfire on them."

"What if they—we—don't have any choice?"

"I don't give a damn what choice you have," Turco said. "I'm not talking for a while. I've got more work to do."

Porter listened to the final click with a sinking feeling. She was a tough one. How would he outwit her? He smiled grimly at his chutzpah for even thinking he could. She'd committed herself all the way—and now, perhaps, she was feeling the power of her position. One lonely woman, holding the key to a world's existence. He wondered how it felt.

Then he shivered, and the sweat in his suit felt very, very cold. If he would have a grave for someone to walk over . . .

For the first time, she realized they wouldn't accede to her demands. They were more traitorous than even she could have imagined. Or—the thought was too horrible to accept—she'd misinterpreted the evidence, and they weren't at fault. Perhaps a madman in the Psyche crew had sought revenge and caused the whole mess. But that didn't fit the facts. It would have taken at least a dozen people to set all the psychotropic vials and release them at once—a concerted preplanned effort. She shook her head. Besides, she had the confidential reports a friend had accidentally plugged into while troubleshooting a Hexamon computer plex. There was no doubt about who was responsible, just uncertainty about the exact procedure. Her evidence for Farmer Kollert's guilt was circumstantial but not baseless.

She sealed her suit and helmet and went outside the bubble again, just to watch the stars for a few minutes. The lead-gray rock under her feet was pitted by eons of micrometeoroids. Rills several kilometers across attested to the rolling impacts of other asteroids, any one of which would have caused a major disaster on Earth. Earth had been hit before, not often by pieces as big as Psyche, but several times at least, and had survived. Earth would survive Psyche's impact, and life would start anew. Those plants and animals—even humans—that survived would eventually build back to the present level, and perhaps it would be a better world, more daunted by the power of past evil. She might be a force for positive regeneration.

The string of bubbles across Psyche's surface was serenely lovely in the starlight. The illumination brightened slowly as Earth rose above the Vlasseg pole, larger now than the Moon. She had a few more hours to make the optimum correction. Just above the Earth was a tiny moving point of light—Porter in his cargo vessel. He was lining up with the smaller bore hole to send signals, if he had to.

Again she wanted to cry. She felt like a little child, full of hatred and frustration, but caught now in something so immense and inexorable that all passion was dwarfed. She couldn't believe she was the controlling factor, that she held so much power. Surely something was behind her, some impersonal, objective force. Alone she was nothing, and her crime would be unbelievable—just as Porter had said. But with a cosmic justification, the agreeing nod of some vast all-seeing God, she was just a tool, bereft of responsibility.

She grasped the guide wires strung between the bubbles and pulled herself back to the airlock hatch. With one gloved hand she pressed the button. Under her palm she felt the metal vibrate for a second, then stop. The hatch was still closed. She pressed again and nothing happened.

Porter listened carefully for a full minute, trying to pick up the weak signal. It had cut off abruptly a few minutes before, during his final lineup with the bore hole through the Vlasseg pole. He called his director and asked if any signals had been received from Turco. Since he was out of line of sight now, the Moon had to act as a relay.

"Nothing," Lunar Guidance said. "She's been silent for an hour."

"That's not right. We've only got an hour and a half left. She should be playing the situation for all it's worth. Listen, LG, I received a weak signal from Psyche several minutes ago. It could have been a freak, but I don't think so. I'm going to move back to where I picked it up."

"Negative, Porter. You'll need all your reaction mass in case Plan A doesn't go off properly."

"I've got plenty to spare, LG. I have a bad feeling about this. Something's gone wrong on Psyche." It was clear to him the instant he said it. "Jesus Christ, LG, the signal must have come from Turco's area on Psyche! I lost it just when I passed out of line of sight from her bubble."

Lunar Guidance was silent for a long moment. "Okay, Porter, we've got clearance for you to regain that signal."

"Thank you, LG." He pushed the ship out of its rough alignment and coasted slowly away from Psyche until he could see the equatorial ring of domes and bubbles. Abruptly his receiver again picked up the weak signal. He locked his tracking antenna to it, boosted it, and cut in the communications processor to interpolate through the hash.

"This is Turco. William Porter, listen to me! This is Turco. I'm locked out. Something has malfunctioned in the control bubble. I'm locked out..."

"I'm getting you, Turco," he said. "Look at my spot above the Vlasseg pole. I'm in line of sight again." If her suit was a standard model, her transmissions would strengthen in the direction she was facing.

"God bless you, Porter. I see you. Everything's gone wrong down here. I can't get back in."

"Try again, Turco. Do you have any tools with you?"

"That's what started all this, breaking in with a chisel and a pry bar. It must have weakened something, and now the whole mechanism is frozen. No, I left the bar inside. No tools. Jesus, this is awful."

"Calm down. Keep trying to get in. I'm relaying your signal to Lunar Guidance and Earth." That settled it. There was no time to waste now. If she didn't turn on the positioning motors soon, any miss would be too close for comfort. He had to set off the internal charges within an hour and a half for the best effect.

"She's outside?" Lunar Guidance asked when the transmissions were relayed. "Can't get back in?"

"That's it," Porter said.

"That cocks it, Porter. Ignore her and get back into position. Don't bother lining up with the Vlasseg pole, however. Circle around to the Janacki pole bore hole and line up for code broadcast there. You'll have a better chance of getting the code through, and you can prepare for any further action."

"I'll be cooked, LG."

"Negative—you're to relay code from an additional thousand kilometers and boost yourself out of the path just before detonation. That will occur—let's see—about four point three seconds after the charges receive the code. Program your computer for sequencing; you'll be too busy."

"I'm moving, LG." He returned to Turco's wavelength. "It's out of your hands now," he said. "We're blowing the charges. They may not be enough, so I'm preparing to detonate myself against the Janacki pole crater. Congratulations, Turco."

"I still can't get back in, Porter."

"I said, congratulations. You've killed both of us and ruined Psyche for any future projects. You know that she'll go to pieces when she drops below Roche's limit? Even if she misses, she'll be too close to survive. You know, they might have gotten it all straightened out in a few administrations. Politicos die, or get booted out of office — even Naderites. I say you've cocked it good. Be happy, Turco." He flipped the switch viciously and concentrated on his approach program display.

Farmer Kollert was slumped in his chair, eyes closed but still awake, half listening to the murmurs in the control room. Someone tapped him on the shoulder, and he jerked up in his seat.

"I had to be with you, Farmer." Gestina stood over him, a nervous smile making her dimples obvious. "They brought me here to be with you."

"Why?" he asked.

Her voice shook. "Because our house was destroyed. I got out just in time. What's happening, Farmer? Why do they want to kill me? What did I do?"

The team officer standing beside her held out a piece of paper, and Kollert took it. Violence had broken out in half a dozen Hexamon centers, and numerous officials had had to be evacuated. Geshels weren't the only ones involved — Naderites of all classes seemed to share indignation and rage at what was happening. The outbreaks weren't organized — and that was even more disturbing. Wherever transmissions had reached the unofficial grapevines, people were reacting.

Gestina's large eyes regarded him without comprehension, much less sympathy. "I had to be with you, Farmer," she repeated. "They wouldn't let me stay."

"Quiet, please," another officer said. "More transmissions coming in."

"Yes," Kollert said softly. "Quiet. That's what we wanted. Quiet and peace and sanity. Safety for our children to come."

"I think something big is happening," Gestina said. "What is it?"

Porter checked the alignment again, put up his visual shields, and instructed the processor to broadcast the coded signal. With no distinguishable pause, the ship's engines started to move him out of the path of the particle blast.

Meanwhile Giani Turco worked at the hatch with a bit of metal brac-
ing she had broken off her suitpack. The sharp edge just barely fit into
the crevice, and by gouging and prying she had managed to force the
door up half a centimeter. The evacuation mechanism hadn't been activated, so frosted air hissed from the crack, making the work doubly difficult. The Moon was rising above the Janacki pole.

Deep below her, seven prebalanced but unchecked charges, mounted
on massive fittings in their chambers, began to whir. Four processors
checked the timings, concurred, and released safety shields.

Six of the charges went off at once. The seventh was late by ten thou-
sandths of a second, its blast muted as the casing melted prematurely.
The particle shock waves streamed out through the bore holes, now pressure release valves, and formed a long neck and tail of flame and ionized
particles that grew steadily for a thousand kilometers, then faded. The
tail from the Vlasseg pole was thinner and shorter, but no less spectacular. The asteroid shuddered, vibrations rising from deep inside to pull
the ground away from Turco's boots, then swing it back to kick her away
from the bubble and hatch. She floated in space, disoriented, ripped free
of the guide wires, her back to the asteroid, faceplate aimed at peaceful
stars, turning slowly as she reached the top of her arc.

Her leisurely descent gave her plenty of time to see the secondary
plume of purple and white and red forming around the Janacki pole. The
stars were blanked out by its brilliance. She closed her eyes. When she
opened them again, she was nearer the ground, and her faceplate had polarized against the sudden brightness. She saw the bubble still intact, and
the hatch wide open now. It had been jarred free. Everything was vibrat-
ing . . . and with shock she realized the asteroid was slowly moving out
from beneath her. Her fall became a drawn-out curve, taking her away
from the bubble toward a ridge of lead-gray rock, without guide wires,
where she would bounce and continue on unchecked. To her left, one
dome ruptured and sent a feathery wipe of debris into space. Pieces of
rock and dust floated past her, shaken from Psyche's weak surface grip.
Then her hand was only a few meters from a guide wire torn free and
swinging outward. It came closer like a dancing snake, hesitated, rippled
again, and came within reach. She grabbed it and pulled herself down.

"Porter, this is Lunar Guidance. Earth says the charges weren't
enough. Something went wrong."

"She held together, LG," Porter said in disbelief. "She didn't break up. I've got a fireworks show like you've never seen before."

"Porter, listen. She isn't moving fast enough. She'll still impact."

"I *heard* you, LG," Porter shouted. "I heard! Leave me alone to get things done." Nothing more was said between them.

Turco reached the hatch and crawled into the airlock, exhausted. She closed the outer door and waited for equalization before opening the inner. Her helmet was off and floating behind as she walked and bounced and guided herself into the control room. If the motors were still functional, she'd fire them. She had no second thoughts now. Something had gone wrong, and the situation was completely different.

In the middle of the kilometers-wide crater at the Janacki pole, the bore hole was still spewing debris and ionized particles. But around the perimeter, other forces were at work. Canisters of reaction mass were flying to a point three kilometers above the crater floor. The Beckmann drive engines rotated on their mountings, aiming their nodes at the canister's rendezvous point.

Porter's ship was following the tail of debris down to the crater floor. He could make out geometric patterns of insulating material. His computers told him something was approaching a few hundred meters below. There wasn't time for any second guessing. He primed his main cargo and sat back in the seat, lips moving, not in prayer, but repeating some stray, elegant line from the Burgess novel, a final piece of pleasure.

One of the canisters struck the side of the cargo ship just as the blast began. A brilliant flare spread out above the crater, merging with and twisting the tail of the internal charges. Four canisters were knocked from their course and sent plummeting into space. The remaining six met at the assigned point and were hit by beams from the Beckmann drive nodes. Their matter was stripped down to pure energy.

All of this, in its lopsided, incomplete way, bounced against the crater floor and drove the asteroid slightly faster.

When the shaking subsided, Turco let go of a grip bar and asked the computers questions. No answers came back. Everything except minimum life support was out of commission. She thought briefly of returning to her tug, if it was still in position, but there was nowhere to go. So she walked and crawled and floated to a broad view-window in the bubble's dining room. Earth was rising over the Vlasseg pole again,

filling half her view, knots of storm and streaks of brown continent twisting slowly before her. She wondered if it had been enough — it hadn't
felt right. There was no way of knowing for sure, but the Earth looked
much too close.

"It's too close to judge," the president said, deliberately standing with
his back to Kollert. "She'll pass over Greenland, maybe just hit the
upper atmosphere."

The terrorist team officers were packing their valises and talking to
each other in subdued whispers. Three of the president's security men
looked at the screen with dazed expressions. The screen was blank except for a display of seconds until accession of picture. Gestina was
asleep in the chair next to Kollert, her face peaceful, hands wrapped together in her lap.

"We'll have relay pictures from Iceland in a few minutes," the president said. "Should be quite a sight." Kollert frowned. The man was almost cocky, knowing he would come through it untouched. Even with
survival uncertain, his government would be preparing explanations.
Kollert could predict the story: a band of lunar terrorists, loosely tied
with Giani Turco's father and his rabid spacefarers, was responsible for
the whole thing. It would mean a few months of ill feeling on the Moon,
but at least the Nexus would have found its scapegoats.

A communicator beeped in the room, and Kollert looked around
for its source. One of the security men reached into a pocket and
pulled out a small earplug, which he inserted. He listened for a few
seconds, frowned, then nodded. The other two gathered close, and they
whispered.

Then, quietly, they left the room. The president didn't notice they
were gone, but to Kollert their absence spoke volumes.

Six Nexus police entered a minute later. One stood by Kollert's chair,
not looking at him. Four waited by the door. Another approached the
president and tapped him on the shoulder. The president turned.

"Sir, fourteen desks have requested your impeachment. We're instructed to put you under custody, for your own safety."

Kollert started to rise, but the officer beside him put a hand on his
shoulder.

"May we stay to watch?" the president asked. No one objected.

Before the screen was switched on, Kollert asked, "Is anyone going to get Turco, if it misses?"

The terrorist team leader shrugged when no one else answered. "She may not even be alive."

Then, like a crowd of children looking at a horror movie, the men and women in the communications center grouped around the large screen and watched the dark shadow of Psyche blotting out stars.

From the bubble window, Turco saw the sudden aurorae, the spray of ionized gases from the Earth's atmosphere, the awesomely rapid passage of the ocean below, and the blur of white as Greenland flashed past. The structure rocked and jerked as the Earth exerted enormous tidal strains on Psyche.

Sitting in the plastic chair, numb, tightly gripping the arms, Giani looked up—down—at the bright stars, feeling Psyche die beneath her.

Inside, the still-molten hollows formed by the charges began to collapse. Cracks shot outward to the surface, where they became gaping chasms. Sparks and rays of smoke jumped from the chasms. In minutes the passage was over. Looking closely, she saw roiling storms forming over Earth's seas and the spreading shock wave of the asteroid's sudden atmospheric compression. Big winds were blowing, but they'd survive.

It shouldn't have gone this far. They should have listened reasonably, admitted their guilt—

Absolved, girl, she wanted her father to say. She felt him very near. *You've destroyed everything we worked for—a fine architect of Pyrrhic victories.* And now he was at a great distance, receding.

The room was cold, and her skin tingled.

One huge chunk rose to block out the sun. The cabin screamed, and the bubble was filled with sudden flakes of air.

View from a Height

JOAN D. VINGE

The enormity of space implies an isolation so vast that it will dwarf any experience felt by earlier pioneers. In American history the famous Frederick Turner thesis—that the frontier shaped the national character—may account for the development, in the twentieth century, of a unique culture that exploded out into the world, transforming it. Though few Americans went to their frontier, the prospect of an untamed horizon seems to have acted in profound ways on the conventional communities of the East Coast. Would a similar deep-space frontier transform the culture on Earth? What sort of person would be drawn to the profound loneliness of space? In this story the answer has unforeseen aspects.

Saturday, the 7th

I want to know why those pages were missing! How am I supposed to keep up with my research if they leave out pages—?

(Long sighing noise.)

Listen to yourself, Emmylou: You're listening to the sound of fear. It was an oversight, you know that. Nobody did it to you on purpose. Relax, you're getting Fortnight Fever. Tomorrow you'll get the pages, and an apology too, if Harvey Weems knows what's good for him.

But still, five whole pages; and the table of contents. How could you miss *five* pages? And the table of contents.

How do I know there hasn't been a coup? The Northwest's finally taken over completely, and they're censoring the media— And like the Man without a Country, everything they send me from now on is going to have holes cut in it.

In *Science?*

Or maybe Weems has decided to drive me insane—?

Oh, my God... it would be a short trip. Look at me. I don't have any fingernails left.

(*"Arrwk. Hello, beautiful. Hello? Hello?"*)

("Ozymandias! Get out of my hair, you devil." *Laughter.* "Polly want a cracker? Here... gently! That's a boy.")

It's beautiful when he flies. I never get tired of watching him, or looking at him, even after twenty years. Twenty years.... What did the *psittacidae* do, to win the right to wear a rainbow as their plumage? Although the way we've hunted them for it, you could say it was a mixed blessing. Like some other things.

Twenty years. How strange it sounds to hear those words, and know they're true. There are gray hairs when I look in the mirror. Wrinkles starting. And Weems is bald! Bald as an egg, and all squinty behind his spectacles. How did we get that way, without noticing it? Time is both longer and shorter than you think, and usually all at once.

Twelve days is a long time to wait for somebody to return your call. Twenty years is a long time gone. But I feel somehow as though it was only last week that I left home. I keep the circuits clean, going over them and over them, showing those mental home movies until I could almost step across, sometimes, into that other reality. But then I always look down, and there's that tremendous abyss full of space and time, and I realize I can't, again. You can't go home again.

Especially when you're almost one thousand astronomical units out in space. Almost there, the first rung of the ladder. Next Thursday is the day. Oh, that bottle of champagne that's been waiting for so long. Oh, the parallax view! I have the equal of the best astronomical equipment in all of near-Earth space at my command, and a view of the universe that no one has ever had before; and using them has made me the only astrophysicist ever to win a PhD in deep space. Talk about your fieldwork.

Strange to think that if the Forward Observatory had massed less than its thousand-plus tons, I would have been replaced by a machine. But because the installation is so large, I in my infinite human flexibility, even with my infinite human appetite, become the most efficient legal tender. And the farther out I get, the more important my own ability to judge what happens, and respond to it, becomes. The first—and maybe the last—manned interstellar probe, on a one-way journey into infinity... into a universe unobscured by our own system's gases and dust... equipped with eyes that see everything from gamma to ultralong wavelengths, and ears that listen to the music of the spheres.

And Emmylou Stewart, the captive audience. Adrift on a star... if you hold with the idea that all the bits of inert junk drifting through space, no matter how small, have star potential. Dark stars, with brilliance in their secret hearts, only kept back from letting it shine by Fate, which denied them the critical mass to reach their kindling point.

Speak of kindling: the laser beam just arrived to give me my daily boost, moving me a little faster, so I'll reach a little deeper into the universe. Blue sky at bedtime; I always was a night person. I'm sure they didn't design the solar sail to filter light like the sky... but I'm glad it happened to work out that way. Sky-blue was always my passion—the color, texture, fluid purity of it. This color isn't exactly right; but it doesn't matter, because I can't remember how anymore. This sky is a sun catcher. A big blue parasol. But so was the original, from where I used to stand. The sky is a blue parasol... did anyone ever say that before, I wonder? If anyone knows, speak up—

Is anyone even listening? Will anyone ever be?

("Who cares, anyway? Come on, Ozzie—climb aboard. Let's drop down to the observation porch while I do my meditation, and try to remember what days were like.")

Weems, damn it, I want satisfaction!

Sunday, the 8th

That idiot. That intolerable moron—how could he do that to me? After all this time, wouldn't you think he'd know me better than that? To keep me waiting for twelve days, wondering and afraid: twelve days of all the possible stupid paranoias I could weave with my idle hands and mind, making myself miserable, asking for trouble—

And then giving it to me. God, he must be some kind of sadist! If I could only reach him, and hurt him the way I've hurt these past hours—

Except that I know the news wasn't his fault, and that he didn't mean to hurt me . . . and so I can't even ease my pain by projecting it onto him.

I don't know what I would have done if his image hadn't been six days stale when it got here. What would I have done, if he'd been in earshot when I was listening; what would I have said? Maybe no more than I did say.

What can you say, when you realize you've thrown your whole life away?

He sat there behind his faded blotter, twiddling his pen, picking up his souvenir moon rocks and laying them down—looking for all the world like a man with a time bomb in his desk drawer—and said, "Now don't worry, Emmylou. There's no problem . . ." Went on saying it, one way or another, for five minutes; until I was shouting, "What's *wrong*, damn it?"

"I thought you'd never even notice the few pages . . ." with that sidling smile of his. And while I'm muttering, "I may have been in solitary confinement for twenty years, Harvey, but it hasn't turned my brain to mush," he said,

"So maybe I'd better explain, first—" and the look on his face; oh, the look on his face. "There's been a biomed breakthrough. If you were here on Earth, you . . . well, your body's immune responses could be . . . made normal . . ." And then he looked down, as though he could really see the look on my own face.

Made normal. Made normal. It's all I can hear. I was born with no natural immunities. No defense against disease. No help for it. No. *No, no, no;* that's all I ever heard, all my life on Earth. Through the plastic walls of my sealed room; through the helmet of my sealed suit. . . . And now it's all changed. They could cure me. But I can't go home. I knew this could happen; I knew it had to happen someday. But I chose to ignore that fact, and now it's too late to do anything about it.

Then why can't I forget that I could have been f-free....

...I didn't answer Weems today. Screw Weems. There's nothing to say. Nothing at all.

I'm so tired.

Monday, the 9th

Couldn't sleep. It kept playing over and over in my mind.... Finally took some pills. Slept all day, feel like hell. Stupid. And it didn't go away. It was waiting for me, still waiting, when I woke up.

It isn't fair —!

I don't feel like talking about it.

Tuesday, the 10th

Tuesday, already. I haven't done a thing for two days. I haven't even started to check out the relay beacon, and that damn thing has to be dropped off this week. I don't have any strength; I can't seem to move, I just sit. But I have to get back to work. Have to...

Instead I read the printout of the article today. Hoping I'd find a flaw! If that isn't the greatest irony of my entire life. For two decades I prayed that somebody would find a cure for me. And for two more decades I didn't care. Am I going to spend the next two decades hating it, now that it's been found?

No... hating myself. I could have been free, they could have cured me; if only I'd stayed on Earth. If only I'd been patient. But now it's too late... by twenty *years*.

I want to go home. I want to go home.... But you can't go home again. Did I really say that, so blithely, so recently? *You* can't: you, Emmylou Stewart. You are in prison, just like you have always been in prison.

It's all come back to me so strongly. Why me? Why must I be the ultimate victim — In all my life I've never smelled the sea wind, or plucked berries from a bush and eaten them, right there! Or felt my parents' kisses against my skin, or a man's body. . . . Because to me they were all deadly things.

I remember when I was a little girl, and we still lived in Victoria—I was just three or four, just at the brink of understanding that I was the only prisoner in my world. I remember watching my father sit polishing his shoes in the morning, before he left for the museum. And me smiling, so deviously, "Daddy . . . I'll help you do that, if you let me come out—"

And he came to the wall of my bubble and put his arms into the hugging gloves, and said, so gently, "No." And then he began to cry. And I began to cry too, because I didn't know why I'd made him unhappy. . . .

And all the children at school, with their "spaceman" jokes, pointing at the freak; all the years of insensitive people asking the same stupid questions every time I tried to go out anywhere . . . worst of all, the ones who weren't stupid, or insensitive. Like Jeffrey . . . no, I will not think about Jeffrey! I couldn't let myself think about him then. I could never afford to get close to a man, because I'd never be able to touch him. . . .

And now it's too late. Was I controlling my fate, when I volunteered for this one-way trip? Or was I just running away from a life where I was always helpless; helpless to escape the things I hated, helpless to embrace the things I loved?

I pretended this was different, and important . . . but was that really what I believed? No! I just wanted to crawl into a hole I couldn't get out of, because I was so afraid.

So afraid that one day I would unseal my plastic walls, or take off my helmet and my suit; walk out freely to breathe the air, or wade in a stream, or touch flesh against flesh . . . and die of it.

So now I've walled myself into this hermetically sealed tomb for a living death. A perfectly sterile environment, in which my body will not even decay when I die. Never having really lived, I shall never really die, dust to dust. A perfectly sterile environment; in every sense of the word.

I often stand looking at my body in the mirror after I take a shower. Hazel eyes, brown hair in thick waves with hardly any gray . . . and a good figure; not exactly stacked, but not unattractive. And no one has ever seen it that way but me. Last night I had the Dream again . . . I haven't had it for such a long time . . . this time I was sitting on a carved wooden beast in the park beside the Provincial Museum in Victoria; but not as a child in my suit. As a college girl, in white shorts and a bright cotton shirt, feeling the sun on my shoulders, and — Jeffrey's arms around my waist.... We stroll along the bayside hand in hand, under the Victorian lampposts with their bright hanging flower baskets, and everything I do is fresh and spontaneous and full of the moment. But always, always, just when he holds me in his arms at last, just as I'm about to... I wake up.

When we die, do we wake out of reality at last, and all our dreams come true? When I die... I will be carried on and on into the timeless depths of uncharted space in this computerized tomb, unmourned and unremembered. In time all the atmosphere will seep away; and my fair corpse, lying like Snow White's in inviolate sleep, will be sucked dry of moisture, until it is nothing but a mummified parchment of shriveled leather and bulging bones....

("*Hello? Hello, baby? Good night. Yes, no, maybe... Awk. Food time!*")

("Oh, Ozymandias! Yes, yes, I know... I haven't fed you, I'm sorry. I know, I know...")

(*Clinks and rattles.*)

Why am I so selfish? Just because I can't eat, I expect him to fast, too.... No. I just forgot.

He doesn't understand, but he knows something's wrong; he climbs the lamp pole like some tripodal bem, using both feet and his beak, and stares at me with that glass-beady bird's eye, stares and stares and mumbles things. Like a lunatic! Until I can hardly stand not to shut him in a cupboard, or something. But then he sidles along my shoulder and kisses me — such a tender caress against my cheek, with that hooked prehensile beak that could crush a walnut like a grape — to let me know that he's worried, and he cares. And I stroke his feathers to thank him and tell him that it's all right... but it's not. And he knows it.

Does he ever resent his life? Would he, if he could? Stolen away from his own kind, raised in a sterile bubble to be a caged bird for a caged human....

I'm only a bird in a gilded cage. I want to go home.

Wednesday, the 11th

Why am I keeping this journal? Do I really believe that sometime some alien being will find this, or some starship from Earth's glorious future will catch up to me ... glorious future, hell. Stupid, selfish, shortsighted fools. They ripped the guts out of the space program after they sent me away, no one will ever follow me now. I'll be lucky if they don't declare me dead and forget about me.

As if anyone would care what a woman all alone on a lumbering space probe thought about day after day for decades, anyway. What monstrous conceit.

I did lubricate the bearings on the big scope today. I did that much. I did it so that I could turn it back toward Earth ... toward the sun ... toward the whole damn system. Because I can't even see it, all crammed into the space of two moon diameters, even Pluto; and too dim and small and far away below me for my naked eyes, anyway. Even the sun is no more than a gaudy star that doesn't even make me squint. So I looked for them with the scope. . . .

Isn't it funny how when you're a child you see all those drawings and models of the solar system with big, lumpy planets and golden wakes streaming around the sun. Somehow you never get over expecting it to look that way in person. And here I am, one thousand astronomical units north of the solar pole, gazing down from a great height ... and it doesn't look that way at all. It doesn't look like anything; even through the scope. One great blot of light, and all the pale tiny diamond chips of planets and moons around it, barely distinguishable from half a hundred undistinguished stars trapped in the same arc of blackness. So meaningless, so insignificant ... so disappointing.

Five hours I spent, today, listening to my journal, looking back and trying to find — something, I don't know, something I suddenly don't have anymore.

I had it at the start. I was disgusting; Pollyanna grad student skipping and singing through the rooms of my very own observatory. It seemed like heaven, and a lifetime spent in it couldn't possibly be long enough for all that I was going to accomplish, and discover. I'd never be bored, no, not me. . . .

And there was so much to learn about the potential of this place, before I got out to where it supposedly would matter, and there would be new things to turn my wonderful extended senses toward ... while I could still communicate easily with my dear mentor Dr. Weems, and the world. (Who'd ever have thought, when the lecherous old goat was my thesis advisor at Harvard, and making jokes to his other grad students about "the lengths some women will go to protect their virginity," that we would have to spend a lifetime together.)

There was Ozymandias's first word . . . and my first birthday in space, and my first anniversary . . . and my doctoral degree at last, printed out by the computer with scrolls made of little *x*'s and taped up on the wall. . . .

Then day and night and day and night, beating me black and blue with blue and black . . . my fifth anniversary, my eighth, my decade. I crossed the magnetopause, to become truly the first voyager in interstellar space . . . but by then there was no one left to *talk* to anymore, to really share the experience with. Even the radio and television broadcasts drifting out from Earth were diffuse and rare; there were fewer and fewer contacts with the reality outside. The plodding routines, the stupefying boredom — until sometimes I stood screaming down the halls just for something new; listening to the echoes that no one else would ever hear and pretending they'd come to call; trying so hard to believe there was something to hear that wasn't *my* voice, *my* echo, or Ozymandias making a mockery of it.

("*Hello, beautiful. That's a crock. Hello, hello?*")

("*Ozymandias, get* away *from me —*")

But always I had that underlying belief in my mission: that I was here for a purpose, for more than my own selfish reasons, or NASA's (or whatever the hell they call it now), but for Humanity, and Science. Through meditation I learned the real value of inner silence and thought that by creating an inner peace I had reached equilibrium with the outer silences. I thought that meditation had disciplined me, I was in touch with my self and with the soul of the cosmos. . . . But I haven't been able to meditate since — it happened. The inner silence fills up with my own anger screaming at me, until I can't remember what peace sounds like.

And what have I really discovered, so far? Almost nothing. Nothing worth wasting my analysis or all my fine theories — or my freedom — on. Space is even emptier than anyone dreamed, you could count on both hands the bits of cold dust or worldlet I've passed in all this time, lost souls falling helplessly through near-perfect vacuum . . . all of us together. With my absurdly long astronomical tape measure I have fixed precisely the distance to NGC 2419 and a few other features, and from that made new estimates about a few more distant ones. But I have not detected a miniature black hole insatiably vacuuming up the vacuum; I have not pierced the invisible clouds that shroud the ultralong wavelengths like fog; I have not discovered that life exists beyond the Earth in even the most tentative way. Looking back at the solar system, I see nothing to show definitively that we even exist, anymore. All I hear anymore when I scan is electromagnetic noise, no coherent thought. Only Weems every twelfth night, like the last man alive.... Christ, I still haven't answered him.

Why bother? Let him sweat. Why bother with any of it. Why waste my precious time.

Oh, my precious time.... Half a lifetime left that could have been mine, on Earth.

Twenty years—I came through them all all right. I thought I was safe. And after twenty years, my facade of discipline and self-control falls apart at a touch. What a self-deluded hypocrite I've been. Do you know that I said the sky was like a blue parasol eighteen years ago? And probably said it again fifteen years ago, and ten, and five—

Tomorrow I pass 1000 AUs.

Thursday, the 12th

I burned out the scope. I burned out the scope. I left it pointing toward the Earth, and when the laser came on for the night, it shone right down the scope's throat and burned it out. I'm so ashamed.... Did I do it on purpose, subconsciously?

("*Good night starlight. Arrk. Good night. Good...*")

("Damn it, I want to hear another human voice—!")

(*Echoing, "voice, voice, voice, voice..."*)

When I found out what I'd done, I ran away. I ran and ran through the halls... But I only ran in a circle: this observatory, my prison, myself... I can't escape. I'll always come back in the end, to this green-walled room with its desk and its terminals, its cupboards crammed with a hundred thousand dozens of everything, toilet paper and magnetic tape and oxygen tanks. . . . And I can tell you exactly how many steps it is to my bedroom or how long it took me to crochet the afghan on the bed . . . how long I've sat in the dark and silence, setting up an exposure program or listening for the feeble pulse of a radio galaxy two billion light-years away. There will never be anything different, or anything more.

When I finally came back here, there was a message waiting. Weems, grinning out at me half-bombed from the screen — "Congratulations," he cried, "on this historic occasion! Emmylou, we're having a little celebration here at the lab; mind if we join you in yours, one thousand astronomical units from home — ?" I've never seen him drunk. They really must have meant to do something nice for me, planning it all six days ahead. . . .

To celebrate I shouted obscenities I didn't even know I knew at him, until my voice was broken and my throat was raw.

Then I sat at my desk for a long time with my jackknife lying open in my hand. Not wanting to die — I've always been too afraid of death for that — but wanting to hurt myself. I wanted to make a fresh hurt, to take my attention off the terrible thing that is sucking me into myself like an imploding star. Or maybe just to punish myself, I don't know. But I considered the possibility of actually cutting myself quite calmly; while some separate part of me looked on in horror. I even pressed the knife against my flesh . . . and then I stopped and put it away. It hurts too much.

I can't go on like this. I have duties, obligations, and I can't face them. What would I do without the emergency automechs? . . . But it's the rest of my life, and they can't go on doing my job for me forever —

Later.

I just had a visitor. Strange as that sounds. Stranger yet — it was Donald Duck. I picked up half of a children's cartoon show today, the first coherent piece of nondirectional, unbeamed television broadcast I've recorded in months. And I don't think I've ever been happier to see anyone in my life. What a nice surprise, so glad you could drop by. . . . Ozymandias loves him; he hangs upside down from his swing under the cabinet with a cracker in one foot, cackling away and saying, "Give us a kiss, *smack-smack-smack.*" . . . We watched it three times. I even smiled, for a while; until I remembered myself. It helps. Maybe I'll watch it again until bedtime.

Friday, the 13th

Friday the Thirteenth. Amusing. Poor Friday the Thirteenth, what did it ever do to deserve its reputation? Even if it had any power to make my life miserable, it couldn't hold a candle to the rest of this week. It seems like an eternity since last weekend.

I repaired the scope today; replaced the burned-out parts. Had to suit up and go outside for part of the work... I haven't done any outside maintenance for quite a while. Odd how both exhilarating and terrifying it always is when I first step out of the air lock, utterly alone, into space. You're entirely on your own, so far away from any possibility of help, so far away from anything at all. And at that moment you doubt yourself, suddenly, terribly... just for a moment.

But then you drag your umbilical out behind you and clank along the hull in your magnetized boots that feel so reassuringly like lead ballast. You turn on the lights and look for the trouble, find it, and get to work; it doesn't bother you anymore.... When your life seems to have torn loose and be drifting free, it creates a kind of sea anchor to work with your hands; whether it's doing some mindless routine chore or the most intricate of repairs.

There was a moment of panic, when I actually saw charred wires and melted metal, when I imagined the damage was so bad that I couldn't repair it again. It looked so final, so — masterful. I clung there by my feet and whimpered and clenched my hands inside my gloves, like a great shining baby, for a while. But then I pulled myself down and began to pry here and unscrew there and twist a component free... and little by little I replaced everything. One step at a time; the way we get through life.

By the time I'd finished I felt quite calm, for the first time in days; the thing that's been trying to choke me to death this past week seemed to falter a little at my demonstration of competence. I've been breathing easier since then; but I still don't have much strength. I used up all I had just overcoming my own inertia.

But I shut off the lights and hiked around the hull for a while afterwards — I couldn't face going back inside just then: looking at the black convex dish of the solar sail I'm embedded in, up at the radio antenna's smaller dish occluding stars as the observatory's cylinder wheels endlessly at the hub of the spinning parasol....

That made me dizzy, and so I looked out into the starfields that lie on every side. Even with my own poor, unaugmented senses there's so much more to see out here, unimpeded by atmosphere or dust, undominated by any sun's glare. The brilliance of the Milky Way, the depths of star and nebula and farthest galaxy breathlessly suspended... as I am. The realization that I'm lost for eternity in an uncharted sea.

Strangely, although that thought aroused a very powerful emotion when it struck me, it wasn't a negative one at all: it was from another scale of values entirely; like the universe itself. It was as if the universe itself stretched out its finger to touch me. And in touching me, singling me out, it only heightened my awareness of my own insignificance.

That was somehow very comforting. When you confront the absolute indifference of magnitudes and vistas so overwhelming, the swollen ego of your self-important suffering is diminished....

And I remembered one of the things that was always so important to me about space — that here *any*one has to put on a spacesuit before they step outside. We're all aliens, no one better equipped to survive than another. I am as normal as anyone else, out here.

I must hold on to that thought.

Saturday, the 14th

There is a reason for my being here. There is a reason.

I was able to meditate earlier today. Not in the old way, the usual way, by emptying my mind. Rather by letting the questions fill up the space, not fighting them; letting them merge with my memories of all that's gone before. I put on music, that great mnemonic stimulator; letting the images that each tape evoked free-associate and interact.

And in the end I could believe again that my being here was the result of a free choice. No one forced me into this. My motives for volunteering were entirely my own. And I was given this position because

NASA believed that I was more likely to be successful in it than anyone else they could have chosen.

It doesn't matter that some of my motives happened to be unresolved fear or wanting to escape from things I couldn't cope with. It really doesn't matter. Sometimes retreat is the only alternative to destruction, and only a madman can't recognize the truth of that. Only a madman.... Is there anyone "sane" on Earth who isn't secretly a fugitive from something unbearable somewhere in their life? And yet they function normally.

If they ran, they ran toward something, too, not just away. And so did I. I had already chosen a career as an astrophysicist before I ever dreamed of being a part of this project. I could have become a medical researcher instead, worked on my own to find a cure for my condition. I could have grown up hating the whole idea of space and "spacemen," stumbling through life in my damned ugly sterile suit....

But I remember when I was six years old, the first time I saw a film of suited astronauts at work in space... they looked just like me! And no one was laughing. How could I help but love space, then?

(And how could I help but love Jeffrey, with his night-black hair, and his blue flightsuit with the starry patch on the shoulder. Poor Jeffrey, poor Jeffrey, who never even realized his own dream of space before they cut the program out from under him.... I will not talk about Jeffrey. I will not.)

Yes, I could have stayed on Earth, and waited for a cure! I knew even then there would have to be one, someday. It was both easier and harder to choose space, instead of staying.

And I think the thing that really decided me was that those people had faith enough in me and my abilities to believe that I could run this observatory and my own life smoothly for as long as I lived. Billions of dollars and a thousand tons of equipment resting on me; like Atlas holding up his world.

Even Atlas tried to get rid of his burden; because no matter how vital his function was, the responsibility was still a burden to him. But he took his burden back again too, didn't he; for better or worse....

I worked today. I worked my butt off getting caught up on a week's worth of data processing and maintenance, and I'm still not finished. Discovered while I was at it that Ozymandias had used those missing five pages just like the daily news: crapped all over them. My sentiments exactly! I laughed and laughed.

I think I may live.

Sunday, the 15th

The clouds have parted.

That's not rhetorical — among my fresh processed data is a series of photo reconstructions in the ultralong wavelengths. And there's a gap in the obscuring gas up ahead of me, a break in the clouds that extends thirty or forty light-years. Maybe fifty! Fantastic. What a view. What a view I have from here of everything, with my infinitely extended vision: of the way ahead, of the passing scene — or looking back toward Earth.

Looking back. I'll never stop looking back and wishing it could have been different. That at least there could have been two of me, one to be here, one who could have been normal, back on Earth; so that I wouldn't have to be forever torn in two by regrets —

("Hello. What's up, Doc? Avast!")

("Hey, watch it! If you drink, don't fly.")

Damn bird . . . If I'm getting maudlin, it's because I had a party today. Drank a whole bottle of champagne. Yes, I had *the* party . . . we did, Ozymandias and I. Our private 1000 AU celebration. Better late than never, I guess. At least we did have something concrete to celebrate — the photos. And if the celebration wasn't quite as merry as it could have been, still I guess it will probably seem like it was when I look back on it from the next one, at 2000 AUs. They'll be coming faster now, the celebrations. I may even live to celebrate 8000. What the hell, I'll shoot for 10,000 —

After we finished the champagne . . . Ozymandias thinks '98 was a great year, thank God he can't drink as fast as I can . . . I put on my Strauss waltzes, and the *Barcarolle:* oh, the Berlin Philharmonic; their touch is what a lover's kiss must be. I threw the view outside onto the big screen, a ballroom of stars, and danced with my shadow. And part of the time I wasn't dancing above the abyss in a jumpsuit and headphones, but waltzing in yards of satin and lace across a ballroom floor in nineteenth-century Vienna. What I wouldn't give to be *there* for a moment out of time. Not for a lifetime, or even a year, but just for an evening; just for one waltz.

Another thing I shall never do. There are so many things we can't do, any of us, for whatever the reasons—time, talent, life's callous whims. We're all on a one-way trip into infinity. If we're lucky, we're given some life's work we care about, or some person. Or both, if we're very lucky.

And I do have Weems. Sometimes I see us like an old married couple, who have grown to a tolerant understanding over the years. We've never been soul mates, God knows, but we're comfortable with each others' silences. . . .

I guess it's about time I answered him.

The Voyage That Lasted Six Hundred Years

DON WILCOX

This energetic 1940 story has the distinction of being the first full treatment of the idea of the generation starship. The concept had been proposed in 1929 by J. D. Bernal and treated obliquely in the works of Olaf Stapledon and in Lawrence Manning's haunting story "The Living Galaxy" (1934). Robert Heinlein's influential "Universe" and "Common Sense" of 1941 added the cultural loss of memory about the ship's mission—a significant development of the idea that spurred many variations. Although Cox's story is not strong on physical details, it does present the sociology of the concept, its human impact, with a sense of humor, tragedy, and gritty realism, which puts it well ahead of its day. It is still provocative today.

I

They gave us a gala send-off, the kind that keeps your heart bobbing up at your tonsils.

"It's a long, long way to the Milky Way!" the voices sang out. The band thundered the chorus over and over. The golden trumpaphones blasted our eardrums wide open. Thousands of people clapped their hands in time.

There were thirty-three of us — that is, there were supposed to be. As it turned out, there were thirty-five.

We were a dazzling parade of red, white, and blue uniforms. We marched up the gangplank by couples, every couple a man and wife, every couple young and strong, for the selection had been rigid.

Captain Sperry and his wife and I — I being the odd man — brought up the rear. Reporters and cameramen swarmed at our heels. The microphones stopped us. The band and the crowd hushed.

"This is Captain Sperry telling you good-by," the amplified voice boomed. "In behalf of the thirty-three, I thank you for your grand farewell. We'll remember this hour as our last contact with our beloved Earth."

The crowd held its breath. The mighty import of our mission struck through every heart.

"We go forth into space to live — and to die," the captain said gravely. "But *our children's children*, born in space and reared in the light of our vision, will carry on our great purpose. And in centuries to come, *your children's children* may set forth for the Robinello planets, knowing that you will find an American colony already planted there."

The captain gestured good-by and the multitude responded with a thunderous cheer. Nothing so daring as a six-century nonstop flight had ever been undertaken before.

An announcer nabbed me by the sleeve and barked into the microphone,

"And now one final word from Professor Gregory Grimstone, the one man who is supposed to live down through the six centuries of this historic flight and see the journey through to the end."

"Ladies and gentlemen," I choked, and the echo of my swallow blobbed back at me from distant walls, "as Keeper of the Traditions, I give you my word that the S. S. *Flashaway* shall carry your civilization through to the end, unsoiled and unblemished!"

A cheer stimulated me and I drew a deep breath for a burst of oratory. But Captain Sperry pulled at my other sleeve.

"That's all. We're set to slide out in two minutes."

The reporters scurried down the gangplank and made a center rush through the crowd. The band struck up. Motors roared suddenly.

One lone reporter who had missed out on the interviews blitzkrieged up and caught me by the coattail.

"Hold it, Butch. Just a coupla words so I can whip up a column of froth for the *Star*—Well, I'll be damned! If it ain't 'Crackdown' Grimstone!"

I scowled. The reporter before me was none other than Bill Broscoe, one of my former pupils at college and a star athlete. At heart I knew that Bill was a right guy, but I'd be the last to tell him so.

"Broscoe!" I snarled. "Tardy as usual. You finally flunked my history course, didn't you?"

"Now, Crackdown," he whined, "don't go hopping on me. I won that Thanksgiving game for you, remember?"

He gazed at my red, white, and blue uniform.

"So you're off for Robinello," he grinned.

"Son, this is my last minute on Earth, and *you* have to haunt me, of all people—"

"So you're the one that's taking the refrigerated sleeper, to wake up every hundred years—"

"And stir the fires of civilization among the crew—yes. Six hundred years from now when your bones have rotted, I'll still be carrying on."

"Still teaching 'em history? God forbid!" Broscoe grinned.

"I hope I have better luck than I did with you."

"Let 'em off easy on dates, Crackdown. Give them 1066 for William the Conqueror and 2066 for the *Flashaway* take off. That's enough. Taking your wife, I suppose?"

At this impertinent question I gave Broscoe the cold eye.

"Pardon me," he said, suppressing a sly grin—proof enough that he had heard the devastating story about how I missed my wedding and got the air. "Faulty alarm clock, wasn't it? Too bad, Crackdown. And you always ragged *me* about being tardy!"

With this jibe Broscoe exploded into laughter. Some people have the damnedest notions about what constitutes humor. I backed into the entrance of the space ship uncomfortably. Broscoe followed.

Zzzzippp!

The automatic door cut past me. I jerked Broscoe through barely in time to keep him from being bisected.

"Tardy as usual, my friend," I hooted. "You've missed your gangplank! That makes you the first castaway in space."

We took off like a shooting star, and the last I saw of Bill Broscoe, he stood at a rear window cursing as he watched the Earth and the moon fall away into the velvety black heavens. And the more I laughed at him, the madder he got. No sense of humor.

Was that the last time I ever saw him? Well, no, to be strictly honest, I had one more unhappy glimpse of him.

It happened just before I packed myself away for my first one hundred years' sleep.

I had checked over the "Who's Who aboard the *Flashaway*" — the official register — to make sure that I was thoroughly acquainted with everyone on board; for these sixteen couples were to be the great-grandparents of the next generation I would meet. Then I had promptly taken my leave of Captain Sperry and his wife, and gone directly to my refrigeration plant, where I was to suspend my life by instantaneous freezing.

I clicked the switches, and one of the two huge horizontal wheels — one in reserve, in the event of a breakdown — opened up for me like a door opening in the side of a gigantic doughnut, or better, a tubular merry-go-round. There was my nook waiting for me to crawl in.

Before I did so, I took a backward glance toward the ballroom. The one-way glass partition, through which I could see but not be seen, gave me a clear view of the scene of merriment. The couples were dancing. The journey was off to a good start.

"A grand gang," I said to myself. No one doubted that the ship was equal to the six-hundred-year journey. The success would depend upon the people. Living and dying in this closely circumscribed world would put them to a severe test. All credit, I reflected, was due the planning committee for choosing such a congenial group.

"They're equal to it," I said optimistically. If their children would only prove as sturdy and adaptable as their parents, my job as Keeper of the Traditions would be simple.

But how, I asked myself, as I stepped into my life-suspension merry-go-round, would Bill Broscoe fit into this picture? Not a half-bad guy. Still —

My final glance through the one-way glass partition slew me. Out of the throng I saw Bill Broscoe dancing past with a beautiful girl in his arms. The girl was Louise — *my* Louise — the girl I had been engaged to marry!

In a flash it came to me — but not about Bill. I forgot him on the spot. About Louise.

Bless her heart, she'd come to find me. She must have heard that I had signed up for the *Flashaway*, and she had come aboard, a stowaway, to forgive me for missing the wedding — to marry me! Now —

A warning click sounded, a lid closed over me, my refrigerator merry-go-round whirled — Blackness!

II

In a moment—or so it seemed — I was again gazing into the light of the refrigerating room. The lid stood open.

A stimulating warmth circulated through my limbs. Perhaps the machine, I half-consciously concluded, had made no more than a preliminary revolution.

I bounded out with a single thought. I must find Louise. We could still be married. For the present I would postpone my entrance into the ice. And since the machine had been equipped with *two* merry-go-round freezers as an emergency safeguard — ah! happy thought — perhaps Louise would be willing to undergo life suspension with me!

I stopped at the one-way glass partition, astonished to see no signs of dancing in the ballroom. I could scarcely see the ballroom, for it had been darkened.

Upon unlocking the door (the refrigerator room was my own private retreat), I was bewildered. An unaccountable change had come over everything. What it was, I couldn't determine at the moment. But the very air of the ballroom was different.

A few dim green lightbulbs burned along the walls — enough to show me that the dancers had vanished. Had time enough elapsed for night to come on? My thoughts spun dizzily. Night, I reflected, would consist simply of turning off the lights and going to bed. It had been agreed in our plan that our twenty-four-hour Earth day would be maintained for the sake of regularity.

But there was something more intangible that struck me. The furniture had been changed about, and the very walls seemed *older*. Something more than minutes had passed since I left this room.

Strangest of all, the windows were darkened.

In a groggy state of mind I approached one of the windows in hopes of catching a glimpse of the solar system. I was still puzzling over how much time might have elapsed. Here, at least, was a sign of very recent activity.

"Wet Paint" read the sign pinned to the window. The paint was still sticky. What the devil—

The ship, of course, was fully equipped for blind flying. But aside from the problems of navigation, the crew had anticipated enjoying a wonderland of stellar beauty through the portholes. Now, for some strange reason, every window had been painted opaque.

I listened. Slow measured steps were pacing in an adjacent hallway. Nearing the entrance, I stopped, halted by a shrill sound from somewhere overhead. It came from one of the residential quarters that gave on the ballroom balcony.

It was the unmistakable wail of a baby.

Then another baby's cry struck up; and a third, from somewhere across the balcony, joined the chorus. Time, indeed, must have passed since I left this roomful of dancers.

Now some irate voices of disturbed sleepers added rumbling basses to the symphony of wailings. Grumbles of "Shut that little devil up!" and poundings of fists on walls thundered though the empty ballroom. In a burst of inspiration I ran to the records room, where the ship's "Who's Who" was kept.

The door to the records room was locked, but the footsteps of some sleepless person I had heard now pounded down the dimly lighted hallway. I looked upon the aged man. I had never seen him before. He stopped at the sight of me; then snapping on a brighter light, came on confidently.

"Mr. Grimstone?" he said, extending his hand. "We've been expecting you. My name is William Broscoe—"

"Broscoe!"

"William Broscoe, the second. You knew my father, I believe."

I groaned and choked.

"And my mother," the old man continued, "always spoke very highly of you. I'm proud to be the first to greet you."

He politely overlooked the flush of purple that leaped into my face. For a moment nothing that I could say was intelligible.

He turned a key and we entered the records room. There I faced the inescapable fact. My full century had passed. The original crew of the *Flashaway* were long gone. A completely new generation was on the register.

Or, more accurately, three new generations: the children, the grand-children, and the great-grandchildren of the generation I had known.

One hundred years had passed—and I had lain so completely suspended, owing to the freezing, that only a moment of my own life had been absorbed.

Eventually I was to get used to this; but on this first occasion I found it utterly shocking—even embarrassing. Only a few minutes ago, as my experience went, I was madly in love with Louise and had hopes of yet marrying her.

But now—well, the leather-bound "Who's Who" told all. Louise had been dead twenty years. Nearly thirty children now alive aboard the S. S. *Flashaway* could claim her as their great-grandmother. These carefully recorded pedigrees proved it.

And the patriarch of that fruitful tribe had been none other than Bill Broscoe, the fresh young athlete who had always been tardy for my history class. I gulped as if I were swallowing a baseball.

Broscoe—tardy! And I had missed my second chance to marry Louise—by a full century!

My fingers turned the pages of the register numbly. William Broscoe II misinterpreted my silence.

"I see you are quick to detect our trouble," he said, and the same deep conscientious concern showed in his expression that I had remembered in the face of his mother, upon our grim meeting after my alarm clock had failed and I had missed my own wedding.

Trouble? Trouble aboard the S. S. *Flashaway*, after all the careful advance planning we had done, and after all our array of budgeting and scheduling and vowing to stamp our systematic ways upon the oncoming generations? This, we had agreed, would be the world's most unique colonizing expedition; for every last trouble that might crop up on the six-hundred-year voyage had already been met and conquered by advance planning.

"They've tried to put off doing anything about it until your arrival," Broscoe said, observing respectfully that the charter invested in me the authority of passing upon all important policies. "But this very week three new babies arrived, which brings the trouble to a crisis. So the captain ordered a blackout of the heavens as an emergency measure."

"Heavens?" I grunted. "What have the heavens got to do with babies?"

"There's a difference of opinion on that. Maybe it depends upon how susceptible you are."

"Susceptible—to what?"

"The romantic malady."

I looked at the old man, much puzzled. He took me by the arm and led me toward the pilots' control room. Here were unpainted windows that revealed celestial glories beyond anything I had ever dreamed. Brilliant planets of varied hues gleamed through the blackness, while close at hand—almost close enough to touch—were numerous large moons, floating slowly past as we shot along our course.

"Some little show," the pilot grinned, "and it keeps getting better."

He proceeded to tell me just where we were and how few adjustments in the original time schedules he had had to make, and why this nonstop flight to Robinello would stand unequaled for centuries to come.

And I heard virtually nothing of what he said. I simply stood there, gazing at the unbelievable beauty of the skies. I was hypnotized, enthralled, shaken to the very roots. One emotion, one thought dominated me. I longed for Louise.

"The romantic malady, as I was saying," William Broscoe resumed, "may or may not be a factor in producing our large population. Personally, I think it's pure buncombe."

"Pure buncombe," I echoed, still thinking of Louise. If she and I had had moons like these—

"But nobody can tell Captain Dickinson anything..."

There was considerable clamor and wrangling that morning as the inhabitants awakened to find their heavens blacked out. Captain Dickinson was none too popular anyway. Fortunately for him, many of the people took their grouches out on the babies who had caused the disturbance in the night.

Families with babies were supposed to occupy the rear staterooms — but there weren't enough rear staterooms. Or rather, there were too many babies.

Soon the word went the rounds that the Keeper of the Traditions had returned to life. I was duly banqueted and toasted and treated to lengthy accounts of the events of the past hundred years. And during the next few days many of the older men and women would take me aside for private conferences and spill their worries into my ears.

III

"What's the world coming to?" these granddaddies and grandmothers would ask. And before I could scratch my head for an answer, they would assure me that this expedition was headed straight for the rocks.

"It's all up with us. We've lost our grip on our original purposes. The Six-Hundred-Year Plan is nothing but a dead scrap of paper."

I'll admit things looked plenty black. And the more parlor conversations I was invited in on, the blacker things looked. I couldn't sleep nights.

"If our population keeps on increasing, we'll run out of food before we're halfway there," William Broscoe II repeatedly declared. "We've got to have a compulsory program of birth control. That's the only thing that will save us."

A delicate subject for parlor conversations, you think? This older generation didn't think so. I was astonished, and I'll admit I was a bit proud as well, to discover how deeply imbued these old graybeards were with *Flashaway* determination and patriotism. They had missed life in America by only one generation, and they were unquestionably the staunchest of flag wavers on board.

The younger generations were less outspoken, and for the first week I began to deplore their comparative lack of vision. They, the possessors of families, seemed to avoid these discussions about the oversupply of children.

"So you've come to check up on our American traditions, Professor Grimstone," they would say casually. "We've heard all about this great purpose of our forefathers, and I guess it's up to us to put it across. But gee whiz, Grimstone, we wish we could have seen the Earth! What's it like, anyhow?"

"Tell us some more about the Earth . . ."

"All we know is what we get secondhand . . ."

I told them about the Earth. Yes, they had books galore, and movies and phonograph records, pictures and maps; but these things only excited their curiosity. They asked me questions by the thousands. Only after I had poured out several encyclopedia-loads of Earth memories did I begin to break through their masks.

Back of this constant questioning, I discovered, they were watching me. Perhaps they were wondering whether they were not being subjected to more rigid discipline here on shipboard than their cousins back on Earth. I tried to impress upon them that they were a chosen group, but this had little effect. It stuck in their minds that *they* had had no choice in the matter.

Moreover, they were watching to see what I was going to do about the population problem, for they were no less aware of it than their elders.

Two weeks after my "return" we got down to business.

Captain Dickinson preferred to engineer the matter himself. He called an assembly in the movie auditorium. Almost everyone was present.

The program began with the picture of the Six-Hundred-Year Plan. Everyone knew the reels by heart. They had seen and heard them dozens of times, and were ready to snicker at the proper moments—such as when the stern old committee chairman, charging the unborn generations with their solemn obligations, was interrupted by a friendly fly on his nose.

When the films were run through, Captain Dickinson took the rostrum, and with considerable bluster he called upon the Clerk of the Council to review the situation. The clerk read a report which went about as follows:

To maintain a stable population, it was agreed in the original Plan that families should average two children each. Hence, the original 16 families would bring forth approximately 32 children; and assuming that they were fairly evenly divided as to sex, they would eventually form 16 new families. These 16 families would, in turn, have an average of two children each—another generation of approximately 32.

By maintaining these averages, we were to have a total population, at any given time, of 32 children, 32 parents, and 32 grandparents. The great-grandparents may be left out of account, for owing to the natural span of life they ordinarily die off before they accumulate in any great numbers.

The three living generations, then, of 32 each would give the *Flashaway* a constant active population of 96, or roughly, 100 persons.

The Six-Hundred-Year Plan has allowed for some flexibility in these figures. It has established the safe maximum at 150 and the safe minimum at 75.

If our population shrinks below 75, it is dangerously small. If it shrinks to 50, a crisis is at hand.

But if it grows above 150, it is dangerously large; and if it reaches the 200 mark, as we all know, a crisis may be said to exist.

The clerk stopped for an impressive pause, marred only by the crying of a baby from some distant room.

"Now, coming down to the present-day facts, we are well aware that the population has been dangerously large for the past seven years—"

"Since we entered this section of the heavens," Captain Dickinson interspersed with a scowl.

"From the first year in space, the population plan has encountered some irregularities," the clerk continued. "To begin with, there were not sixteen couples, but seventeen. The seventeenth couple"—here the clerk shot a glance at William Broscoe—"did not belong to the original compact, and after their marriage they were not bound by the sacred traditions—"

"I object!" I shouted, challenging the eyes of the clerk and the captain squarely. Dickinson had written that report with a touch of malice. The clerk skipped over a sentence or two.

"But however the Broscoe family may have prospered and multiplied, our records show that nearly all the families of the present generation have exceeded the per-family quota."

At this point there was a slight disturbance in the rear of the auditorium. An anxious-looking young man entered and signaled to the doctor. The two went out together.

"*All* the families," the clerk amended. "Our population this week passed the two hundred mark. This concludes the report."

The captain opened the meeting for discussion, and the forum lasted far into the night. The demand for me to assist the Council with some legislation was general. There was also hearty sentiment against the captain's blacked-out heavens from young and old alike.

This, I considered, was a good sign. The children craved the fun of watching the stars and planets; their elders desired to keep up their serious astronomical studies.

"Nothing is so important to the welfare of this expedition," I said to the Council on the following day, as we settled down to the job of thrashing out some legislation, "as to maintain our interests in the outside world. Population or no population, we must not become ingrown!"

I talked of new responsibilities, new challenges in the form of contests and campaigns, new leisure-time activities. The discussion went on for days.

"Back in my times—" I said for the hundredth time; but the captain laughed me down. My times and these times were as unlike as black and white, he declared.

"But the principle is the same!" I shouted. "We had population troubles, too."

They smiled as I referred to twenty-first-century relief families who were overrun with children. I cited the fact that some industrialists who paid heavy taxes had considered giving every relief family an automobile as a measure to save themselves money in the long run; for they had discovered that relief families with cars had fewer children than those without.

"That's no help," Dickinson muttered. "You can't have cars on a spaceship."

"You can play bridge," I retorted. "Bridge is an enemy of the birthrate too. Bridge, cars, movies, checkers—they all add up to the same thing. They lift you out of your animal natures—"

The Councilmen threw up their hands. They had bridged and checkered themselves to death.

"Then try other things," I persisted. "You could produce your own movies and plays—organize a little theater—create some new drama—"

"What have we got to dramatize?" the captain replied sourly. "All the dramatic things happen on the Earth."

September • 50 cents

analog
SCIENCE FACT ⌂· SCIENCE FICTION

A LIFE FOR THE STARS by James Blish
A story of the industrial cities of space

An "Okie" city (Scranton, Pennsylvania) lofting, wrapped in the gauzy protective shield of its "spindizzy" field, which is also its motive source. Cover of *Analog*, September, 1962. An "Okie" story by James Blish appears in this volume. *Painting by Solonevich (collection of Sam Moskowitz).*

"The Thousand-Year Ark." Cover of *Science Fiction Plus*, April, 1953, illustrating the article "Interstellar Flight" by Leslie R. Shepherd of the British Interplanetary Society. A hollowed-out asteroid contains the ark, a world unto itself, in which several generations will live until the vessel reaches a solar system containing a natural world suitable for colonization. "The Voyage That Lasted Six Hundred Years," in this volume, presents such a project. *Painting by Alex Schomburg (collection of Sam Moskowitz).*

"The Problem of Space Flying." Cover of *Science Wonder Stories*, August, 1929. The first full-color depiction of a man-made satellite ever published. The human figures are gazing at a space station and astronomical observatory, which is solar-powered through collecting mirrors. *Painting by Frank R. Paul (collection of Sam Moskowitz).*

Chesley Bonestell

Overall view of the Space Station, at the time of the arrival of one of the
supply ships. At the extreme left is the Third Stage of one of the rocket
ships which originally established the station; next to the Third Stage,
one of the small space taxis. . . . The station itself, with a space taxi just
leaving its landing berth, is at the right. The men in space suits near the
Third Stage and near the Observatory are floating freely, but the two men
on the outside of the station are secured by lines hooked to holding rings

on the station. These two men follow the rotation of the Space Station and if not fastened to it would be thrown off tangentially.

The Space Station is 1,075 miles above the Pacific Ocean, above a point 800 miles south by east of the Galapagos Islands. The visual angle of the picture is 50 degrees, the horizon 3,000 miles away, and the area of the picture about 4 million square miles. From *Across the Space Frontier*, edited by Cornelius Ryan, 1953. *Painting by Chesley Bonestell.*

Interior of a rotating Bernal Sphere. Everything is held down by centrifugal acceleration as a substitute for gravity. Gerard K. O'Neill, *The High Frontier* (New York: Morrow; Bantam, 1978). *Painting by Donald Davis.*

A view down the length of a space colony twenty miles long by four miles in diameter. An eclipse of the sun by the moon is visible through one long window. Gerard K. O'Neill, *The High Frontier* (New York: Morrow; Bantam, 1976, 1978). *Painting by Donald Davis.*

The interior of a "mostly countryside" hollowed-out asteroid, with sunplate run by an artificial power source at one end. The exterior of the asteroid is shown at the top of the painting. Cover of *The Sunspacers Trilogy* by George Zebrowski, 1996. *Painting by Bob Eggleton.*

This shocked me. Somehow it took all the starch out of this colossal adventure to hear the captain give up so easily.

"All our drama is secondhand," he grumbled. "Our ship's course is cut-and-dried. Our world is bounded by walls. The only dramatic things that happen here are births and deaths."

A doctor broke in on our conference and seized the captain by the hand.

"Congratulations, Captain Dickinson, on the prize crop of the season! Your wife has just presented you with a fine set of triplets — three boys!"

That broke up the meeting. Captain Dickinson was so busy for the rest of the week that he forgot all about his official obligations. The problem of population limitation faded from his mind.

I wrote out my recommendations and gave them all the weight of my dictatorial authority. I stressed the need for more birth control forums, and recommended that the heavens be made visible for further studies in astronomy and mathematics.

I was tempted to warn Captain Dickinson that the *Flashaway* might incur some serious dramas of its own — poverty, disease, and the like — unless he got back on the track of the Six-Hundred-Year Plan in a hurry. But Dickinson was preoccupied with some family washings when I took my leave of him, and he seemed to have as much drama on his hands as he cared for.

I paid a final visit to each of the twenty-eight great-grandchildren of Louise, and returned to my ice.

IV

My chief complaint against my merry-go-round freezer was that it didn't give me any rest. One whirl into blackness, and the next thing I knew I popped out of the open lid again with not so much as a minute's time to reorganize my thoughts.

Well, here it was 2266 — two hundred years since the takeoff.

A glance through the one-way glass told me it was daytime in the ballroom.

As I turned the key in the lock I felt like a prizefighter on a vaudeville tour who, having just trounced the tough local strongman, steps back in the ring to take on his cousin.

A touch of a headache caught me as I reflected that there should be four more returns after this one — if all went according to plan. *Plan!* That word was destined to be trampled underfoot.

Oh, well (I took a deep optimistic breath), the *Flashaway* troubles would all be cleared up by now. Three generations would have passed. The population should be back to normal.

I swung the door open, stepped through, locked it after me.

For an instant I thought I had stepped in on a big movie "take" — a scene of a stricken multitude. The big ballroom was literally strewn with people — if creatures in such a deplorable state could be called people.

There was no movie camera. This was the real thing.

"Grimstone's come!" a hoarse voice cried out.

"Grimstone! Grimstone!" Others caught up the cry. Then — "Food! Give us food! We're starving! For God's sake — "

The weird chorus gathered volume. I stood dazed, and for an instant I couldn't realize that I was looking upon the population of the *Flashaway.*

Men, women, and children of all ages and all states of desperation joined in the clamor. Some of them stumbled to their feet and came toward me, waving their arms weakly. But most of them hadn't the strength to rise.

In that stunning moment an icy sweat came over me.

"Food! Food! We've been waiting for you, Grimstone. We've been holding on — "

The responsibility that was strapped to my shoulders suddenly weighed down like a locomotive. You see, I had originally taken my job more or less as a lark. That Six-Hundred-Year Plan had looked so airtight. I, the Keeper of the Traditions, would have a snap.

I had anticipated many a pleasant hour acquainting the oncoming generations with noble sentiments about George Washington; I had pictured myself filling the souls of my listeners by reciting the Gettysburg address and lecturing upon the mysteries of science.

But now those pretty bubbles burst on the spot, nor did they ever re-form in the centuries to follow.

And as they burst, my vision cleared. My job had nothing to do with theories or textbooks or speeches. My job was simply to get to

Robinello — to get there with enough living, able-bodied, sane human beings to start a colony.

Dull blue starlight sifted through the windows to highlight the big roomful of starved figures. The mass of pale blue faces stared at me. There were hundreds of them. Instinctively I shrank as the throng clustered around me, calling and pleading.

"One at a time!" I cried. "First I've got to find out what this is all about. Who's your spokesman?"

They designated a handsomely built, if undernourished, young man. I inquired his name and learned that he was Bob Sperry, a descendant of the original Captain Sperry.

"There are eight hundred of us now," Sperry said.

"Don't tell me the food has run out!"

"No, not that — but six hundred of us are not entitled to regular meals."

"Why not?"

Before the young spokesman could answer, the others burst out with an unintelligible clamor. Angry cries of "That damned Dickinson!" and "Guns!" and "They'll shoot us!" were all I could distinguish.

I quieted them and made Bob Sperry go on with his story. He calmly asserted that there was a very good reason that they shouldn't be fed, all sentiment aside; namely, because they had been born outside the quota.

Here I began to catch a gleam of light.

"By Captain Dickinson's interpretation of the Plan," Sperry explained, "there shouldn't be more than two hundred of us altogether."

This Captain Dickinson, I learned, was a grandson of the one I had known.

Sperry continued, "Since there are eight hundred, he and his brother — his brother being Food Superintendent — launched an emergency measure a few months ago to save food. They divided the population into the two hundred who had a right to be born, and the six hundred who had not."

So the six hundred starving persons before me were theoretically the excess population. The vigorous ancestry of the sixteen — no, seventeen — original couples, together with the excellent medical care that had reduced infant mortality and disease to the minimum, had wrecked the original population plan completely.

"What do you do for food? You must have *some* food!"

"We live on charity."

The throng again broke in with hostile words. Young Sperry's version was too gentle to do justice to their outraged stomachs. In fairness to the two hundred, however, Sperry explained that they shared whatever food they could spare with these, their less fortunate brothers, sisters, and offspring.

Uncertain what should or could be done, I gave the impatient crowd my promise to investigate at once. Bob Sperry and nine other men accompanied me.

The minute we were out of hearing of the ballroom, I gasped,

"Good heavens, men, how is it that you and your six hundred haven't mobbed the storerooms long before this?"

"Dickinson and his brother have got the drop on us."

"Drop? What kind of drop?"

"Guns!"

I couldn't understand this. I had believed these new generations of the *Flashaway* to be relatively innocent of any knowledge of firearms.

"What kind of guns?"

"The same kind they use in our Earth-made movies—that make a loud noise and kill people by the hundreds."

"But there aren't any guns aboard! That is—"

I knew perfectly well that the only firearms the ship carried had been stored in my own refrigerator room, which no one could enter but myself. Before the voyage, one of the planning committee had jestingly suggested that if any serious trouble ever arose, I should be master of the situation by virtue of one hundred revolvers.

"They made their own guns," Sperry explained, "just like the ones in our movies and books."

Inquiring whether any persons had been shot, I learned that three of their number, attempting a raid on the storerooms, had been killed.

"We heard three loud bangs, and found our men dead with bloody skulls."

Reaching the upper end of the central corridor, we arrived at the captain's headquarters.

The name of Captain Dickinson carried a bad flavor for me. A century before, I had developed a distaste for a certain other Captain Dickinson, his grandfather. I resolved to swallow my prejudice. Then the door opened, and my resolve stuck in my throat. The former Captain Dickinson had merely annoyed me; but this one I hated on sight.

"Well?" the captain roared at the eleven of us.

Well uniformed and neatly groomed, he filled the doorway with an impressive bulk. In his right hand he gripped a revolver. The gleam of that weapon had a magical effect upon the men. They shrank back respectfully. Then the captain's cold eye lighted on me.

"Who are *you?*"

"Gregory Grimstone, Keeper of the Traditions."

The captain sent a quick glance toward his gun and repeated his "Well?"

For a moment I was fascinated by that intricately shaped piece of metal in his grip.

"Well!" I echoed. "If 'well' is the only reception you have to offer, I'll proceed with my official business. Call your Food Superintendent."

"Why?"

"Order him out! Have him feed the entire population without further delay!"

"We can't afford the food," the captain growled.

"We'll talk that over later, but we won't talk on empty stomachs. Order out your Food Superintendent!"

"Crawl back in your hole!" Dickinson snarled.

At that instant another bulky man stepped into view. He was almost the identical counterpart of the captain, but his uniform was that of the Food Superintendent. Showing his teeth with a sinister snarl, he took his place beside his brother. He too jerked his right hand up to flash a gleaming revolver.

I caught one glimpse—and laughed in his face! I couldn't help it.

"You fellows are good!" I roared. "You're damned good actors! If you've held off the starving six hundred with nothing but those two imitations of revolvers, you deserve an Academy award!"

The two Dickinson brothers went white.

Back of me came low mutterings from ten starving men.

"Imitations—dumb imitations—what the hell?"

Sperry and his nine comrades plunged with one accord. For the next ten minutes the captain's headquarters was simply a whirlpool of flying fists and hurtling bodies.

I have mentioned that these ten men were weak from lack of food. That fact was all that saved the Dickinson brothers; for ten minutes of lively exercise was all the ten men could endure, in spite of the circumstances.

But ten minutes left an impression. The Dickinsons were the worst beaten-up men I have ever seen, and I have seen some bad ones in my time. When the news echoed through the ship, no one questioned the ethics of ten starved men attacking two overfed ones.

Needless to say, before two hours passed, every hungry man, woman, and child ate to his gizzard's content. And before another hour passed, some new officers were installed. The S. S. *Flashaway*'s trouble was far from solved; but for the present the whole eight hundred were one big family picnic. Hope was restored, and the rejoicing lasted through many thousand miles of space.

There was considerable mystery about the guns. Surprisingly, the people had developed an awe of the movie guns as if they were instruments of magic.

Upon investigating, I was convinced that the captain and his brother had simply capitalized on this superstition. They had a sound enough motive for wanting to save food. But once their gun bluff had been established, they had become uncompromising oppressors. And when the occasion arose that their guns were challenged, they had simply crushed the skulls of their three attackers and faked the noises of explosions.

But now the firearms were dead. And so was the Dickinson regime.

But the menacing problem of too many mouths to feed still clung to the S. S. *Flashaway* like a hungry ghost determined to ride the ship to death.

Six full months passed before the needed reform was forged.

During that time everyone was allowed full rations. The famine had already taken its toll in weakened bodies, and seventeen persons—most of them young children—died. The doctors, released from the Dickinson regime, worked like Trojans to bring the rest back to health.

The reform measure that went into effect six months after my arrival consisted of outright sterilization.

The compulsory rule was sterilization for everyone except those born "within the quota" — and that quota, let me add, was narrowed down one half from Captain Dickinson's two hundred to the most eligible one hundred. The disqualified one hundred now joined the ranks of the six hundred.

And that was not all. By their own agreement, every within-the-quota family, responsible for bearing the *Flashaway's* future children, would undergo sterilization operations after the second child was born.

The seven hundred out-of-quota citizens, let it be said, were only too glad to submit to the simple sterilization measures in exchange for a right to live their normal lives. Yes, they were to have three squares a day. With an assured population decline in prospect for the coming century, this generous measure of food would not give out. Our surveys of the existing food supplies showed that these seven hundred could safely live their four-score years and die with full stomachs.

Looking back on that six months' work, I was fairly well satisfied that the doctors and the Council and I had done the fair, if drastic, thing. If I had planted seeds for further trouble with the Dickinson tribe, I was little concerned about it at the time.

My conscience was, in fact, clear — except for one small matter. I was guilty of one slightly act of partiality.

I incurred this guilt shortly before I returned to the ice. The doctors and I, looking down from the balcony into the ballroom, chanced to notice a young couple who were obviously very much in love.

The young man was Bob Sperry, the handsome, clear-eyed descendant of the *Flashaway's* first and finest captain, the lad who had been the spokesman when I first came upon the starving mob.

The girl's name — and how it had clung in my mind! — was Louise Broscoe. Refreshingly beautiful, she reminded me for all the world of my own Louise (mine and Bill Broscoe's).

"It's a shame," one of the doctors commented, "that fine young blood like that has to fall outside the quota. But rules are rules."

With a shrug of the shoulders he had already dismissed the matter from his mind — until I handed him something I had scribbled on a piece of paper.

"We'll make this one exception," I said perfunctorily. "If any question ever arises, this statement relieves you doctors of all responsibility. This is my own special request."

V

One hundred years later my rash act came back to haunt me — and how! Bob Sperry had married Louise Broscoe, and the births of their two children had raised the unholy cry of "Favoritism!"

By the year 2366, Bob Sperry and Louise Broscoe were gone and almost forgotten. But the enmity against me, the Keeper of the Traditions who played favorites, had grown up into a monster of bitter hatred waiting to devour me.

It didn't take me long to discover this. My first contact after I emerged from the ice set the pace.

"Go tell your parents," I said to the gang of brats that were playing ball in the spacious ballroom, "that Grimstone has arrived."

Their evil little faces stared at me a moment, then they snorted.

"Faw! Faw! Faw!" and away they ran.

I stood in the big bleak room wondering what to make of their insults. On the balcony some of the parents craned over the railings at me.

"Greetings!" I cried. "I'm Grimstone, Keeper of the Traditions. I've just come —"

"Faw!" the men and women shouted at me. "Faw! Faw!"

No one could have made anything friendly out of those snarls. "Faw," to them, was simply a vocal manner of spitting poison.

Uncertain what this surly reception might lead to, I returned to my refrigerator room to procure one of the guns. Then I returned to the volley of catcalls and insults, determined to carry out my duties, come what might.

When I reached the forequarter of the ship, however, I found some less hostile citizens who gave me a civil welcome. Here I established myself for the extent of my 2366–67 sojourn, an honored guest of the Sperry family.

This, I told myself, was my reward for my favor to Bob Sperry and Louise Broscoe a century ago. For here was their grandson, a fine upstanding gray-haired man of fifty, a splendid pilot and the father of a beautiful twenty-one-year-old daughter.

"Your name wouldn't be Louise by any chance?" I asked the girl as she showed me into the Sperry living room.

"Lora-Louise," the girl smiled. It was remarkable how she brought back memories of one of her ancestors of three centuries previous.

Her dark eyes flashed over me curiously.

"So you are the man that we Sperries have to thank for being here!"

"You've heard about the quotas?" I asked.

"Of course. You're almost a god to our family."

"I must be a devil to some of the others," I said, recalling my reception of catcalls.

"Rogues!" the girl's father snorted, and he thereupon launched into a breezy account of the past century.

The sterilization program, he assured me, had worked—if anything, too well. The population was the lowest in *Flashaway* history. It stood at the dangerously low mark of *fifty*!

Besides the sterilization program, a disease epidemic had taken its toll. In addition three ugly murders, prompted by jealousies, had spotted the record. And there had been one suicide.

As to the character of the population, Pilot Sperry declared gravely that there had been a turn for the worse.

"They fight each other like damned anarchists," he snorted.

The Dickinsons had made trouble for several generations. Now it was the Dickinsons against the Smiths; and these two factions included four-fifths of all the people. They were about evenly divided—twenty on each side—and when they weren't actually fighting each other, they were "fawing" at each other.

These bellicose factions had one sentiment in common: they both despised the Sperry faction. And—here my guilt cropped up again—their hatred stemmed from my special favor of a century ago, without which there would be no Sperrys now. In view of the fact that the Sperry faction lived in the forequarter of the ship and held all the important offices, it was no wonder that the remaining forty citizens were jealous.

All of which gave me enough to worry about. On top of that, Lora-Louise's mother gave me one other angle of the setup.

"The trouble between the Dickinsons and the Smiths has grown worse since Lora-Louise has become a young lady," Mrs. Sperry confided to me.

We were sitting in a breakfast nook. Amber starlight shone softly through the porthole, lighting the mother's steady imperturbable gray eyes.

"Most girls have married at eighteen or nineteen," her mother went on. "So far, Lora-Louise has refused to marry."

The worry in Mrs. Sperry's face was almost imperceptible, but I understood. I had checked over the "Who's Who" and I knew the seriousness of this population crisis. I also knew that there were four young unmarried men with no other prospects of wives except Lora-Louise.

"Have you any choice for her?" I asked.

"Since she must marry—and I know she *must*—I have urged her to make her own choice."

I could see that the ordeal of choosing had been postponed until my coming, in hopes that I might modify the rules. But I had no intention of doing so. The *Flashaway* needed Lora-Louise. It needed the sort of children she would bear.

That week I saw the two husky Dickinson boys. Both were in their twenties. They stayed close together and bore an air of treachery and scheming. Rumor had it that they carried weapons made from table knives.

Everyone knew that my coming would bring the conflict to a head. Many thought I would try to force the girl to marry the older Smith—"Batch," as he was called in view of his bachelorhood. He was past thirty-five, the oldest of the four unmarried men.

But some argued otherwise. For Batch, though a splendid specimen physically, was slow of wit and speech. It was common knowledge that he was weak-minded.

For that reason, I might choose his younger cousin, "Smithy," a roly-poly overgrown boy of nineteen who spent his time bullying the younger children.

But if the Smiths and the Dickinsons could have their way about it, the Keeper of the Traditions should have no voice in the matter. Let me insist that Lora-Louise marry, said they; but whom she should marry was none of my business.

They preferred a fight as a means of settlement. A free-for-all between the two factions would be fine. A showdown of fists among the four contenders would be even better.

Best of all would be a battle of knives that would eliminate all but one of the suitors. Not that either the Dickinsons or the Smiths needed to admit that was what they preferred; but their barbaric tastes were plain to see.

Barbarians! That's what they had become. They had sprung too far from their native civilization. Only the Sperry faction, isolated in their monasteries of control boards, physicians' laboratories, and record rooms, kept alive the spark of civilization.

The Sperrys and their associates were human beings out of the twenty-first century. The Smiths and the Dickinsons had slipped. They might have come out of the Dark Ages.

What burned me up more than anything else was that obviously both the Smiths and the Dickinsons looked forward with sinister glee toward dragging Lora-Louise down from her height to their own barbaric levels.

One night I was awakened by the sharp ringing of the pilot's telephone. I heard the snap of a switch. An *emergency* signal flashed on throughout the ship.

Footsteps were pounding toward the ballroom. I slipped into a robe, seized my gun, made for the door.

"The Dickinsons are murdering up on them!" Pilot Sperry shouted to me from the door of the control room.

"I'll see about it," I snapped.

I bounded down the corridor. Sperry didn't follow. Whatever violence might occur from year to year within the hull of the *Flashaway*, the pilot's code demanded that he lock himself up at the controls and tend to his own business.

It was a free-for-all. Under the bright lights they were going to it, tooth and toenail.

Children screamed and clawed, women hurled dishes, old tottering granddaddies edged into the fracas to crack at each other with canes.

The appalling reason for it all showed in the center of the room — the roly-poly form of young "Smithy" Smith. Hacked and stabbed, his nightclothes ripped, he was a veritable mess of carnage.

I shouted for order. No one heard me, for in that instant a chase thundered on the balcony. Everything else stopped. All eyes turned on the three racing figures.

Batch Smith, fleeing in his white nightclothes, had less than five yards' lead on the two Dickinsons. Batch was just smart enough to run when he was chased, not smart enough to know he couldn't possibly outrun the younger Dickinsons.

As they shot past blazing lights, the Dickinsons' knives flashed. I could see that their hands were red with Smithy's blood.

"*Stop!*" I cried. "Stop or I'll *shoot!*"

If they heard, the words must have been meaningless. The younger Dickinson gained ground. His brother darted back in the opposite direction, crouched, waited for his prey to come around the circular balcony.

"Dickinson! Stop or I'll shoot you dead!" I bellowed.

Batch Smith came on, his eyes white with terror. Crouched and waiting, the older Dickinson lifted his knife for the killing stroke.

I shot.

The crouched Dickinson fell in a heap. Over him tripped the racing form of Batch Smith, to sprawl headlong. The other Dickinson leaped over his brother and pounced down upon the fallen prey, knife upraised.

Another shot went home.

Young Dickinson writhed and came toppling down over the balcony rail. He lay where he fell, his bloody knife sticking up through the side of his neck.

It was ugly business trying to restore order. However, the magic power of firearms, which had become only a dusty legend, now put teeth into every word I uttered.

The doctors were surprisingly efficient. After many hours of work behind closed doors, they released their verdicts to the waiting groups. The elder Dickinson, shot through the shoulder, would live. The younger Dickinson was dead. So was Smithy. But his cousin, Batch Smith, although too scared to walk back to his stateroom, was unhurt.

The rest of the day the doctors devoted to patching up the minor damages done in the free fight. Four-fifths of the *Flashaway* population were burdened with bandages, it seemed. For some time to come both the warring parties were considerably sobered over their losses. But most of all they were disgruntled because the fight had settled nothing.

The prize was still unclaimed. The two remaining contenders, backed by their respective factions, were at a bitter deadlock.

Nor had Lora-Louise's hatred for either the surviving Dickinson or Smith lessened in the slightest.

Never had a duty been more oppressive to me. I postponed my talk with Lora-Louise for several days, but I was determined that there should be no more fighting. She must choose.

We sat in an alcove next to the pilot's control room, looking out into the vast sky. Our ship, bounding at a terrific speed though it was, seemed to be hanging motionless in the tranquil star-dotted heavens.

"I must speak frankly," I said to the girl. "I hope you will do the same."

She looked at me steadily. Her dark eyes were perfectly frank, her full lips smiled with childlike simplicity.

"How old are you?" she asked.

"Twenty-eight," I answered. I'd been the youngest professor on the college faculty. "Or you might say three hundred and twenty-eight. Why?"

"How soon must you go back to your sleep?"

"Just as soon as you are happily married. That's why I must insist that you—"

Something very penetrating about her gaze made my words go weak. To think of forcing this lovely girl—so much like the Louise of my own century—to marry either the brutal Dickinson or the moronic Smith—

"Do you really want me to be *happily* married?" she asked.

I don't remember that any more words passed between us at the time.

A few days later she and I were married—and most happily!

The ceremony was brief. The entire Sperry faction and one representative from each of the two hostile factions were present. The aged captain of the ship, who had been too ineffectual in recent years to apply any discipline to the fighting factions, was still able with vigorous voice to pronounce us man and wife.

A year and a half later I took my leave.

I bid fond good-by to the "future captain of the *Flashaway*," who lay on a pillow kicking and squirming. He gurgled back at me. If the boasts and promises of the Sperry grandparents and their associates were to be taken at full value, this young prodigy of mine would in time become an accomplished pilot and a skilled doctor as well as a stern but wise captain.

Judging from his talents at the age of six months, I was convinced he showed promise of becoming Food Superintendent as well.

I left reluctantly but happily.

VI

The year 2466 was one of the darkest in my life. I shall pass over it briefly.

The situation I found was all but hopeless.

The captain met me personally and conveyed me to his quarters without allowing the people to see me.

"Safer for everyone concerned," he muttered. I caught glimpses as we passed through the shadows. I seemed to be looking upon ruins.

Not until the captain had disclosed the events of the century did I understand how things could have come to such a deplorable state. And before he finished his story, I saw that I was helpless to right the wrongs.

"They've destroyed 'most everything," the hard-bitten old captain rasped. "And they haven't overlooked *you*. They've destroyed you completely. *You are an ogre.*"

I wasn't clear on his meaning. Dimly in the back of my mind the hilarious farewell of four centuries ago still echoed.

"The *Flashaway* will go through!" I insisted.

"They destroyed all the books, phonograph records, movie films. They broke up clocks and bells and furniture —"

And I was supposed to carry this interspatial outpost of American civilization through *unblemished*! That was what I had promised so gayly four centuries ago.

"They even tried to break out the windows," the captain went on. "'Oxygen be damned!' they'd shout. They were mad. You couldn't tell them anything. If they could have got into this end of the ship, they'd have murdered us and smashed the control boards to hell."

I listened with bowed head.

"Your son tried like the devil to turn the tide. But God, what chance did he have? The dam had busted loose. They wanted to kill each other. They wanted to destroy each other's property and starve each other out. No captain in the world could have stopped either faction. They had to get it out of their systems . . ."

He shrugged helplessly. "Your son went down fighting . . ." For a time I could hear no more. It seemed but minutes ago that I had taken leave of the little tot.

The war — if a mania of destruction and murder between two feuding factions could be called a war — had done one good thing, according to the captain. It had wiped the name of Dickinson from the records.

Later I turned through the musty pages to make sure. There were Smiths and Sperrys and a few other names still in the running, but no Dickinsons. Nor were there any Grimstones. My son had left no living descendants.

To return to the captain's story, the war (he said) had degraded the bulk of the population almost to the level of savages. Perhaps the comparison is an insult to the savage. The instruments of knowledge and learning having been destroyed, beliefs gave way to superstitions, memories of past events degenerated into fanciful legends.

The rebound from the war brought a terrific superstitious terror concerning death. The survivors crawled into their shells, almost literally; the brutalities and treacheries of the past hung like storm clouds over their imaginations.

As year after year dropped away, the people told and retold the stories of destruction to their children. Gradually the legend twisted into a strange form in which all the guilt for the carnage *was placed upon me!*

I was the one who had started all the killing! I, *the ogre,* who slept in a cave somewhere in the rear of the ship, came out once upon a time and started all the trouble.

I, the Traditions Man, dealt death with a magic weapon; I cast the spell of killing upon the Smiths and the Dickinsons that kept them fighting until there was nothing left to fight for.

"But that was years ago," I protested to the captain. "Am I still an ogre?" I shuddered at the very thought.

"More than ever. Stories like that don't die out in a century. They grow bigger. You've become the symbol of evil. I've tried to talk the silly notion down, but it has been impossible. My own family is afraid of you."

I listened with sickening amazement. I was the Traditions Man: or rather the "Traddy Man"—the bane of every child's life.

Parents, I was told, would warn them, "If you don't be good, the Traddy Man will come out of his cave and get you!"

And the Traddy Man, as every grown-up knew, could storm out of his cave without warning. He would come with a strange gleam in his eye. That was his evil will. When the bravest, strongest men would cross his path, he would hurl instant death at them. Then he would seize the most beautiful woman and marry her.

"Enough!" I said. "Call your people together. I'll dispel their false ideas—"

The captain shook his head wisely. He glanced at my gun.

"Don't force me to disobey your orders," he said. "I can believe you're not an ogre—but they won't. I know this generation. You don't. Frankly, I refuse to disturb the peace of this ship by telling the people you have come. Nor am I willing to terrorize my family by letting them see you."

For a long time I stared silently into space.

The captain dismissed a pilot from the control room and had me come in.

"You can see for yourself that we are straight on our course. You have already seen that all the supplies are holding up. You have seen that the population problem is well cared for. What more do you want?"

What more did I want! With the whole population of the *Flashaway* steeped in ignorance—immorality—superstition—savagery!

Again the captain shook his head. "You want us to be like your friends of the twenty-first century. *We can't be.*"

He reached in his pocket and pulled out some bits of crumpled papers.

"Look. I save every scrap of reading matter. I learned to read from the primers and charts that your son's grandparents made. Before the destruction, I tried to read about the Earth-life. I still piece together these torn bits and study them. But I can't piece together the Earth-life that they tell about. All I really know is what I've seen and felt and breathed right here in my native *Flashaway* world.

"That's how it's bound to be with all of us. We can't get back to your notions about things. Your notions haven't any real truth for us. You don't belong to our world," the captain said with honest frankness.

"So I'm an outcast on my own ship."

"That's putting it mildly. You're a menace and a troublemaker—*an ogre*. It's in their minds as tight as the bones in their skulls."

The most I could do was secure some promises from him before I went back to the ice. He promised to keep the ship on its course. He promised to do his utmost to fasten the necessary obligations upon those who would take over the helm.

"Straight relentless navigation!" We drank a toast to it. He didn't pretend to appreciate the purpose or the mission of the *Flashaway*, but he took my word for it that it would come to some good.

"To Robinello in 2666!" Another toast. Then he conducted me back, in utmost secrecy, to my refrigerator room.

I awoke to the year 2566, keenly aware that I was not Gregory Grimstone, the respected Keeper of the Traditions. If I was anyone at all, I was the Traddy Man–the ogre.

But perhaps by this time—and I took hope with the thought—I had been completely forgotten.

I tried to get through the length of the ship without being seen. I had watched through the one-way glass for several hours for a favorable opportunity, but the ship seemed to be in a continual state of daylight, and shabby-looking people roamed about as aimlessly as sheep in a meadow.

The few persons who saw me as I darted toward the captain's quarters shrieked as if they had been knifed. In their world there was no such thing as a strange person. I was the impossible, the unbelievable. My name, obviously, had been forgotten.

I found three men in the control room. After minutes of tension, during which they adjusted themselves to the shock of my coming, I succeeded in establishing speaking terms. Two of the men were Sperrys.

But at the very moment I should have been concerned with solidifying my friendship, I broke the calm with an excited outburst. My eye caught the position of the instruments and I leaped from my seat.

"How long have you been going *that way?*"

"Eight years."

"Eight—" I glanced at the huge automatic chart overhead. It showed the long straight line of our centuries of flight with a tiny shepherd's crook at the end. Eight years ago we had turned back sharply.

"That's sixteen years lost, gentlemen!"

I tried to regain my poise. The three men before me were perfectly calm, to my astonishment. The two Sperry brothers glanced at each other. The third man, who had introduced himself as Smith, glared at me darkly.

"It's all right," I said. "We won't lose another minute. I know how to operate—"

"No you don't!" Smith's voice was harsh and cold. I had started to reach for the controls. I hesitated. Three pairs of eyes were fixed on me.

"We know where we're going," one of the Sperrys said stubbornly, "We've got our own destination."

"This ship is bound for Robinello!" I snapped. "We've got to colonize. The Robinello planets are ours—America's. It's our job to clinch the claim and establish the initial settlement—"

"Who said so?"

"America!"

"*When?*" Smith's cold eyes tightened.

"Five hundred years ago."

"That doesn't mean a thing. Those people are all dead."

"I'm one of those people!" I growled. "And I'm not dead by a damned sight!"

"Then you're out on a limb."

"Limb or no limb, the plan goes through!" I clutched my gun. "We haven't come five hundred years in a straight line for nothing!"

"The plan is dead," one of the Sperrys snarled. "We've killed it."

His brother chimed in, "This is our ship and we're running it. We've studied the heavens and we're out on our own. We're through with this straight-line stuff. We're going to see the universe."

I didn't want to kill the men. But I saw no other way out. Was there any other way? Three lives weren't going to stand between the *Flashaway* and her destination.

Seconds passed, with the four of us breathing hard. Eternity was about to descend on someone. Any of the three might have been splendid pioneers if they had been confronted with the job of building a colony. But in this moment, their lack of vision was as deadly as any deliberate sabotage. I focused my attack on the most troublesome man of the three.

"Smith, I'm giving you an order. Turn back before I count ten or I'll kill you. One . . . two . . . three . . ."

Not the slightest move from anyone.

"Seven . . . eight . . . nine . . ."

Smith leaped at me — and fell dead at my feet.

The two Sperrys looked at the faint wisp of smoke from the weapon. I barked another sharp command, and one of the Sperrys marched to the controls and turned the ship back toward Robinello.

VII

For a year I was with the Sperry brothers constantly, doing my utmost to bring them around to my way of thinking. At first I watched them like hawks. But they were not treacherous. Neither did they show any inclination to avenge Smith's death. Probably this was due to a suppressed hatred they had held toward him.

The Sperrys were the sort of men, being true children of space, who bided their time. That's what they were doing now. That was why I couldn't leave them and go back to my ice.

As sure as the *Flashaway* could cut through the heavens, those two men were counting the hours until I returned to my rest. The minute I was gone, they would turn back toward their own goal.

And so I continued to stay with them for a full year. If they contemplated killing me, they gave no indication. I presume I would have killed them with little hesitation, had I had any pilots whatsoever that I could entrust with the job of carrying on.

There were no other pilots, nor were there any youngsters old enough to break into service.

Night after night I fought the matter over in my mind. There was a full century to go. Perhaps one hundred and fifteen or twenty years. And no one except the two Sperrys and I had any serious conception of a destination!

These two pilots and I—*and one other*, whom I had never for a minute forgotten. If the *Flashaway* was to go through, it was up to me and *that one other*—

I marched back to the refrigerator room, people fleeing my path in terror. Inside the retreat I touched the switches that operated the auxiliary merry-go-round freezer. After a space of time the operation was complete.

Someone very beautiful stood smiling before me, looking not a minute older than when I had packed her away for safekeeping two centuries before.

"Gregory," she breathed ecstatically. "Are my three centuries up already?"

"Only two of them, Lora-Louise." I took her in my arms. She looked up at me sharply and must have read the trouble in my eyes.

"They've all played out on us," I said quietly. "It's up to us now."

I discussed my plan with her and she approved.

One at a time we forced the Sperry brothers into the icy retreat, with repeated promises that they would emerge within a century. By that time Lora-Louise and I would be gone—but it was our expectation that our children and grandchildren would carry on.

And so the two of us, plus firearms, plus Lora-Louise's sense of humor, took over the running of the *Flashaway* for its final century.

As the years passed, the native population grew to be less afraid of us. Little by little a foggy glimmer of our vision filtered into their numbed minds.

The year is now 2600. Thirty-three years have passed since Lora-Louise and I took over. I am now sixty-two, she is fifty-six. Or if you prefer, I am 562, she is 256. Our four children have grown up and married.

We have realized down through these long years that we would not live to see the journey completed. The Robinello planets have been visible for some time; but at our speed they are still sixty or eighty years away.

But something strange happened nine or ten months ago. It has changed the outlook for all of us — even me, the crusty old Keeper of the Traditions.

A message reached us through our radio receiver!

It was a human voice speaking in our own language. It had a fresh vibrant hum to it and a clear-cut enunciation. It shocked me to realize how sluggish our own brand of the King's English had become in the past five-and-a-half centuries.

"Calling the S. S. *Flashaway!*" it said. "Calling the S. S. *Flashaway!* We are trying to locate you, S. S. *Flashaway.* Our instruments indicate that you are approaching. If you can hear us, will you give us your exact location?"

I snapped on the transmitter. "This is the *Flashaway.* Can you hear us?"

"Dimly. Where are you?"

"On our course. Who's calling?"

"This is the American colony on Robinello," came the answer. "American colony, Robinello, established in 2550 — fifty years ago. We're waiting for you, *Flashaway.*"

"How the devil did you get there?" I may have sounded a bit crusty but I was too excited to know what I was saying.

"Modern spaceships," came the answer. "We've cut the time from the earth to Robinello down to six years. Give us your location. We'll send a fast ship out to pick you up."

I gave them our location. That, as I said, was several months ago. Today we are receiving a radio call every five minutes as their ship approaches.

One of my sons, supervising the preparations, has just reported that all persons aboard are ready to transfer—including the Sperry brothers, who have emerged successfully from the ice. The eighty-five *Flashaway* natives are scared half to death and at the same time as eager as children going to a circus.

Lora-Louse has finished packing our boxes, bless her heart. That teasing smile she just gave me was because she noticed the "Who's Who aboard the *Flashaway*" tucked snugly under my arm.

Redeemer

GREGORY BENFORD

Here we meet the ironies of history, as later developments overtake earlier ones. A slow, relativistic starship is overtaken by a faster one. A great-grandson catches up with his great-grandmother. Human failure and foibles overtake hopes and dreams. And yet something good may come of it after all, in unexpected ways.

He had trouble finding it. The blue-white exhaust plume was a long trail of ionized hydrogen scratching a line across the black. It had been a lot harder to locate out here than Central said it would be.

Nagara came up on the *Redeemer* from behind, their blind side. They wouldn't have any sensors pointed aft. No point in it when you're on a one-way trip, not expecting visitors and haven't seen anybody for seventy-three years.

He boosted in with the fusion plant, cutting off the translight to avoid overshoot. The translight rig was delicate and still experimental and it had already pushed him over seven light-years out from Earth. And anyway, when he got back to Earth there would be an accounting, and he would have to pay off from his profit anything he spent for overexpenditure of the translight hardware.

The ramscoop vessel ahead was running hot. It was a long cylinder, fluted fore and aft. The blue-white fire came boiling out of the aft throat, pushing *Redeemer* along at a little below a tenth of light velocity. Nagara's board buzzed. He cut in the null-mag system. The ship's skin, visible outside, fluxed into its superconducting state, gleaming like chrome. The readout winked and Nagara could see on the sim-board his ship slipping like a silver fish through the webbing of magnetic field lines that protected *Redeemer.*

The field was mostly magnetic dipole. He cut through it and glided in parallel to the hot exhaust streamer. The stuff was spitting out a lot of UV and he had to change filters to see what he was doing. He came up along the aft section of the ship and matched velocities. The magnetic throat up ahead sucked in the interstellar hydrogen for the fusion motors. He stayed away from it. There was enough radiation up there to fry you for good.

Redeemer's midsection was rotating but the big clumsy-looking lock aft was stationary. Fine. No trouble clamping on.

The couplers seized *clang* and he used a waldo to manually open the lock. He would have to be fast now, fast and careful.

He pressed a code into the keyin plate on his chest to check it. It worked. The slick aura enveloped him, cutting out the ship's hum. Nagara nodded to himself.

He went quickly through the *Redeemer's* lock. The pumps were still laboring when he spun the manual override to open the big inner hatch. He pulled himself through in the zero-g with one powerful motion, through the hatch and into a cramped suitup room. He cut in his magnetos and settled to the grid deck.

As Nagara crossed the deck a young man came in from a side hatchway. Nagara stopped and thumped off his protective shield. The man didn't see Nagara at first because he was looking the other way as he came through the hatchway, moving with easy agility. He was studying the subsystem monitoring panels on the far bulkhead. The status phosphors were red but they winked green as Nagara took three steps forward and grabbed the man's shoulder and spun him around. Nagara was grounded and the man was not. Nagara hit him once in the stomach and then shoved him against a bulkhead. The man gasped for breath. Nagara stepped back and put his hand into his coverall pocket and when it came out there was a dart pistol in it. The man's eyes didn't register anything at first and when they did he just stared at the pistol, getting his breath back, staring as though he couldn't believe either Nagara or the pistol was there.

"What's your name?" Nagara demanded in a clipped, efficient voice.

"What? I—"

"Your name. Quick."

"I . . . Zak."

"All right, Zak, now listen to me. I'm inside now and I'm not staying long. I don't care what you've been told. You do just what I say and nobody will blame you for it."

". . . nobody . . . ?" Zak was still trying to unscramble his thoughts and he looked at the pistol again as though that would explain things.

"Zak, how many of you are manning this ship?"

"Manning? You mean crewing?" Confronted with a clear question, he forgot his confusion and frowned. "Three. We're doing our five-year stint. The Revealer and Jacob and me."

"Fine. Now, where's Jacob?"

"Asleep. This isn't his shift."

"Good." Nagara jerked a thumb over his shoulder. "Personnel quarters that way?

"Uh, yes."

"Did an alarm go off through the whole ship, Zak?"

"No, just on the bridge."

"So I didn't wake up Jacob?"

"I . . . I suppose not."

"Fine, good. Now, where's the Revealer?"

So far it was working well. The best way to handle people who might give you trouble right away was to keep them busy telling you things before they had time to decide what they should be doing. And Zak plainly was used to taking orders.

"She's in the forest."

"Good. I have to see her. You lead the way, Zak."

Zak automatically half turned to kick down the hatchway he'd come in through, and then the questions came out. "What—who *are* you? How—"

"I'm just visiting. We've got faster ways of moving now, Zak. I caught up with you."

"A faster ramscoop? But we —"

"Let's go, Zak." Nagara waved the dart gun and Zak looked at it a moment and then, still visibly struggling with his confusion, he kicked off and glided down the drift tube.

The forest was one-half of a one-hundred-meter-long cylinder, located near the middle of the ship and rotating to give one g. The forest was dense with pines and oak and tall bushes. A fine mist hung over the treetops, obscuring the other half of the cylinder, a gardening zone that hung over their heads. Nagara hadn't been in a small cylinder like this for decades. He was used to seeing a distant green carpet overhead, so far away you couldn't make out individual trees, and shrouded by the cottonball clouds that accumulated at the zero-g along the cylinder axis. This whole place felt cramped to him.

Zak led him along footpaths and into a bamboo-walled clearing. The Revealer was sitting in lotus position in the middle of it. She was wearing a Flatlander robe and cowl just like Zak. He recognized it from a historical fax readout.

She was a plain-faced woman, wrinkled and wiry, her hands thick and callused, the fingers stubby, the nails clipped off square. She didn't go rigid with surprise when Nagara came into view and that bothered him a little. She didn't look at the dart pistol more than once, to see what it was, and that surprised him, too.

"What's your name?" Nagara said as he walked into the bamboo-encased silence.

"I am the Revealer." A steady voice.

"No, I meant your name."

"That is my name."

"I mean —"

"I am the Revealer for this stage of our exodus."

Nagara watched as Zak stopped halfway between them and then stood uncertainly, looking back and forth.

"All right, When they freeze you back down, what'll they call you then?"

She smiled at this. "Michele Astanza."

Nagara didn't show anything in his face. He waved the pistol at her and said, "Get up."

"I prefer to sit."

"And I prefer you stand."

"Oh."

He watched both of them carefully. "Zak, I'm going to have to ask you to do a favor for me."

Zak glanced at the Revealer and she moved her head a few millimeters in a nod. He said, "Sure."

"This way." Nagara gestured with the pistol to the woman.

The woman nodded to herself as if this confirmed something and got up and started down the footpath to the right, her steps so soft on the leafy path that Nagara could not hear them over the tinkling of a stream on the overhead side of the cylinder. Nagara followed her. The trees trapped the sound in here and made him jumpy.

He knew he was taking a calculated risk by not getting Jacob, too. But the odds against Jacob waking up in time were good and the whole point of doing it this way was to get in and out fast, exploit surprise. And he wasn't sure he could handle the three of them together. That was just it—he was doing this alone so he could collect the whole fee, and for that you had to take some extra risk. That was the way this thing worked.

The forest gave onto some cornfields and then some wheat, all the UV phosphorus netted above. The three of them skirted around the nets and through a hatchway in the big aft wall. Whenever Zak started to say anything Nagara cut him off with a wave of the pistol. Then Nagara saw that with some time to think Zak was adding some things up and the lines around his mouth were tightening, so Nagara asked him some questions about the ship's design. That worked. Zak rattled on about quintuple-redundant fail-safe subsystems he'd been repairing until they were at the entrance to the freezing compartment.

It was bigger than Nagara had thought. He had done all the research he could, going through old faxes of *Redeemer's* prelim designs, but plainly the Flatlanders had changed things in some later design phase.

One whole axial section of *Redeemer* was given over to the freeze-down vaults. It was at zero-g because otherwise the slow compression of tissues in the corpses would do permanent damage. They floated in their translucent compartments, like strange fish in endless rows of pale blue-white aquariums.

The vaults were stored in a huge array, each layer a cylinder slightly larger than the one it enclosed, all aligned along the ship's axis. Each cylinder was two compartments thick, a corpse in every one, and the long cylinders extended into the distance until the chilly fog steaming off them blurred the perspective and the eye could not judge the size of the things. Despite himself Nagara was impressed. There were thousands upon thousands of Flatlanders in here, all dead and waiting for the promised land ahead, circling Tau Ceti. And with seventy-five more years of data to judge by, Nagara knew something this Revealer couldn't reveal: the failure rate when they thawed them out would be thirty percent.

They had come out on the center face of the bulwark separating the vault section from the farming part. Nagara stopped them and studied the front face of the vault array, which spread away from them radially like an immense spiderweb. He reviewed the old plans in his head. The axis of the whole thing was a tube a meter wide, the same translucent organiform. Liquid nitrogen flowed in the hollow walls of the array and the phosphor light was pale and watery.

"That's the DNA storage," Nagara said, pointing at the axial tube.

"What?" Zak said. "Yes, it is."

"Take them out."

"What?"

"They're in fail-safe self-refrigerated canisters, aren't they?"

"Yes."

"That's fine." Nagara turned to the Revealer. "You've got the working combinations, don't you?"

She had been silent for some time. She looked at him steadily and said, "I do."

"Let's have them."

"Why should I give them?"

"I think you know."

"Not really."

He knew she was playing some game but he couldn't see why. "You're carrying DNA material for over ten thousand people. Old genotypes, undamaged. It wasn't so rare when you collected it seventy-five years ago, but it is now. I want it."

"It is for our colony."

"You've got enough corpses here."

"We need genetic diversity."

"The System needs it more than you. There's been a war. A lot of radiation damage."

"Who won?"

"Us. The Outskirters."

"That means nothing to me."

"We're the environments in orbit around the sun, not sucking up to Earth. We knew what was going on. We're mostly in Bernal spheres. We got the jump on—"

"You've wrecked each other genetically, haven't you? That was always the trouble with your damned cities. No place to dig a hole and hide."

Nagara shrugged. He was watching Zak. From the man's face Nagara could tell he was getting to be more insulted than angry—outraged at somebody walking in and stealing their future. And from the way his leg muscles were tensing against a foothold Nagara guessed Zak was also getting more insulted than scared, which was trouble for sure. It was a lot better if you dealt with a man who cared more about the long odds against a dart gun at this range than about some principle. Nagara knew he couldn't count on Zak ignoring all the Flatlander nonsense the Revealer and others had pumped into him.

They hung there in zero-g, nobody moving in the wan light, the only sound a gurgling of liquid nitrogen. The Revealer was saying something and there was another thing bothering Nagara. Some sound, but he ignored it.

"How did the planetary enclaves hold out?" the woman was asking. "I had many friends—"

"They're gone."

Something came into the woman's face. "You've lost man's *birthright?*"

"They sided with the—"

"Abandoned the planets altogether? Made them unfit to *live* on? All for your awful cities—" and she made a funny jerky motion with her right hand.

That was it. When she started moving that way, Nagara saw it had to be a signal and he jumped to the left. He didn't take time to place his boots right and so he picked up some spin but the important thing was to get away from that spot fast. He heard a *chuung* off to the right and a dart smacking into the bulkhead, and when he turned his head to the right and up behind him, a burly man with black hair and the same Flatlander robes and a dart gun was coming at him on a glide.

Nagara had started twisting his shoulder when he leaped, and now the differential angular momentum was bringing his shooting arm around. Jacob was already aiming again. Nagara took the extra second to make his shot and allow for the relative motions. His dart gun puffed and Nagara saw it take Jacob in the chest, just right. The man's face went white and he reached down to pull the dart out, but by that time the nerve inhibitor had reached the heart and abruptly Jacob stopped plucking at the dart and his fingers went slack and the body drifted on in the chilly air, smacking into a vault door and coming to rest.

Nagara wrenched around to cover the other two. Zak was coming at him. Nagara leaped away, braked. He turned and Zak had come to rest against the translucent organiform, waiting.

"That's a lesson," Nagara said evenly. "Here's another."

He touched the keyin on his chest and his force screen flickered on around him, making him look metallic. He turned it off in time to hear the hollow boom that came rolling through the ship like a giant's shout.

"That's a sample. A shaped charge. My ship set it off two hundred meters from *Redeemer*. The next one's keyed to go on impact with your skin. You'll lose pressure too fast to do anything about it. My force field comes on when the charge goes, so it won't hurt me."

"We've never seen such a field," the woman said unsteadily.

"Outskirter invention. That's why we won."

He didn't bother watching Zak. He looked at the woman as she clasped her thick worker's hands together and began to realize what choices were left. When she was done with that she murmured, "Zak, take out the canisters."

The woman sagged against a strut. Her robes clung to her and made her look gaunt and old.

"You're not giving us a chance, are you?" she said.

"You've got a lot of corpses here. You'll have a big colony out at Tau Ceti." Nagara was watching Zak maneuver the canisters onto a mobile carrier. The young man was going to be all right now, he could tell that. There was the look of weary defeat about him.

"We need the genotypes for insurance. In a strange ecology there will be genetic drift."

"The System has worse problems right now."

"With Earth dead, you people in the artificial worlds are *finished*," she said savagely, a spark returning. "That's why we left. We could see it coming."

Nagara wondered if they'd have left at all if they'd known a faster-than-light drive would come along. But no, it wouldn't have made any difference. The translight transition cost too much and only worked for small ships. He narrowed his eyes and made a smile without humor.

"I know quite well why you left. A bunch of scum-lovers. Purists. Said Earth was just as bad as the cylinder cities, all artificial, all controlled. Yeah, I know. You Flatties sold off everything you had and built *this*—" His voice became bitter. "Ransacked a fortune—*my* fortune."

For once she looked genuinely curious, uncalculating. "Yours?"

He flicked a glance at her and then back at Zak. "Yeah. I would've inherited some of your billions you made out of those smelting patents."

"You—"

"I'm one of your great-grandsons."

Her face changed. "No."

"It's true. Stuffing the money into this clunker made all your descendants have to bust ass for a living. And it's not so easy these days."

"I . . . didn't . . ."

He waved her into silence. "I knew you were one of the mainstays, one of the rich Flatlanders. The family talked about it a lot. We're not doing so well now. Not as well as you did, not by a thousandth. I thought that would mean you'd get to sleep right through, wake up at Tau Ceti. Instead"—he laughed—"they've got you standing watch."

"Someone has to be the Revealer of the word, grandson."

"Great-grandson. Revealer? If you'd 'revealed' a little common sense to that kid over there, he would've been alert and I wouldn't be in here."

She frowned and watched Zak, who was awkwardly shifting the squat modular canisters stenciled GENETIC BANK: MAX SECURITY. "We are not military types," she replied.

Nagara grinned. "Right. I was looking through the family records and I thought up this job. I figured you for an easy setup. A max of three or four on duty, considering the size of the life support systems and redundancies. So I got the venture capital together for a translight and here I am."

"We're not your kind. Why can't you give us a chance, grandson?"

"I'm a businessman."

She had a dry, rasping laugh. "A few centuries ago everybody thought space colonies would be the final answer. Get off the stinking old Earth and everything's solved. Athens in the sky. But look at you—a paid assassin. A 'businessman.' You're no grandson of *mine.*"

"Old ideas." He watched Zak.

"Don't you see it? The colony environments aren't a social advance. You need discipline to keep life-support activated. Communication and travel have to be regulated for simple safety. So you don't get democracies, you get strong men. And then they turned on *us*—on Earth."

"You were out of date," he said casually, not paying much attention.

"Do you ever read any history?"

"No." He knew this was part of her spiel—he'd seen it on a fax from a century ago—but he let her go on to keep her occupied. Talkers never acted when they could talk.

"They turned Earth into a handy preserve. The Berbers and Normans had it the same way a thousand years ago. They were seafarers. They depopulated Europe's coastline by raids, taking what or who they wanted. You did the same to us, from orbit, using solar lasers. But to—"

"Enough," Nagara said. He checked the long bore of the axial tube. It was empty. Zak had the stuff secured on the carrier. There wasn't any point in staying here any longer than necessary.

"Let's go," he said.

"One more thing," the woman said.

"What?"

"We went peacefully, I want you to remember that. We have no defenses."

"Yeah," Nagara said impatiently.

"But we have huge energies at our disposal. The scoop fields funnel an enormous flux of relativistic particles. We could've temporarily altered the magnetic multipolar fields and burned your sort to death."

"But you didn't."

"No, we didn't. But remember that."

Nagara shrugged. Zak was floating by the carrier ready to take orders, looking tired. The kid had been easy to take, too easy for him to take any pride in doing it. Nagara liked an even match. He didn't even mind losing if it was to somebody he could respect. Zak wasn't in that league, though.

"Let's go," he said.

The loading took time, but he covered Zak on every step and there were no problems. When he cast off from *Redeemer* he looked around by reflex for a planet to sight on, relaxing now, and it struck him that he was more alone than he had ever been, the stars scattered like oily jewels on velvet were the nearest destination he could have. That woman in *Redeemer* had lived with this for years. He looked at the endless long night out here, felt it as a shadow that passed through his mind, and then he punched in instructions and *Redeemer* dropped away, its blue-white arc a fuzzy blade that cut the darkness, and he slipped with a hollow clapping sound into translight.

He was three hours from his dropout point when one of the canisters strapped down behind the pilot's couch gave a warning buzz from thermal overload. It popped open.

Nagara twisted around and fumbled with the latches. He could pull the top two access drawers a little way out, and when he did, he saw that inside there was a store of medical supplies. Boxes and tubes and fluid cubes. Cheap stuff. No DNA manifolds.

Nagara sat and stared at the complete blankness outside. *We could've temporarily altered the magnetic multipolar fields and burned your sort to death,* she had said. *Remember that.*

If he went back she would be ready. They could rig some kind of aft sensor and focus the ramscoop fields on him when he came tunneling in through the flux. Fry him good.

They must have planned it all from the first. Something about it, about the way she'd looked, told him it had been the old woman's idea.

The risky part of it had been the business with Jacob. That didn't make sense. But maybe she'd known Jacob would try something and since she couldn't do anything about it, she used it. Used it to relax him, make him think the touchy part of the job was done so that he didn't think to check inside the stenciled canisters.

He looked at the medical supplies. Seventy-three years ago the woman had known they couldn't protect themselves from what they didn't know, ships that hadn't been invented yet. So on her five-year watch she had arranged a dodge that would work even if some System ship caught up to them. Now the Flatlanders knew what to defend against.

He sat and looked out at the blankness and thought about that.

When he popped out into System space, the A47 sphere was hanging up to the left at precisely the relative coordinates and distance he'd left it.

A47 was big and inside there were three men waiting to divide up and classify and market the genotypes. When he told them what was in the canisters, it would be all over, his money gone and theirs and no hope of his getting a stake again. And maybe worse than that. Maybe a lot worse.

He squinted at A47 as he came in for rendezvous. It looked different. Some of the third quadrant damage from the war wasn't repaired yet. The skin that had gleamed once was smudged now, and twisted gray girders stuck out of the ports. It looked pretty beat up. It was the best high-tech fortress they had and A47 had made the whole difference in the war. It broke the African shield by itself. But now it didn't look like so much. All the dots of light orbiting in the distance were pretty nearly the same or worse and now they were all that was left in the system.

Nagara turned his ship about to vector on the landing bay, listening to the rumble as the engines cut in. The console phosphors rippled blue, green, yellow as Central reffed him.

This next part was going to be pretty bad. Damned bad. And out there his great-grandmother was on the way still, somebody he could respect now, and for the first time he thought the Flatlanders probably were going to make it. In the darkness of the cabin something about the thought made him smile.

Bindlestiff

JAMES BLISH

We take a giant step into the future with this story, and ask, What can you do with a flying city? James Blish explored the answers to this question in a variety of ways through his "Okie" stories, collected into a novel, *Earthman, Come Home* (1957), which became part of a tetralogy, *Cities in Flight* (1970). The care and loving attention that Blish lavished on these novels, together with his emphasis on economic, political, and irrational motivations, still make a breathtaking narrative, as the very first line of this story demonstrates.

I

Even to the men of the flying city, the Rift was awesome beyond all human experience. Loneliness was natural between the stars, and starmen were used to it—the star density of the average cluster was more than enough to give a veteran Okie claustrophobia; but the enormous empty loneliness of the Rift was unique.

To the best of Mayor Amalfi's knowledge, no Okie city had ever crossed the Rift before. The City Fathers, who knew everything, agreed. Amalfi was none too sure that it was wise, for once, to be a pioneer.

Ahead and behind, the walls of the Rift shimmered, a haze of stars too far away to resolve into individual points of light. The walls curved gently toward a starry floor, so many parsecs "beneath" the keel of the city that it seemed to be hidden in a rising haze of star dust.

"Above," there was nothing; a nothing as final as the slamming of a door — it was the intergalactic gap.

The Rift was, in effect, a valley cut in the face of the galaxy. A few stars swam in it, light-millennia apart — stars which the tide of human colonization could never have reached. Only on the far side was there likely to be any inhabited planet, and, consequently, work for a migratory city.

On the near side there were the Earth police. They would not chase Amalfi's city across the Rift; they were busy consolidating their conquests of Utopia and the Duchy of Gort, barbarian planets whose ties with Earth were being forcibly reestablished. But they would be happy to see the city turn back — there was a violation of a Vacate order still on the books, and a little matter of a trick —

Soberly, Amalfi contemplated the oppressive chasm which the screens showed him. The picture came in by ultrawave from a string of proxy robots, the leader of which was already parsecs out across the gap. And still the far wall was featureless, just beginning to show a faintly granular texture which gave promise of resolution into individual stars at top magnification.

"I hope the food holds out," he muttered. "I never expected the cops to chase us this far."

Beside him, Mark Hazleton, the city manager, drummed delicately upon the arm of his chair. "No reason why it shouldn't," he said lazily. "Of course the oil's low, but the *Chlorella* crop is flourishing. And I doubt that we'll be troubled by mutation in the tanks. Aren't ultronic nexi supposed to vary directly with star density?"

"Sure," Amalfi said, irritated. "We won't starve if everything goes right. If we hadn't been rich enough to risk crossing, I'd of let us be captured and paid the fine instead. But we've never been as long as a year without planet-fall before, and this crossing is going to take all of the four years the Fathers predicted. The slightest accident, and we'll be beyond help."

"There'll be no accident," Hazleton said confidently.

"There's fuel decomposition — we've never had a flash fire but there's always a first time. And if the Twenty-Third Street spindizzy conks out again — "

He stopped abruptly. Through the corner of his eye, a minute pinprick of brightness poked insistently into his brain. When he looked directly at the screen, it was still there. He pointed.

"Look — is that a cluster? No, it's too small. If that's a free-floating star, it's close."

He snatched up a phone. "Give me Astronomy. Hello, Jake. Can you figure me the distance of a star from the source of an ultraphone broadcast?"

"Why, yes," the phone said. "Wait, and I'll pick up your image. Ah — I see what you mean; something at 10:00 o'clock center, can't tell what yet. Dinwiddie pickups on your proxies? Intensity will tell the tale." The astronomer chuckled like a parrot on the rim of a cracker barrel. "Now if you'll just tell me how many proxies you have, and how far they — "

"Five. Full interval."

"Hm-m-m. Big correction." There was a long, itching silence. "Amalfi?"

"Yeah."

"About ten parsecs, give or take 0.4. I'd say you've found a floater, my boy."

"Thanks." Amalfi put the phone back and drew a deep breath. "What a relief."

"You won't find any colonists on a star that isolated," Hazleton reminded him.

"I don't care. It's a landing point, possibly a fuel or even a food source. Most stars have planets; a freak like this might not, or it might have dozens. Just cross your fingers."

He stared at the tiny sun, his eyes aching from sympathetic strain. A star in the middle of the Rift — almost certainly a wild star, moving at four hundred or five hundred k.p.s. It occurred to him that a people living on a planet of that star might remember the moment when it burst through the near wall and embarked upon its journey into the emptiness.

"There might be people there," he said. "The Rift was swept clean of stars once, somehow. Jake claims that that's an overdramatic way of putting it, that the mean motions of the stars probably opened the gap naturally. But either way that sun must be a recent arrival, going at quite a clip, since it's moving counter to the general tendency. It could have been colonized while it was still passing through a populated area. Runaway stars tend to collect hunted criminals as they go by, Mark."

"Possibly," Hazleton admitted. "By the way, that image is coming in from your lead proxy, 'way out across the valley. Don't you have any outriggers? I ordered them sent."

"Sure. But I don't use them except for routine. Cruising the Rift lengthwise would be suicide. We'll take a look if you like."

He touched the board. On the screen, the far wall was wiped away. Nothing was left but thin haze; down at that end, the Rift turned, and eventually faded out into a rill of emptiness, soaking into the sands of the stars.

"Nothing there. Lots of nothing."

Amalfi moved the switch again.

On the screen, apparently almost within hallooing distance, a city was burning.

Space flight got its start, as a war weapon, amid the collapse of the great Western culture of Earth. In the succeeding centuries it was almost forgotten. The new culture, that vast planar despotism called by historiographers the Bureaucratic State, did not think that way.

Not that the original Soviets or their successors forbade space travel. They simply never thought of it. Space flight had been a natural, if late, result of Western thought patterns, which had always been ambitious for the infinite, but the geometrically flat dialectic of the succeeding culture could not include it. Where the West had soared from the rock like a sequoia, the Soviets spread like lichens, tightening their grip, satisfied to be at the very bases of the pillars of sunlight the West had sought to ascend.

The coming of the spindizzy—the antigravity generator, or gravitron—spelled the doom of the flat culture, as the leveling menace of the nuclear reactor had cut down the soaring West. Space flight returned; not, this time, as a technique of tiny ships and individual adventure, but as a project of cities.

There was no longer any reason why a man-carrying vehicle to cross space needed to be small, cramped, organized fore and aft, penurious of weight. The spindizzy could lift anything, and protect it, too. Most important, its operation was rooted in a variation of the value of c as a limit. The overdrive, the meteor screen, and antigravity had all arrived in one compact package, labeled "$G = (2PC)^2/(BU)^2$".

Every culture has its characteristic mathematic, in which historiographers can see its inevitable form. This one, couched in the algebra of the Magian culture, pointing toward the matrix mechanics of the new Nomad era, was a Western discovery. Blackett had found the essential relationship between gravity and magnetism, and Dirac had explained why it had not been detected before. Yet despite all of the minority groups butchered or "concentrated" by the Bureaucratic State, only the pure mathematicians went unsuspected about the destruction of that State, innocent even in their own minds of revolutionary motives.

The exodus began.

At first it was logical enough. The Aluminum Trust, the Thorium Trust, the Germanium Trust put their plants aloft bodily, to mine the planets. The Steel Trust made it possible for the rest, for it had turned Mars into the Pittsburgh of the solar system, and lulled the doubts of the State.

But the Thorium Trust's Plant No. 8 never came back. The revolution against the planar culture began as simply as that.

The first of the Okie cities soared away from the solar system, looking for work among the colonists — colonists left stranded among the stars by the ebb tide of Western civilization. The new culture began among these nomad cities, and before long Earth was virtually deserted.

But Earth laws, though much changed, survived. It was still possible to make a battleship, and the Okies were ungainly. Steam shovels, by and large, had been more characteristic of the West than tanks had been, but in a fight between the two the outcome was predictable; that situation never changed. The cities were the citizens — but there were still police.

And in the Rift, where there were no police, a city was burning.

It was all over in a few minutes. The city bucked and toppled in a maelstrom of lightning. Feeble flickers of resistance spat around its edges — and then it no longer had any edges. Sections of it broke off, and melted like wraiths. From its ardent center, a few hopeless life ships shot out into the gap; whatever was causing the destruction let them go. No conceivable life ship could live long enough to cross the Rift.

Amalfi cut in the audio circuit, filling the control room with a howl of static. Far behind the wild blasts of sound, a tiny voice was shouting desperately:

"Rebroadcast if anyone hears us. Repeat: we have the fuelless drive. We're destroying our model and evacuating our passenger. Pick him up if you can. We're being blown up by a bindlestiff. Rebroadcast if—"

Then there was nothing left but the skeleton of the city, glowing whitely, evaporating in the blackness. The pale, innocent light of the guide beam for a Bethe blaster played over it, but it was still impossible to see who was wielding the weapon. The Dinwiddie circuits in the proxy were compensating for the glare, so that nothing was coming through to the screen that did not shine with its own light.

The terrible fire died slowly, and the stars brightened. As the last spark flared and went out, a shadow loomed against the distant star wall. Hazleton drew his breath in sharply.

"*Another* city! So some outfits really do go bindlestiff. And we thought we were the first out here!"

Amalfi nodded, feeling a little sick. That one city should destroy another was bad enough. But it was even more of a wrench to realize that the whole scene was virtually ancient history. Ultrawave transmission was faster than light, but by no means instantaneous; the dark city had destroyed its smaller counterpart nearly two years ago, and must now be beyond pursuit. It was even beyond identification, for no orders could be sent now to the proxy which would result in any action until another two years had passed.

"You'd think some heavy thinker on Earth would've figured out a way to make Diracs compact enough to be mounted in a proxy," he grumbled. "They haven't got anything better to do back there."

Hazleton had no difficulty in penetrating to the speech's real meaning. He said, "Maybe we can still smoke 'em out, boss."

"Not a chance. We can't afford a side jaunt."

"Well, I'll send out a general warning on the Dirac," Hazleton said. "It's barely possible that the cops will be able to invest the Rift before the 'stiff gets out."

"That'll trap *us* neatly, won't it? Besides, that bindlestiff isn't going to leave the Rift."

"Eh? How do you know?"

"Did you hear what the SOS said about a fuelless drive?"

"Sure," Hazleton said uneasily, "but the guy who knows how to build it must be dead by now, even if he escaped the burning."

"We can't be sure of that—and that's the one thing that the 'stiff has to make sure of. If they get ahold of it, 'stiffs won't be a rarity any more. There'll be widespread piracy throughout the galaxy!"

"That's a big statement, Amalfi."

"Think, Mark. Pirates died out a thousand years ago on Earth when sailing ships were replaced by fueled ships. The fueled ships were faster—but couldn't themselves become pirates, because they had to touch civilized ports regularly to coal up. We're in the same state. But if that bindlestiff can actually get its hands on a fuelless drive—"

Hazleton stood up, kneading his hands uneasily. "I see what you mean. Well, there's only one place where a life ship could go out here, and that's the wild star. So the 'stiff is probably there, too, by now." He looked thoughtfully at the screen, now glittering once more only with anonymous stars. "Shall I send out the warning or not?"

"Yes, send it out. It's the law. But I think it's up to us to deal with the 'stiff; we're familiar with ways of manipulating strange cultures, whereas the cops would just smash things up if they did manage to get here in time."

"Check. Our course as before, then."

"Necessarily."

Still the city manager did not go. "Boss," he said at last, "that outfit is heavily armed. They could muscle in on us with no trouble."

"Mark, I'd call you yellow if I didn't know you were just lazy," Amalfi growled. He stopped suddenly and peered up the length of Hazleton's figure to his long, horselike face. "Or are you leading up to something?"

Hazleton grinned like a small boy caught stealing jam. "Well, I did have something in mind. I don't like 'stiffs, especially killers. Are you willing to entertain a small scheme?"

"Ah," Amalfi said, relaxing. "That's better. Let's hear it."

II

The wild star, hurling itself through the Rift on a course that would not bring it to the far wall for another ten thousand Earth years, carried with it six planets, of which only one was even remotely Earthlike. That

planet shone deep chlorophyll green on the screens long before it had
grown enough to assume a recognizable disk shape. The proxies called
in now, arrived one by one, circling the new world like a swarm of ten-
meter footballs, eying it avidly.

It was everywhere the same: savagely tropical, in the throes of a geological period roughly comparable to Earth's Carboniferous era. Plainly,
the only planet would be nothing but a way station; there would be no
work for pay there.

Then the proxies began to pick up weak radio signals.

Nothing, of course, could be made of the language; Amalfi turned
that problem over to the City Fathers at once. Nevertheless, he continued to listen to the strange gabble while he warped the city into an orbit.
The voices sounded ritualistic, somehow.

The City Fathers said: "THIS LANGUAGE IS A VARIANT OF PATTERN G,
BUT THE SITUATION IS AMBIGUOUS. GENERALLY WE WOULD SAY THAT THE
RACE WHICH SPEAKS IT IS INDIGENOUS TO THE PLANET, A RARE CASE BUT
BY NO MEANS UNHEARD OF. HOWEVER, THERE ARE TRACES OF FORMS
WHICH MIGHT BE DEGENERATES OF ENGLISH, AS WELL AS STRONG EVI-
DENCES OF DIALECT MIXTURES SUGGESTING A TRIBAL SOCIETY. THIS
LATTER FACT IS NOT CONSONANT WITH THE POSSESSION OF RADIO NOR
WITH THE UNDERLYING SAMENESS OF THE PATTERN. UNDER THE CIRCUM-
STANCES WE MUST POSITIVELY FORBID ANY MACHINATIONS BY MR. HAZLE-
TON ON THIS VENTURE."

"I didn't ask them for advice," Amalfi said. "And what good is a lesson
in etymology at this point? Still, Mark, watch your step —"

"'Remember Thor V,'" Hazleton said, mimicking the mayor's father-
bear voice to perfection. "All right. Do we land?"

For answer, Amalfi grasped the space stick, and the city began to
settle. Amalfi was a true child of space, a man with an intuitive understanding of the forces and relationships which were involved in astronautics; in delicate situations he invariably preferred to dispense with
instruments. Sensitively he sidled the city downward, guiding himself
mainly by the increasingly loud chanting in his earphones.

At four thousand meters there was a brief glitter from amid the dark-
green waves of the treetops. The proxies converged upon it slowly, and
on the screens a turreted roof showed; then two, four, a dozen. There
was a city there—a homebody, grown from the earth. Closer views

showed it to be walled, the wall standing just inside a clear ring where nothing grew; the greenery between the towers was a camouflage.

At three thousand, a flight of small ships burst from the city like frightened birds, trailing feathers of flame. "Gunners!" Hazleton snapped into his mike. "Posts!"

Amalfi shook his head, and continued to bring his city closer to the ground. The fire-tailed birds wheeled around them, dipping and flashing, weaving a pattern in smoky plumes; yet an Earthman would have thought, not of birds, but of the nuptial flight of drone bees.

Amalfi, who had never seen a bird or a bee, nevertheless sensed the ceremony in the darting cortege. With fitting solemnity he brought the city to a stop beside its jungle counterpart, hovering just above the tops of the giant cycads. Then, instead of clearing a landing area with the usual quick scythe of the mesotron rifles, he polarized the spindizzy screen.

The base and apex of the Okie city grew dim. What happened to the giant ferns and horsetails directly beneath it could not be seen—they were flattened into synthetic fossils in the muck in a split second—but those just beyond the rim of the city were stripped of their fronds and splintered, and farther out, in a vast circle, the whole forest bowed low away from the city, to a clap of sunlit thunder.

Unfortunately, the Twenty-Third Street spindizzy, always the weakest link, blew out at the last minute and the city dropped the last five meters in free fall. It arrived on the surface of the planet rather more cataclysmically than Amalfi had intended. Hazleton hung on to his bucket seat until City Hall had stopped swaying, and then wiped blood from his nose with a judicious handkerchief.

"That," he said, "was one dramatic touch too many. I'd best go have that spindizzy fixed again, just in case."

Amalfi shut off the controls with a contented gesture. "If that bindlestiff should show," he said, "they'll have a tough time amassing any prestige *here* for a while. But go ahead, Mark, it'll keep you busy."

The mayor eased his barrel-shaped bulk into the lift shaft and let himself be slithered through the friction fields to the street. Outside, the worn facade of City Hall shone with sunlight, and the City's motto—MOW YOUR LAWN, LADY?—was clear even under its encrustation of verdigris.

Amalfi was glad that the legend could not be read by the local folk—it would have spoiled the effect.

Suddenly he was aware that the chanting he had been hearing for so long through the earphones was thrilling through the air around him. Here and there, the sober, utilitarian faces of the Okie citizens were turning to look down the street, and traces of wonder, mixed with amusement and an unaccountable sadness, were in those faces. Amalfi turned.

A procession of children was coming toward him: children wound in mummylike swatches of cloth down to their hips, the strips alternately red and white. Several free-swinging panels of many-colored fabric, as heavy as silk, swirled about their legs as they moved.

Each step was followed by a low bend, hands outstretched and fluttering, heads rolling from shoulder to shoulder, feet moving in and out, toe-heel-toe, the whole body turning and turning again. Bracelets of objects like dried pods rattled at wrists and bare ankles. Over it all the voices chanted like water flutes.

Amalfi's first wild reaction was to wonder why the City Fathers had been puzzled about the language. *These were human children.* Nothing about them showed any trace of alienage.

Behind them, tall black-haired men moved in less agile procession, sounding in chorus a single word which boomed through the skirl and pitter of the children's dance at wide-spaced intervals. The men were human, too; their hands, stretched immovably out before them, palms up, had five fingers, with fingernails on them; their beards had the same topography as human beards; their chests, bared to the sun by a symbolical rent which was torn at the same place in each garment, and marked identically by a symbolical wound rubbed on with red chalk, showed ribs where ribs ought to be, and the telltale tracings of clavicles beneath the skin.

About the women there might have been some doubt. They came at the end of the procession, all together in a huge cage drawn by lizards. They were all naked and filthy and sick, and could have been any kind of animal. They made no sound, but only stared out of purulent eyes, as indifferent to the Okie city and its owners as to their captors. Occasionally they scratched, reluctantly, wincing from their own claws.

The children deployed around Amalfi, evidently picking him out as the leader because he was the biggest. He had expected as much; it was but one more confirmation of their humanity. He stood still while they made a circle and sat down, still chanting and shaking their wrists. The men, too, made a circle, keeping their faces toward Amalfi, their hands outstretched. At last that reeking cage was drawn into the double ring, virtually to Amalfi's feet. Two male attendants unhitched the docile lizards and led them away.

Abruptly the chanting stopped. The tallest and most impressive of the men came forward and bent, making that strange gesture with fluttering hands over the street. Before Amalfi quite realized what was intended, the stranger had straightened, placed some heavy object in his hand, and retreated, calling aloud the single word the men had been intoning before. Men and children responded together in one terrific shout, and then there was silence.

Amalfi was alone in the middle of the circle, with the cage. He looked down at the thing in his hand.

It was — a key.

Miramon shifted nervously in the chair, the great black sawtoothed feather stuck in his topknot bobbing uncertainly. It was a testimony of his confidence in Amalfi that he sat in it at all, for in the beginning he had squatted, as was customary on his planet. Chairs were the uncomfortable prerogatives of the gods.

"I myself do not believe in the gods," he explained to Amalfi, bobbing the feather. "It would be plain to a technician, you understand, that your city was simply a product of a technology superior to ours, and you yourselves to be men such as we are. But on this planet religion has a terrible force, a very immediate force. It is not expedient to run counter to public sentiment in such matters."

Amalfi nodded. "From what you tell me, I can believe that. Your situation is unique. What, precisely, happened 'way back then?"

Miramon shrugged. "We do not know," he said. "It was nearly eight thousand years ago. There was a high civilization here then — the priests and the scientists agree on that. And the climate was different; it got cold regularly every year, I am told, although how men could survive such a thing is difficult to understand. Besides, there were many more stars — the ancient drawings show *thousands* of them, though they fail to agree on the details."

"Naturally. You're not aware that your sun is moving at a terrific rate?"

"Moving?" Miramon laughed shortly. "Some of our more mystical scientists have that opinion—they maintain that if the planets move, so must the sun. It is an imperfect analogy, in my opinion. Would we still be in this trough of nothingness if we were moving?"

"Yes, you would—you are. You underestimate the size of the Rift. It's impossible to detect any parallax at this distance, though in a few thousand years you'll begin to suspect it. But while you were actually among the stars, your ancestors could see it very well, by the changing positions of the neighboring suns."

Miramon looked dubious. "I bow to your superior knowledge, of course. But, be that as it may—the legends have it that for some sin of our people, the gods plunged us into this starless desert, and changed our climate to perpetual heat. This is why our priests say that we are in Hell, and that to be put back among the cool stars again, we must redeem our sins. We have no Heaven as you have defined the term— when we die, we die damned; we must win 'salvation' right here in the mud. The doctrine has its attractive features, under the circumstances."

Amalfi meditated. It was reasonably clear, now, what had happened, but he despaired of explaining it to Miramon—hard common sense sometimes has a way of being impenetrable. This planet's axis had a pronounced tilt, and the concomitant amount of libration. That meant that, like Earth, it had a Draysonian cycle: every so often, the top wobbled, and then resumed spinning at a new angle. The result, of course, was a disastrous climatic change. Such a thing happened on Earth roughly once every twenty-five thousand years, and the first one in recorded history had given birth to some extraordinary silly legends and faiths—sillier than those the Hevians entertained, on the whole.

Still, it was miserable bad luck for them that a Draysonian overturn had occurred almost at the same time that the planet had begun its journey across the Rift. It had thrown a very high culture, a culture entering its ripest phase, back forcibly into the Interdestructional phase without the slightest transition.

The planet of He was a strange mixture now. Politically the regression had stopped just before barbarism—a measure of the lofty summits this race had scaled at the time of the catastrophe—and was now in reverse, clawing through the stage of warring city-states. Yet the basics of the scientific techniques of eight thousand years ago had not been forgotten; now they were exfoliating, bearing "new" fruits.

Properly, city-states should fight each other with swords, not with missile weapons, chemical explosives, and supersonics — and flying should be still in the dream stage, a dream of flapping wings at that; not already a jet-propelled fact. Astronomical and geological accident had mixed history up for fair.

"What would have happened to me if I'd unlocked that cage?" Amalfi demanded suddenly.

Miramon looked sick. "Probably you would have been killed — or they would have tried to kill you, anyhow," he said, with considerable reluctance. "That would have been releasing Evil again upon us. The priests say that it was women who brought about the sins of the Great Age. In the bandit cities, to be sure, that savage creed is no longer maintained — which is one reason why we have so many deserters to the bandit cities. You can have no idea of what it is like to do your duty to the race each year as our law requires. Madness!"

He sounded very bitter. "This is why it is hard to make our people see how suicidal the bandit cities are. Everyone on this world is weary of fighting the jungle, sick of trying to rebuild the Great Age with handfuls of mud, of maintaining social codes which ignore the presence of the jungle — but most of all, of serving in the Temple of the Future. In the bandit cities the women are clean, and do not scratch one."

"The bandit cities don't fight the jungle?" Amalfi asked.

"No. They prey on those who do. They have given up the religion entirely — the first act of a city which revolts is to slay its priests. Unfortunately, the priesthood is essential; and our beast-women must be borne, since we cannot modify one tenet without casting doubt upon all — or so they tell us. It is only the priesthood which keeps us fighting, only the priesthood which teaches us that it is better to be men than mud puppies. So we — the technicians — follow the rituals with great strictness, stupid through some of them are, and consider it a matter of no moment that we ourselves do not believe in the gods."

"Sense in that," Amalfi admitted. Miramon, in all conscience, was a shrewd apple. If he was representative of as large a section of Hevian thought as he believed himself to be, much might yet be done on this wild and untamed world.

"It amazes me that you knew to accept the key as a trust," Miramon said. "It was precisely the proper move — but how could you have guessed that?"

Amalfi grinned. "That wasn't hard. I know how a man looks when he's dropping a hot potato. Your priest made all the gestures of a man passing on a sacred trust, but he could hardly wait until he'd got it over with. Incidentally, some of those women are quite presentable now that Dee's bathed 'em and Medical has taken off the under layers. Don't look so alarmed, we won't tell your priests — I gather that we're the foster fathers of He from here on out."

"You are thought to be emissaries from the Great Age," Miramon agreed gravely. "What you *actually* are, you have not said."

"True. Do you have migratory workers here? The phrase comes easily in your language; yet I can't see how — "

"Surely, surely. The singers, the soldiers, the fruit pickers — all go from city to city, selling their services." Suddenly the Hevian got it. "Do you ... do you imply ... that your resources are *for sale*? For sale to *us*?"

"Exactly, Miramon."

"But how shall we pay you?" Miramon gasped. "All of what we call wealth, all that we have, could not buy a length of the cloth in your sash!"

Amalfi thought about it, wondering principally how much of the real situation Miramon could be expected to understand. It occurred to him that he had persistently underestimated the Hevian so far; it might be profitable to try the full dose — and hope that it wasn't lethal.

"It's this way," Amalfi said. "In the culture we belong to, a certain metal, called germanium, serves for money. You have enormous amounts of it on your planet, but it's very hard to obtain, and I'm sure you've never even detected it. One of the things we would like is your permission to mine for that metal."

Miramon's pop-eyed skepticism was comical. "Permission?" he squeaked. "Please, Mayor Amalfi — is your ethical code as foolish as ours? Why do you not mine this metal without permission and be done with it?"

"Our law enforcement agencies would not allow it. Mining your planet would make us rich — almost unbelievably rich. Our assays show, not only fabulous amounts of germanium, but also the presence

of certain drugs in your jungle — drugs which are known to be anti-
agapics—"

"Sir?"

"Sorry, I mean that, used properly, they cure death."

Miramon rose with great dignity.

"You are mocking me," he said. "I will return at a later date and perhaps we may talk again."

"Sit down, please," Amalfi said contritely. "I had forgotten that death
is not everywhere known to be a disease. It was conquered so long ago —
before space flight, as a matter of fact. But the pharmaceuticals involved
have always been in very short supply, shorter and shorter as man spread
throughout the galaxy. Less than a two thousandth of one percent of our
present population can get the treatment now, and an ampoule of any
anti-agapic, even the most inefficient ones, can be sold for the price the
seller asks. Not a one of the anti-agapics has ever been synthesized, so if
we could harvest here —"

"That is enough, it is not necessary that I understand more," Miramon said. He squatted again, reflectively. "All this makes me wonder if
you are not from the Great Age after all. Well — this is difficult to think
about reasonably. Why would your culture object to your being rich?"

"It wouldn't, as long as we got it honestly. We shall have to show that
we worked for our riches. We'll need a written agreement. A permission."

"That is clear," Miramon said. "You will get it, I am sure. I cannot
grant it myself. But I can predict what the priests will ask you to do to
earn it."

"What, then? This is just what I want to know. Let's have it."

"First of all, you will be asked for the secret of this . . . this cure for
death. They will want to use it on themselves, and hide it from the rest
of us. Wisdom, perhaps; it would make for more desertions otherwise —
but I am sure they will want it."

"They can have it, but we'll see to it that the secret leaks out. The City
Fathers know the therapy. What next?"

"You must wipe out the jungle."

Amalfi sat back, stunned. Wipe out the jungle! Oh, it would be easy
enough to lay waste almost all of it — even to give the Hevians energy
weapons to keep those wastes clear — but sooner or later, the jungle

would come back. The weapons would disintegrate in the eternal moisture, the Hevians would not take proper care of them, would not be able
to repair them—how would the brightest Greek have repaired a shattered
X-ray tube, even if he had known how? The technology didn't exist.

No, the jungle would come back. And the cops would come to He to
see whether or not the Okie city had fulfilled its contract—and would
find the planet as raw as ever. Good-by to riches. This was jungle climate. There would be jungles here until the next Draysonian catastrophe, and that was that.

"Excuse me," he said, and reached for the control helmet. "Give me
the City Fathers," he said into the mouthpiece.

"SPEAK," the spokesman vodeur said after a while.

"How would you go about wiping out a jungle?"

There was a moment's silence. "SODIUM FLUOSILICATE SPRAY WOULD
SERVE. IN A WET CLIMATE IT WOULD CREATE FATAL LEAF BLISTER. ALSO
THERE IS A FORGOTTEN COMPOUND, 2,4-D, WHICH WOULD SERVE FOR
STUBBORN SECTIONS. OF COURSE THE JUNGLE WOULD RETURN."

"That's what I meant. Any way to make the job stick?"

"NO, UNLESS THE PLANET EXHIBITS DRAYSONIANISM."

"*What?*"

"NO, UNLESS THE PLANET EXHIBITS DRAYSONIANISM. IN THAT CASE ITS
AXIS MIGHT BE REGULARIZED. IT HAS NEVER BEEN TRIED, BUT THEORETI-
CALLY IT IS QUITE SIMPLE; A BILL TO REGULARIZE EARTH'S AXIS WAS DE-
FEATED BY THREE VOTES IN THE EIGHTY-SECOND COUNCIL, OWING TO
THE OPPOSITION OF THE CONSERVATION LOBBY."

"Could the city handle it?"

"NO. THE COST WOULD BE PROHIBITIVE. *MAYOR AMALFI, ARE YOU CONTEM-
PLATING TIPPING THIS PLANET? WE FORBID IT!* EVERY INDICATION SHOWS—"

Amalfi tore the helmet from his head and flung it across the room.
Miramon jumped up in alarm.

"*Hazleton!*"

The city manager shot through the door as if he had been kicked
through it on roller skates. "Here, boss—what's the—"

"Get down below and turn off the City Fathers—*fast*, before they
catch on and do something! Quick, man—"

Hazleton was already gone. On the other side of the control room,
the phones of the helmet squawked dead data in italic capitals.

Then, suddenly, they went silent.

The City Fathers had been turned off, and Amalfi was ready to move a world.

III

The fact that the City Fathers could not be consulted—for the first time in two centuries—made the job more difficult than it need have been, barring their conservatism. Tipping the planet, the crux of the job, was simple enough in essence; the spindizzy could handle it. But the side effects of the medicine might easily prove to be worse than the disease.

The problem was seismological. Rapidly whirling objects have a way of being stubborn about changing their positions. If that energy were overcome, it would have to appear somewhere else—the most likely place being multiple earthquakes.

Too, very little could be anticipated about the gravitics of the task. The planet's revolution produced, as usual, a sizable magnetic field. Amalfi did not know how well that field would take to being tipped with relation to the space lattice which it distorted, nor just what would happen when the spindizzies polarized the whole gravity field. During "moving day" the planet would be, in effect, without magnetic moment of its own, and since the Calculator was one of the City Fathers, there was no way of finding out where the energy would reappear, in what form, or in what intensity.

He broached the latter question to Hazleton. "If we were dealing with an ordinary case, I'd say it would show up as velocity," he pointed out. "In which case we'd be in for an involuntary junket. But this is no ordinary case. The mass involved is . . . well, it's planetary, that's all. What do you think, Mark?"

"I don't know what to think," Hazleton admitted. "When we move the city, we change the magnetic moment of its component atoms; but the city itself doesn't revolve, and doesn't have a *gross* magnetic moment. Still—we could control velocity; suppose the energy reappears as heat, instead? There'd be nothing left but a cloud of gas."

Amalfi shook his head. "That's a bogey. The gyroscopic resistance may show up as heat, sure, but not the magnetogravitic. I think we'd be safe to expect it to appear as velocity, just as in ordinary spindizzy operation. Figure the conversion equivalency and tell me what you get."

Hazleton bent over his slide rule, the sweat standing out along his forehead and above his mustache in great heavy droplets. Amalfi could understand the eagerness of the Hevians to get rid of the jungle and its eternal humidity—his own clothing had been sopping ever since the city had landed here.

"Well," the city manager said finally, "unless I've made a mistake somewhere, the whole kit and kaboodle will go shooting away from here at about half the speed of light. That's not too bad—less than cruising speed for us. We could always loop around and bring it back into its orbit."

"Ah, but could we? Remember, we don't control it! It appears automatically when we turn on the spindizzies. We don't even know in which direction we're going to move."

"Yes we do," Hazleton objected. "Along the axis of spin, of course."

"Cant? And torque?"

"No problem—yet there is. I keep forgetting we're dealing with a planet instead of electrons." He applied the slipstick again. "No soap. Can't be answered without the Calculator and he's turned off. But if we can figure a way to control the flight, it won't matter in the end. There'll be perturbations of the other planets when this one goes massless, whether it moves or not, but nobody lives there anyhow."

"All right, go figure a control system. I've got to get the Geology men to—"

The door slid back suddenly, and Amalfi looked over his shoulder. It was Anderson, the perimeter sergeant. The man was usually blasé in the face of all possible wonders, unless they threatened the city. "What's the matter?" Amalfi said, alarmed.

"Sir, we've gotten an ultrawave from some outfit claiming to be refugees from another Okie—claim they hit a bindlestiff. They've crash-landed on this planet up north and they're being mobbed by one of the local bandit towns. They were holding 'em off and yelling for help, and then they stopped transmitting."

Amalfi heaved himself to his feet. "Did you get a bearing?" he demanded.

"Yes, sir."

"Give me the figures. Come on, Mark. We need those boys."

They grabbed a cab to the edge of the city, and went the rest of the way on foot, across the supersonics-cleared strip of bare turf which surrounded the Hevian town. The turf felt rubbery; Amalfi suspected that some rudimentary form of friction field was keeping the mud in a state of stiff gel. He had visions of foot soldiers sinking suddenly into liquid ooze as defenders turned off the fields, and quickened his pace.

Inside the gates, the guards summoned a queer, malodorous vehicle which seemed to be powered by the combustion of hydrocarbons, and they were shot through the streets toward Miramon. Throughout the journey, Amalfi clung to a cloth strap in an access of nervousness. He had never traveled right *on* the surface at any speed before, and the way things zipped past him made him jumpy.

"Is this bird out to smash us up?" Hazleton demanded petulantly. "He must be doing all of four hundred kilos an hour."

"I'm glad you feel the same way," Amalfi said, relaxing a little. "Actually I'll bet he's doing less than two hundred. It's just the way the—"

The driver, who had been holding his car down to a conservative fifty out of deference to the strangers, wrenched the machine around a corner and halted neatly before Miramon's door. Amalfi got out, his knees wobbly. Hazleton's face was a delicate puce.

"I'm going to figure a way to make our cabs operate outside the city," he muttered. "Every time we make a new planet-fall, we have to ride in ox carts, on the backs of bull kangaroos, in hot-air balloons, steam-driven airscrews, things that drag you feet first and face down through tunnels, or whatever else the natives think is classy transportation. My stomach won't stand much more."

Amalfi grinned and raised his hand to Miramon, whose expression suggested laughter smothered with great difficulty.

"What brings you here?" the Hevian said. "Come in. I have no chairs, but—"

"No time," Amalfi said. He explained the situation quickly. "We've got to get those men out of there, if they're still alive. This bindlestiff is a bandit city, like the ones you have here, but it has all the stuff we have and more besides. It's vital to find out what these survivors know about it. Can you locate the town that's holding them? We have a fix on it."

Miramon went back into his house—actually, like all the other living quarters in the town, it was a dormitory housing twenty-five men of the same trade or profession—and returned with a map. The map-making conventions of He were anything but self-explanatory, but after a while Hazleton figured out the symbolism involved. "That's your city, and here's ours," he said, pointing. "Right? And this peeled orange is a butterfly grid. I've always claimed that was a lot more faithful to spherical territory than our parabolic projection, boss."

"Easier still to express what you want to remember as a topological relation," Amalfi grunted. "Show Miramon where the signals came from."

"Up here, on this wing of the butterfly."

Miramon frowned. "That can only be Fabr-Suithe. A very bad place to approach, even in the military sense. However, we shall have to try. Do you know what the end result will be?"

"No; what?"

"The bandit cities will come out in force to hinder the Great Work. They do not fear you now—they fear nothing, we think they take drugs—but they have seen no reason to risk probable huge losses by attacking you. When *you* attack one of them, they will have that reason; they learn hatred very quickly."

Amalfi shrugged. "We'll chance it. We'll pick our own town up and go calling; if they don't want to deliver up these Okies—"

"Boss—"

"Eh?"

"How are you going to get us off the ground?"

Amalfi could feel his ears turning red, and swore. "I forgot that Twenty-Third Street machine. And we can't get anything suitable into a Hevian rocket—a pile would fit easily enough, but a frictionator or a dismounted spindizzy wouldn't, and there'd be no point in taking popguns—Maybe we could gas them."

"Excuse me," Miramon said, "but it is not certain that the priests will authorize the use of the rockets. We had best drive over to the temple directly and ask."

"Belsen and bebop!" Amalfi said. It was the oldest oath in his repertoire.

Talk, even with electrical aid, was impossible in the rocket. The whole machine roared like a gigantic tamtam to the vibration of the jets. Morosely Amalfi watched Hazleton connecting the mechanism in the nose with the power leads from the pile—no mean balancing feat, considering the way the rocket pitched in its passage through the tortured Hevian air currents. The reactor itself had not been filled all the way, since its total capacity could not have been used, and the heavy water sloshed and foamed in the transparent cube.

There had been no difficulty with the priests about the little rocket task force itself. To the end of his life Amalfi was sure that the straight-faced Miramon had invented the need for religious permission, just to get the two Okies back into the ground car again. Still, the discomforts of that ride were small compared to this one.

The pilot shifted his feet on the treadles and the deck pitched. Metal rushed back under Amalfi's nose, and he found himself looking through misty air at a crazily canted jungle. Something long, thin, and angry flashed over it and was gone. At the same instant there was a piercing in-human shriek, sharp enough to dwarf for a long instant the song of the rocket.

Then there were more of the same: *ptsouiiirrr! ptsouiiirrr! ptsouiiirrr!* The machine jerked to each one and now and then shook itself violently, twisting and careening across the jungle top. Amalfi had never felt so help-less before in his life. He did not even know what the noise was; he could only be sure that it was ill-tempered. The coarse *blaam* of high explosive, when it began, was recognizable — the city had often had occasion to blast on jobs — but nothing in his experience went *kerchowkerchowkerchowker-chowkerchow* like a demented vibratory drill, and the invisible thing that screamed its own pep yell as it flew — *eeeeeeeeyowKRCHKackackarack-arackaracka* — seemed wholly impossible.

He was astonished to discover that the hull around him was stippled with small holes, real holes with the slipstream fluting over them. It took him what seemed to be three weeks to realize that the whooping and cheerleading which meant nothing to him was riddling the ship and threatening to kill him any second.

Someone was shaking him. He lurched to his knees, trying to un-freeze his eyeballs.

"Amalfi! Amalfi!" The voice, though it was breathing on his ear, was parsecs away. "Pick your spot, quick! They'll have us shot down in a —"

Something burst outside and threw Amalfi to the deck. Doggedly he crawled to the port and peered down through the shattered plastic. The bandit Hevian city swooped past, upside down. He was sick suddenly, and the city was lost in a web of tears. The second time it came, he managed to see which building had the heaviest guard, and pointed, choking.

The rocket threw its tailfeathers over the nearest cloud and bored beak-first for the ground. Amalfi hung on to the edge of the suddenly blank deck port, his own blood spraying back in a fine mist into his face from his cut fingers.

"*Now!*"

Nobody heard, but Hazleton saw his nod. A blast of pure heat blew through the upended cabin as the pile blew off the shielded nose of the rocket. Even through the top of his head, the violet-white light of that soundless concussion nearly blinded Amalfi, and he could feel the irradiation of his shoulders and chest. He would have no colds for the next two or three years, anyhow — every molecule of histamine in his blood must have been detoxified at that instant.

The rocket yawed wildly, and then came under control again. The ordnance noises had already quit, cut off at the moment of the flash.

The bandit city was blind.

The sound of the jets cut off, and Amalfi understood for the first time what an "aching void" might be. The machine fell into a steep glide, the air howling dismally outside it. Another rocket, under the guidance of one of Hazleton's assistants, dived down before it, scything a narrow runway in the jungle with a mesotron rifle — for the bandit towns kept no supersonic no-plant's-land between themselves and the rank vegetation.

The moment the rocket stopped moving, Amalfi and a hand-picked squad of Okies and Hevians were out of it and slogging through the muck. From inside the bandit city drifted a myriad of screams — human screams now, screams of agony and terror, from men who thought themselves blinded for life. Amalfi had no doubt that many of them were. Certainly anyone who had had the misfortune to be looking at the sky when the pile had converted itself into photons would never see again.

But the law of chance would have protected most of the renegades, so speed was vital. The mud built up heavy pads under his shoes, and the jungle did not thin out until they hit the town's wall itself.

The gates had been rusted open years ago, and were choked with greenery. The Hevians hacked their way through it with practiced knives and cunning.

Inside, the going was still almost as thick. The city proper presented a depressing face of proliferating despair. Most of the buildings were completely enshrouded in vines, and many were halfway toward ruins. Iron-hard tendrils had thrust their way between stones, into windows, under cornices, up drains and chimney funnels. Poison-green, succulent leaves plastered themselves greedily upon every surface, and in shadowed places there were huge blood-colored fungi which smelled like a man six days dead; the sweetish taint hung heavily in the air. Even the paving blocks had sprouted — inevitably, since, whether by ignorance or lazi-ness, most of them had been cut from green wood.

The screaming began to die into whimpers. Amalfi did his best to keep from inspecting the inhabitants. A man who believes he has just been blinded permanently is not a pretty sight, even when he is wrong. Yet it was impossible not to notice the curious mixture of soiled finery and gleamingly clean nakedness; it was as if two different periods had mixed in the city, as if a gathering of Hruntan nobles had been sprinkled with Noble Savages. Possibly the men who had given in completely to the jungle had also slid back far enough to discover the pleasures of bathing — if so, they would shortly discover the pleasures of the mud wal-low, too, and would not look so noble after that.

"Amalfi, here they are — "

The mayor's suppressed pity for the blinded men evaporated when he got a look at the imprisoned Okies. They had been systematically mauled to begin with, and after that sundry little attentions had been paid to them which combined the best features of savagery and deca-dence. One of them, mercifully, had been strangled by his comrades early in the "trial." Another, a basket case, should have been rescued, for he could still talk rationally, but he pleaded so persistently for death that Amalfi had him shot in a sudden fit of sentimentality. Of the other three men, all could walk and talk, but two were mad. The catatonic was car-ried out on a stretcher, and the manic was gagged and led gingerly away.

"How did you do it?" asked the rational man in Russian, the dead uni-versal language of deep space. He was a human skeleton, but he radiated a terrific personal force. He had lost his tongue early in the "question-ing," but had already taught himself to talk by the artificial method — the result was inhuman, but it was intelligible. "They were coming down to kill us as soon as they heard your jets. Then there was a sort of a flash, and they all started screaming — a pretty sound, let me tell you."

"I'll bet," Amalfi said. "That 'sort of a flash' was a photon explosion. It was the only way we could figure on being sure of getting you out alive.

We thought of trying gas, but if they had had gas masks they would have been able to kill you anyhow."

"I haven't seen any masks, but I'm sure they have them. There are traveling volcanic gas clouds in this part of the planet, they say; they must have evolved some absorption device—charcoal is well known here. Lucky we were so far underground, or we'd be blind, too, then. You people must be engineers."

"More or less," Amalfi agreed. "Strictly, we're miners and petroleum geologists, but we've developed a lot of sidelines since we've been aloft—like any Okie. Here's our rocket—crawl in. It's rough, but it's transportation. How about you?"

"Agronomists. Our mayor thought there was a field for it out here along the periphery—teaching the abandoned colonies and the off-shoots how to work poisoned soil and manage low-yield crops without heavy machinery. Our sideline was wax-mans."

"What are those?" Amalfi said, adjusting the harness around the wasted body.

"Soil-source antibiotics. It was those the bindlestiff wanted—and got. The filthy swine. They can't bother to keep a reasonably sanitary city; they'd rather pirate some honest outfit for drugs when they have an epidemic. Oh, and they wanted germanium, too, of course. They blew us up when they found we didn't have any—we'd converted to a barter economy as soon as we got out of the last commerce lanes."

"What about your passenger?" Amalfi said with studied nonchalance.

"Dr. Beetle? Not that that was his name, I couldn't pronounce *that* even when I had my tongue. I don't imagine he survived; we had to keep him in a tank even in the city, and I can't quite see him living through a life-ship journey. He was a Myrdian, smart cookies all of them, too. That no-fuel drive of his—"

Outside, a shot cracked, and Amalfi winced. "We'd best get off— they're getting their eyesight back. Talk to you later. Hazleton, any incidents?"

"Nothing to speak of, boss. Everybody stowed?"

"Yep. Kick off."

There was a volley of shots, and then the rocket coughed, roared, and stood on its tail. Amalfi pulled a deep sigh loose from the acceleration and turned his head toward the rational man.

He was still securely strapped in, and looked quite relaxed. A brass-nosed slug had come through the side of the ship next to him and had neatly removed the top of his skull.

IV

Working information out of the madmen was a painfully long, anxious process. The manic was a three-hundred-fifty-hour case, and even after he had been returned to a semblance of rationality he could contribute very little.

The life ship had not come to He because of the city's Dirac warning, he said. The life ship and the burned Okie had not had any Dirac equipment. The life ship had come to He, as Amalfi had predicted, because it was the only possible planet-fall in the desert of the Rift. Even so, the refugees had had to use deep sleep and strict starvation rationing to make it.

"Did you see the 'stiff again?"

"No, sir. If they heard your Dirac warning, they probably figured the police had spotted them and scrammed—or maybe they thought there was a military base or an advanced culture here on the planet."

"You're guessing," Amalfi said gruffly. "What happened to Dr. Beetle?"

The man looked startled. "The Myrdian in the tank? He got blown up with the city, I guess."

"He wasn't put off in another life ship?"

"Doesn't seem very likely. But I was only a pilot. Could be that they took him out in the mayor's gig for some reason."

"You don't know anything about his no-fuel drive?"

"First I heard of it."

Amalfi was far from satisfied; he suspected that there was still a short circuit somewhere in the man's memory. The city's auditors insisted that he had been cleared, however, and Amalfi had to accept the verdict. All that remained to be done was to get some assessment of the weapons available to the bindlestiff; on this subject the manic was ignorant, but the city's analyst said cautiously that something might be extracted from the catatonic within a month or two.

Amalfi accepted the figure, since it was the best he had. With Moving Day so close, he couldn't afford to worry overtime about another problem. He had already decided that the simplest answer to vulcanism, which otherwise would be inevitable when the planet's geophysical balance was changed, was to reinforce the crust. All over the surface of He, drilling teams were sinking long, thin, slanting shafts, reaching toward the stress fluid of the world's core. The shafts interlocked intricately, and thus far only one volcano had been created by the drilling—in general the lava pockets which had been tapped had already been anticipated and the flow had been bled off into half a hundred intersecting channels without ever reaching the surface. After the molten rock had hardened, the clogged channels were drilled again, with mesotron rifles set to the smallest possible dispersion.

None of the shafts had yet tapped the stress fluid; the plan was to complete them all simultaneously. At that point, specific areas, riddled with channel intersections, would give way, and immense plugs would be forced up toward the crust, plugs of iron, connected by ferrous cantilevers through the channels between. The planet of He would wear a cruel corset, permitting not the slightest flexure—it would be stitched with threads of steel, steel that had held even granite in solution for millennia.

The heat problem was tougher, and Amalfi was not sure whether or not he had hit upon the solution. The very fact of structural resistance would create high temperatures, and any general formation of shear planes would cut the imbedded girders at once. The method being prepared to cope with that was rather drastic, and its aftereffects unknown.

On the whole, however, the plans were simple, and putting them into effect had seemed heavy but relatively simple labor. Some opposition, of course, had been expected from the local bandit towns.

But Amalfi had not expected to lose nearly twenty percent of his crews during the first month.

It was Miramon who brought in the news of the latest camp found slaughtered. Amalfi was sitting under a tree fern on high ground overlooking the city, watching a flight of giant dragonflies and thinking about heat transfer in rock.

"You are sure they were adequately protected?" Miramon asked cautiously. "Some of our insects—"

Amalfi thought the insects, and the jungle, almost disturbingly beautiful. The thought of destroying it all occasionally upset him. "Yes, they were," he said shortly. "We sprayed out the camp areas with dicoumarins and fluorine-substituted residuals. Besides—do any of your insects use explosives?"

"Explosives! There was dynamite used? I saw no evidence—"

"No. That's what bothers me. I don't like all those felled trees you describe. We used to use TDX to get a cutting blast; it has a property of exploding in a flat plane."

Miramon goggled. "Impossible. An explosion has to expand evenly in the open."

"Not if it's a piperazo-hexybitrate built from polarized carbon atoms. Such atoms can't move in any direction but at right angles to the gravity radius. That's what I mean. You people are up to dynamite, but not to TDX."

He paused, frowning. "Of course some of our losses have just been by bandit raids, with arrows and crude bombs—your friends from Fabr-Suithe and their allies. But these camps where there was an explosion and no crater to show for it—"

He fell silent. There was no point in mentioning the gassed corpses. It was hard even to think about them. Somebody on this planet had a gas which was a regurgitant, a sternutatory, and a vesicant all in one. The men had been forced out of their masks—which had been designed solely to protect them from volcanic gases—to vomit, had taken the stuff into their lungs by convulsive sneezing, and had blistered into great sacs of serum inside and out. That, obviously, had been the multiple benzene ring Hawkesite; very popular in the days of the Hruntan Empire, when it had been called "polybathroom-floorine" for no discoverable reason. But what was it doing on He?

There was only one possible answer, and for a reason which he did not try to understand, it made Amalfi breathe a little easier. All around him, the jungle sighed and swayed, and humming clouds of gnats made rainbows over the dew-laden pinnae of the fern. The jungle, almost always murmurously quiet, had never seemed like a real enemy; now Amalfi knew that that intuition had been right. The real enemy had declared itself, stealthily, but with a stealth which was naïveté itself in comparison with the ancient guile of the jungle.

"Miramon," Amalfi said tranquilly, "we're in a spot. That city I told you about—the bindlestiff—is already here. It must have landed before we arrived, long enough ago to hide itself thoroughly. Probably it came down at night in some taboo area. The men in it have leagued themselves with Fabr-Suithe, anyhow, that much is obvious."

A moth with a two-meter wingspread blundered across the clearing, piloted by a gray-brown nematode which had sunk its sucker above the ganglion between the glittering creature's pinions. Amalfi was in a mood to read parables into things, and the parasitism reminded him anew of how greatly he had underestimated the enemy. The bindlestiff evidently knew, and was skillful at, the secret of manipulating a new culture; a shrewd Okie never attempts to overwhelm a civilization, but instead pilots it, as indetectably as possible, doing no apparent harm, adding no apparent burden, but turning history deftly and tyrannically aside at the crucial instant—

Amalfi snapped the belt switch of his ultraphone. "Hazleton?"

"Here, boss." Behind the city manager's voice was the indistinct rumble of heavy mining. "What's up?"

"Nothing yet. Are you having any trouble out there?"

"No. We're not expecting any, either, with all this artillery."

"Famous last words," Amalfi said. "The 'stiff's here, Mark."

There was a short silence. In the background, Amalfi could hear the shouts of Hazleton's crew. When the city manager's voice came in again, it was moving from word to word very carefully, as if it expected each one to break under its weight. "You imply that the 'stiff was already on He when our Dirac broadcast went out. Right? I'm not sure these losses of ours can't be explained some other way, boss; the theory . . . uh . . . lacks elegance."

Amalfi grinned tightly. "A heuristic criticism," he said. "Go to the foot of the class, Mark, and think it over. Thus far they've outthought us six ways for Sunday. We may be able to put your old plan into effect yet, but if it's to work, we'll have to provoke open conflict."

"How?"

"Everybody here knows that there's going to be a drastic change when we finish what we're doing, but we're the only ones who know exactly what we're going to do. The 'stiffs will have to stop us, whether they've got Dr. Beetle or not. So I'm forcing their hand. Moving Day is hereby advanced by one thousand hours."

"What! I'm sorry, boss, but that's flatly impossible."

Amalfi felt a rare spasm of anger. "That's as may be," he growled. "Nevertheless, spread it around; let the Hevians hear it. And just to prove that I'm not kidding, Mark, I'm turning the City Fathers back on at that time. If you're not ready to spin by then, you may well swing instead."

The click of the belt switch to the "Off" position was unsatisfying. Amalfi would much have preferred to conclude the interview with something really final—a clash of cymbals, for instance. He swung suddenly on Miramon.

"What are you goggling at?"

The Hevian shut his mouth, flushing. "Your pardon. I was hoping to understand your instructions to your assistant, in the hope of being of some use. But you spoke in such incomprehensible terms that it sounded like a theological dispute. As for me, I never argue about politics or religion." He turned on his heel and stamped off through the trees.

Amalfi watched him go, cooling off gradually. This would never do. He must be getting to be an old man. All during the conversation he had felt his temper getting the better of his judgment, yet he had felt sodden and inert, unwilling to make the effort of opposing the momentum of his anger. At this rate, the City Fathers would soon depose him and appoint some stable character to the mayoralty—not Hazleton, certainly, but some unpoetic youngster who would play everything by empirics. Amalfi was in no position to be threatening anyone else with liquidation, even as a joke.

He walked toward the grounded city, heavy with sunlight, sunk in reflection. He was now about a thousand years old, give or take fifty; strong as an ox, mentally alert and "clear," in good hormone balance, all twenty-eight senses sharp, his own special psi faculty—orientation—still as infallible as ever, and all in all as sane as a compulsively peripatetic starman could be. The anti-agapics would keep him in this shape indefinitely, as far as anyone knew—but the problem of *patience* had never been solved.

The older a man became, the more quickly he saw answers to tough questions; and the less likely he was to tolerate slow thinking among his associates. If he were sane, his answers were generally right answers; if he were unsane, they were not; but what mattered was the speed of the thinking itself. In the end, both the sane and the unsane became equally dictatorial.

It was funny; before death had been conquered, it had been thought that memory would turn immortality into a Greek gift, because not even the human brain could remember a practical infinity of accumulated facts. Nowadays, however, nobody bothered to remember many *things*. That was what the City Fathers and like machines were for; they stored facts. Living men memorized nothing but processes, throwing out obsolete ones for new ones as invention made it necessary. When they needed facts, they asked the machines.

In some cases, even processes were thrown out, if there were simple, indestructible machines to replace them — the slide rule, for instance. Amalfi wondered suddenly if there were a single man in the city who could multiply, divide, take square root, or figure pH in his head or on paper. The thought was so novel as to be alarming — as alarming as if an ancient astrophysicist had seriously wondered how many of his colleagues could run an abacus.

No, memory was no problem. But it was very hard to be patient after a thousand years.

The bottom of a port drifted into his field of view, plastered with brown tendrils of mud. He looked up. The port was a small one, and in a part of the perimeter of the city a good distance away from the section where he had intended to go on board. Feeling like a stranger, he went in.

Inside, the corridor rang with bloodcurdling shrieks. It was as if someone were flaying a live dinosaur, or, better, a pack of them. Underneath the awful noises there was a sound like water being expelled under high pressure, and someone was laughing madly. Alarmed, Amalfi hunched his bull shoulders and burst through the nearest door.

Surely there had never been such a place in the city. It was a huge, steamy chamber, walled with some ceramic substance placed in regular tiles. The tiles were slimy, and stained; hence, old — very old.

Hordes of nude women ran aimlessly back and forth in it, screaming, battering at the wall, dodging wildly, or rolling on the mosaic floor. Every so often a thick stream of water caught one of them, bowling her howling away or driving her helplessly. Amalfi was soaking wet almost at once. The laughter got louder. Overhead, long banks of nozzles sprayed needles of mist into the air.

The mayor bent quickly, threw off his muddy shoes, and stalked the laughter, his toes gripping the slippery mosaic. The heavy column of water swerved toward him, then was jerked away again.

"John! Do you need a bath so badly? Come join the party!"

It was Dee Hazleton, the Utopian girl who had become the city manager's companion shortly before the crossing of the Rift had been undertaken. She was as nude as any of her victims, and was gleefully plying an enormous hose.

"Isn't this fun? We just got a new batch of these creatures. I got Mark to connect the old fire hose and I've been giving them their first wash."

It did not sound much like the old Dee, who had been full of solemn thoughts about politics — she had been a veritable commissar when Amalfi had first met her. He expressed his opinions of women who had lost their inhibitions so drastically. He went on at some length, and Dee made as if to turn the hose on him again.

"No, you don't," he growled, wresting it from her. It proved extremely hard to manage. "Where is this place, anyhow? I don't recall any such torture chamber in the plans."

"It was a public bath, Mark says. It's in the oldest part of the city, and Mark says it must have been just shut off when the city went aloft for the first time. I've been using it to sluice off these women before they're sent to Medical. The water is pumped in from the river to the west, so there's no waste involved."

"Water for bathing!" Amalfi said. "The ancients certainly were wasteful. Still I'd thought the static jet was older than that."

He surveyed the Hevian women, who were now huddling, temporarily reprieved, in the warmest part of the echoing chamber. None of them shared Dee's gently curved ripeness, but, as usual, some of them showed promise. Hazleton was prescient; it had to be granted. Of course it had been expectable that the Hevian would turn out to be human, for only eleven nonhuman civilizations had ever been discovered, and of these only the Lyrans and the Myrdians had any brains to speak of.

But to have had the Hevians turn over complete custody of their women to the Okies, without so much as a conference, at first contact — after Hazleton had proposed using any possible women as bindlestiff-bait — a proposal advanced before it had been established that there even was such a place as He —

Well, that was Hazleton's own psi gift — not true clairvoyance, but an

ability to pluck workable plans out of logically insufficient data. Time
after time only the seemingly miraculous working out of Hazleton's
plans had prevented his being shot by the blindly logical City Fathers.

"Dee, come to Astronomy with me," Amalfi said with sudden energy.
"I've got something to show you. And for my sake put on something, or
the men will think I'm out to found a dynasty."

"All right," Dee said reluctantly. She was not yet used to the odd Okie
standards of exposure, and sometimes appeared nude when it wasn't customary—a compensation, Amalfi supposed, for her Utopian upbring-
ing, where she had been taught that nudity had a deleterious effect upon
the purity of one's politics. The Hevian women moaned and hid their
heads while she put on her shorts—most of them had been stoned for in-
advertently covering themselves at one time or another, for in Hevian
society women were not people but reminders of damnation, doubly evil
for the slightest secrecy.

History, Amalfi thought, would be more instructive a teacher if it
were not so stupefyingly repetitious. He led the way up the corridor,
searching for a lift, Dee's wet soles padding cheerfully behind him.

In Astronomy, Jake was as usual peering wistfully at a nebula somewhere out on the marches of no-when, trying to make ellipses out of spirals without recourse to the Calculator. He looked up as Amalfi and the
girl entered.

"Hello," he said, dismally. "Amalfi, I really need some help here. How
can a man work without facts? If only you'd turn the City Fathers back
on—"

"Shortly. How long has it been since you looked back the way we
came, Jake?"

"Not since we started across the Rift. Why, should I have? The Rift is
just a scratch in a saucer; you need real distance to work on basic
problems."

"I know that. But let's take a look. I have an idea that we're not as
alone in the Rift as we thought."

Resignedly, Jake went to his control desk and thumbed buttons.
"What do you expect to find?" he demanded, his voice petulant. "A haze
of iron filings, or a stray meson? Or a fleet of police cruisers?"

"Well," Amalfi said, pointing to the screen, "those aren't wine bottles."

The police cruisers, so close that the light of He's sun twinkled on their sides, shot across the screen in a brilliant stream, long tails of false photons striping the Rift behind them.

"So they aren't," Jake said, not much interested. "Now may I have my scope back, Amalfi?"

Amalfi only grinned. Cops or no cops, he felt young again.

Hazleton was mud up to the thighs. Long ribands of it trailed behind him as he hurtled up the lift shaft to the control tower. Amalfi watched him coming, noting the set whiteness of the city manager's face as he looked up at Amalfi's bending head.

"What's this about cops?" Hazleton demanded while still in flight. "The message didn't get to me straight. We were raided, all hell's broken loose everywhere. I nearly didn't get here straight myself." He sprang into the chamber, his boots shedding gummy clods.

"I saw the fighting. Looks like the Moving Day rumor reached the 'stiffs, all right."

"Sure. What's this about cops?"

"The cops are here. They're coming in from the northwest quadrant, already off overdrive, and should be here day after tomorrow."

"Surely they're not after us," Hazleton said. "And I can't see why they should come all this distance after the 'stiffs. They must have had to use deep sleep to make it. And we didn't say anything about the no-fuel drive in our alarm 'cast—"

"We didn't have to," Amalfi said. "Someday I must tell you the parable of the diseased bee—as soon as I figure out what a bee is. In the meantime things are breaking fast. We have to keep an eye on every-thing, and be able to jump in any direction no matter which item on the agenda comes up first. How bad is the fighting?"

"Very bad. At least five of the local bandit towns are in on it, includ-ing Fabr-Suithe, of course. Two of them mount heavy stuff, about con-temporary with the Hruntan Empire in its heyday . . . ah, I see you know that already. Well, it's supposed to be a holy war on us. We're meddling with the jungle and interfering with their chances for salvation-through-suffering, or something—I didn't stop to dispute the point."

"That's bad; it will convince some of the civilized towns, too—I doubt that Fabr-Suithe really believes the religious line, they've thrown all that overboard, but it makes wonderful propaganda."

"You're right there. Only a few of the civilized towns, the ones that have been helping us from the beginning, are putting up a stiff fight. Almost everyone else, on both sides, is sitting it out waiting for us to cut each other's throat. Our handicap is that we lack mobility. If we could persuade all the civilized towns to come in on our side we wouldn't need it, but so many of them are scared."

"The enemy lacks mobility, too, until the bindlestiff is ready to take a direct hand," Amalfi said thoughtfully. "Have you seen any signs that the tramps are in on the fighting?"

"Not yet. But it can't be long now. And we don't even know where they are!"

"They'll be forced to locate themselves today or tomorrow, I'm certain. Right now I want you to muster all the rehabilitated women we have on hand and get ready to spring your scheme. As soon as I get a fix on the bindlestiff I'll locate the nearest participating bandit town, and you can do the rest."

Hazleton's eyes, very weary until now, began to glitter with amusement. "And how about Moving Day?" he said. "You know, of course — you know everything — that not one of your stress-fluid plugs is going to hold with the work this incomplete."

"I'm counting on it," Amalfi said tranquilly. "We'll spin when the time comes. If a few plugs spring high, wide, and tall, I won't weep."

"How—"

The Dinwiddie Watch blipped sharply, and both men turned to look at the screen. There was a fountain of green dots on it. Hazleton took three quick steps and turned on the coordinates, which he had had readjusted to the butterfly grid.

"Well, where are they?" Amalfi demanded.

"Right smack in the middle of the southwestern continent, in that vine jungle where the little chigger-snakes nest—the ones that burrow under your fingernails. There's supposed to be a lake of boiling mud on that spot."

"There probably is—they could be under it with a medium-light screen."

"All right, we've got them placed—but what are they shooting up?"

"Mines, I suspect," Amalfi said.

"That's dandy," Hazleton said bitterly. "They'll leave an escape lane for themselves, of course, but we'll never be able to find it. They've got us under a plutonium umbrella, Amalfi."

"We'll get out. Go plant your women, Mark. And—put some clothes on 'em first. They'll make more of a show that way."

"You bet they will," the city manager said feelingly. He went out.

Amalfi went out on the balcony. At moments of crisis, his old predilection for seeing and hearing and breathing the conflict, with his senses unfiltered and unheightened by any instruments, became too strong to resist. There was good reason for the drive, for that matter; excitement of the everyday senses had long ago been shown to bring his orientation sense to its best pitch.

From the balcony of City Hall, most of the northwest quadrant of the perimeter was visible. There were plenty of battle noises rattling the garish tropical sunset there, and even an occasional tiny toppling figure. The city had adopted the local dodge of clearing and gelling the mud at its rim, and had returned the gel to the morass state at the first sign of attack; but the jungle men had broad skis, of some metal no Hevian could have fashioned so precisely. Disks of red fire marked bursting TDX shells, scything the air like death's own winnows. No gas was in evidence, but Amalfi knew that there would be gas before long.

The city's retaliatory fire was largely invisible, since it emerged below the top of the perimeter. There was a Bethé fender out, which would keep the wall from being scaled—until one of the projectors was knocked out; and plenty of heavy rifles were being kept hot. But the city had never been designed for warfare, and many of its most efficient destroyers had their noses buried in the earth, since their intended function was only to clear a landing area. Using an out-and-out Bethé blaster was, of course, impossible where there was an adjacent planetary mass.

He sniffed the scarlet edges of the struggle appraisingly. Under his fingers on the balcony railing were three buttons, which he had had placed there four hundred years ago. They had set in motion different things at different times. But each time, they had represented choices of action which he would have to make when the pinch came; he had never had reason to have a fourth button installed.

Rockets screamed overhead. Bombs followed, crepitating bursts of noise and smoke and flying metal. He did not look up; the very mild spindizzy screen would fend off anything moving that rapidly. Only slow-moving objects, like men, could sidle through a polarized gravitic field. He looked out to the horizon, touching the buttons very delicately.

Suddenly the sunset snuffed itself out. Amalfi, who had never seen a tropical sunset before coming to He, felt a vague alarm, but as far as he could see the abrupt darkness was natural, if startling. The fighting went on, the flying disks of TDX much more lurid now against the blackness.

After a while there was a dogfight far aloft, identifiable mostly by traceries of jet trails and missiles. The jungle jammered derision and fury without any letup.

Amalfi stood, his senses reaching out slowly, feeling the positions of things. It was hard work, for he had never tried to grasp a situation at such close quarters before, and the trajectory of every shell tried to capture his attention.

About an hour past midnight, at the height of the heaviest raid yet, he felt a touch at his elbow.

"Boss—"

Amalfi heard the word as if it had been uttered at the bottom of the Rift. The still-ascending fountain of space mines had just been touched, and he was trying to reach the top of it; somewhere up there the trumpet flattened into a shell encompassing the whole of He, and it was important to know how high up that network of orbits began.

But the utter exhaustion of the voice touched something deeper. He said, "Yes, Mark."

"It's done. We lost almost everybody. But we caused a very nice riot." A ghost of animation stirred in the voice for a moment. "You should have been there."

"I'm—almost there now. Good . . . work, Mark. Get . . . some rest."

"Sure. But—"

Something very heavy described a searing hyperbola in Amalfi's mind, and then the whole city was a scramble of magnesium-white and ink. As the light faded, there was a formless spreading and crawling, utterly beyond any detection but Amalfi's.

"Gas alarm, Mark," he heard himself saying. "Hawkesite . . . barium suits for everybody."

"Yes. Right. Boss, you'll kill yourself running things this way."

Amalfi found that he could not answer. He had found the town where the women had been dropped. Nothing clear came through, but there was certainly a riot there, and it was not entirely within the town itself. Tendrils of movement were being turned back from the Okie city, and were weaving out from places where there had been no sign of activity before.

At the base of the mine fountain, something else new was happening. A mass rose slowly, and there was a thick flowing around it. Then it stopped, and there was a sense of doors opening, heavy potentials moving out into tangled desolation. The tramps were leaving their city. The unmistakable, slightly nauseating sensation of a spindizzy field under medium drive domed the boiling of the lake of mud.

Dawn coming now. The riot in the town where the women were still would not come clear, but it was getting worse rather than better. Abruptly there was no town there at all, but a boiling, mushrooming pillar of radioactive gas — the place had been bombed. The struggle moved back toward the area of tension that marked the location of the bindlestiff.

Amalfi's own city was shrouded in sick orange mist, lit with flashes of no-color. The gas could not pass the spindizzy screen in a body, but it diffused through, molecule by heavy molecule. He realized suddenly that he had not heeded his own gas warning, and that there was probably some harm coming to him; but he could not localize it. He moved slightly, and instantly felt himself incased. What—

Barium paste. Hazleton had known that Amalfi could not leave the balcony, and evidently had plastered him with the stuff in default of trying to get a suit on him. Even his eyes were covered, and a feeling of distension in his nostrils bespoke a Kolman respirator.

The emotional and gravitic tensions in the bindlestiff city continued to gather; it would soon be unbearable. Above, just outside the space mines, the first few police vessels were sidling in cautiously. The war in the jungle had already fallen into meaninglessness. The abduction of the women from the Hevian town by the tramps had collapsed all Hevian rivalry; bandits and civilized towns alike were bent now upon nothing but the destruction of Fabr-Suithe and its allies. Fabr-Suithe could hold them off for a long time, but it was clearly time for the bindlestiff to leave — time for it to make off with its women and its anti-agapics and its germanium, time for it to lose itself in the Rift before the Earth police could invest all of He.

The tension knotted suddenly, painfully, and rose away from the boiling mud. The 'stiff was taking off. Amalfi pressed the button—the only one, this time, that had been connected to anything.

Moving Day began.

V

It began with six pillars of glaring white, forty miles in diameter, that burst through the soft soil at every compass point of He. Fabr-Suithe had sat directly over the site of one of them. The bandit town was nothing but a flake of ash in a split second, a curled flake borne aloft on the top of a white-hot piston.

The pillars lunged roaring into the heavens, fifty, a hundred, two hundred miles, and burst at their tops like popcorn. The sky burned thermite-blue with steel meteors. Outside, the space mines, cut off from the world of which they had been satellites by the greatest spindizzy screen of all time, fled into the Rift.

And when the meteors had burned away, the sun was growing.

The world of He was on overdrive, its magnetic moment transformed, expressed as momentum; it was the biggest city ever flown. There was no time to feel alarmed. The sun flashed by and was dwindling to a point before the fact could be grasped. It was gone. The far wall of the Rift began to swell, and separate into individual points of light.

Appalled, Amalfi fought to grasp the scale of speed. He failed. The planet of He was moving, that was all he could comprehend; its speed gulped light-years like gnats. Even to think of controlling so stupendous a flight was ridiculous.

Stars began to wink past He like fireflies. Then they were all behind.

The surface of the saucer that was the galaxy receded.

"Boss, we're going out of the—"

"I know it. Get me a fix on the Hevian sun before it's too late."

Hazleton worked feverishly. It took him only three minutes, but during those three minutes, the massed stars receded far enough so that the gray scar of the Rift became plain, as a definite mark on a spangled ground. The Hevian sun was less than an atom in it.

"Got it. But we can't swing the planet back. It'll take us two thousand years to cross to the next galaxy. We'll have to abandon He, boss, or we're sunk."

"All right. Get us aloft. Full drive."

"Our contract—"

"Fulfilled—take my word for it. Spin!"

The city screamed and sprang aloft. The planet of He did not dwindle—it simply vanished, snuffed out in the intergalactic gap. It was the first of the pioneers.

Amalfi took the controls, the barium casing cracking and falling away from him as he moved. The air still stank of Hawkesite, but the concentration of the gas already had been taken down below the harmful level by the city's purifiers. The mayor began to edge the city away from the vector of He's movement and the city's own, back toward the home lens.

Hazleton stirred restlessly.

"Your conscience bothering you, Mark?"

"Maybe," Hazleton said. "Is there some escape clause in our contract that lets us run off like this? If there is I missed it, and I read the fine print pretty closely."

"No, no escape clause," Amalfi said, shifting the space stick delicately. "The Hevians won't be hurt. The spindizzy screen will protect them from loss of heat and atmosphere—their volcanoes will supply more heat than they'll need, and their technology is up to artificial UV generation. But they won't be able to put out enough UV to keep the jungle alive. By the time they reach the Andromedan star that suits them, they'll understand the spindizzy principle well enough to set up a proper orbit. Or maybe they'll like roaming better by then, and decide to be an Okie planet. Either way, we did what we promised to do, fair and square."

"We didn't get paid," the city manager pointed out. "And it'll take our last reserves to get back to any part of our own galaxy. The bindlestiff got off, and got carried 'way out of range of the cops in the process—with plenty of dough, women, everything."

"No, they didn't," Amalfi said. "They blew up the moment we moved He."

"All right," Hazleton said resignedly. "You could detect that; I'll take your word for it. But you'd better be able to explain it."

"It's not hard to explain. The 'stiffs had captured Dr. Beetle. I was pretty sure they would. They came to He for no other reason. They needed the fuelless drive, and they knew Dr. Beetle had it, because of the agronomists' SOS. So they snatched him when he landed — notice how they made a big fuss about the *other* agronomist life ship, to divert our attention? — and worked the secret out of him."

"So?"

"So," Amalfi said, "they forgot that any Okie city always has passengers like Dr. Beetle — people with big ideas only partially worked out, ideas that need the finishing touches that can only be provided by some other culture. After all, a man doesn't take passage on an Okie city unless he's a third-rate sort of person, hoping to make his everlasting fortune on some planet where the people know less than he does."

Hazleton scratched his head ruefully. "That's right. We had the same experience with the Lyrian invisibility machine. It didn't work, until we took that Hruntan physicist on board; he had the necessary extra knowledge — but he couldn't have discovered the principle himself, either."

"Exactly. The 'stiffs were in too much of a hurry. They didn't carry their stolen fuelless drive with them until they found some culture which could perfect it. They tried to use it right away — they were lazy. And they tried to use it inside the biggest spindizzy field ever generated. It blew up. If we hadn't left them parsecs behind in a split second, it would have blown up He at the same time."

Hazleton sighed and began to plot the probable point at which the city would return to its own galaxy. It turned out to be a long way away from the Rift, in an area that, after a mental wrench to visualize it backwards from the usual orientation, promised a fair population.

"Look," he said, "we'll hit about where the last few waves of the Acolytes settled — remember the Night of Hadjjii?"

Amalfi didn't, since he hadn't been born then, nor had Hazleton; but he remembered the history, which was what the city manager had meant. With a sidelong glance, he leaned forward, resumed the helmet he had cast aside a year ago, and turned on the City Fathers.

The helmet phone shrilled with alarm. "All right, all right," he growled. "What is it?"

"MAYOR AMALFI, HAVE YOU TIPPED THIS PLANET?"

"No," Amalfi said. "We sent it on its way as it was."

There was a short silence, humming with computation. "VERY WELL.
WE MUST NOW SELECT THE POINT AT WHICH WE LEAVE THE RIFT. STAND
BY FOR DETERMINATION."

Amalfi and Hazleton grinned at each other. Amalfi said, "We're coming in on the last Acolyte stars. Give us a determination for the present
setup there, please—"

"YOU ARE MISTAKEN. THAT AREA IS NOWHERE NEAR THE RIFT. WE WILL
GIVE YOU A DETERMINATION FOR THE FAR RIFT WALL: STAND BY."

Amalfi removed the headset gently.

"That," he said, moving the phone away from his mouth, "was long
ago—and far away."

Open Loops

STEPHEN BAXTER

Inhabiting the high vacuum brings forth ready analogies to evolutionary leaps. Once fish ventured up onto land, carrying as much of the ocean with them as they could. They still held fluids inside for bodily regulation and to thwart dehydration. Space stations will probably follow similar strategies, creating an almost claustrophobic air. In Baxter's story, written for this volume, we see the implications of such evolutionary metaphors painted against the full cosmological landscape.

I*t began, in fact, with a supernova: thus, from the beginning, it was a causal chain shaped by stupendous violence.*

The star was a blue supergiant, twenty times the mass of Earth's sun, fifty thousand times as bright. It had formed a mere million years ago.

Nevertheless there was life here.

It had come drifting on the interstellar winds from older, more stable systems, and taken root on worlds which cautiously skirted the central fire.

But the hydrogen fuel in the star's fusing core was already exhausted.

The core of the star, clogged with helium ash, began to burn that ash itself, helium nuclei fusing to carbon. And the carbon compacted to neon, the neon to oxygen . . . At last, iron nuclei snowed, inert, on the center of the star.

The core's free-fall implosion took fractions of a second. The star's outer layers were suddenly suspended over an effective vacuum.

They collapsed inward, the infalling layers crashing onto the rigid core remnant, and rebounded violently. The reflected shock wave was hurled out of the center of the star, dragging away the star's outer layers with it . . .

For a week, the dying star outshone its galaxy.

For forty years the expanding shell of matter traveled, preceded by a sleet of electromagnetic radiation: gamma rays, X rays, visible light. A human eye might have seen a brilliant blue-white star grow suddenly tremendously luminous: fifty times as bright as the moon, as bright as all the other stars in the sky combined.

But Earth did not exist, nor even, yet, the sun. The garish light of the supernova washed, instead, over the thin tendrils of a gas cloud: cold, inert, stable.

And in any event no human telescope could have detected, rushing before the light storm, a single, delicate, spidery silhouette.

A fleeing craft.

Scale: Exp 1

In the confines of *Ehricke's* airlock Oliver Greenberg put on his gloves and snapped home the connecting rings. Then he lifted his helmet over his head.

The ritual of the suit checklist was oddly comforting. In fact, it was just the old shuttle EVA routine he'd undergone a half-dozen times, in an orbiter-class airlock just like this.

But the *Ehricke* was no dinged-up old orbiter, and right now he was far from low Earth orbit.

He felt his heart hammer under his suit's layers.

Mike Weissman, on the hab module's upper deck, was monitoring him. "EV1, you have a go for depress."

Greenberg turned the depress switch on the control panel. "Valve to zero." He heard a distant hiss. "Let's motor." He twisted the handle of the outer airlock hatch and pushed.

Oliver Greenberg gazed out into space.

He moved out through the airlock's round hatchway. There was a handrail and two slide wires that ran the length of the curving hull, and Greenberg tethered himself to them. It was a routine he'd practiced a hundred times in the sims at Houston, a dozen times in LEO. There was no reason why now should be any different.

No reason, except that the Earth wasn't where it should be.

In LEO, the Earth had been a bright floor beneath him all the time, as bright as a tropical sky. But out here, Earth was all of five million kilometers away, reduced to a blue button the size of a dime three or four arm's lengths away, and Greenberg was suspended in a huge three-hundred-sixty-degree planetarium just studded with stars, stars everywhere...

Everywhere, that is, except for one corner of the sky blocked by a vaguely elliptical shadow, sharp-edged, one rim picked out by the sun.

It was Ra-Shalom: Greenberg's destination.

He was looking along the length of the *Ehricke*'s hab module. It was a tight cylinder, just ten meters long and seven wide, home to four crew for this year-long jaunt. The outer hull was crammed with equipment, sensors and antennas clustered over powder-white and gold insulating blankets. At the back of the hab module he could see the bulging upper domes of the big cryogenic fuel tanks, and when he turned the other way, there was the Earth-return module, an Apollo-sized capsule stuck sideways under the canopy of the big aerobrake.

The whole thing was just a collection of cylinders and boxes and canopies, thrown together as if at random, a ropy piece of shit.

But in a vessel such as this, Americans planned to sail to Mars.

Not Oliver Greenberg, though.

One-small-step time, he thought.

He pulled himself tentatively along the slide wire and made his way to the PMU station, on the starboard side of the hab module. The Personal Maneuvering Unit was a big backpack shaped like the back and arms of an armchair, with foldout head and leg rests on a tubular frame. Greenberg ran a quick check of the PMU's systems. It was old shuttle technology, cannibalized from the Manned Maneuvering Units that had enabled crew to shoot around orbiter cargo bays. But today, it was being put to a use its designers never dreamed of.

He turned around, and backed into the PMU.

"*Ehricke*, EV1," he said. "Suit latches closed."

"Copy that."

He pulled the PMU's arms out around him and closed his gloved hands around the hand controllers on the end of the arms. He unlatched the folded-up body frame. He rested his neck against the big padded rest, and settled his feet against the narrow footpads at the bottom of the frame, so he was braced. Today's EVA was just a test reconnaissance, but a full field expedition to Ra could last all of eight hours; the frame would help him keep his muscle movements down, and so reduce resource wasteage.

Greenberg released his tethers. A little spring-loaded gadget gave him a shove in the back, gentle as a mother's encouraging pat, and he floated away from the bulkhead.

. . . suddenly he didn't have hold of anything, and he was *falling*.

Oh, shit, he thought.

He had become an independent spacecraft. The spidery frame of the PMU occulted the dusting of stars around him.

He tested out his propulsion systems.

He grasped his right-hand controller and pushed it left. There was a soft tone in his helmet as the thruster worked; he saw a faint sparkle of exhaust crystals to his right. In response to the thrust, he tipped a little to the left. He had four big fuel tanks on his back, and twenty-four small reaction control system nozzles. In fact he had two systems, a heavy-duty hot gas bipropellant system — kerosene and nitric acid — for the big orbital changes he would have to make to reach Ra, and a cold-gas nitrogen thruster for close control at the surface of the rock.

When he started moving, he just kept on going, until he stopped himself with another blip of his thrusters.

Greenberg tipped himself up so he was facing Ra-Shalom, with the *Ehricke* behind him.

"*Ehricke*, I'm preparing to head for Ra."

"We copy, Oliver."

He fired his kerosene thruster and felt a small, firm shove in the small of his back. Computer graphics started to scroll across the inside of his faceplate, updating burn parameters. He was actually changing orbit here, and he would have to go through a full rendezvous procedure to reach Ra.

That was what had got him this job, in fact. Greenberg had flown several of the missions which docked a shuttle orbiter with the old *Mir*, and then with *Alpha*. He had even been chief astronaut for a while.

Then the *VentureStar* had outdated his piloting skills, and he was grounded, at age fifty.

NASA was full of younger guys now, preparing for the LMP, the Lunar-Mars Program that was at the heart of NASA's current strategy, inspired by the evidence the sample-return probes had come up with of life on Mars.

This mission, a year-long jaunt to the near-Earth asteroid Ra-Shalom, was a shakedown test of the technologies that would be needed to get to Mars. Ra provided an intermediate goal, between lunar flights of a few weeks and the full Mars venture that would take years, setting major challenges in terms of life-support loop closure and systems reliability.

But there was also, he was told, good science to be done here.

Not that he gave a shit about that.

He was only here, tinkering with plumbing and goddamn pea plants, because nobody else in the office had wanted to be distracted from the competition for places on the Mars flights to come.

The angle of the sun was changing, and the slanting light changed Ra from a flat silhouette to a potato-shaped rock in space, fat and solid. Ra's surface was crumpled, split by ravines, punctured by craters of all sizes. There was one big baby that must have been a kilometer across, its walls spreading around the cramped horizon.

The rock was more than three kilometers long, spinning on its axis once every twenty hours. It was as black as coal dust. Ra-Shalom was a C-type asteroid—carbonaceous, fat with light elements, coated by carbon deposits. It had probably formed at the chilly outer rim of the asteroid belt. Ra was like a folded-over chunk of the moon, its beat-up surface a record of this little body's dismal, violent history.

At a computer prompt, he prepared for his final burn. "Ready for terminal initiation."

"Copy that, Oliver."

One last time the kerosene thrusters fired, fat and full.

"Okay, EV1, *Ehricke*. Coming up to your hundred-meter limit."

"Copy that."

He came to a dead stop a hundred meters from the surface of Ra-Shalom. The asteroid's complex, battered surface was like a wall in front of him. He felt no tug of gravity — Ra's g was less than a thousandth of Earth's — it would take him more than two minutes to fall to the surface from here, compared with a few seconds on Earth.

He was comfortable. The suit was quiet, warm, safe. He could hear the whir of his backpack's twenty-thousand rpm fan. But he missed the squeaks and pops on the radio which he got used to in LEO as he drifted over UHF stations on the ground.

He blipped his cold-gas thrusters and drifted forward. This wasn't like coming in for a landing; it was more like walking toward a cliff face, which bulged gently out at him, its coal-like blackness oppressive. He made out more detail, craters overlaid on craters down to the limit of visibility.

He tweaked his trajectory once more, until he was heading for the center of a big crater, away from any sharp-edged crater walls or boulder fields. Then he just let himself drift in, at a meter a second. If he used the thrusters anymore, he risked raising dust clouds that wouldn't settle. There were four little landing legs at the corners of his frame; they popped out now, little spear-shaped penetrators designed to dig into the surface and hold him there.

The close horizon receded, and the cliff face turned into a wall that cut off half the universe.

He collided softly with Ra-Shalom.

The landing legs, throwing up dust, dug into the regolith with a grind that carried through the PMU structure. The dust hung about him. Greenberg was stuck here, clinging to the wall inside his PMU frame like a mountaineer to a rock face.

He turned on his helmet lamp. Impact glass glimmered.

Unexpectedly, wonder pricked him. Here was the primordial skin of Ra-Shalom, as old as the solar system, just centimeters before his face. He reached out and pushed his gloved hand into the surface, a monkey paw probing.

The surface was thick with regolith: a fine rock flour, littered with glassy agglutinates, asteroid rock shattered by eons of bombardment. His fingers went in easily enough for a few centimeters — he could feel the stuff crunching under his pressure, as if he were digging into compacted snow—but then he came up against much more densely packed material, tamped down by the endless impacts.

He closed his fist and pulled out his hand. A cloud of dust came with it, gushing into his face like a hail of meteorites. He looked at the material he'd dug out. There were a few bigger grains here, he saw: it was breccia, bits of rock smashed up in multiple impacts, welded back together by impact glass. There was no gravity to speak of; the smallest movement sent the fragments drifting out of his palm.

His glove, pristine white a moment ago, was already caked black with dust. He knew the blackness came from carbon-rich compounds. There were hydrates too: water, locked up in the rock, just drifting around out here. In fact rocks like Ra were the only significant water deposits between Earth and Mars. It might prove possible to use the rock's resources to close the loops of mass and energy circulating in *Ehricke*'s life support, even on this preliminary jaunt.

Ra could probably even support some kind of colony, off in the future. So it was said.

Greenberg had always preferred to leave the sci-fi stuff to the wackos in the fringe study groups in NASA, and focus on his checklist. Still, it was a nice thought.

He allowed himself a moment to savor this triumph. Maybe he would never get to Mars. But he was, after all, the first human to touch the surface of another world since Apollo 17.

He pushed his hand back into the pit he'd dug, ignoring the fresh dust he raised.

The cloud was scattered, thin and dark, across ten light-years. It was gas laced with dust grains—three-quarters hydrogen, the rest helium, some trace elements—visible only to any observers as a shadow against the stars.

When the supernova's gale of heavy particles washed over it, the cloud's stability was lost. It began to fall in on itself.

In a ghostly inverse of the inciting supernova explosion, the core of the cloud heated up as material rained in upon it, its rotation speeding up, an increasingly powerful electromagnetic field whipping through the outer debris. The core began to glow, first at infrared wavelengths, and then in visible light.

It was the first sunlight.

Scale: Exp 2

Oliver Greenberg was bored.

He was actually glad to get the call from Gita Weissman about the balky rock splitter in shaft 7, even though the lost time would mean they weren't going to make quota this month.

At least it made a change from the usual CELSS problems, CELSS for closed environment and life-support systems, a term nobody used except him anymore. Even after a century, nobody had persuaded a pea plant to grow nice straight roots in microgravity, and the loss from the mass loops in the hydroponic tanks continued at a stubborn couple of percent a month, despite the new generation of supercritical water oxidizers they used to reduce their solid wastes.

It's still about pea plants and plumbing, he thought dismally.

He started clambering into his skinsuit, hauling the heavy fabric over his useless legs.

He took a last glance around the glass-wall displays of his hab module. It shocked him when the displays showed him he was the only one of Ra's two thousand inhabitants on the surface.

Well, hell, it suited him out here, even if it had stranded him in this lonely assignment, monitoring the systems that watched near-Ra space. Most of the inhabitants of Ra had been born up here, and lived their lives encased in the fused-regolith walls of old mine shafts. They didn't know any better.

Greenberg, though, preferred to keep a weather eye on the stars, unchanged since his Iowa boyhood. He even liked seeing Earth swim past on its infrequent close approaches, like a blue liner on a black ocean, approaching and receding. It made him nostalgic. Even if he couldn't go home anymore.

Suited up, he shut down the glass-wall displays. The drab green walls of the hab module were revealed, with their equipment racks and antique bathroom and galley equipment and clumsy-looking up-down visual cues. This was just an old space station module, dragged out here and stuck to the surface of Ra-Shalom, covered over with a couple of meters of regolith. He was tethered in the rim shadow of Helin Crater, the place he'd landed on that first jaunt in the *Ehricke*. And that had been all of a hundred years ago, my God.

He pushed his way through the diaphragm lock set in the floor of his hab module. He was at the top of shaft 2, one of the earliest they'd dug out, with those first clumsy drill-blast-muck miners. It was a rough cylinder ten meters across, lined with regolith glass and hung with lamps and tethers; it descended beneath him, branching and curving.

He grabbed hold of a wall spider, told it his destination, and let it haul him on down into the tunnel along its stay wires.

Thus, clinging to his metal companion, he descended into the heart of Ra-Shalom.

His legs dangled uselessly, and so he set his suit to tuck them up to his chest. He was thinking of taking the surgeons' advice and opting for amputation. What the hell. He was a hundred and fifty years old, give or take; he wasn't going to start complaining.

Anyhow, apart from that, the surgeons were preserving him pretty well. They were treating him to a whole cocktail of growth hormones and DHEA and melatonin treatments and beta-carotene supplements, not to mention telomere therapy and the glop those little nanomachines had painted on the surface of his shriveled-up brain to keep him sharp.

These guys were good at keeping you alive.

This asteroid was *small*. A stable population was important, and a heavy investment in training needed a long payback period to be effective. So the birthrate was low, and a lot of research was directed to human longevity.

He understood the logic. Still, he missed the sound of children playing, every now and again. The youngsters here didn't seem to mind that, which made them a little less than human, in his view. But maybe that was part of the adjustment humans were having to make, as they learned to life off-Earth.

In fact he missed his own kids, his daughters, even though, astonishingly, they were now both old ladies themselves.

The surgeons had even managed to repair some of the cumulative microgravity damage he'd suffered over the years. For instance, his skeletal and cardiac muscles were deeply atrophied. Until they found a way to stabilize it, his bone calcium had continued to wash out in his urine, at a half percent a month. At last, the surgeons said, the inner spongy bone, the trabeculae, had vanished altogether, without hope of regeneration.

He never had been too conscientious about his time in the treadmills. It had left him a cripple, on Earth.

So, at age eighty, he'd left Earth.

Even then they had been closing down the cans — the early stations starting with *Mir* and *ISS*, that had relied completely on materials brought up from Earth. In retrospect it just didn't make sense to haul material up from Earth at great expense, when it was already *here*, just floating around in the sky, in rocks like Ra.

So he'd come back to come out to Ra-Shalom, the place that had made him briefly famous.

He suspected the surgeons liked to have him around, as a control experiment. The youngsters were heavily treated from birth, up here, to enable them to endure a lifetime of microgravity. Not a one of them could land on Earth, of course, or even Mars. But not too many of them showed a desire to do any such thing.

The wall spider, scuttling busily, brought him to the mine face, the terminus of shaft 7. It was a black, dusty wall, like a coal face. There was dust everywhere, floating in the air.

There were five or six people here, in their brightly colored skinsuits, scraping their way around the stalled miner. Their suits were seamless and without folds, to guard against the dust. They were all tall, their limbs spindly as all hell, their skeletal structures pared down as far as they would go.

The miner itself clung to the walls with a dozen fat legs, with the balky rock splitter itself held out on a boom before the face. It was a radial-axial design with a percussive drill, powered by hydraulics, with a drill feed, a radial splitter, and a loader. But for now it was inert.

One of the youngsters came up to him. It was Gita Weissman, Mike's granddaughter. She grinned through her translucent faceplate; her skinsuit was what they used to call Day-Glo orange.

"Dust," she said. "It's always the dust."

"Yeah."

"Grab a pump. We want to get this baby back on line or we'll miss quota again."

He started to prepare a vacuum pump tube.

The "dust" was surface rock flour: half of it invisible to the naked eye, abrasive and electrostatically sticky. Despite their best efforts it had got all the way through the interior workings of Ra, coating every surface.

A lot of Earthbound experience was worthless up here. No machine, for example, which used its own weight for leverage was going to be any use up here. Nevertheless, some terrestrial technologies, like coal gasification, had proven to be good bases for development of systems that gave a low capital investment and a fast payback.

Greenberg remembered how they'd celebrated when the ore processors had first started up, and water had come trickling out of crushed and heated asteroid cinder. It had touched, he supposed, something deep and human, some atavistic response to the presence of water here, the stuff of life in this ancient rock from space.

Whatever, it had been one terrific party.

And this rock, and many others like it, had proven to be as rich as those old sci-fi-type dreamers, who Greenberg used to laugh at, had hoped. Ra was fat with water—twenty percent of its mass, locked up in hydrate minerals and in subsurface ice. It exported kerogen, a tarry petrochemical compound found in oil shales, which contained a good balance of nutrients: primordial soup, they called it. Ra pumped out hydrogen, methane, kerosene, and methanol for propellants, and carbon monoxide, hydrogen, and methane combinations to support metal processing…

And so on.

Ra was just a big volatiles warehouse floating around in the sky. And with the big surface mass drivers that Greenberg called softball pitchers, Ra products were shipped to places that were volatile-poor—like Mars, lacking nitrogen, and the moon, dry as a desert. It was a *lot* cheaper to export them from a rock floating around up here than from all the way at the bottom of Earth's gravity well.

To Greenberg's great surprise, Ra's inhabitants had become rich.

The first justification for opening up the rocks had been to make them serve as short-term resource factories to aid in the colonization of the moon, Mars, and beyond. But it wasn't working out like that. Sure, the gravity well colonies were in place, but they were hardly thriving; they were always going to be dependent on key volatiles shipped in from somewhere else. And they didn't have much to trade; Ra could purchase high-grade metals much more cheaply from other rocks.

There were actually more humans living in the rocks now than on the moon or Mars. And Ra had more trade with other rocks than anybody else — even Earth . . .

He saw there was one articulated joint on the splitter boom that was giving particular problems; its prophylactic cover had been taken off, revealing a knobby joint with big, easily replaced parts, already half dismantled, like the knee joint of a *T. rex*.

The youngsters were talking about more advances in technology. Like nanotech miners which would chomp their way through the rock without any human intervention at all. Greenberg kind of hoped it wouldn't be for a while, though; he preferred machinery big enough to see, and wrestle with. It gave him a purpose, a reason to use the upper-body strength he'd brought up from Earth.

The workers got out of the way of him, and, whistling, he moved into the balky joint with his vacuum line.

Screw Mars, he thought as he worked; he *liked* it here.

The remnant of the cloud molded itself into a flattened, rotating disk. Solid particles condensed: ices of water and hydrocarbons in the cooler, outer rim, but only rocky debris in the hot, churning heart of the nebula. Planetesimals formed, massive, misshapen bodies that collided and accreted as they raced around the new Sun.

And, out of the collisions, planets grew: rocky worlds in the hot center, volatile-fat giants farther out. A powerful wind blew from the Sun, violently ejecting the amniotic remnants of the birth cloud. Planetesimals rained down on the surfaces of the new worlds, leaving scars that would persist for billions of years.

The gravity of young Jupiter plucked at the belt of planetesimals farther in, preventing their coalescence into larger bodies. So, in the gap between Jupiter and Mars, the planetesimals survived as asteroids: rocky chunks closest to the sun, volatile-rich snowballs at the outer rim, molded by impacts with one another, melted by radioactivity and electrical induction.

And it was to the asteroids that the starship came: after billions of years drifting like a seed between the stars, still running from the supernova, exhausted, depleted, its ancient machinery cradling the generations that swarmed within, evolving, never understanding their plight.

Scale: Exp 3

The nanobugs woke him; with reluctance he swam up from dreams of sunlit days with his daughters on the beaches of Galveston.

He emerged into a gritty, unwelcome reality. Here he was: half a man, with his whole lower body replaced by the gleaming box he called his PMU, pipes and tubes everywhere, still rattling around inside his clumsy old hab module.

Not that there could be much left of his original home. That old NASA stuff had mostly worn out after a decade, let alone a thousand years. But the Weissmans, or anyhow the robots they'd assigned to keeping him alive, quietly rebuilt this old box around him, just as they rebuilt him continually, nanobugs crawling through his body while he slept away the years.

Well, the hell with it. He dug out a packet of food—the label said chicken soup, and as far as he was concerned that was what it was—and he shoved it into the rehydration drawer of his galley.

He moved to a window, the little nitrogen reaction-control squirters on his PMU hissing softly. The window gave onto a shaft cut through the regolith, which had a massive lid that would swing down on him in case of a solar flare or some such. It gave him a good view of the surface of Ra-Shalom, and a slice of the nightside of Earth, and a handful of stars.

Water-blue light glared out of Ra.

When he'd first come here, Ra had been just a lump of dirty carbonaceous stone. Now, the old craters and ravines transformed into a patchwork of windows, roofed over with some kind of smart membrane.

Greenberg could see into the lenslike surface of one of the crater windows. And right now, a few minutes from the aerobraking of *Toutatis*, the Weissmans were swimming up from the big spherical ocean they were building in the hollowed-out interior of Ra, swimming up to watch a light show hardly any of them understood, probably.

The Weissmans came in a variety of shapes. There were even still a few standard-issue four-limbed humans around. But the most common morphology was something like a mermaid, with the legs—useless, heavy distractions in microgravity—replaced by a kind of fish tail, useful for swimming around in the air, or the interior ocean. A lot of them had gills and never came out of the water at all, and some were covered with fur that streamlined and warmed their bodies.

The Weissmans had done away with every part of the body which wasn't needed in microgravity. And some had gone further. Some didn't have hands, or arms. In an age of ubiquitous and one hundred percent reliable machinery—machinery which could manufacture other machinery—human beings, it seemed, didn't need to be tool-makers anymore.

To Greenberg, they looked like nothing so much as seals.

It was their choice, or their progenitors' anyhow. But what Greenberg couldn't figure was what they *did* all day.

Greenberg himself still had work to do, in these rare intervals of wake-fulness: monitoring Ra's external systems, checking the import of volatile and metal-rich cargoes.

But maybe the Weissmans were just being kind. There were probably gigantic smart systems that backed up every action he took. He was a kind of museum piece, he supposed: the first human to rendezvous with an asteroid, all those years ago, a living totem for the Weissmans of Ra.

He finished the soup and let go of the packet, and a domestic bot—a fussy little bastard like a trash can with attitude thrusters—came hissing out of its corner and grabbed the bag.

Greenberg felt sour, grumpy, and isolated.

He studied Earth, which swam past on one of its closest approaches to the rock in years.

He remembered from his first orbital missions aboard the shuttle, all those centuries ago, how the coastal rims of the continents would just glow with artificial light. Greenberg had supposed, then, that it would go on, that the Earth would just get richer and fatter and brighter.

But it hadn't worked out that way. Earth, in fact, grew darker every time he looked.

Once the expansion into the near-Earth rocks had begun, it wasn't long before a move farther out followed: first to Phobos and Deimos, the cap-tured asteroids that circled Mars, and then out into the main belt itself. Vesta, one of the biggest of the main belt rocks, had been the first to be extensively colonized, and now it was the hub of farther expansion, little archipelagoes of busy mines and colonization scattered across the belt.

And, so Greenberg understood, there were some pioneers who had gone even farther afield: to the comets out in the Oort Cloud, and the

Kuiper Belt, where billions of ice moons the size of Ganymede swam through the darkness.

Of course the techniques they used nowadays made Ra look primitive. Those universal fabricators, for instance, that sucked in asteroid ore at one end and pumped out whatever you wanted at the other, using something called molecular beam epitaxy to spray atoms and molecules directly onto a substrate. Greenberg didn't understand any of these new gadgets, even the stuff you could *see*.

It was strange for Greenberg to remember now how much agonizing there had been when he was growing up about the depletion of Earth's resources, the needs to close the loops of mass and energy, as if Earth itself was one big CELSS. Nobody worried about that anymore; the solar system had worked out to be just too rich in resources; those loops would stay open for a long time yet.

It took a long time for the economics and demographics and such to work out, but it had all been pretty much inevitable, it seemed to Greenberg. It was just *so* much cheaper to send resources skimming between the rocks than to haul them out of the planets' big gravity wells. The colonies on Mars and the Moon had shriveled and died, and Earth— growing poorer, its population steadily declining—had turned into a kind of huge theme park: a museum of the human species, but studded with pits of abject poverty in the darkened ruins of the old cities. Nobody knew what was happening in those pits.

And nobody much cared, because beyond old Earth there were too many people even to *count*.

If you knew where to look, the sky was full of inhabited rocks, with their little orbital necklaces of solar power stations, and habitats studding their surfaces or buried inside, green and blue, the old colors of life. It was estimated that for every person alive when Greenberg was born, there were a *billion* human souls now. That was a hell of a thought. And when he considered some of the assholes he used to have to work with back in those days, a dismaying one.

In Ra there was a whole bunch of little Weissmans, though not all of them used Mike's old name any more, and so in his head Greenberg thought of them all as Weissmans; it made it easier to love them. Mike would have been pleased, anyhow. There were no Greenbergs, though.

His line had finished with a great-grandchild, a male, who had got caught up in the New AIDS epidemic of the twenty-second century, and died childless. It was ironic. Here was Greenberg, perhaps the oldest surviving human, and not one of all those teeming trillions floating around the system could claim direct descent from him.

On the other hand, by the laws of statistics, there ought to be a billion Einsteins out there. Nobody knew what they were all doing. They sure weren't working together.

All those pious dreams of the space buffs of some kind of giant solar system civilization had never been remotely likely. *There were just too many people.* The human race had gathered into a billion small-town-sized tribes and splintered, shaping and seeking goals unimaginable to an Earth-born geezer like him.

It seemed to him, in fact, that he was watching the end of the species, as a unitary whole: two million years out of Africa, the race had escaped from the cradle and was growing, to where the hell nobody could even guess.

. . . and now here came *Toutatis* on its aerobraking pass.

The rock looked like a comet glowing in the thin upper air of Earth, streaking by in a perfect straight line *below* Greenberg. It made the cities and oceans of Earth glow like the day — it must have been a remarkable sight from down there — and asteroid light played on his own face, the ancient bones of his eye sockets.

The encounter was over in seconds. The trail of scorched air soon dissipated and dimmed, and *Toutatis*, its orbit subtly altered, passed on toward its next encounter. It was going to take fifty years to nudge *Toutatis* into its final low Earth orbit, but planning projects on that kind of time scale didn't seem to trouble the inhabitants of *Toutatis*, or anybody else.

The show was over. The people of Ra-Shalom drifted away from their blue watery windows and returned to their mysterious business within.

Greenberg had never meant to live for a thousand years. It was ridiculous. Nobody else had stuck around like this. It was just that he would have had to have *chosen* when to die, and that was something he had never expected to face when he grew up, and he just had no instinct for it.

Anyhow, if he let himself die, he would have missed *this*.

Greenberg, with a sigh, turned away from the window and went to his instrument consoles.

It was a massive asteroid, big enough to have dragged itself into a sphere, with planetlike layers of internal structure, rich in metals, rocks, and volatiles. It was bathed by the light of a sun only three times as far away as from Earth.

The guardians considered carefully. It was, after all, to be the repository of all that was left of their designers' species, until even this new young sun guttered and died.

They were machines designed to plan for billions of years. They had already nursed their fragile cargo across such deserts of time. Now, looking to the future, they must plan for evolution, even the loss of mind.

It was a good home, rich in energy and resources.

The guardians were satisfied. They closed themselves down.

Within the rock, history continued.

Scale: Exp 4

It was to be quite a day, as the last of Ra's ore was transmuted, and Greenberg made sure the Weissmans woke him up to see it. In the event he nearly missed it, it took so long to put him together again.

Greenberg's window was the same old tunnel through fused regolith, but the view beyond changed as he watched, the last of the gray-black old crap literally dissolving before his eyes, to be replaced by a sharp, tight blue curve of watery horizon.

Too damn sharp, he thought. He wondered if those asshole nanobugs had changed his eyes on him again while he'd slept. But even his naps lasted a century at a time, longer than he had once expected to live; they had time.

Anyhow, his new eyes showed him a blue world, the landscape softly pulsing, with Greenberg's NASA-style space station hab module stuck stubbornly to the side under its crust of regolith, like a leech clinging to flesh. Ra was just water now, encased by some smart membrane that held the whole thing in place and collected solar energy and regulated temperature and stuff. It looked like a little clone of Earth, in fact, and Greenberg thought it somehow appropriate that today the tired, depopulated old Earth itself was over somewhere on the far side of the sun, invisible, forgotten, the last traces of man being scraped off by the returned glaciers.

Under the pulsing surface of Ra he could make out dark brown shapes, graceful and lithe: people, Weissmans, whole schools of them flipping around the interior. And now here came a child, wriggling up to the membrane, pushing its disturbingly human face up to the wall, peering out—with curiosity or indifference, he couldn't tell which—at the stars. It broke his unreconstructed twentieth-century heart to see that little girl's face stuck on the end of such a fat, unnatural body.

An adult came by and chivvied the kid away, into the deeper interior; Greenberg saw their sleek shapes disappear into the misty blue.

The Weissmans had been working on making their environment as simple and durable as they could. They were planning for the long haul, it seemed. So, the whole rock had been transformed into this spherical ocean, and the biosphere had been cut down to essentially two components: Weissmans, posthumans, swimming around in a population of something that was descended from blue-green algae. The algae, feeding on sunlight, were full of proteins, vitamins, and essential amino acids. And the humans ate the algae, drank the water, breathed in oxygen, breathed out carbon dioxide to feed the algae.

When people died, their bodies were allowed to drift down to the center of the world, where supercritical water reactors worked to break down their residues and return their body masses to the ecosystem.

Their loops were as closed as they could be. The loss that entropy dictated was made up by the energy steadily gathered by that smart membrane, and a few nanobugs embedded there. Greenberg understood that research was going on to eliminate the last few technological components of the system: maybe those supercritical water reactors could be replaced by something organic, and maybe even the surface membrane and the last nanobugs could be done away with. For instance, a few meters of water would serve as a radiation shield.

It was a kind of extreme end result, Greenberg supposed, of the technology evolution that had begun all the way back with John Glenn in his cramped little Mercury tin can, breathing in canned air for his few orbits of the home planet.

But the Weissmans were not much like John Glenn.

He didn't know any of their names. He didn't care to. For a long time now, longer than he cared to think, there had been hardly anybody alive who remembered him from one waking period to the next, from one of his "days" to another. Hell of a thing. He preferred to talk to machines, in fact.

Greenberg didn't even know if the Weissmans were still human anymore.

The last of the true humans, as *he* recognized them, had been leaving the system for millennia.

It had been necessary. For a time, as the human population grew exponentially, it looked as if even the solar system's vast resources were in danger of depletion.

So somebody had to leave, to open up the loops once more.

There was a whole variety of ways to go, all of them based on pushing people-laden rocks out of the system. You could mount a big mass driver on the back of your rock and use its substance as reaction mass. Close to the Sun, you could use its heat to just boil off volatiles. You could use a solar sail. You could use Jupiter's powerful electromagnetic field as a greater mass driver. And so on. There was even a rumor of an antimatter factory, out in the Kuiper Belt somewhere.

Greenberg's favorite method was the most resolutely low-tech. Just nudge your rock out of its stable orbit, let it whip through the gravity fields of Jupiter and Saturn a few times, and you could slingshot your way out of the system for free. Of course it might take you ten thousand years to reach your destination, at Barnard's Star or E Eradini or E Indi. But what the hell; you probably had with you more water than in the whole of the Atlantic Ocean.

Greenberg accepted the necessity of the migration. But to him it had been a drain, not just on the system's titanic population but also on the human spirit.

The solar system had been left a drab, depopulated place. All the engineering types had gone, leaving behind the navel-gazing seals of Ra, and similar relics scattered around the system.

The Weissmans, turned in on themselves, had their own interests. They were probing into a lot of areas well beyond his expertise. Like the possibility of tapping into zero-point field energy, the energy of the vacuum itself, so dense you could — it was said — boil all the oceans of Earth with the energy contained in a coffee cup of empty space. Then there was the compact energy stored in the topological defects, little packets of space that had got tangled up and folded over in the Big Bang, containing some of the monstrous primeval energies within, just waiting to be tapped and opened up . . .

Research and development, carried on by a community of goddamn seals, with no hands or tools. Greenberg didn't know how they did it. It was one of the many things about the Weissmans he didn't understand.

He did know they were trying to extend their consciousness. Mind, it seemed, was a quantum process, intimately bound to the structure of space and time. And in space, after ten thousand years free of the distortions of the muddy pond of atmosphere at the bottom of Earth's gravity well, consciousness — the Weissmans claimed — was taking a huge evolutionary leap forward, to new realms of power and control and depth.

Maybe.

To Greenberg, it was all very well to dream of superminds of the future, but right now he suspected there was nobody left, for instance, who could push an asteroid out of its orbit, where once the children of man had rearranged worlds almost at will.

And, Greenberg was coming to realize, that might make a big difference in the future.

He still had some of his old monitoring systems, or patiently reconstructed copies anyhow. He studied Ra's evolving trajectory around the sun.

And, gradually, he'd learned something that had disturbed him to his core.

Near-Earth asteroids wandered in steadily from the main belt, their orbits tweaked by the gravity of Jupiter, Venus, Mars, and Earth itself. They hung around for thirty megayears or so, their paths slowly evolving. Then they would encounter one of three fates, with equal probability: they would hit Earth, or hit Venus, or be slingshot out of the system altogether.

The cratering record on Earth showed this had been going on for billions of years. The smaller the object type, the more frequent the collision. Every few thousand years, for instance, Earth would be hit by an object a hundred meters or so across, big enough to dig out a new

Meteor Crater, as in Arizona, where the Apollo moonwalkers had once trained. Earth had actually suffered a few fresh strikes like that while Greenberg had been observing.

And every few tens of millions of years, a much larger body would strike.

Such an object had struck the Earth sixty-five million years ago, at Chicxulub in Mexico. It had caused the extinction of most of the species extant at that time.

It was known as the dinosaur killer.

Earth was overdue for another impact like that.

Near-Earth asteroid orbits were pretty much chaotic. It was like the weather used to be, back when he lived in a place that had weather. But as computers got smarter, the path of Ra-Shalom was pushed out, in the computer's digital imagination, farther and farther. Finally it became clear to Greenberg what Ra's ultimate fate would be.

Ra wasn't going to hit Venus or be thrown out of the system to the stars. Ra was going to hit Earth.

Ra was the next dinosaur killer.

It was a long time ahead: all of a million years from now. But it worried him that right now, nobody seemed to know how to deflect this damn rock.

Whenever he got the chance, he sounded off about the dinosaur-killer problem. The Weissmans told him they had plans to deal with it, when the time came. Greenberg wasn't sure whether he believed that.

And he wasn't sure he wanted to be around to see this chewed-up rock auger in on the surface of the planet where he was born.

Within the confines of the tiny world, civilizations fell and rose; by turns, the refugee race fell to barbarism, or dreamed of the stars. The guardians had planned for this.

But the little world was not stable. This they had not anticipated.

Its orbit was close to a resonance with that of Jupiter: it circled the sun three times in each of Jupiter's stately years. The powerful tug of Jupiter worked on the asteroid's trajectory, millennium after millennium.

Quite suddenly, the orbit's ellipticity increased. The asteroid started to swing deep into the warm heart of the solar system.

There was nothing the inhabitants could do to steer their rock. Some adapted. Many died. Superstitions raged.

For the first time, the asteroid dipped within the orbit of Earth.

Scale: Exp 5

... crossing time in unimaginable jumps, drifting between sleeping and walking, eroding toward maximum entropy like some piece of lunar rock...

He never knew, he didn't understand, he couldn't believe how much time had passed. A hundred thousand years? It was a joke.

But even the sky was changing.

The nearby stars, for instance: Alpha Centauri and Barnard's Star and Sirius and Procyon and Tau Ceti, names from the science fiction of his youth. You could see the changes in the light, the stain of oxygen and carbon, chlorophyll green. Even from here you could *see* how humans, or posthumans anyhow, had changed the stars themselves.

And to think he used to be awed by the vehicle assembly building at Canaveral.

And the expansion must be continuing, farther out, inexorably. On it would go, he thought dimly, a growing mass of humanity filling up the sphere centered on Sol, chewing up stars and planets and asteroids, until the outer edge of the inhabited sphere had to move at the speed of light to keep up, and *then* what would happen, he wanted to know?

But none of that made a difference here, in the ancient system of Sol, the dead heart of human expansion. It was hard for him to trace the passing of the years because so little changed anymore, even on the heroic timescales of his intervals of consciousness.

Conditions in a lot of the inhabited rocks had converged, in fact, so that the worlds came to resemble one another. Most of them finished up with the kind of simple, robust ecosystem that sustained Ra, even though their starting points might have been very different. It was like the way a lot of diverse habitats on Earth—forests and jungles and marshes— would, with the passage of time, converge into a peat bog, the same the world over, as if they were drawn to an attractor in some ecological phase space.

And most of the rocks, drifting between uninhabited gravity wells, were about as interesting as peat bogs, as far as Greenberg was concerned.

Meanwhile, slowly but inexorably, life was dying back, here in the solar system, which had once hosted billions of jewel-like miniature worlds.

There were a lot of ways for a transformed asteroid to be destroyed: for instance, a chance collision with another object. Even a small impact on a fragile bubble world like Ra could puncture it fatally. But nobody around seemed capable of pushing rocks aside any more.

But the main cause of the die-back was simple ecological failure.

An asteroid wasn't a planet; it didn't have the huge buffers of mass and energy that Earth had. A relatively small amount of matter circulated in each mass loop, and so the whole thing was only marginally stable, and not always self-recovering.

It had even happened here, on Ra-Shalom. Greenberg had woken once to find that concentrations of the amino acid called lysine had crashed. The Weissmans were too busy dreaming their cetacean dreams to think too much about the systems that were keeping them alive. Many died before a new stability was reached. It drove Greenberg crazy.

But the Weissmans didn't seem too upset. *You have to think of it as apoptosis,* they said to him. *The cells in the hands of an archaic-form human embryo will die back in order to sculpt out tool-making fingers. Death is necessary, sometimes, so that life can progress. It is apoptosis, not necrosis . . .*

Greenberg just couldn't see that argument at all.

And in the meantime, Ra was still on its course to become the next dinosaur killer. The predictions just got tighter and tighter. And still, nobody seemed to be concerned about doing anything about it.

When what the Weissmans said to him made no sense at all—when they deigned to speak to him—Greenberg felt utterly isolated.

But then, all humans were alone.

Nobody had found nonterrestrial life *anywhere*, in the solar system or beyond, above prokaryotes: single-celled creatures without internal structures such as nuclei, mitochondria, and chloroplasts. Mars was typical, it had turned out: just a handful of crude prokaryote-type bugs shivering deep in volcanic vents, waiting out an ice age that would never end. Only on Earth, it seemed, had life made the big, unlikely jump to eukaryotic structure, and then to multicelled organisms and the future.

It seemed that back when he was born Earth had been one little world holding all the life there was, to all intents and purposes. And it would have stayed that way if his generation and a couple before, Americans and Russians, hadn't risked their lives to enter space in converted ICBMs and ridiculous little capsules.

Makes you think, he reflected. The density of all life, forever, was in our hands. And we never knew it. Probably would have scared us to death if we had.

For if we'd failed, if we'd turned ourselves to piles of radioactive ash, there would now be no life, no mind, anywhere.

Gravitational tweaks by Earth and Venus gradually wore away the asteroid's energy, and its orbit diminished. The process took a hundred million years.

At last, the asteroid with its fragile cargo settled into a circle, a close shadow of Earth's orbit. Its random walk across the solar system was complete.

The inhabitants adapted. They even flourished, here in the warmer heart of the solar system.

For a time, it seemed that a long and golden afternoon lay ahead of the refugees within the rock. Once more, they forgot what lay beyond the walls of their world . . .

But there seemed to be something in the way.

Scale: Exp 6

We have an assignment for you.

He came swimming up from a sleep as deep as death. He wondered, in fact, if he was truly in any sense alive, between these vivid flashes of consciousness.

. . . and Earth, ocean blue, swam before Ra, a fat crescent cupping a darkened ocean hemisphere, huge and beautiful, just as he'd seen it long ago, from a shuttle cargo bay.

In his vision there was water everywhere: the skin of Earth, the droplet body of Ra-Shalom, and in his own eyes.

We have an assignment for you. A mission.

"What are you talking about? Are you going to push this damn rock out of the way? I can't believe you've let it go this far."

This has happened before. There has been much necrosis.

"Hell, I know that ..."

He looked up at a transformed sky.

Everywhere now, the stars were *green*.

There was old Rigel, for instance, one of the few stars he could name when he was a kid, down there in Orion, at the hunter's left boot. Of course all the constellations had swum around now. But Rigel was still a blue supergiant, sixty thousand times more luminous than the sun.

But now even old Rigel had been turned emerald green, by a titanic Dyson cloud twice the diameter of Pluto's orbit.

Not only that, the people up there were starting to adjust the evolution of their giant star. Rigel only had a few million years of stable life — compared to Sol's billions — before it would slide off the Main Sequence and rip itself apart as a supernova.

But the people up there were *managing* Rigel, managing a goddamn supergiant, deflecting its evolution into realms of light and energy never before seen in the history of the universe. And that emerald color, visible even to a naked archaic human eye, was the symbol of that achievement.

It was a hell of a thing, a Promethean triumph, monkey paws digging into the collapsing heart of a supergiant.

Nobody knew how far humans had got from Earth, or what technical and other advances they had achieved, out there on the rim. But if we don't have to fear supernovas, he thought, we don't have to fear *anything*.

We've come a long way, he thought, since the last time I climbed into the belly of a *VentureStar*, down there at Canaveral, and breathed in my last lungful of sea air ...

... *an assignment*, the Weissmans were saying to him.

Earth swam close, and was growing closer.

We want to right the ancient necrosis as far as we can. We want you to help us.

"Me? Why me?"

It is appropriate. You are an ambassador from exponent zero. This is a way of closing the loop, in a sense. The causal loop. Do you accept?

"I don't know what you're talking about. I accept. I don't know what you mean . . ."

. . . the walls of the hab module dissolved around him. Suddenly he didn't have hold of anything, and he was falling.

Oh, shit, he thought.

But there were shadows around him, struts and blocks. And a heavy, liquid mass at his lower body he hadn't felt for a long time.

Legs. He had legs.

His breathing was loud in his ears. Oxygen hissed over his face.

He was back in his shuttle-era pressure suit, and he was encased in his PMU once more, the original model, its spidery frame occluding the dusting of stars around him.

He grasped his right-hand controller. It worked. There was a soft tone in his helmet; he saw a faint sparkle of exhaust crystals, to his left.

Still, Earth swam before him.

It is time.

"Wait — what — "

Earth was gone.

Ra-Shalom sailed through the space where the Earth had been, its meniscus shimmering with slow, complex waves as it rolled, the life at its heart a dim green knot against the blue.

My God, he thought. *They pushed Earth aside.* I didn't know they got so powerful —

"What did you do? Is it destroyed?"

No. Earth is in a stable orbit around Jupiter. The ice will return, for now. But later, when the sun starts to die, Earth will be preserved, as it would not have been . . .

"Later?"

We must plan for exponent seven, eight, nine. Even beyond. The future is in our hands. It always has been.

"But how — "

Goodbye, the Weissmans said, a tinny voice in the headphones in his Snoopy hat. *Goodbye.*

And now there was another hulking mass swimming into view, just visible at the edge of his faceplate.

He worked his altitude thrusters, and began a slow yaw. Strange, he didn't seem to have forgotten any of the old skills he had practiced in the sims at Houston, and in LEO, all those years ago.

He faced the new object.

It was an asteroid. It looked like Ra-Shalom — at any rate, how that rock had looked when he first approached it — but it was a lot bigger, a neat sphere. The sun's light slanted across craters and ravines, littered with coal-dust regolith. And there was a structure there, he saw: tracings of wire and paneling, but up and abandoned, and a big affair that stuck out from the rock, a spiderweb of wires and threads. Maybe it was an antenna. Or a solar sail.

Artifacts.

It looked like the remains of a ship, in fact. But not human.

Not human. My God, he thought.

And now the light changed: to the stark planes of the sun's eternal glow was added a new, softer glow.

Water-blue.

He turned, clumsily, blipping his altitude thrusters.

Earth was *back*, a fat crescent, directly ahead of him. This is a hell of a light show, he thought.

But Earth looked different. It had spun around on its axis. Before he'd been over the Pacific; now he could make out, in a faint dawn glow, the familiar shapes of the continents — North and South America, painted over the ocean under bubbling wisps of cloud.

There were no lights, anywhere. And the arrangement of continents didn't look right. Earth didn't match his memories of schoolroom globes, under the Stars and Stripes, back in Iowa.

The Atlantic looked too skinny, for instance.

This new rock was heading for Earth, just like Ra-Shalom had been. It couldn't be more than a few minutes from reaching the atmosphere. And it looked to him as if it were going to hit somewhere in Mexico...

Oh, he thought. I get it.

This was the dinosaur killer, the original, destined to gouge out a two-hundred-kilometer crater at Chicxulub, and to have its substance rained around the planet.

He shielded his eyes with a gloved hand, and studied the stars.

They were different. The stars were bone-white: no green anywhere.

He was displaced in time, a long way. This was not the far future but the deep past.

He turned again to face the plummeting rock, with its fragile cargo of artifacts.

One last time the kerosene thrusters fired, fat and full. The asteroid started to approach him, filling his sky. The suit was quiet, warm, safe.

He just let himself drift in, at a meter or so a second. The close horizon receded, and the cliff face turned into a wall that cut off half the universe.

He collided softly with the rock. Dust sprays were thrown up from around the PMU's penetrator legs. Greenberg was stuck there, clinging to the surface like a mountaineer to a rock face.

He turned on his helmet lamp. Impact glass glimmered a few centimeters from his face. He reached out and pushed his gloved hand into the compacted-snow surface, a monkey paw probing.

. . . there was something here. Something alive, something sentient, inside the rock. He could feel it, though he couldn't tell how.

Maybe the Weissmans were using him as some kind of conduit, he thought. Maybe they wanted to save some of whatever was here from the destruction of the rock, take it with them to whatever future awaited mankind.

Or maybe it was just him.

He smiled. He was a million years old, after all; maybe a little of the Weissmans had rubbed off on him.

He took a handful of dust and pulled out his hand. A cloud of dust came with it that gushed into his face like a hail of meteorites, glittering particles following dead straight lines.

He sensed acceptance. Forgiveness. He wondered how far they'd come, how long they'd traveled. What they were fleeing.

Anyhow, it was over now.

"You weren't alone," he said. "And neither were we." He pushed his hand back into the pit he'd dug, ignoring the fresh dust clouds he raised.

The light of Earth billowed around him.

Spomelife:
The Universe and the Future

ISAAC ASIMOV

An early advocate of habitats in space, Asimov embraced a particularly American view of their potential for social change. Perhaps the dominance of the skylife idea by Americans arises from their assumption that small communities are crucial to a burgeoning originality. The European vision is much more constrained and orderly, typically foreseeing habitats as outposts under distant Earthly regulation. Necessarily, this makes interesting plots harder to find. Asimov, as usual, sees farther in this early essay.

L et me begin by coining an uneuphonious word — *spome* — and defining it.

A spome is any system, substantially closed with respect to matter, that is capable of supporting human life for an indefinitely long period of time.

The earth is a spome and, at present, is the only spome known to exist. Its qualifications for spomehood are obvious. It has supported human life for well over a million years, if we count the hominids generally, and will continue to do so for the foreseeable future, barring the effects of man's own willful folly.

Furthermore, it is substantially closed with respect to matter. The matter that is added in the form of meteoroid infall or lost in the form of atmospheric leakage is not significant. It does not affect earth's spomic characteristics, nor is it likely to in the foreseeable future.

But a spome cannot be closed with respect to energy.

Life is a process whereby relatively unorganized components of the environment are made more organized. That means that life involves a continuing decrease of entropy and can exist only at the expense of a continuing, and even greater, increase of entropy in the environment generally.

If the earth were closed with respect to energy, mankind, and life generally, would see to it that in a relatively short time, enough oxygen and organic matter would be degraded to carbon dioxide and other wastes to render the earth uninhabitable.

The energy of the sun makes all the difference. It enters the earth system, keeps the atmosphere stirred up and the oceans liquid; it makes the rain fall; and most important, solar energy is utilized by green plants to reconvert carbon dioxide and water into organic substances and free oxygen.

The entropy of the environment, pushed upward by the activities of life, is pushed downward again by the energy of the sun. An equilibrium has been maintained for some billions of years at the expense of the vastly increasing entropy of the sun — which has room for additional entropy increase for some additional billions of years.

Beyond the sun we need not go. For all we know, there are processes that reverse the entropy increase of the sun, and of stars generally, and keep the universe in stable equilibrium forever, as some astronomers have believed, but that need not concern us. The sun will endure, substantially in its present form, for some ten billion years and that, on the human scale, is an indefinitely long period of time. Earth may therefore certainly be regarded as a spome.

If the earth were the only spome that could exist, the subject of spomology would be trivial. It would be comprehended by such sciences as geography and geology. But it may be that the earth is merely the only spome that exists so far, and that many others can exist in conception or potentiality. In that case, the subject increases in interest.

It is possible — indeed, it is certain — that elsewhere among the stars (but *not* in our own solar system) there may be other spomes. That is, there may be planets sufficiently like the earth in general characteristics, with a sun sufficiently like our own sun, to serve as habitable planets and therefore as spomes. The figure I have used is a possible 640,000,000 in our galaxy alone.

And yet all 640,000,000 lumped together do not in themselves suffice to make spomology a truly interesting study, for they are all merely so many earths. From the broad standpoint of the spomologist, if you see one earthlike planet, you have seen them all. Since we have all indeed seen one earthlike planet, our own, we have seen them all and can forget about them.

What we want, if we are to make spomology interesting, are spomes that are drastically different from the earth. And if we make the subject interesting, we may find — who knows — that it is valuable as well.

Suppose we ask ourselves what makes earth a spome and Jupiter or Mercury nonspomes? If we want to express the difference most succinctly, it is a matter of mass. Jupiter is too massive; Mercury is insufficiently massive. The difference in mass involves, one way or another, almost every quality that goes to make or not make a spome.

If a planet is insufficiently massive, it cannot hold either an atmosphere or an ocean of a volatile liquid. If it is too massive, it will hold hydrogen and helium and produce a poisonous atmosphere and, at best, an ammoniated ocean. In neither case can it be a spome.

If it is very massive, that is probably because it is far distant from its primary and can accumulate matter with little competition from the greater body, and at a temperature low enough to make the dancing molecules of hydrogen (the major component of matter) sufficiently sluggish to be captured. Under such conditions, the planet is too cold to be a spome.

If the planet is insufficiently massive, it is because it is too close to the primary, so that accumulating matter is lost to the greater body and many of the more common elements are, at that distance from the primary, too nimble and elusive to be captured. Alternately, the body is forming too close to a large planet which competes successfully for matter, so that the body itself is a satellite rather than a planet. In the former case, the body is too hot to be a spome, in the latter too cold.

There are exceptions to these rules, of course; known exceptions within our solar system. Our moon seems too large for its place in the system, whereas Pluto seems too small. This departure from regularity leads to theories that the moon is a captured planet and Pluto an escaped satellite.

On the other hand, assuming a sun of the proper type, it is quite reasonable to hope that there is a good chance that a planet of the proper mass would be bound to form at the right distance from that sun and with the proper chemical composition to lead to spomehood.

We might say, then, that the search for a spome is the search for a body of appropriate mass.

But all this is in the course of nature. It works as we are looking for "natural spomes," for spomes ready-made. Let us now add the factor of human intelligence. Only God may make a tree, according to Joyce Kilmer, but perhaps spomes can be made by fools like us. (No, I didn't invent the word in order to be able to make that statement.)

The problem is: Can we make an "artificial spome"? Can we take a body of drastically wrong mass and make a spome of it? In one direction, let's not even try. Bodies too massive to be spomes are quite rare (there are only five in the solar system, counting the sun itself, as compared with many thousands of bodies that are insufficiently massive to serve as natural spomes). The too-massive bodies are, in addition, too dangerous to play with, thanks to their strong gravitational fields and their inevitably enormous atmospheres.

If we look in the direction of bodies insufficiently massive for spomehood, we find at once that the closest body to us, the moon, is an example of the class.

The problem boils down, then, to the conversion of small bodies into spomes, and the specific version of the problem is, inevitably: Can we make the moon into a spome?

The moon is certainly not a spome now. Thanks to its low mass, it has neither an atmosphere nor free water. But let us consider essentials and not accidentals. An atmosphere can be kept from diffusing out into space by the force of a sufficiently strong gravitational field, but, on a smaller scale, it can be kept from doing so by physical barriers as well.

In other words, we can distinguish two general varieties of spomes: external and internal. An external spome is one with an atmosphere and ocean held to the outer surface of the body by a gravitational field, so that men can live on that outer surface. An internal spome is one with air and water held within an airtight cavity and with men living on the inner surface. Inevitably, natural spomes are external ones, while artificial spomes must be internal.

Suppose, then, we hollow out a cavity under the moon's surface and supply it with air, water, and the other necessities of life. We might have to begin with capital from the earth, but it is possible that eventually water could be baked out of silicate hydrates in the body of the moon. From such water, oxygen could be formed.

Given a sufficient supply of energy, and a mass of variegated chemical composition such as the moon (or even a much smaller body) the basic chemical requirements can be met on the spot.

Energy is the key, and we are used to thinking of the sun as the energy source. In nature, the only source of energy in quantities large enough to support a natural spome does, in fact, happen to be a star like our sun, but a star—any star—is an incredibly wasteful source. Hardly any of its radiation is stopped by a planet, and only a small fraction of that which is stopped is used. A much smaller source, used with much greater efficiency, will serve the purpose.

A roaring wood fire, whose energy production is a completely contemptible fraction of that of the sun, will warm us in winter at a time when all the sun is insufficient. On the scale that would be sufficient for an internal spome, an ordinary fire is not enough, however. Fortunately, something much better is in sight.

On the large scale of spomehood, only hydrogen fusion can be relied on as an energy source through an indefinite future. It is large-scale hydrogen fusion that powers the sun, and it may be small-scale hydrogen fusion that will power the earth some day.

I foresee, then—although not in the immediate future—the possibility of the moon being honeycombed immediately below its surface by a growing system of caverns, supplied with all basic materials from the moon itself, and all its energy requirements would be supplied by fusion power plants. It would be seeded with plant and animal life (and, inevitably, with microscopic life as well) and inhabited by men, women, and children; families who may know no other life, and want none.

The advantages are obvious. The moon will have a controlled environment designed specifically for man; man will have what he wants and needs (in many vital respects) and not merely what he can get. What's more, he will have the advantage of a fresh start. As the United States managed to prosper and flourish partly because it was freed of many of the choking traditions of Europe's bitter past, so the moon, it may be hoped, will be freed of the incubus of earth's past mistakes.

Some disadvantages are also obvious. However confidently we rely on scientific and technological advance, it seems certain that we can never do anything to alter the moon's gravity. The inhabitants of the moon will always be under a gravitational pull only one-sixth that of the earth.

Undoubtedly, they can get used to it, and people born on the moon, knowing no other, will consider such a gravitational force natural. Will men suffer as a result, however, particularly in the transitional period when they may be shuttling between the earth and the moon? Will muscles weakened and bones softened under the influence of lower gravity be able to withstand a return to earth?

The problem might not arise in fullest intensity. Men on the moon could keep in condition with exercise or in centrifuges. Perhaps only a few specialists would need to condition themselves for possible trips to earth, whereas the general population of the moon would find it no hardship at all to remain away from the earth permanently.

Another disadvantage is that an internal spome is liable to accidental catastrophes of a sort to which external spomes are immune. An atmosphere and ocean held to the surface by gravity are absolutely secure. Barring catastrophe on an astronomic scale, nothing can alter the gravitational force and nothing can cause the atmosphere and ocean of an external spome to be lost.

On an internal spome, on the other hand, a cavern punctured by a large meteorite, or ruptured by a landslide, loses its air at once and its water more slowly. Nevertheless, it is to be expected that men will be ingenious enough to minimize the chances of such catastrophes. Furthermore, the cavern of an internal spome will undoubtedly be compartmentalized so that a local catastrophe can be confined to its immediate neighborhood.

Nor is catastrophe in itself a bar to spomehood. There are catastrophes on earth, too. We suffer periodically from the effects of hurricanes, blizzards, tornadoes, floods, and drought, to none of which the moon would be subject. A patriotic moonman might well argue that it was the earth rather than the moon that fell short of ideal spomehood through catastrophe.

But what about the psychological difficulties? Can men really learn to live for extended periods in what is essentially, after all, a cavern? Can they bear to be born and to die there? The answer, in my opinion, is the heartiest possible affirmative. If the cavern is large and comfortable, why not?

It is a mistake to underestimate the flexibility of mankind. Man has already demonstrated abilities to make enormous adjustments. A city such as New York represents, in a way, almost as artificial a spome, one almost as divorced from man's original environment as the moon would be. Yet man has made the transition from hut to skyscraper over an insignificant period of time. Indeed, a peasant immigrant can adjust adequately to New York in his own lifetime.

Why should we imagine a moonman would be horrified at being "cooped up"? I think it would be much more likely that he would think with horror of a world like the earth, where men had to cling precariously to an outer surface, exposed to the vagaries of an unpredictable and changeable climate. A moonman might no more want to live on earth than a New Yorker would want to live in a cave.

Of course, in thinking of an internal spome, we must fight our prejudices. It is easy to fall into the trap of thinking, vaguely, that an external spome is "natural" and an internal spome "artificial" and that what is natural is good and what is artificial is bad.

The argument might even be advanced that a "true" spome can only be one in which life could develop spontaneously out of nonliving matter, as it did on earth. A world that had to be engineered and seeded by a species that already had two to three billion years of evolution behind it might seem no true spome at all, but one that was only able to imitate spomehood through an initially parasitic dependence on a true spome.

But if that argument is advanced, where does Homo sapiens stand? Life did not develop on dry land. The only portion of the earth that is a "natural" spome, in the sense that life arose there spontaneously from simple chemicals, is the ocean. It was only little by little that certain types of living things emerged onto the dry land, a habitat as hostile to the creatures of the sea then as the moon seems to us now.

Some fishy philosopher, if we can imagine one, might well have shaken his head at the foolish creatures who chose to emerge on land. It would seem a bad exchange to move from the equable environment of the ocean to the violent extremes of the open air; from a plenitude of water to the perennial threat of dessication; from a gravitation-free three-dimensional world to a gravity-ridden two-dimensional world.

Nor are these dangers unrealistic ones, or these disadvantages of the dry land imaginary. Life first invaded the land some 425,000,000 years ago, yet even today, the ocean remains much richer in life than dry land is, area for area. Land animals had to evolve for millions of years before they could develop limbs strong enough to lift them clear of the ground and make both size and rapid movement simultaneously possible. It was some two hundred million years before creatures evolved who possessed internal thermostats and external insulation so that the equable temperature of the ocean might be imperfectly restored. Man himself rose to his hind feet a million and a half years ago and still pays his respects to gravity with flat feet, slipped disks, sinus trouble, potbellies, and numerous other ailments. And to this day he must live in dread of falling, a dread we are usually unaware of only because we are so accustomed to it.

No, no, if we are going to sneer at the moon as an unnatural habitat, we must sneer with precisely equal intensity at the continents of the earth. We live on a portion of the earth artificially seeded from the truly spomic portion; and despite everything, land life remains less rich and, in some respects and by some criteria, less comfortable and less successful than ocean life.

Yet need we be sorry that our ancestors emerged from sea to land? With all land's dangers and discomforts, it opened the way to advances not possible in the sea. In hindsight, we can see that the ocean was a dead end, whereas land offered a new and brighter horizon.

Nor are we being parochial when we argue in this way. Air is far less viscous than water. In water, a creature must either travel slowly or it must be streamlined. The most highly developed sea creatures, the squids, sharks, and fish, are highly streamlined. The land creatures that return to the sea are streamlined in proportion to the extent to which they have returned, if you think of the otter, penguin, seal, sea cow, and finally, the whale.

A streamlined body implies short, stubby appendages, if any, with an exception for the squid's highly specialized tentacles. In low-viscosity air, on the other hand, it is possible to be fast-moving and irregularly shaped at the same time, so that land animals can have elaborate appendages. It is to this that man owes his priceless hands.

Consider how, were the porpoise indeed as intelligent as man, the lack of hands would hamper the exhibiting of that intelligence! If we ever learn to communicate with porpoises, we may find ourselves with fluked philosophers on our hands; introverts who can think but not do.

Then, too, one can deal with fire only in air and never in water. Only a land creature, therefore, could conceivably develop the technology that begins with the discovery of fire. It is certainly possible to argue that man's advancing technology is not an unalloyed good, but I doubt that even the most inveterate yearner after the good old days before the building of Blake's "dark, satanic mills" could possibly wish to retreat to the days before the discovery of how to start and use a fire.

To use a chemical analogy, the passage from sea to land involved a "phase change" in the progress of life; most or even all of us cannot help but consider that desirable.

Is it possible, then, that the passage from an external "natural" spome to an internal "artificial" spome might likewise involve a desirable phase change? I hate to undertake the role of prophet here; foresight in such matters is as difficult as hindsight is easy. Nevertheless, I will try.

It seems to me, for instance, that however difficult the initial passage from an external spome to an internal one, the end would be a partial cancellation of the difficulties introduced by the previous great life-adventure. In an internal spome, man would return to the equable environment and lower gravity of the sea, without abandoning the low-viscosity environment of the air. An internal spome would have, after a fashion, the best of both land and sea and the worst of neither. Surely something great may come of that.

If we begin with an internal spome on the moon, victory and success there can only inspire attempts at expansion, at forming spomes out of other medium-sized bodies such as Mars and the larger satellites of Jupiter. In particular, though, there may be a movement to internal spomes on smaller and smaller bodies — that is, on the asteroids that exist by the thousand in the space between the orbits of Mars and Jupiter.

Why the asteroids?

Well, consider the matter of efficiency. With the best will in the world, and with all the technological advances likely in the foreseeable future, it would seem that mankind could not burrow very deeply into the skin of the earth, or into the skin of even a smaller body such as Mars or the moon. We may sink narrow bores to the mantle in time to come, but if we are thinking of internal spomes, of large, comfortable, and well-appointed caverns, the outer couple of miles is the most that we may consider. (Earth's internal heat, perhaps that of Mars and the moon too, would make deeper caverns uncomfortable anyway.)

This means that virtually all the volume of a planet is unused and serves the men of the spome only by supplying them with the source of a gravitational field.

The asteroids, however, can be spomified completely. They can be riddled and honeycombed. They have no internal heat for discomfort and no significant gravity to make more difficult the shifting of mass. Nor need the caverns be buttressed more than minimally to counter possible collapse. If we except the very largest, *all* of an asteroid can be used. (A nickel-iron asteroid might be difficult to work with, and its composition might not be suitable as a source of raw material for anything except the ferrous metals, but, judging by the ratio of iron meteorites to stony ones, we can hope that less than 10 percent of the asteroids will be metallic.)

Nor need an asteroid be considered too small to make an ample spome. Some years ago, I wrote a story about such an asteroidal spome, in which an earthman visiting the asteroid expressed surprise that the inhabitants had room to grow tobacco. His guide to the asteroid replied:

We are not a small world, Dr. Lamorak; you judge us by two-dimensional standards. The surface area of Elsevere [the asteroid] is only three-fourths that of the State of New York, but that's irrelevant. Remember, we can occupy, if we wish, the entire interior of Elsevere.

A sphere of 50 miles radius has a volume of well over half a million cubic miles. If all of Elsevere were occupied by levels of 50 feet apart, the total surface area within the planetoid would be 56,000,000 square miles and that is equal to the total land area of earth. And none of these square miles, doctor, would be unproductive.

In the story I deliberately dismissed one serious problem that would inevitably arise on an asteroidal spome in order that I might concentrate on the sociological point I was trying to make. I avoided any consideration of the fact that the gravitational field on an asteroid is negligible by supplying my storybook spome with artificial gravity.

In real life, as opposed to science fiction, an artificial gravity field cannot be set up merely with a wave of the typewriter. One conceivable possibility would be to set the asteroidal spome into rapid rotation. The centrifugal effect would be analogous to a gravitational field directed outward in every direction from the axis of rotation, with some important side effects. The gravitational field so set up would vary markedly with distance from the axis and there would be very noticeable Coriolis effects. The smaller the spome, the greater the angular velocity required for a given maximum centrifugal effect and the more pronounced the variations in the effect and in the obtrusiveness of Coriolis effects.

It seems to me that spinning the spome would not be worth the energy expended and the problems produced. Why not, instead, accept null gravity as a condition of life? Life has, in the past, switched from the essential null gravity of the oceans to the gravity slavery of the land and survived. Why not the switch back?

To be sure, the switch from null-g to g was made over eons of time, and the bodies of the creatures making the switch had to undergo elaborate and glacially slow changes through the force of natural selection. Mankind obviously lacks the time to proceed in this fashion.

But it is not in space science and engineering alone that mankind is experiencing great advances in technology. Biology is undergoing its own revolutionary breakthroughs. It is reasonable to hope that by the time man reaches the point where he can reach the asteroids with a supply of energy sufficient to set up a spome, he will also have learned enough about genetics to engage in meaningful tissue engineering. Why may we not suppose that the changes necessary to fit a human body for null gravity can be guided by intelligence rather than left to the colossal blindness of a nature that knows only random change?

A null-gravity body may well be designed differently from our own, but not necessarily radically so. Bones and muscles may be smaller and legs shorter, but I would guess that this would not go to extremes. To whatever extent weight may disappear, the body will still have to handle inertial mass, which would be the same on an asteroid as on the earth.

A null-gravity body would, it seems to me, become utterly graceful in its maneuverings, gaining some of the three-dimensional skills of the fish and birds. We would have a human species capable of flight without having to sacrifice the infinitely useful hand for the sake of a wing.

Land animals might require similar adaptations but, except perhaps for pets, dwellers on the asteroidal spomes could do without them. Plants could be grown at null-g without much trouble. Fish could still be cultivated. Algae culture and the chemical industry might combine to produce food items with the taste and texture of meat if that were desired.

To be sure, a null-g man could never come to earth, or even visit a world as small as the moon, but that should be no more a hardship to him than the fact that we can no longer breathe underwater is to us (except when we are drowning).

If we concentrate on this state of affairs, it would seem that there would be two species of man, g and null-g. We are g, of course, as would be the colonists on such large spomes as Mars, the moon, the large satellites of Jupiter, and so on. The inhabitants of the asteroidal spomes would be null-g.

It would not be so much merely the passage from external spome to internal spome that would represent the second phase change of evolution, as the passage from g to null-g. Might it not be that the future will belong to the null-g? That we g's of earth will now reach a dead end, while the null-g's of the asteroids will find a new and glorious horizon opening up for them? They may advance, leaving the discarded things of earth behind them while we, no more able to follow them than a fish could us, remain as oblivious as fish to their greater glories.

Consider —

First, the null-g species may well outnumber us as time goes on. Honeycombed asteroids may support a larger population, all taken together, than the mere outer skin of the large spomes inhabited by g's. The fact that null-g might be smaller in body (though not in brain) would serve to make their possible numbers still greater.

Second, the nature of the null-g environment will make it certain that they will far outstrip us in variability and versatility. The g people will exist as one large glob (earth's population) with small offshoots on Mars, the moon, and elsewhere, but the null-g's will be divided among a thousand or more worlds.

The situation will resemble that which once contrasted the Roman civilization with the Greek. The Romans wrought tremendous feats in law and government, in architecture and engineering, in military offense and defense. There was, however, something large, heavy, and inflexible about Roman civilization; it was Rome, wherever it was.

The Greeks, on the other hand, reaching far lesser material heights, had a life and verve in their culture that attracts us even today, across a time lapse of 2,500 years. No other culture ever had the spark of that of the Greeks, and part of the reason was that there was no Greece, really, only a thousand Greek city-states, each with its own government, its own customs, its own form of living, loving, worshiping, and dying. As we look back on the days of Greece, the brilliance of Athens tends to drown out the rest, but each town had something of its own to contribute. The endless variety that resulted gave Greece a glory that nothing before or since has been able to match; certainly not our own civilization of humanity-en-masse.

The null-g's may be the Greeks all over again. A thousand worlds, all with a common history and background, and each with its own way of developing and expressing that history and background. The richness of life represented by all the different null-g worlds may far surpass what is developed, by that time, on an earth rendered smaller and more uniform than ever by technological advance.

A third difference, and the really crucial one, in my opinion, can best be explained if I now turn to the subject of spaceships.

In the light of what I have already said, we can see that a spaceship is not exactly a spome, for a spome must be capable of supporting human life indefinitely. It is rather a "spomoid," something that is capable of serving a spomelike function temporarily.

Spomoids have performed notably well on a number of occasions already and have at this writing supported two men in reasonable comfort for as long as two weeks.

It is the obvious intention of the human race to explore the solar system by means of spomoids even before any extraterrestrial spomes are established; and, in fact, even if it turns out that the establishment of extraterrestrial spomes is unfeasible. By stages, we might even reach Pluto.

But there we would have to come to a halt. Beyond Pluto lie the stars, and the distances there involved are so enormous that the techniques that will have sufficed for the solar system will be completely useless to meet the new situation.

To reach even the nearer stars will involve one of three alternatives:

(1) Straightforward flight from here to the nearer stars and back, the time required being anywhere from a generation to a century or more.

(2) Flight at velocities near that of light, thus introducing a time-dilatation effect, so that the duration of the flight will seem to the astronaut to be no more than a few months or years. In that case, however, on returning to earth, he will find that the time lapse here has been anywhere from a generation to a century or more.

(3) Flight with astronauts frozen into suspended animation, the effect being the same as in case 2.

None of these alternatives is pleasing. The astronaut will either have to expose himself to the perils and uncertainties of freezing over long periods of time, or be willing to expend the energies required to reach extremely high velocities. It may well prove that freezing for decades is unfeasible and that the energy demands for time dilatation are prohibitive. If alternative 1 is chosen as the simplest, the astronaut must not only spend most or all his life on the star ship; he may also have to be prepared to bring up children and grandchildren who will in turn have to take over the star ship and spend their lives on it.

As for those who wait on earth, there are no alternatives. A star ship leaving for a neighboring star may not get back for a hundred years. The original astronauts may shorten the time for themselves by time dilatation, or by freezing, and return scarcely aged, but that does not affect the observers at home. The star ship will still not have returned for a century, and no one in the crowd that waves good-by will be in the crowd that waves hello.

Under the circumstances, stellar exploration would never be a popular exercise for anyone, either on the ship or at home. A few expeditions may set off as tours de force, but earthmen, unable to follow them, unable to see the results in their own lifetimes, will lose interest.

But let's consider under what conditions such voyages might become popular.

The longer the exploring trip within the solar system, the more elaborate the spomoid will have to be. By the time the outermost planets are reached, space voyages will have become years in length and a spomoid capable of supporting a crew for years will, of necessity, have a recycling mechanism that would require little further sophistication to serve a crew indefinitely.

The trend in space exploration, then, will be from the spomoid to the spome and, certainly, where stellar exploration is concerned, nothing less than an elaborate spome will be required.

Not only is a star ship a spome, but it is an internal spome, and one of an extreme type. In assembling a crew for a star ship, we are asking earthmen and women to make the transfer from an external spome to an extremely internal one and we may be asking too much.

To be sure, I have been talking about the establishment of spomes — *but by stages!* The change from the external spome of the earth to an internal spome on the moon is, in many ways, a mild one. There is still the chance of communication with earth, there is still the sight of the earth in the sky, even if only on a television set within the cavern, and, finally, the possibility of returning to earth someday.

It is then the men of the moon, accustomed to a mild internal spome, who will go on to spomify Mars and Ganymede. And it will be the far distant colonists, further divorced from the earth by the mere fact that it is not forever hanging in the sky like a large balloon, who will make the further step to the asteroids and the null-g phase change.

Little by little the inhabitants of spomes would get over any longing for blue skies, open air, the stretch of ocean, the intricate world of mountains, rivers, and animals.

But even a colonist from the moon or Mars would not feel at home on a star ship, which would be null-g, unless it was rapidly rotated — with all the problems that would introduce.

No, the proper crew for a star ship would be null-g people, and there would be no need to recruit them, for an asteroidal spome would be a star ship in itself. Working upward from a primitive spaceship and downward from the earth, we meet in the middle at the equation: asteroidal spome = star ship.

Under such conditions, a voyage to the stars could be made without hardships whatever. If an asteroid were fitted with rocket motors and made to veer out of its course and away from the sun (the escape velocity from the sun is considerably less in the asteroid belt than it is in earth's vicinity), what would it matter to the null-g inhabitants of the asteroid?

They had always been in a null-g internal spome, and they would still be in a null-g internal spome. They wouldn't be leaving home; they would be taking home with them. What matter how long the trip to a star? How many generations lived and died? There would be no change in their way of life.

To be sure, they would be leaving the sun, but what of that? A dweller of the asteroids would not depend on the sun for anything. Properly space-suited, he might emerge from the asteroid and observe the sun as a tiny, glowing marble in the sky, but nothing more. He may miss that sight and idealize "the sun of home," but such idealizations will evoke nothing more than a nostalgic thought, like the modern city dweller's occasional sigh for the "old home town."

The star ship turning out of its orbit might simply be taking the third and final step in the weaning of life. Once life-forms were weaned from the ocean. With the establishment of extraterrestrial spomes, life-forms will have been weaned from the earth. With the star ships, they will be weaned from the solar system.

But why should the asteroids bother to become star ships? What do they gain? A number of things:

First, the satisfaction of curiosity — the basic, itching desire to know. Why not see what the universe looks like? What's out there anyway?

Second, the desire for freedom — why circle the sun uselessly forever, when you can take your place as an independent portion of the universe, bound to no star?

Third, the usefulness of knowledge — since a trip of this sort is bound to add to the information possessed and this new information will surely be applied to the problem of adding to the security and comfort of the spome.

Nor need such a journey be dull and uneventful. True, it may take hundreds or even thousands of years to reach a star, and generations may live without seeing one at close quarters, but does this mean there is nothing at all to see?

I can't really guess what phenomena await the ship and what beauties of nature the travelers will find to admire. One thing seems certain, however: the universe must be better populated than would appear.

We see the stars because they advertise themselves so brilliantly; but small stars are far more numerous than large ones, and dim stars far more numerous than bright ones. Surely bodies that are so small and dim that they can't be seen, except at close quarters indeed, are the most numerous of all.

Perhaps no generation will pass without some dark world coming into view, some material body the star ship may pause to investigate. If the body is large, the star ship couldn't land, but it could still fly by, take up a temporary orbit, observe, and nose it out. If the body is small enough to have a negligible gravity, it can be mined and made to serve as a source of minerals to replace the small inevitable losses suffered by any spome, however efficient the cycling.

When the neighborhood of a star is reached, with its lighted planets, observations might be particularly intense and particularly interesting. The system may contain external spomes: earthlike planets bearing life — even, perhaps, intelligent life.

What a rare phenomenon that would be in terms of human lifetimes! How fortunate the generation granted such a sight!

Silently, they would observe, watch, and eventually, pass on as the unbearably attractive lure of open space beckoned — and back on the inhabited planet, creatures might talk excitedly of flying saucers — No! I am not advancing this as a serious explanation of the reports of flying saucers here on earth.

The neighborhood of a star might offer a chance for refueling, too. I can conceive that the deuterium supplies needed for the fusion reactors might be picked up in the space the ship passes through, but such deuterium is spread out incredibly thinly. It would be more concentrated within a stellar system. The neighborhood of a star might then be not only a means of seeing a rare sight, but also a chance to stock up on deuterium — enough to last another million years or so.

If an asteroidal belt were encountered about some star, a landfall might, in a sense, be made. The star ship could take up some appropriate orbit. Other asteroids could then be made into spomes. The colony would divide and new ones would be set up. Eventually one or more of them — or all of them — would set off as star ships themselves. Perhaps an old, old star ship, worn past the worthwhileness of repair, can be abandoned on such occasions — undoubtedly with much more trauma than ever the sun and earth were abandoned.

In fact, there might almost be an "alternation of generations" over the eons as far as the star ships were concerned. There would be a motile generation in which the star ships moved steadily across the vastness of space but in which population increase would have to be tightly controlled. There would then be a sessile generation after an asteroid belt was encountered, when for a long period of time there would be no motion, but the population would proliferate.

With the conclusion of each sessile generation, there would be a proliferation of star ships. As the years passed and lengthened into the hundreds of millennia, the star ships would begin to swarm over the universe — all of it their home.

And every once in a while, perhaps, two spomes would meet by arrangement.

That, I imagine, would involve a ritual of incomparable importance. There would be no flash-by with a hail and farewell. The spomes, having contacted each other in a deliberate search over vast distances, would be brought to a stand relative to each other and preparations would be made for a long stay.

Each would have compiled its own records, which it could make available to the other. There would be descriptions by each of sectors of space never visited by the other. New theories and novel interpretations of old ones would be expounded. Literature and works of art could be exchanged, differences in custom explained.

Most of all there would be the opportunity for a cross-flow of genes. An exchange of population (either temporary or permanent) might be an inevitable accomplishment of any such meeting.

And yet it may happen that such cross-flows will become impossible in an increasing number of cases. Long isolation may allow the development of varieties that may no longer be interfertile. The meeting of spomes will have to endure long enough, certainly, for a check on whether the two populations are compatible. If not, intellectual cross-fertilization will have been carried on, at any rate.

Eventually, perhaps, space will carry a load of innumerable varieties of null-g intelligences, all alike in that space is their home (and, indeed, "space-home" is what the shortened "spome" stands for); in that they are intelligent; and in that they are descended from the inhabitants of some planet that may no longer exist in their memory even as a component of legend, and from which the initial load of humanity may long since have vanished.

It may even be that Homo sapiens will not be the only species to make the transition to a star-ship culture. Perhaps there is a crucial point, reached by every intelligence, from which two roads branch off, one leading to the true conquest of space and the other to a slow withering on the planetary vine.

Out there, perhaps, are many creatures waiting for man to join them. And when we do, we may find ourselves united with them not in terms of material body resemblances, but in the life we lead and in the intellect we cultivate.

Is this, then, the consequence of the new phase change that will make space exploration truly possible? Or am I only stumbling in a vain attempt to see the unseeable? Perhaps the essential point of the phase change is as far beyond my grasp as the smell of a rose is beyond the grasp of a fish or a Beethoven symphony beyond the grasp of a chimpanzee.

But I tried!

Reef

PAUL J. McAULEY

In another story expressly written for this volume, we see the prospects for taking habitats into extreme environments. At the rim of the solar system lie great riches of light elements. Opening the inner portion of sunspace will probably require moving closer to the sun the light, volatile elements necessary for both life and for rocket fuel. This assumes the outer system is essentially a refrigerator holding raw materials, but it may not be so.

Margaret Henderson Wu was riding a proxy by telepresence deep inside Tigris Rift when Dzu Sho summoned her. The others in her crew had dropped out one by one and only she was left, descending slowly between rosy, smoothly rippled cliffs scarcely a hundred meters apart. These were pavements of the commonest vacuum organism, mosaics made of hundreds of different strains of the same species. Here and there bright red whips stuck out from the pavement; a commensal species which deposited iron sulphate crystals within its integument.

The pavement seemed to stretch endlessly below her. No probe or proxy had yet reached the bottom, still more than thirty kilometers away.

Microscopic flecks of sulfur-iron complexes, sloughed cells, and excreted globules of carbon compounds and other volatiles made a kind of vacuum smog or snow. The vacuum organisms deposited nodes and intricate lattices of reduced metals, too. Somewhere far below, these deposits, probably by some trick of superconductivity, had set up a broad-band electromagnetic resonance which pulsed like a giant's slow heartbeat.

All this futzed the telepresence link between operators and their proxies. One moment Margaret was experiencing the 320-degree panorama of the little proxy's microwave radar, the perpetual tug of vacuum on its mantle, the tang of extreme cold, a mere thirty degrees above absolute zero, the complex taste of the vacuum smog (burnt sugar, hot rubber, tar), the minute squirts of hydrogen from the folds of the proxy's puckered nozzle as it maintained its orientation relative to the cliff face during its descent, with its tentacles retracted in a tight ball around the relay piton. The next, she was back in her cradled body in warm blackness, phosphenes floating in her vision and white noise in her ears while the transmitter searched for a viable waveband, locked on and—*pow*—she was back, falling past rippled pink pavement.

The alarm went off, flashing an array of white stars over the panorama. Her number two, Srin Kerenyi, said in her ear, "You're wanted, boss."

Margaret killed the alarm and the audio feed. She was already a kilometer below the previous bench mark, and she wanted to get as deep as possible before she implanted the telemetry relay. She swiveled the proxy on its long axis, increased the amplitude of the microwave radar. Far below were intimations of swells and bumps jutting from the plane of the cliff face, textured mounds like brain coral, randomly orientated chimneys. And something else, clouds of organic matter perhaps—

The alarm again. Srin had overridden the cutout.

Margaret swore and dove at the cliff, unfurling the proxy's tentacles and jamming the piton into pinkness rough with black papillae, like a giant's tongue quick frozen against the ice. The piton's spikes fired automatically. Recoil sent the little proxy tumbling over its long axis until it reflexively stabilized itself with judicious squirts of gas. The link rastered, came back, cut out completely. Margaret hit the switch which turned the tank into a chair; the mask lifted away from her face.

Srin Kerenyi was standing in front of her. "Dzu Sho wants to talk with you, boss. Right now."

The job had been offered as a sealed contract. Science crews had been informed of the precise nature of their tasks only when the habitat was under way. But it was good basic pay with promises of fat bonuses on completion, and when she had won the survey contract, Margaret Henderson Wu brought with her most of the crew from her previous job, and nursed a small hope that this would be a change in her family's luck.

The *Ganapati* was a new habitat founded by an alliance of two of the Commonwealth's oldest patrician families. It was of standard construction, a basaltic asteroid cored by a gigawatt X-ray laser, spun up by vented rock vapor to give 0.2 gee on the inner surface of its hollowed interior, factories and big reaction motors dug into the stern. With its AIs rented out for information crunching, and refineries synthesizing exotic plastics from cane-sugar biomass and gengeneered oilseed rape precursors, the new habitat had enough income to maintain the interest on its construction loan from the Commonwealth Bourse, but not enough to attract new citizens and workers. It was still not completely fitted out, had less than a third of its optimal population.

Its Star Chamber, young and cocky and eager to win independence from their families, had taken a big gamble. They were chasing a legend.

Eighty years ago, an experiment in accelerated evolution of chemo-autotrophic vacuum organisms had been set up on a planetoid in the outer edge of the Kuiper Belt. The experiment had been run by a shell company registered on Ganymede but covertly owned by the Democratic Union of China. In those days, companies and governments of Earth were not allowed to operate in the Kuiper Belt, which had been claimed and ferociously defended by outer-system cartels. That hegemony ended in the Quiet War, but the Quiet War also destroyed all records of the experiment; even the Democratic Union of China disappeared, absorbed into the Pacific Community.

There were over fifty thousand objects with diameters greater than a hundred kilometers in the Kuiper Belt, and a billion more much smaller, the plane of their orbits stretching beyond those of Neptune and Pluto. The experimental planetoid, Enki, named for one of the Babylonian gods of creation, had been lost among them. It became a legend, like the Children's Habitat, or the ghost comet, or the pirate ship crewed by the reanimated dead, or the worker's paradise of Fiddler's Green.

And then, forty-five years after the end of the Quiet War, a data miner recovered enough information to reconstruct Enki's eccentric orbit. She sold it to the *Ganapati*. The habitat bought time on the Uranus deep-space telescopic array and confirmed that the planetoid was where it was supposed to be, currently more than seven thousand million kilometers from the sun.

Nothing more was known. The experiment could have failed almost as soon as it had begun, but if it had worked, the results would win the *Ganapati* platinum-rated credit on the Bourse. Margaret and the rest of the science crews would, of course, receive only their fees and bonuses, less deductions for air and food and water taxes, and anything they bought with scrip in the habitat's stores; the indentured workers would not even get that. Like every habitat in the Commonwealth, the *Ganapati* was structured like an ancient Greek republic, ruled by shareholding citizens, who lived in the landscaped parklands of the inner surface, and run by indentured and contract workers, who were housed in the under-croft of malls and barracks tunneled into the *Ganapati*'s rocky skin.

On the long voyage out, the science crews were on minimal pay, far less than that of the unskilled techs who worked the farms and refineries, or of the servants who maintained the citizens' households. There were food shortages on the *Ganapati* because so much biomass was being used to make exportable biochemicals. Any foodstuffs other than basic rations were expensive, and prices were carefully manipulated by the habitat's Star Chamber. When the *Ganapati* reached Enki and the con-tracts of the science crews were activated, food prices increased accord-ingly. Techs and household servants suddenly found themselves unable to afford anything other than dole yeast. Resentment bubbled over into skirmishes and knife fights, and a small riot which the White Mice, the undercroft's police, subdued with gas. Margaret had had to take time off to bail out several of her crew, had given them an angry lecture about threatening everyone's bonuses.

"We got to defend our honor," one of the men said.

"Don't be a fool," Margaret told him. "The citizens play workers against science crews to keep both sides in their places, and still turn a good profit from increases in food prices. Just be glad you can afford the good stuff now, and keep out of trouble."

"They were calling you names, boss," the man said. "On account you're —"

Margaret stared him down. She was standing on a chair, but even so she was a good head shorter than the gangling outers. She said, "I'll fight my own fights. I always have. Just think of your bonuses and keep quiet. It will be worth it. I promise you."

And it was worth it, because of the discovery of the reef.

At some time in the deep past, Enki had suffered an impact which remelted it and split it into two big pieces and thousands of fragments. One lone fragment still orbited Enki, a tiny moonlet where the AI which had controlled the experiment lived. The big pieces were drawn together again by their feeble gravity fields, but cooled before coalescence was completed, leaving a vast deep chasm, Tigris Rift, at the lumpy equator.

Margaret's crew discovered that the vacuum organisms had proliferated wildly in the deepest part of the Rift, deriving energy by oxidation of elemental sulfur and ferrous iron, converting carbonaceous material into useful organic chemicals. There were crusts and sheets, things like thin scarves folded into fragile vases and chimneys, organ-pipe clusters, whips, delicate fretted laces. Some fed on others, one crust slowly overgrowing and devouring another. Others appeared to be parasites, sending complex veins ramifying through the thalli of their victims. Water-mining organisms recruited sulfur oxidizers, trading precious water for energy and forming warty outgrowths like stromaliths. Some were more than a hundred meters across, surely the largest prokaryotic colonies in the known Solar System.

All this variety, and after only eighty years of accelerated evolution! Wild beauty won from the cold and the dark. The potential to feed billions. The science crews would get their bonuses, all right; the citizens would become billionaires.

Margaret spent all her spare time exploring the reef by proxy, pushing her crew hard to overcome the problems of penetrating the depths of the Rift. Although she would not admit it even to herself, she had fallen in love with the reef. She would even have explored in person if the Star Chamber allowed it, but as in most habitats, the *Ganapati*'s citizens did not like their workers going where they themselves would not.

Clearly, the experiment had far exceeded its parameters, but no one knew why. The AI which had overseen the experiment shut down thirty years ago. There was still heat in its crude proton-beam fission pile, but it had been overgrown by the very organisms it manipulated.

Its task had been simple. Colonies of a dozen species of slow-growing chemoautotrophs were introduced into a part of the Rift rich with sulfur and ferrous iron. Thousands of random mutations were induced. Most colonies died, and those few which thrived were sampled, mutated, and reintroduced in a cycle repeated every hundred days.

But the AI had selected only for fast growth, not for adaptive radiation, and the science crews held heated seminars about the possible cause of the unexpected richness of the reef. Very few believed that it was simply a result of accelerated evolution. Many terrestrial bacteria divided every twenty minutes in favorable conditions, and certain bacteria were known to have evolved from being resistant to an antibiotic to becoming obligately dependent upon it as a food source in less than five days, or only three hundred and sixty generations. But that was merely a biochemical adaptation. The fastest division rate of the vacuum organisms in the Rift was less than once a day, and while that still meant more than thirty thousand generations since the reef was seeded, half a million years in human terms, the evolutionary radiation in the reef was the equivalent of Neanderthal Man's evolving to fill every mammalian niche from bats to whales.

Margaret's survey crew explored and sampled the reef for more than thirty days. Cluster analysis suggested that they had identified less than ten percent of the species which had formed from the original seed population. And now deep radar suggested that there were changes in the unexplored regions in the deepest part of Tigris Rift, which the proxies had not yet successfully penetrated.

Margaret pointed this out at the last seminar.

"We're making hypotheses on incomplete information. We don't know everything that's out there. Sampling suggests that complexity increases away from the surface. There could be thousands more species in the deep part of the Rift."

At the back of the room, Opie Kindred, the head of the genetics crew, said languidly, "We don't need to know everything. That's not what we're paid for. We've already found several species which perform better than present commercial cultures. The *Ganapati* can make money from them and we'll get full bonuses. Who cares how they got there?"

Arn Nivedta, the chief of the biochemist crew, said, "We're all scientists here. We prove our worth by finding out how things work. Are your mysterious experiments no more than growth tests, Opie? If so, I'm disappointed."

The genetics crew had set up an experimental station on the surface of the *Ganapati*, off limits to everyone else.

Opie smiled. "I'm not answerable to you."

This was greeted with shouts and jeers. The science crews were tired and on edge, and the room was hot and poorly ventilated.

"Information should be free," Margaret said. "We all work toward the same end. Or are you hoping for extra bonuses, Opie?"

There was a murmur in the room. It was a tradition that all bonuses were pooled and shared out between the various science crews at the end of a mission.

Opie Kindred was a clever, successful man, yet somehow soured, as if the world was a continual disappointment. He rode his team hard, was quick to find failure in others. Margaret was a natural target for his scorn, a squat, muscle-bound, unedited dwarf from Earth who had to take drugs so that she could survive in microgravity, who grew hair in all sorts of unlikely places. He stared at her with disdain and said, "I'm surprised at the tone of this briefing, Dr. Wu. Wild speculations built on nothing at all. I have sat here for a hour and heard nothing useful. We are paid to get results, not generate hypotheses. All we hear from your crew is excuses, when what we want are samples. It seems simple enough to me. If something is upsetting your proxies, then you should use robots. Or send people in and handpick samples. I've worked my way through almost all you've obtained. I need more material, especially in light of my latest findings."

"Robots need transmission relays too," Srin Kerenyi pointed out.

Orly Higgins said, "If you ride them, to be sure. But I don't see the need for human control. It is a simple enough task to program them to go down, pick up samples, return."

She was the leader of the crew which had unpicked the AI's corrupted code, and was an acolyte of Opie Kindred.

"The proxies failed whether or not they were remotely controlled,"

Margaret said, "and on their own they are as smart as any robot. I'd love to go down there myself, but the Star Chamber has forbidden it for the usual reasons. They're scared we'll get up to something if we go where they can't watch us."

"Careful, boss," Srin Kerenyi whispered. "The White Mice are bound to be monitoring this."

"I don't care," Margaret said. "I'm through with trying polite requests. We need to get down there, Srin."

"Sure, boss. But getting arrested for sedition isn't the way."

"There's some interesting stuff in the upper levels," Arn Nivedta said. "Commercial stuff, as you pointed out, Opie."

Murmurs of agreement throughout the crowded room. The reef could make the *Ganapati* the richest habitat in the Outer System, where expansion was limited by the availability of fixed carbon. Even a modest-sized comet nucleus, ten kilometers in diameter, say, and salted with only one-hundredth of one percent carbonaceous material, contained fifty million tons of carbon, mostly as methane and carbon monoxide ice, with a surface dusting of tarry long-chain hydrocarbons. And the mass of some planetoids consisted of up to fifty percent methane ice. But most vacuum organisms converted simple carbon compounds into organic matter using the energy of sunlight captured by a variety of photosynthetic pigments, and so could grow only on the surfaces of planetoids. No one had yet developed vacuum organisms which, using other sources of energy, could efficiently mine planetoid interiors. But that was what accelerated evolution appeared to have produced in the reef. It could enable exploitation of the entire volume of objects in the Kuiper Belt, and beyond, in the distant Oort Cloud.

Arn Nivedta waited for silence, and added, "If the reef species test out, of course. What about it, Opie? Are they commercially viable?"

"We have our own ideas about commercialism," Opie Kindred said. "I think you'll find that we hold the key to success here."

Boos and catcalls at this from both the biochemists and the survey crew. The room was polarizing. Margaret saw one of her crew unsheathe a sharpened screwdriver, and she caught the man's hand and squeezed it until he cried out. "Let it ride," she told him. "Remember that we're scientists."

"We hear of indications of more diversity in the depths, but we can't seem to get there. One might suspect," Opie said, his thin upper lip lifting in a supercilious curl, "sabotage."

"The proxies are working in the upper part of the Rift," Margaret said, "and we are working hard to get them operative farther down."

"Let's hope so," Opie Kindred said. He stood, and around him his crew stood, too. "I'm going back to work, and so should all of you. Especially you, Dr. Wu. Perhaps you should be attending to your proxies instead of planning useless expeditions."

And so the seminar broke up in uproar, with nothing productive coming from it and lines of enmity drawn through the community of scientists.

"Opie is scheming to come out of this on top," Arn Nivedta said to Margaret afterward. He was a friendly, enthusiastic man, tall even for an outer, and as skinny as a rail. He stooped in Margaret's presence, trying to appear less tall. He said, "He wants desperately to become a citizen, and so he thinks like one."

"Well, my god, we all want to be citizens," Margaret said. "Who wants to live like this?"

She gestured, meaning the crowded bar, its rock walls and low ceiling, harsh lights and the stink of spilled beer and too many people in close proximity. Her parents had been citizens, once upon a time. Before their run of bad luck. It was not that she wanted those palmy days back—she could scarcely remember them—but she wanted more than this.

She said, "The citizens sleep in silk sheets and eat real meat and play their stupid games, and we have to do their work on restricted budgets. The reef is the discovery of the century, Arn, but god forbid that the citizens should begin to exert themselves. We do the work, they fuck in rose petals and get the glory."

Arn laughed at this.

"Well, it's true!"

"It's true we have not been as successful as we might like," Arn said mournfully.

Margaret said reflectively, "Opie's a bastard, but he's smart, too. He picked just the right moment to point the finger at me."

Loss of proxies was soaring exponentially, and the proxy farms of the *Ganapati* were reaching a critical point. Once losses exceeded reproduction, the scale of exploration would have to be drastically curtailed, or the seed stock would have to be pressed into service, a gamble the *Ganapati* could hardly afford.

And then, the day after the disastrous seminar, Margaret was pulled back from her latest survey to account for herself in front of the chairman of the *Ganapati*'s Star Chamber.

"We are not happy with the progress of your survey, Dr. Wu," Dzu Sho said. "You promise much, but deliver little."

Margaret shot a glance at Opie Kindred, and the man smiled. He was immaculately dressed in gold-trimmed white tunic and white leggings. His scalp was oiled and his manicured fingernails were painted with something that split light into rainbows. Margaret, fresh from the tank, wore loose, grubby work grays. There was sticky electrolyte paste on her arms and legs and shaven scalp, the reek of sour sweat under her breasts and in her armpits.

She contained her anger and said, "I have submitted daily reports on the problems we encountered. Progress is slow but sure. I have just established a relay point a full kilometer below the previous datum point."

Dzu Sho waved this away. Naked, as smoothly fat as a seal, he lounged in a blue gel chair. He had a round, hairless head and pinched features, like a thumbprint on an egg. The habitat's lawyer sat behind him, a young woman neat and anonymous in a gray tunic suit. Margaret, Opie Kindred, and Arn Nivedta sat on low stools, supplicants to Dzu Sho's authority. Behind them, half a dozen servants stood at the edge of the grassy space.

This was in an arbor of figs, ivy, bamboos, and fast-growing banyan at the edge of Sho's estate. Residential parkland curved above, a patchwork of spindly, newly planted woods and meadows and gardens. Flyers were out, triangular rigs in primary colors pirouetting around the weightless axis. Directly above, mammoths the size of large dogs grazed an emerald-green field. The parkland stretched away to the ring lake and its slosh barrier, three kilometers in diameter, and the huge farms which dominated the inner surface of the habitat. Fields of lentils, wheat, cane fruits, tomatoes, rice, and exotic vegetables for the tables of the citizens, and fields and fields and fields of sugar cane and oilseed rape for the biochemical industry and the yeast tanks.

Dzu Sho said, "Despite the poor progress of the survey crew, we have what we need, thanks to the work of Dr. Kindred. This is what we will discuss."

Margaret glanced at Arn, who shrugged. Opie Kindred's smile deepened. He said, "My crew has established why there is so much diversity here. The vacuum organisms have invented sex."

"We know they have sex," Arn said. "How else could they evolve?"

His own crew had shown that the vacuum organisms could exchange genetic material through pilli, microscopic hollow tubes grown between cells or hyphal strands. It was analogous to the way in which genes for antibiotic resistance spread through populations of terrestrial bacteria.

"I do not mean genetic exchange, but genetic recombination," Opie Kindred said. "I will explain."

The glade filled with flat plates of color as the geneticist conjured charts and diagrams and pictures from his slate. Despite her anger, Margaret quickly immersed herself in the flows of data, racing ahead of Opie Kindred's clipped explanations.

It was not normal sexual reproduction. There was no differentiation into male or female, or even into complementary mating strains. Instead, it was mediated by a species which aggressively colonized the thalli of others. Margaret had already seen it many times, but until now she had thought that it was merely a parasite. Instead, as Opie Kindred put it, it was more like a vampire.

A shuffle of pictures, movies patched from hundreds of hours of material collected by roving proxies. Here was a colony of the black crustose species found all through the explored regions of the Rift. Time speeded up. The crustose colony elongated its ragged perimeter in pulsing spurts. As it grew, it exfoliated microscopic particles. Margaret's viewpoint spiraled into a close-up of one of the exfoliations, a few cells wrapped in nutrient-storing strands.

Millions of these little packages floated through the vacuum. If one landed on a host thallus, it injected its genetic payload into the host cells. The view dropped inside one such cell. A complex of carbohydrate and protein strands webbing the interior like intricately packed spiderwebs. Part of the striated cell wall drew apart, and a packet of DNA coated in hydrated globulins and enzymes burst inward. The packet contained the genomes of both the parasite and its previous victim. It latched onto protein strands and crept along on ratcheting microtubule claws until it fused with the cell's own circlet of DNA.

The parasite possessed an enzyme which snipped strands of genetic material at random lengths. These recombined, forming chimeric cells which contained genetic information from both sets of victims, with the predator species' genome embedded among the native genes like an interpenetrating text.

The process repeated itself in flurries of coiling and uncoiling DNA strands as the chimeric cells replicated. It was a crude, random process. Most contained incomplete or noncomplementary copies of the genomes and were unable to function, or contained so many copies that transcription was halting and imperfect. But a few out of every thousand were viable, and a few of those were more vigorous than either of their parents. They grew from a few cells to a patch, and finally overgrew the parental matrix in which they were embedded. There were pictures which showed every stage of this transformation in a laboratory experiment.

"This is why I have not shared the information until now," Opie Kindred said, as the pictures faded around him. "I had to ensure by experimental testing that my theory was correct. Because the procedure is so inefficient, we had to screen thousands of chimeras until we obtained a strain which overgrew its parent."

"A very odd and extreme form of reproduction," Arn said. "The parent dies so that the child might live."

Opie Kindred smiled. "It is more interesting than you might suppose."

The next sequence showed the same colony, now clearly infected by the parasitic species—leprous black spots mottled its pinkish surface. Again time speeded up. The spots grew larger, merged, shed a cloud of exfoliations.

"Once the chimera overgrows its parent," Opie Kindred said, "the genes of the parasite, which have been reproduced in every cell of the thallus, are activated. The host cells are transformed. It is rather like an RNA virus, except that the virus does not merely subvert the protein- and RNA-making machinery of its host cell. It takes over the cell itself. Now the cycle is completed, and the parasite sheds exfoliations that will in turn infect new hosts.

"Here is the motor of evolution. In some of the infected hosts, the parasitic genome is prevented from expression, and the host becomes resistant to infection. It is a variation of the Red Queen's race. There is an evolutionary pressure upon the parasite to evolve new infective forms, and then for the hosts to resist them, and so on. Meanwhile, the host species benefit from new genetic combinations which by selection incrementally improve growth. The process is random but continuous, and takes place on a vast scale. I estimate that millions of recombinant cells are produced each hour, although perhaps only one in ten million are viable, and of those only one in a million are significantly more efficient at growth than their parents. But this is more than sufficient to explain the diversity we have mapped in the reef."

Arn said, "How long have you known this, Opie?"

"I communicated my findings to the Star Chamber just this morning," Opie Kindred said. "The work has been very difficult. My crew has to work under very tight restraints, using Class One containment techniques, as with the old immunodeficiency plagues."

"Yah, of course," Arn said. "We don't know how the exfoliations might contaminate the ship."

"Exactly," Opie Kindred said. "That is why the reef is dangerous."

Margaret bridled at this. She said sharply, "Have you tested how long the exfoliations survive?"

"There is a large amount of data about bacterial spore survival. Many survive thousands of years in vacuum close to absolute zero. It hardly seems necessary—"

"You didn't bother," Margaret said. "My God, you want to destroy the reef and you have no *evidence*. You didn't *think*."

It was the worst of insults in the scientific community. Opie Kindred colored, but before he could reply, Dzu Sho held up a hand, and his employees obediently fell silent.

"The Star Chamber has voted," Dzu Sho said. "It is clear that we have all we need. The reef is dangerous, and must be destroyed. Dr. Kindred has suggested a course of action which seems appropriate. We will poison the sulfur-oxidizing cycle and kill the reef."

"But we don't know—"

"We haven't found—"

Margaret and Arn had spoken at once. Both fell silent when Dzu Sho held up a hand again. He said, "We have isolated strains which are commercially useful. Obviously, we can't use the organisms we have isolated because they contain the parasite within every cell. But we can synthesize useful gene sequences and splice them into current commercial strains of vacuum organism to improve quality."

"I must object," Margaret said. "This is a unique construct. The chances of it evolving again are minimal. We must study it further. We might be able to discover a cure for the parasite."

"It is unlikely," Opie Kindred said. "There is no way to eliminate the parasite from the host cells by gene therapy, because they are hidden within the host chromosome, shuffled in a different pattern in every cell of the trillions of cells that make up the reef. However, it is quite easy to produce a poison that will shut down the sulfur-oxidizing metabolism common to the different kinds of reef organism."

"Production has been authorized," Sho said. "It will take, what did you tell me, Dr. Kindred?"

"We require a large quantity, given the large biomass of the reef. Ten days at least. No more than fifteen."

"We have not studied it properly," Arn said. "So we cannot yet say what and what is not possible."

Margaret agreed, but before she could add her objection, her earpiece trilled, and Srin Kerenyi's voice said apologetically, "Trouble, boss. You better come at once."

The survey suite was in chaos, and there was worse chaos in the Rift. Margaret had to switch proxies three times before she found one she could operate. All around her, proxies were fluttering and jinking, as if caught in strong currents instead of floating in vacuum in virtual free fall.

This was at the four-thousand-meter level, where the nitrogen-ice walls of the Rift were sparsely patched with faux yellow and pink marblings that followed veins of sulfur and organic contaminants. The taste of the vacuum smog here was strong, like burnt rubber coating Margaret's lips and tongue.

As she looked around, a proxy jetted toward her. It overshot and rebounded from a gable of frozen nitrogen, its nozzle jinking back and
forth as it tried to stabilize its position.

"Fuck," its operator, Kim Nieye, said in Margaret's ear. "Sorry, boss.
I've been through five of these, and now I'm losing this one."

On the other side of the cleft, a hundred meters away, two specks
tumbled end over end, descending at a fair clip toward the depths. Margaret's vision color-reversed, went black, came back to normal. She said,
"How many?"

"Just about all of them. We're using proxies that were up in the table-
lands, but as soon as we bring them down, they start going screwy too."

"Herd some up and get them to the sample pickup point. We'll need
to do dissections."

"No problem, boss. Are you okay?"

Margaret's proxy had suddenly upended. She couldn't get its trim
back. "I don't think so," she said, and then the proxy's nozzle flared, and
with a pulse of gas the proxy shot away into the depths.

It was a wild ride. The proxy expelled all its gas reserves, accelerating
as straight as an arrow. Coralline formations blurred past, and then long
stretches of sulfur-eating pavement. The proxy caromed off the narrowing walls and began to tumble madly.

Margaret had no control. She was a helpless but exhilarated passenger. She passed the place where she had set the relay and continued to
fall. The link started to break up. She lost all sense of proprioception, although given the tumbling fall of the proxy, that was a blessing. Then the
microwave radar started to go, with swathes of raster washing across the
false-color view. Somehow the proxy managed to stabilize itself, so it was
falling headfirst toward the unknown regions at the bottom of the Rift.
Margaret glimpsed structures swelling from the walls. And then everything went away, and she was back, sweating and nauseous on the couch.

It was bad. More than ninety-five percent of the proxies had been lost.
Most, like Margaret's, had been lost in the depths. A few, badly damaged
by collision, had stranded among the reef colonies, but proxies which
tried to retrieve them went out of control too, and were lost. It was clear
that some kind of infective process had affected them. Margaret had several dead proxies collected by a sample robot and ordered that the survivors should be regrouped and kept above the deep part of the Rift

where the vacuum organisms proliferated. And then she went to her suite in the undercroft and waited for the Star Chamber to call her before them.

The Star Chamber took away Margaret's contract, citing failure to perform and possible sedition (that remark in the seminar had been recorded). She was moved from her suite to a utility room in the lower level of the undercroft and put to work in the farms.

She thought of her parents.

She had been here before.

She thought of the reef.

She couldn't let it go.

She would save it if she could.

Srin Kerenyi kept her up-to-date. The survey crew and its proxies were restricted to the upper level of the reef. Manned teams under Opie Kindred's control were exploring the depths—he was trusted where Margaret was not—but if they discovered anything, it wasn't communicated to the other science crews.

Margaret was working in the melon fields when Arn Nivedta found her. The plants sprawled from hydroponic tubes laid across gravel beds, beneath blazing lamps hung in the axis of the farmlands. It was very hot, and there was a stink of dilute sewage. Little yellow ants swarmed everywhere. Margaret had tucked the ends of her pants into the rolled tops of her shoesocks, and wore a green eyeshade. She was using a fine paintbrush to transfer pollen to the stigma of the melon flowers.

Arn came bouncing along between the long rows of plants like a pale scarecrow intent on escape. He wore only tight black shorts and a web belt hung with pens, little silvery tools, and a notepad.

He said, "They must hate you, putting you in a shithole like this."

"I have to work, Arn. Work or starve. I don't mind it. I grew up working the fields."

Not strictly true: her parents had been ecosystem designers. But it was how it had ended.

Arn said cheerfully, "I'm here to rescue you. I can prove it wasn't your fault."

Margaret straightened, one hand on the small of her back where a permanent ache had lodged itself. She said, "Of course it wasn't my fault. Are you all right?"

Arn had started to hop about, brushing at one bare long-toed foot and then the other. The ants had found him. His toes curled like fingers. The big toes were opposed. Monkey feet.

"Ants are having something of a population explosion," she said. "We're in the stage between introduction and stabilization here. The cycles will smooth out as the ecosystem matures."

Arn brushed at his legs again. His prehensile big toe flicked an ant from the pad of his foot. "They want to incorporate me into the cycle, I think."

"We're all in the cycle, Arn. The plants grow in sewage; we eat the plants." Margaret saw her supervisor coming toward them through the next field. She said, "We can't talk here. Meet me in my room after work."

Margaret's new room was barely big enough for a hammock, a locker, and a tiny shower with a toilet pedestal. Its rock walls were unevenly coated with dull green fiber spray. There was a constant noise of pedestrians beyond the oval hatch; the air conditioning allowed in a smell of frying oil and ketones despite the filter trap Margaret had set up. She had stuck an aerial photograph of New York, where she had been born, above the head stay of her hammock, and dozens of glossy printouts of the reef scaled the walls. Apart from the pictures, a few clothes in the closet, and the spider plant under the purple grolite, the room was quite anonymous.

She had spent most of her life in rooms like this. She could pack in five minutes, ready to move on to the next job.

"This place is probably bugged," Arn said. He sat with his back to the door, sipping schnapps from a silvery flask and looking at the overlapping panoramas of the reef.

Margaret sat on the edge of her hammock. She was nervous and excited. She said, "Everywhere is bugged. I want them to hear that I'm not guilty. Tell me what you know."

Arn looked at her. "I examined the proxies you sent back. I wasn't quite sure what I was looking for, but it was surprisingly easy to spot."

"An infection," Margaret said.

"Yah, a very specific infection. We concentrated on the nervous system, given the etiology. In the brain we found lesions, always in the same area."

Margaret examined the three-dimensional color-enhanced tomographic scan Arn had brought. The lesions were little black bubbles in the underside of the unfolded cerebellum, just in front of the optic node.

"The same in all of them," Arn said. "We took samples, extracted DNA, and sequenced it." A grid of thousands of colored dots, then another superimposed over it. All the dots lined up.

"A match to Opie's parasite," Margaret guessed.

Arn grinned. He had a nice smile. It made him look like an enthusiastic boy. "We tried that first, of course. Got a match, then went through the library of reef organisms, and got partial matches. Opie's parasite has its fingerprints in the DNA of everything in the reef, but this"—he jabbed a long finger through the projection—"is the pure quill. Just an unlucky accident that it lodges in the brain at this particular place and produces the behavior you saw."

"Perhaps it isn't a random change," Margaret said. "Perhaps the reef has a use for the proxies."

"Teleology," Arn said. "Don't let Opie hear that thought. He'd use it against you. This is evolution. It isn't directed by anything other than natural selection. There is no designer, no watchmaker. Not after the AI crashed, anyway, and it only pushed the ecosystem toward more efficient sulfur oxidation. There's more, Margaret. I've been doing some experiments on the side. Exposing aluminum foil sheets in orbit around Enki. There are exfoliations everywhere."

"Then Opie is right."

"No, no. All the exfoliations I found were nonviable. I did more experiments. The exfoliations are metabolically active when released, unlike bacterial spores. And they have no protective wall. No reason for them to have one, yah? They live only for a few minutes. Either they land on a new host or they don't. Solar radiation easily tears them apart. You can kill them with a picowatt ultraviolet laser. Contamination isn't a problem."

"And it can't infect us," Margaret said. "Vacuum organisms and proxies have the same DNA code as us, the same as everything from Earth, for that matter, but it's written in artificial nucleotide bases. The reef isn't dangerous at all, Arn."

"Yah, but in theory it could infect every vacuum organism ever designed. The only way around it would be to change the base structure of vacuum organism DNA—how much would that cost?"

"I know about contamination, Arn. The mold that wrecked the biome designed by my parents came in with someone or something. Maybe on clothing, or skin, or in the gut, or in some trade goods. It grew on anything with a cellulose cell wall. Every plant was infected. The fields were covered with huge sheets of gray mold; the air was full of spores. It didn't infect people, but more than a hundred died from massive allergic reactions and respiratory failure. They had to vent the atmosphere in the end. And my parents couldn't find work after that."

Arn said gently, "That is the way. We live by our reputations. It's hard when something goes wrong."

Margaret ignored this. She said, "The reef is a resource, not a danger. You're looking at it the wrong way, like Opie Kindred. We need diversity. Our biospheres have to be complicated because simple systems are prone to invasion and disruption, but even so, they aren't one-hundredth as complicated as those on Earth. If my parents' biome had been more diverse, the mold couldn't have found a foothold."

"There are some things I could do without." Arn scratched his left ankle with the toes of his right foot. "Like those ants."

"Well, we don't know if we need the ants specifically, but we need variety, and they contribute to it. They help aerate the soil, to begin with, which encourages stratification and diversity of soil organisms. There are a million different kinds of microbe in a gram of soil from a forest on Earth; we have to make do with less than a thousand. We don't have one-tenth that number of useful vacuum organisms, and most are grown in monoculture, which is the most vulnerable ecosystem of all. That was the cause of the crash of the green revolution on Earth in the twenty-first century. But there are hundreds of different species in the reef. Wild species, Arn. You could seed a planetoid with them and go harvest it a year later. The citizens don't go outside because they have their parklands, their palaces, their virtualities. They've forgotten that the outer system isn't just the habitats. There are millions of small planetoids in the Kuiper Belt. Anyone with a dome and the reef vacuum organisms could homestead one."

She had been thinking about this while working out in the fields. The Star Chamber had given her plenty of time to think.

Arn shook his head. "They all have the parasite lurking in them. Any species from the reef can turn into it. Perhaps even the proxies."

"We don't know enough," Margaret said. "I saw things in the bottom of the Rift, before I lost contact with the proxy. Big structures. And there's the anomalous temperature gradient, too. The seat of change must be down there, Arn. The parasite could be useful, if we can master it. The viruses which caused the immunodeficiency plagues are used for gene therapy now. Opie Kindred has been down there. He's suppressing what he has found."

"Yah, well, it does not much matter. They have completed synthesis of the metabolic inhibitor. I'm friendly with the organics chief. They diverted most of the refinery to it." Arn took out his slate. "He showed me how they have set it up. That is what they have been doing down in the Rift. Not exploring."

"Then we have to do something now."

"It is too late, Margaret."

"I want to call a meeting, Arn. I have a proposal."

Most of the science crews came. Opie Kindred's crew was a notable exception; Arn said that it gave him a bad feeling.

"They could be setting us up," he told Margaret.

"I know they're listening. That's good. I want it in the open. If you're worried about getting hurt, you can always leave."

"I came because I wanted to. Like everyone else here. We're all scientists. We all want the truth known." Arn looked at her. He smiled. "You want more than that, I think."

"I fight my own fights." All around people were watching. Margaret added, "Let's get this thing started."

Arn called the meeting to order and gave a brief presentation about his research into survival of the exfoliations before throwing the matter open to the meeting. Nearly everyone had an opinion. Microphones hovered in the room, and at times three or four people were shouting at one another. Margaret let them work off their frustration. Some simply wanted to register a protest; a small but significant minority were worried about losing their bonuses or even all of their pay.

"Better that than our credibility," one of Orly Higgins's techs said. "That's what we live by. None of us will work again if we allow the *Ganapati* to become a plague ship."

Yells of approval, whistles.

Margaret waited until the noise had died down, then got to her feet. She was in the center of the horseshoe of seats, and everyone turned to watch, more than a hundred people. Their gaze fell upon her like sunlight; it strengthened her. A microphone floated down in front of her face.

"Arn has shown that contamination isn't an issue," Margaret said. "The issue is that the Star Chamber want to destroy the reef because they want to exploit what they've found and stop anyone else using it. I'm against that, all the way. I'm not gengeneered. Microgravity is not my natural habitat. I have to take a dozen different drugs to prevent reabsorption of calcium from my bone, collapse of my circulatory system, fluid retention, all the bad stuff microgravity does to unedited Earth stock. I'm not allowed to have children here, because they would be as crippled as me. Despite that, my home is here. Like all of you, I would like to have the benefits of being a citizen, to live in the parklands and eat real food. But there aren't enough parklands for everyone, because the citizens who own the habitats control production of fixed carbon. The vacuum organisms we have found could change that. The reef may be a source of plague, or it may be a source of unlimited organics. We don't know. What we do know is that the reef is unique and we haven't finished exploring it. If the Star Chamber destroys it, we may never know what's out there."

Cheers at this. Several people rose to make points, but Margaret wouldn't give way. She wanted to finish.

"Opie Kindred has been running missions to the bottom of the Rift, but he hasn't been sharing what he's found there. Perhaps he no longer thinks that he's one of us. He'll trade his scientific reputation for citizenship," Margaret said, "but that isn't our way, is it?"

"NO!" the crowd roared.

And the White Mice invaded the room.

Sharp cracks, white smoke, screams. The White Mice had long flexible sticks weighted at one end. They went at the crowd like farmers threshing corn. Margaret was separated from Arn by a wedge of panicking people. Two techs got hold of her and steered her out of the room, down a corridor filling with smoke. Arn loomed out of it, clutching his slate to his chest.

"They're getting ready to set off the poison," he said as they ran in long loping strides.

"Then I'm going now," Margaret said.

Down a drop pole onto a corridor lined with shops. People were smashing windows. No one looked at them as they ran through the riot. They turned a corner, the sounds of shouts and breaking glass fading. Margaret was breathing hard. Her eyes were smarting, her nose running.

"They might kill you," Arn said. He grasped her arm. "I can't let you go, Margaret."

She shook herself free. Arn tried to grab her again. He was taller, but she was stronger. She stepped inside his reach and jumped up and popped him on the nose with the flat of her hand.

He sat down, blowing bubbles of blood from his nostrils, blinking up at her with surprised, tear-filled eyes.

She snatched up his slate. "I'm sorry, Arn," she said. "This is my only chance. I might not find anything, but I couldn't live with myself if I didn't try."

Margaret was five hundred kilometers out from the habitat when the radio beeped. "Ignore it," she told her pressure suit. She was sure that she knew who was trying to contact her, and she had nothing to say to him.

This far out, the sun was merely the brightest star in the sky. Behind and above Margaret, the dim elongated crescent of the *Ganapati* hung before the sweep of the Milky Way. Ahead, below the little transit platform's motor, Enki was growing against a glittering starscape, a lumpy potato with a big notch at the widest point.

The little moonlet was rising over the notch, a swiftly moving fleck of light. For a moment, Margaret had the irrational fear that she would collide with it, but the transit platform's navigational display showed her that she would fall above and behind it. Falling past a moon! She couldn't help smiling at the thought.

"Priority override," her pressure suit said. Its voice was a reassuring contralto Margaret knew as well as her mother's.

"Ignore it," Margaret said again.

"Sorry, Maggie. You know I can't do that."

"Quite correct," another voice said.

Margaret identified him a moment before the suit helpfully printed his name across the helmet's visor. Dzu Sho.

"Turn back right now," Sho said. "We can take you out with the spectrographic laser if we have to."

"You wouldn't dare," she said.

"I do not believe anyone would mourn you," Sho said unctuously. "Leaving *Ganapati* was an act of sedition, and we're entitled to defend ourselves."

Margaret laughed. It was just the kind of silly, sententious, self-important nonsense that Sho was fond of spouting.

"I am entirely serious," Sho said.

Enki had rotated to show that the notch was the beginning of a groove. The groove elongated as the worldlet rotated farther. Tigris Rift. Its edges ramified in complex fractal branchings.

"I'm going where the proxies fell," Margaret said. "I'm still working for you."

"You sabotaged the proxies. That's why they couldn't fully penetrate the Rift."

"That's why I'm going—"

"Excuse me," the suit said, "but I register a small energy flux."

"Just a tickle from the ranging sight," Sho said. "Turn back now, Dr. Wu."

"I intend to come back."

It was a struggle to stay calm. Margaret thought that Sho's threat was no more than empty air. She was certain that he couldn't override the laser's AI, which would not allow it to be used against human targets. And even if he could, he wouldn't dare kill her in full view of the science crews. Sho was bluffing. He had to be.

The radio silence stretched. Then Sho said, "You're planning to commit a final act of sabotage. Don't think you can get away with it. I'm sending someone after you."

So it had been a bluff. Relief poured through her. Anyone chasing her would be using the same kind of transit platform. She had at least thirty minutes' head start.

Another voice said, "Don't think this will make you a hero."

Opie Kindred. Of course. The man never could delegate. He was on the same trajectory, several hundred kilometers behind but gaining slowly.

"Tell me what you found," she said. "Then we can finish this race before it begins."

Opie Kindred switched off his radio.

"If you had not brought along all this gear," her suit grumbled, "we could outdistance him."

"I think we'll need it soon. We'll just have to be smarter than him."

Margaret studied the schematics of the poison-spraying mechanism — it was beautifully simple, but vulnerable — while Tigris Rift swelled beneath her, a jumble of knife-edge chevron ridges. Enki was so small and the Rift so wide that the walls had fallen beneath the horizon. She was steering toward the Rift's center when the suit apologized and said that there was another priority override.

It was the *Ganapati*'s lawyer. She warned Margaret that this was being entered into sealed court records, and then formally revoked her contract and read a complaint about her seditious conduct.

"You're a contracted worker just like me," Margaret said. "We take orders, but we have a code of professional ethics, too. For the record, that's why I'm here. The reef is a unique organism. I cannot allow it to be destroyed."

Dzu Sho came onto the channel and said, "Off the record, don't think about being picked up."

The lawyer switched channels. "He does not mean it," she said. "He would be in violation of the distress statutes." Pause. "Good luck, Dr. Wu."

Then there was only the carrier wave.

Margaret wished this made her feel better. Plenty of contract workers who went against the wishes of their employers had been disappeared, or killed in industrial accidents. The fire of the mass meeting had evaporated long before the suit had assembled itself around her, and now she felt colder and lonelier than ever.

She fell, the platform shuddering now and then as it adjusted its trim. Opie Kindred's platform was a bright spark moving sideways across the drifts of stars above. Directly below was a vast flow of nitrogen ice with a black river winding through it. The center of the Rift, a cleft two kilometers long and fifty kilometers deep. The reef.

She fell toward it.

She had left the radio channel open. Suddenly, Opie Kindred said, "Stop now and it will be over."

"Tell me what you know."

No answer.

She said, "You don't have to follow me, Opie. This is my risk. I don't ask you to share it."

"You won't take this away from me."

"Is citizenship really worth this, Opie?"

No reply.

The suit's proximity alarms began to ping and beep. She turned them off one by one, and told the suit to be quiet when it complained.

"I am only trying to help," it said. "You should reduce your velocity. The target is very narrow."

"I've been here before," Margaret said.

But only by proxy. The ice field rushed up at her. Its smooth flows humped over one another, pitted everywhere with tiny craters. She glimpsed black splashes where vacuum organisms had colonized a stress ridge. Then an edge flashed past; walls unraveled on either side.

She was in the reef.

The vacuum organisms were everywhere: flat plates jutting from the walls; vases and delicate fans and fretworks; huge blotches smooth as ice or dissected by cracks. In the light cast by the platform's lamps, they did not possess the vibrant primary colors of the proxy link, but were every shade of gray and black, streaked here and there with muddy reds. Complex fans ramified far back inside the milky nitrogen ice, following veins of carbonaceous compounds.

Far above, stars were framed by the edges of the cleft. One star was falling toward her: Opie Kindred. Margaret switched on the suit's radar, and immediately it began to ping. The suit shouted a warning, but before Margaret could look around, the pings dopplered together.

Proxies.

They shot up toward her, tentacles writhing from the black, streamlined helmets of their mantles. Most of them missed, jagging erratically as they squirted bursts of hydrogen to kill their velocity. Two collided in a slow flurry of tentacles.

Margaret laughed. None of her crew would fight against her, and Sho was relying upon inexperienced operators.

The biggest proxy, three meters long, swooped past. The crystalline gleam of its sensor array reflected the lights of the platform. It decelerated, spun on its axis, and dove back toward her.

Margaret barely had time to pull out the weapon she had brought with her. It was a welding pistol, rigged on a long rod with a yoked wire around the trigger. She thrust it up like the torch of the Statue of Liberty just before the proxy struck her.

The suit's gauntlet, arm, and shoulder piece stiffened under the heavy impact, saving Margaret from broken bones, but the collision knocked the transit platform sideways. It plunged through reef growths. Like glass, they had tremendous rigidity but very little lateral strength. Rigid fans and lattices broke away, peppering Margaret and the proxy with shards. It was like falling through a series of chandeliers.

Margaret couldn't close her fingers in the stiffened gauntlet. She stood tethered to the platform with her arm and the rod raised straight up and the black proxy wrapped around them. The proxy's tentacles lashed her visor with slow, purposeful slaps.

Margaret knew that it would only take a few moments before the tentacles' carbon-fiber proteins could unlink; then they would be able to reach the life-support pack on her back.

She shouted at the suit, ordering it to relax the gauntlet's fingers. The proxy was contracting around her rigid arm as it stretched toward the life-support pack. When the gauntlet relaxed, the pressure snapped her fingers closed. Her forefinger popped free of the knuckle. She yelled with pain. And the wire rigged to the welding pistol's trigger pulled taut.

Inside the proxy's mantle, a focused beam of electrons boiled off the pistol's filament. The pistol, designed to work only in high vacuum, began to arc almost immediately, but the electron beam had already heated the integument and muscle of the proxy to more than 400°C. Vapor expanded explosively. The proxy shot away, propelled by the gases of its own dissolution.

Opie was still gaining on her. Gritting her teeth against the pain of her dislocated finger, Margaret dumped the broken welding gear. It only slowly floated away above her, for it still had the same velocity as she did.

A proxy swirled in beside her with shocking suddenness. For a moment, she gazed into its faceted sensor array, and then dots of luminescence skittered across its smooth black mantle, forming letters.

Much luck, boss. SK.

Srin Kerenyi. Margaret waved with her good hand. The proxy scooted away, rising at a shallow angle toward Opie's descending star.

A few seconds later, the cleft filled with the unmistakable flash of laser light.

The radar trace of Srin's proxy disappeared.

Shit. Opie Kindred was armed. If he got close enough, he could kill her.

Margaret risked a quick burn of the transit platform's motor to increase her rate of fall. It roared at her back for twenty seconds; when it cut out, her pressure suit warned her that she had insufficient fuel for full deceleration.

"I know what I'm doing," Margaret told it.

The complex forms of the reef dwindled past. Then there were only huge patches of black staining the nitrogen-ice walls. Margaret passed her previous record depth, and still she fell. It was like free fall; the negligible gravity of Enki did not cause any appreciable acceleration.

Opie Kindred gained on her by increments.

In vacuum, the lights of the transit platform threw abrupt pools of light onto the endlessly unraveling walls. Slowly, the pools of light elongated into glowing tunnels filled with sparkling motes. The exfoliations and gases and organic molecules were growing denser. And, impossibly, the temperature was *rising*, one degree with every five hundred meters. Far below, between the narrowing perspective of the walls, structures were beginning to resolve from the blackness.

The suit reminded her that she should begin the platform's deceleration burn. Margaret checked Opie's velocity and said she would wait.

"I have no desire to end as a crumpled tube filled with strawberry jam," the suit said. It projected a countdown on her visor and refused to switch it off.

Margaret kept one eye on Opie's velocity, the other on the blur of reducing numbers. The numbers passed zero. The suit screamed obscenities in her ears, but she waited a beat more before firing the platform's motor.

The platform slammed into her boots. Sharp pain in her ankles and knees. The suit stiffened as the harness dug into her shoulders and waist.

Opie Kindred's platform flashed past. He had waited until after she had decelerated before making his move. Margaret slapped the release buckle of the platform's harness and fired the piton gun into the nitrogen-ice wall. It was enough to slow her so that she could catch hold of a crevice and swing up into it. Her dislocated finger hurt like hell.

The temperature was a stifling eighty-seven degrees above absolute zero. The atmospheric pressure was just registering — a mix of hydrogen and carbon monoxide and hydrogen sulfide. Barely enough in the whole of the bottom of the cleft to pack into a small box at the pressure of Earth's atmosphere at sea level, but the rate of production must be tremendous to compensate for loss by diffusion into the colder vacuum above.

Margaret leaned out of the crevice. Below, it widened into a chimney between humped pressure flows of nitrogen ice sloping down to the floor of the cleft. The slopes and the floor were packed with a wild pro-liferation of growths, the familiar vases and sheets and laces, and other things, too. Great branching structures like crystal trees. Plates raised on stout stalks. Laminar tiers of plates. Tangles of black wire, hundreds of meters in diameter.

There was no sign of Opie Kindred, but tethered above the growths were the balloons of his spraying mechanism. Each was a dozen meters across, crinkled, flaccid. They were fifty degrees hotter than their sur-roundings, would have to be hotter still before the metabolic inhibitor was completely volatized inside them. When that happened, small ex-plosive devices would puncture them, and the metabolic inhibitor would be sucked into the vacuum of the cleft like smoke up a chimney.

Margaret consulted the plans and started to drop down the crevice, light as a dream, steering herself with the fingers of her left hand. The switching relays which controlled the balloons' heaters were manually controlled because of telemetry interference from the reef's vacuum smog and the broad-band electromagnetic resonance. The crash shelter where they were located was about two kilometers away, a slab of orange foamed plastic in the center of a desolation of abandoned equipment and broken and half-melted vacuum organism colonies.

The crevice widened. Margaret landed between drifts of what looked like giant soap bubbles that grew at its bottom.

And Opie Kindred's platform rose up between two of the half-inflated balloons.

Margaret dropped onto her belly behind a line of giant bubbles that grew along a smooth ridge of ice. She opened a radio channel. It was filled with a wash of static and a wailing modulation, but through the noise she heard Opie's voice faintly calling her name. She ignored it.

He was a hundred meters away and more or less at her level, turning in a slow circle. He couldn't locate her amid the radio noise, and the ambient temperature was higher than the skin of her pressure suit, so she had no infrared image.

She began to crawl along the smooth ridge. The walls of the bubbles were whitely opaque, but she could see shapes curled within them. Like embryos inside eggs.

"Everything is ready, Margaret," Opie Kindred's voice said in her helmet. "I'm going to find you, and then I'm going to sterilize this place. There are things here you know nothing about. Horribly dangerous things. Who are you working for? Tell me that, and I'll let you live."

A thread of red light waved out from the platform and a chunk of nitrogen ice cracked off explosively. Margaret felt it through the tips of her gloves.

"I can cut my way through to you," Opie Kindred said, "wherever you are hiding."

Margaret watched the platform slowly revolve. Tried to guess if she could reach the shelter while he was looking the other way. At the least she would get a good start. All she had to do was bound down the slope between the thickets of vacuum organisms and cross a kilometer of bare, crinkled nitrogen ice without being fried by Opie's laser. Still crouching, she lifted onto the tips of her fingers and toes, like a sprinter on the block. He was turning, turning. She took three deep breaths to clear her head—

—and something crashed into the ice cliff high above! It spun out in a spray of shards, hit the slope below, and spun through toppling clusters of tall black chimneys. For a moment, Margaret was paralyzed with astonishment. Then she remembered the welding gear. It had finally caught up with her.

Opie Kindred's platform slewed around and a red thread waved across the face of the cliff. A slab of ice thundered outward. Margaret bounded away, taking giant leaps and trying to look behind her at the same time.

The slab spun on its axis, shedding huge shards, and smashed into the cluster of the bubbles where she had been crouching. The ice shook like a living thing under her feet and threw her head over heels.

She stopped herself by firing the piton gun. She was on her back, looking up at the slope. High above, the bubbles were venting a dense mix of gas and oily organics. Margaret glimpsed black shapes flying away.

Some smashed into the walls and stuck there, but many more vanished upward among wreaths of thinning fog.

A chain reaction had started. Bubbles were bursting open up and down the length of the cleft.

A cluster exploded under Opie Kindred's platform and he vanished in an outpouring of shapes. The crevice shook. Nitrogen ice boiled into a dense fog. A wind got up for a few minutes. Margaret clung to the piton until it was over.

Opie Kindred had drifted down less than a hundred meters away. The visor of his helmet had been smashed by one of the black things. It was slim, with a hard, shiny exoskeleton. The broken bodies of others jostled among smashed vacuum organism colonies, glistening like beetles in the light of Margaret's suit. They were like tiny, tentacleless proxies, their swollen mantles cased in something like keratin. Some had split open, revealing ridged reaction chambers and complex matrices of black threads.

"Gametes," Margaret said, seized by a sudden wild intuition. "Little rocketships full of DNA."

The suit asked if she was all right.

She giggled. "The parasite turns everything into its own self. Even proxies!"

"I believe that I have located Dr. Kindred's platform," the suit said. "I suggest that you refrain from vigorous exercise, Maggie. Your oxygen supply is limited. What are you doing?"

She was heading toward the crash shelter. "I'm going to switch off the balloon heaters. They won't be needed."

After she shut down the heaters, Margaret insisted on hauling one of the dead creatures onto the transit platform. She shot up between the walls of the cleft, and at last rose into the range of the relay transmitters. Her radio came alive, a dozen channels blinking for attention. Arn was on one, and she told him what had happened.

"Sho wanted to light out of here," Arn said, "but stronger heads prevailed. Come home, Margaret."

"Did you see them? Did you, Arn?"

"Some hit the *Ganapati*." He laughed. "Even the Star Chamber can't deny what happened."

She rose up above the ice fields and continued to rise until the curve of the worldlet's horizon became visible, and then the walls of Tigris Rift. The *Ganapati* was a faint star bracketed between them. She called up deep radar, and saw, beyond the *Ganapati*'s strong signal, thousands of faint traces falling away into deep space.

A random scatter of genetic packages. How many would survive to strike new worldlets and give rise to new reefs?

Enough, she thought. The reef evolved in radical jumps. She had just witnessed its next revolution.

Given time, it would fill the Kuiper Belt.

A Dream of Time

GEORGE ZEBROWSKI

Macrolife (1979), from which this text is excerpted, remains a pioneering novel, and part of a larger mosaic still in the writing. It takes the skylife idea into far futurities. This is a long-view sequence near the novel's conclusion. As with any vision of distant conceptual horizons, it owes as much to dreams as to thought.

Thoughts flowed swiftly. Memory, conscience, planner and cross-roads for all intelligences within its realm, the aggregate's images of macrolife moved like a singing river, its source small and all but impossible, its main flow an inexorable rush across time, its emptying a humiliation before an infinite ocean. It was this humiliation, John sensed, that was intolerable to the vast mind of macrolife; it had not dreamed the dream of time only to die. Its fear became his fear, the terror of something large that had been made small again. He listened and watched.

::*Arising from a liquid environment, intelligent life lived on the land-masses of natural worlds, then left its cradles in mobile environments, at first using these small designs to move from one planet to another; but in time the designs grew larger, until it became possible to plan complete new environments to fit the needs of sentient beings::*

John saw shapes appearing in hundreds of thousands of sunspaces; dead worlds were torn apart by the laser-directed energy of suns. The resulting materials were being used to build a variety of habitats: spheres, tubes, domed-over bowls, egg shapes, clusters of spheres and cylinders, honeycombed asteroids, clear blisters a hundred kilometers across; rings of habitats encircled suns, drinking in the radiant energy.

::These habitats became the containers of further cultural and biological development, consciously directed, replacing endosomatic evolutionary natural selection. The form of macrolife that was known to you began as the child of earth's planetary civilization. The first forms were highly organized land and sea communities; later forms included bases on other planets, as well as an endless series of spacegoing research stations that were capable of reaching any point in the solar system. Asterome, a hollowed-out mass of ore, became the first large space home to leave sunspace, following the brief decline of civilization in that system. Asterome grew quickly, level after level, until it became a true example of macrolife, a mobile world independent of planetary circumstances::

John saw *Asterome* entering and leaving a hundred sunspaces, gathering resources, searching for intelligent life; he saw *Asterome* growing in the light of earthlike suns, double suns, green, red and white trisystems, giant red suns and blue dwarfs; he saw *Asterome's* rocky surface acquire a shell, then another, and half a hundred others, until it became the size he remembered.

::Powered by hydrogen fusion, mini black holes, and occasional accumulations of radiant energy, free of a past ruled by scarcity, macrolife reproduced itself more than a hundred times in the following millennium. Later, the development of materials synthesis made macrolife almost completely independent of agriculture and planetary systems.

::Earth-derived macroforms, like so many of different origin, dispersed into the galaxy, living for their own interests and curiosities, largely ignoring natural worlds as being unfit for viable civilizations. Macrolife's versatility naturally fostered this attitude; being a society that could easily meet the needs of its citizens, it permitted them to live as they pleased, supplying wealth and power beyond the needs of any individual. Most interests were permitted within the social container; only its destruction was

absolutely forbidden. Macrolife fulfilled the needs of beings in search of knowledge and novelty, the miraculous and infinite, while giving safety and adventure::

"How many were failures?" John asked.

::A large number. Not every world was able to isolate and preserve its most progressive and creative elements. In time these worlds destroyed themselves; but the macrolife that remained became the ultimate polis, a means for assimilating the past, utilizing the variety and rebelliousness of the present as a way to further growth and innovation. Thus macrolife secured its own future, and continues to exist::

John saw empty shells floating in the cold of interstellar space, armadas of dead shapes circling suns whose generous outpouring of energy now fled wasted into the dark abyss, past hearts and minds which had been unable to strike a balance between beast and angel.

::Inevitably, earth-derived macrolife came into contact with alien macroforms, resulting in hybrid societies, joining cultures and technologies, as well as genetic heritages through biological engineering::

John saw brightly lit interiors filled with graceful living shapes. The humanoid form was present in shades of brown, gold, black and white; four-legged beings with heavy brows and finely muscled arms strolled together with birdlike figures; water-filled macroforms supported swimming minds of vast size and profound capabilities; zero-g worlds were filled with floating creatures who seemed busy and sympathetic.

::Within the first million years, the galaxy came to be dominated by the mobile life form, swarming in numbers greater than the concentration of stars in some sectors. Raw materials for growth, in the form of gas, dust, debris and dead worlds, were everywhere, although some planetary cultures sought to restrict the gathering of resources within the confines of their solar systems; however, there were too few powerful cultures that were still ruled by scarcity to pose a serious problem in such confrontations::

Suddenly it seemed to John that he was *remembering* the history of macrolife. Then he understood; he had been part of that history, and it was only his extreme individual self of the moment which could not remember; his wider self had never forgotten.

::Macrolife became the galaxy's urban life. Planets became the countryside, with the difference that macrolife was independent of rural support. Each macroworld was different, developing along its own lines,

reproducing to create individual children, growing against the common history of the societal framework, whose stability contained all change. In your history, only the Greek city-states had aspired to such a project, and failed for lack of material success.

::Special relationships arose between some macroworlds and star systems. Many of these contacts were friendly, others hostile, with blame on both sides. Scores of sun systems, once they had developed a workable form of in-system space travel, sought to detain visiting macroforms in order to obtain technical and scientific stores; others sought to seize the starfolk's knowledge of immortality, or learn the legendary recipes for perfect nutrition. Early macroworlders regarded flesh-eaters with contempt, while planet dwellers regarded the starfolk as cannibals, because their foods were identical to their bodily proteins. On more than one occasion, a planetary system managed to destroy a macroworld; reprisals against natural worlds became more common as rising civilizations became aware of the circles of intelligent life existing on the galactic scale. The cry went out that macrolife was an infestation, a despoiler of sun systems. The only solution to this hostility was to bring new cultures into the galactic community as soon as they advanced to a certain level, while taking care to leave those in the nursery state isolated::

"What level was that?" John asked.

::The level at which they could communicate a complaint, thus illustrating the old principle that the surest way to close the gap between a scarcity-ruled civilization and one ruled by affluence is to call attention to the gap. A gap communicated spurs its own closing. Of course, a Type I civilization is one that can use the power of a whole planet to signal its complaint, so it is already on its way to solving its scarcity problems, before moving to Type II, which can use a typical sun for its activities: one such activity is talking to distant equals. Well-disguised observers often visited nursery worlds, not so much to report on what was happening as to gain personal experience of life in the universe. This was an effort to avoid the trained incapacity of specialization so often developed by Type I and II civilizations, the result of isolation from the harsher aspects of life, producing a deadening of personal resourcefulness. Later, when contact was made with previously visited worlds, the results of observation and covert influence served to form a bond between the cultures.

::In time, many natural planets transformed the materials of their sun systems into macroforms. Some launched their planets away from their *suns, taking on the attitudes of macrolife, joining in the vast tide of states; others remained in their sunspaces. Gradually the internal environments of macrolife discarded the gravity-oriented systems of natural worlds. At first, zero-g had been used as an industrial convenience, and for recreation; but as it became less necessary to visit natural worlds directly, many worlds changed over to zero-g interiors. A variety of intelligences adapted to life in these flexible, three-dimensional conditions; for these beings, visits to gravity environments were possible only through the use of exoskeletons to support their frail bodies, or in g-screened flitters. Eventually, the very atmospheres of zero-g worlds became mediums from which nutrients could be drawn directly; internally, macrolife became simpler.*

::Macrolife permeated the galaxy, having come out of the smallest lifeforms, each unit of life growing to become the unit for the next: first the endless series of cells, then organisms in great variety; then intelligent organisms; societies of intelligent organisms, rising and falling as better methods of organization were tried; finally, the first multiorganismic forms capable of freeing themselves from the limits of planetary existence.

::After filling whole galaxies, macrolife exploded outward into the metagalaxy, there to meet others like itself, combining, consolidating, transforming itself. Five million years after the birth of macrolife, all conflict with natural worlds ceased; most planetary civilizations had either destroyed themselves or become part of macrolife, mobile and sunspacebound.

::Eons passed. The new countryside being created by the birth of new suns and planets gave rise to new intelligence, which grew toward maturity unaware of our macrolife; these youths emerged into their galaxies with their own macroforms. For one thing is clear about all intelligence: however limited it may be in its origins, it sets no limits for itself in space-time. Mind sets about transforming itself into whatever form is necessary for the attainment of its desires, even if certain attainments can be possessed only in a world of dreams; in those cases, minds dream, living in synthetic realities tended by servant creations, and this form of mind dies when its suns die, unaware of the end.

::Across billions of years, macrolife became layered according to its time of origin, marked by the birth of new stars. The youngest would often initiate the boldest new projects after learning of the existence of the great circle of civilizations around them. Sometimes it took a long time for a younger group of cultures to learn of the existence of older forms::

"Who are the oldest?" John asked.

::We are nearly certain that we know every one, but there may be older Type III forms hidden from us. Our greatest concern now is to continue our system of conscious organization against entropy, to find a way to outlast the decline of nature. We have unified the universe with our communications and transit web, enabling us to go wherever our worlds exist to receive us; because of this, the mobility of macrolife is no longer as important as it was once. Suns and black holes continue to provide all the power we need, as we prepare to suffer the ruin of nature, the end that will make all the epochs of our labor useless, unless we can survive. We have rediscovered the presence of death.

::But if we can perceive the nature of the problem, if we can make use of what we know of the nature of the universe, knowledge gained through billions of years of comparing universe models against the evidence of observation and experiment, then perhaps we may succeed::

"Where in the universe are we?" John asked.

::We are gathered around a dwarf sun that wanders above the plane of a darkening galaxy, the galaxy you once knew::

The black mirror of the sunscreen revealed a plain of white stars, dull red coals, and massive clouds of gas. He was looking toward the galactic center from above. A strange brightness seemed to be hidden at the galactic core, a glowing fire covered by clouds. The small star, around which this group of macroworlds huddled, might have been an old bridge star to the Magellanic Clouds, or a waif torn loose from one of the great globular clusters.

::The galaxies rotate slowly now, and more mass is swallowed by the growing black hole at each center as rotation slows. In the times since you lived as a simple individual, we have had experience with three kinds of singularities: star-sized black holes; galaxy-core black holes; and the very small black holes that we create for our power generators, the kind that were once part of a younger universe. Some two billion years ahead in time the black holes, star-sized and galaxy-core size, will form with increasing frequency, prefiguring the universal collapse into infinite density and zero volume. Infinite density and zero volume being obvious impossibilities, the collapsed matter of our universe will disappear from the space-time we know; space will close up as it becomes infinitely curved in the vicinity of the titanic black hole's mass::

"What happens then?" John asked, feeling again that he was asking the question of another part of himself.

::Then all the energy of our universe tunnels out into a new space; the universe is wound up in a quantum fireball, expansion begins, entropy decreases. This is possible, we believe, because universes swim in an infinite superspace, each cosmos expanding and contracting in its season. Imagine that in superspace our universe leaves a mark, a point and a track; the track grows longer and shorter as it expands and contracts; each collapse into a black hole means there will be a white-hole remergence. In the case of smaller black holes, reemergence may be elsewhere in the same universe, or not at all if the quantum conditions are wrong, leaving a dense mass and a region of curved space, and only the possibility of a white hole. Each emergent universe may be different; its life cycle may be longer or shorter; the final expansion may be larger or smaller; the mass of particles may vary; there may be more disorder, more energy than matter, or the reverse; there may be a difference in the way that the monoforce breaks up into the other forces.

::Each of the universes in superspace has gone through an indefinite number of births and deaths. We may be the first intelligence to think of surviving the end of our cycle. We have an idea of how this may be done::

"By reaching across superspace to a younger locality?" John asked.

::No, although that is a consideration. Unfortunately, we have no knowledge of the topology of superspace; there would be no way to know which direction to take, even if superspace could be entered directly. There is another way, however, one based on direct physical observations::

Another configuration of macroworlds appeared on the sunscreen, a ring of faint globes circling a dark center. As John watched, one world left its position near the black hole and began to move away. For the first time in his conversation with the aggregate, John sensed an emotion, a feeling of cold dismay; it passed into him suddenly, filling him up as if it was his own. The globe was moving rapidly away from its companions now. Abruptly it exploded into brightness and died.

"What happened?"

::That world has chosen to die::

"But why?"

::Death has been unknown to us, except by choice; now we are rediscovering it. That world saw nothing more to learn in the continuing slow *decline of our universe, one that will fade across a finite time toward a fiery end. Our crisis, John Bulero, is that we have nothing to hope for::*

"But you suggested that there was a solution." The dismay had settled inside him like a massive stone; he felt regret bleeding into him as he waited for the answer.

::There is a way, perhaps, to survive. The giant black hole at the center of our galaxy is rotating. Above the event horizon, which is the point of no return for anything approaching the singularity at sublight speeds, there is an area called the ergosphere, where the surface of the collapsar seems to hover forever. There time stands still. We know because we have stayed in this area for brief periods of time, comparing the passage of time there with time outside. Short periods of time in the ergosphere are large periods of time outside. By circling the singularity within the ergosphere, we can move forward in time at a rapid rate::

"When do we come out of the ergosphere?"

::If we stay in the ergosphere long enough, the time line will link directly to the final black hole of the universe, as all the black holes merge. Then we will be circling within the ergosphere of that giant collapsar; and from there we might be able to pass into the next cycle of nature by moving through the neutral area near the singularity's equator::

"Neutral area?"

::A navigable aperture in a spinning singularity where centrifugal forces balance the crushing effects of gravitational collapse. We need this area because we do not know whether our translight drives or protective fields will function in the singularity::

"What happens then?"

::As we circle the galactic-core hole, we must move away when it begins to acquire other black holes during the universal collapse; we must do this to maintain a position in the ergosphere of the universal black hole. This will take a lot of power, possibly all the power we have, which is another reason we must have a neutral passage, an added safety in case our drives and protective fields are without power.

::Finally, only the last singularity will remain in the universe, carrying us in its very large ergosphere. Collapse will continue toward infinite density in zero volume, until the gravitational radius is reached, pulling us toward the center of the singularity in a matter of seconds; but the contraction will not continue to infinite density; long before the universe becomes

*very small, quantum effects will come into play, preventing ultimate col-
lapse. At a certain radius from the center, expansion into new space will
begin, carrying us with it, behind the white-hole outstream. Black holes,
you see, are passages into the future, white holes the outstream from the
past. If the electric charge and mass of a black hole are sufficiently large,
as they will be in the case of a galaxy core and the universal black hole,
conditions should be normal for us inside the charged fields of our worlds;
it might even be possible to protect ourselves by turning on our translight
drives.*

*::As we emerge into the newly expanding space, the time of the new uni-
verse will become our own; the aperture will close behind us as the mass of
the new universe disperses in the fireball ahead, freeing again the curvature of space. The passage will close much as the place where a straw
pushes through a bubble in the process of formation closes after the input
of gas is finished. Thus the configuration of complex information that is
macrolife, its internal systems of power and consciousness, will survive the
ruin of nature::*

The aggregate was silent for a moment, as if the effort of conveying
the magnitude of this project had been too much. All space-time would
be in anguished convulsion during the final part of the process; all form
would be wiped from the face of nature; all phenomena would perish as
macrolife struggled against dissolution, against the crushing hand of
death, which it had not known since the universe was young.

"Why are worlds dying when there is an answer?" John asked.

*::It may be a false answer. To begin with, it would take all our energy to
maintain and adjust our position within the galactic core hole's ergosphere; energy expenditure would increase as we passed farther into futu-
rity. We will need reserves to maintain our various protective fields against
the possible effects of the white-hole outstream, as well as against the density and temperature of the new universe in its early stages; we may need
to use our tachyon tunneling drives for brief moments, to pass by the effects
at the birth of the next cycle; this last may not be necessary, as the expansion might proceed with us at its outer edge. Still, there may be unforeseen
dangers. What you must understand is that the price of using all our resources and energy on such a venture has created for us what may be an in-
surmountable crisis::*

"Is there a choice?"

::*Death by choice, or death by fate*::

"But wouldn't it be better to die trying, to risk everything on even the smallest hope for success?"

::*Now you know why your extreme individuality has been returned. Our mind is too conscious of difficulties and possible failure, too unused to death, to develop the impetus to risk everything. Caution is the first principle of practical reason, which is finite, dealing with the definable and known. Under the pressure of time and death, you have reappeared to stand apart from our large individuality. Macrolife began to fragment into blocks of worlds, then into single worlds; you are one of the first individuals to reappear inside a single unit. We are forced... I am forced to interpret this as a survival response. You, and others like you, will try to save yourselves, as you must, in the manner of younger intelligences, and you may save macrolife*::

"Then ... my body has not persisted from before." Suddenly John was afraid, as he confronted the thought that he was not himself, that something large had been dreaming him.

::*You have been retrieved from past information; your bodily form, such as it is, has been visualized to be as it was. What you are now remembers the past, even if what you are now is a duplication of an earlier self, an exact copy in everything except that it is a copy. Perhaps you are still your original pattern of complex awareness; I do not know, but that is not the central consideration. You might think it cruel to be brought back to such extreme finitude, to be small and powerless in your self; but I assure you that we may follow your will, because small, narrowly focused systems of past intelligent life were capable of what seem to us now as blind decisions of transcendent potential. What is convincing about this view is the fact that you were not called up entirely through our choice; you have been thrown up at a time when incapacity before death fragments macrolife*::

In the aggregate's containing silence, John wondered about the limits to the size of intelligence. After a point, the parts of a vast mind might begin to separate, as the being broke up into simpler components....

::*This is happening because we are again faced with the possibility of death. Many worlds have already fallen into forgetfulness, with no center of general remembrance; they no longer know who or what they are, and live as dreams in the self-maintaining structure, which provides objects for perception in an energy environment. In time we may disintegrate into billions*

of individual entities as the galactic core holes coalesce and natural history
accelerates toward its point of quantum uncertainty::

"Who are you?" John asked.

::I am one of the larger centers, a hyperpersonal aggregate of historical
individuals. As I acquired facets, I grew more complex, containing whole
worlds of awareness. Only a little while ago . . . I was larger. I know what is
happening, having served those who have fallen away. You were part of
me, and now you know also::

The aggregate sensed his confusion.

::Think of minds, individual bodies, both physical constructs and be-
ings of force, pure patterns of energy. Imagine a vast system of minds
within one macroworld, sustained by a central source of energy. Individ-
uals are facets, but they enter into larger, linked unions, which become
permanent, evolving into still greater minds as they join with other
macroworlds in a conscious design. Imagine large biological masses, teem-
ing with mind-linked individuals, cells of life as large as entire sunspaces::

He thought of warm lighted spaces, where the cold darkness was only
a distant thought; where the eye saw bright violets, blues, greens and yel-
lows, warm orange, and little else; where the universe was new. All gone,
all lost because he had forgotten. Countless joys and tragedies flying up
like sparks, discovering one another, loving, hating, passing . . .

He remembered wanting to witness final things.

Before him now lay the abyss separating all consciousness from the
end of time. Macrolife's spontaneous response to the problem of survival
was a process of fragmentation, a narrowing of perception in the manner
of the ancients who had put blinders on horses before leading them
through danger. Isolated centers of consciousness would revert to local
control; blind to billions of years of critical doubt, these centers of mind
would lead. Alone in a midnight universe of dying worlds, he knew what
had to be done. He did not want to die; therefore, any choice was better
than waiting for the final darkness. . . .

"Is there anyone else like me?" he asked. "Has anyone else re-
awakened?"

The screen showed another sudden star, another world dying after a
final moment of light.

::There is::

Space Stations and Space Habitats: A Selective Bibliography

GARY WESTFAHL

The following list is of novels and anthologies, stories, films and television programs, and nonfiction involving space stations, space habitats, generation starships, and artificial worlds. Fictional works were chosen if they featured an inhabited space structure as a major locale, or if they included unusual images of or ideas about space habitats. Some key stories appearing in cited anthologies are also listed separately. Occasional annotations briefly explain the special importance of a work, or note that a novel is one of several connected works about space habitats. Nonfictional works include a few books for general readers, more substantive contributions from visionaries like J. D. Bernal and Dandridge Cole, and a few pieces about space habitats in science fiction.

Novels and Anthologies

Aldiss, Brian W. *Non-Stop*. London: Faber, 1958.
Anderson, Poul. *Star Ways*. New York: Avalon, 1956.
Asimov, Isaac. *Nemesis*. New York: Doubleday, 1989.

Barnes, John. *Orbital Resonance.* New York: Tor, 1991.

Baxter, Stephen. *Raft.* New York: Penguin, 1992. Originally published in Great Britain in 1991; the first of four connected novels.

Bayley, Barrington J. *Collision Course.* New York: DAW, 1973.

Bear, Greg. *Eon.* New York: Bluejay, 1985. The first of three novels involving an asteroid spaceship.

Beliayev, Aleksandr. *The Struggle in Space.* Trans. Albert Parry. Washington, D. C.: Arfor, 1965. Original Russian language version published in the Soviet Union, 1927–1928.

Benford, Gregory. *Jupiter Project.* New York: Berkley, 1980, 1975. An earlier version appeared in *Amazing Science Fiction* in 1972.

Blish, James. *Cities in Flight.* New York: Avon, 1970. Omnibus of *They Shall Have Stars* (1957), *A Life for the Stars* (1963), *Earthman, Come Home* (1958), and *The Triumph of Time* (1958). The definitive portrait of flying cities in space.

Bova, Ben. *Colony.* New York: Pocket, 1978.

Brunner, John. *Sanctuary in the Sky.* New York: Ace, 1963.

Charbonneau, Louis. *Down to Earth.* London: H. Jenkins, 1967. Interesting depiction of a hollowed-out asteroid with holographic images of normal life.

Cherryh, C. J. [Carolyn Cherry]. *Downbelow Station.* New York: DAW, 1981. One of many Cherryh novels set in a future universe featuring large space stations.

Clarke, Arthur C. *The Fountains of Paradise.* 1978. New York: Ballantine, 1980. This and Charles Sheffield's *The Web between the Worlds* were the two pioneering depictions in science fiction of a space elevator.

———. *Islands in the Sky.* 1952. New York: Signet, 1960.

———. *Rendezvous with Rama.* 1973. New York: Ballantine, 1974. Followed by three sequels about a gigantic alien spacecraft written by Clarke and Gentry Lee.

———. *2001: A Space Odyssey.* Based on a screenplay by Stanley Kubrick and Clarke. New York: Signet, 1968.

Cooper, Edmund. *Seed of Light.* New York: Ballantine, 1959.

Dick, Philip K. *The Crack in Space.* New York: Ace, 1966. Originally published in shortened form as "Cantata 140" in *Magazine of Fantasy and Science Fiction,* 1964.

Forstchen, William R. *Into the Sea of Stars.* New York: Del Rey/
    Ballantine, 1986.
Gail, Otto. *The Stone from the Moon.* Trans. Francis Currier. *Science
    Wonder Quarterly* 1 (Spring, 1930): 294–359, 418–19. Originally
    published in Germany in 1926.
Gibson, William. *Neuromancer.* New York: Ace, 1982.
Gunn, James. *Station in Space.* New York: Bantam, 1958. An unusually
    critical analysis of human expansion into space.
Haldeman, Joe. *Worlds: A Novel of the Near Future.* 1981. New York:
    Pocket, 1982. The first novel in a trilogy featuring an Earth-orbiting
    space habitat.
Harrison, Harry. *Captive Universe.* New York: Putnam, 1969.
Heinlein, Robert A. *Citizen of the Galaxy.* New York: Scribner, 1957.
———. *Orphans in the Sky.* 1963. New York: Signet, 1965. Originally
    published as "Universe" and "Common Sense" in *Astounding
    Science-Fiction,* 1941. The classic generation starship adventure.
Lasswitz, Kurd. *Two Planets. (Auf zwei Planeten.)* Abridged by Erich
    Lasswitz. Trans. Hans H. Rudnick. Afterword by Mark Hillegas.
    Carbondale, Ill.: Southern Illinois University Press, 1971. Originally
    published in German in 1897. Martian invaders of Earth employ
    space stations over the poles as their bases.
Leiber, Fritz. *A Specter Is Haunting Texas.* New York: Walker, 1968. A
    future space-station resident, physiologically altered by life in space,
    visits Earth.
———. *The Wanderer.* New York: Ballantine, 1964.
Leinster, Murray. *The Wailing Asteroid.* 1960. New York: Avon, 1966.
Lesser, Milton. *The Star Seekers.* Philadelphia: Winston, 1953.
Long, Frank Belknap. *This Strange Tomorrow.* New York: Belmont,
    1966.
Lupoff, Richard A. *The Forever City.* New York: Walker, 1987. Features
    a haunting portrayal of the birth and death of a space habitat.
Munro, John. *A Trip to Venus.* London: Jarrold, 1897. Includes a
    prophetic conversation about building "artificial planets" in space.
Niven, Larry. *Ringworld.* New York: Ballantine, 1970. The first of three
    novels involving the huge artificial world.
Nourse, Alan E. *Scavengers in Space.* New York: McKay, 1959.
Panshin, Alexei. *Rite of Passage.* New York: Ace, 1968.

Pellegrino, Charles, and George Zebrowski. *The Killing Star.* New
    York: Avon, 1995.

Pohl, Frederik. *Gateway.* (Book 1 of the Heechee Saga.) 1977. New
    York: Del Rey/Ballantine, 1978. One of five novels featuring the
    Gateway asteroid.

Pournelle, Jerry, ed. *The Endless Frontier.* Vol. 1. New York: Ace,
    1979.

Pournelle, Jerry, with John F. Carr, eds. *The Endless Frontier.* Vol. 2.
    New York: Ace, 1982.

———. *Cities in Space: The Endless Frontier.* Vol. 3. New York: Ace,
    1991.

Reynolds, Mack. *Chaos in Lagrangia.* Ed. Dean Ing. New York: Tor,
    1984.

———. *Satellite City.* New York: Ace, 1975.

Reynolds, Mack, with Dean Ing. *Trojan Orbit.* New York: Baen, 1985. A
    powerful critique of overly optimistic projections of space habitats.

Robinson, Frank. *The Dark beyond the Stars.* New York: Tor, 1991.

Sargent, Pamela. *Earthseed.* New York: Harper, 1983.

———. *Watchstar.* New York: Pocket, 1980. First novel in a trilogy in
    which humanity has made a habitat of a comet.

Scortia, Thomas M. *Earthwreck!* New York: Fawcett Gold Medal, 1974.

Shaw, Bob. *Orbitsville.* New York: Ace, 1975. Novel about an immense
    Dyson sphere.

Sheffield, Charles. *Between the Strokes of Night.* New York: Baen, 1985.

———. *The Web between the Worlds.* New York: Ace, 1979.

Shwartz, Susan, ed. *Habitats.* New York: DAW, 1984.

Silverberg, Robert (as Ivar Jorgenson). *Starhaven.* New York: Avalon,
    1958.

Silverberg, Robert. *World's Fair, 1992.* 1970. New York: Ace, 1982.

Smith, George O. *Venus Equilateral.* Introduction by John W.
    Campbell, Jr. New York: Prime, 1947. Originally published in
    Astounding Science Fiction in 1942, 1943, 1944, and 1945. The first
    prominent space station in modern science fiction.

Steele, Allen. *Clarke County, Space.* New York: Ace, 1990.

Sterling, Bruce. *Schismatrix Plus.* New York: Ace, 1997. Incorporates
    Schismatrix, first published in 1985, and several related stories about
    a future universe featuring space habitats.

Suchariktul, Somtow (S. P. Somtow). *Mallworld.* 1981. New York: Tor,

1984. Portions of the novel appeared as stories in 1979, 1980, and 1981.

Swanwick, Michael. *Vacuum Flowers.* 1987. New York: Ace, 1988.

Tsiolkovsky, Konstantin. *Beyond the Planet Earth.* Trans. V. Talmy. In *The Call of the Cosmos.* By Tsiolkovsky. Ed. V. Dutt. Moscow: Foreign Languages Publishing House, 1960. 161–332. Original Russian language version published in the Soviet Union, 1920. This didactic but fascinating novel introduces many major ideas about future human life in space.

Tubb, E. C. *The Space Born.* New York: Ace, 1956.

Varley, John. *Titan.* 1979. New York: Berkley, 1980. First novel in a trilogy about an immense artificial world.

Vinge, Joan. *The Outcasts of Heaven Belt.* New York: New American Library, 1978.

Walsh, J. M. *Vandals of the Void. Wonder Stories Quarterly* 2 (Summer, 1931): 438–513.

Watkins, William John. *The Centrifugal Rickshaw Dancer.* New York: Popular Library, 1985.

White, James. *Hospital Station.* New York: Ballantine, 1985, 1962. One of several novels featuring the immense Sector General space hospital, perhaps the best known and best developed space habitat in science fiction.

Zebrowski, George. *Macrolife.* New York: Harper, 1979.

———. *The Sunspacers Trilogy.* Clarkston, GA: White Wolf/Borealis, 1996.

Short Stories

Asimov, Isaac. "Strikebreaker." *Isaac Asimov: The Complete Stories.* Vol. 1. New York: Doubleday, 1990. Originally published in *Original Science Fiction Stories,* January 1957.

Ballard, J. G. "Report on an Unidentified Space Station." *Semiotext(e) SF.* Ed. Rudy Rucker, Peter Lambert Wilson, and Robert Anton Wilson. New York: Semiotext(e), 1989. 135–39.

———. "Thirteen for Centaurus." *The Best Short Stories of J. G. Ballard.* New York: Holt, Rinehart, and Winston, 1978. Originally published in *Amazing Stories,* April 1962.

Benford, Gregory. "Dark Sanctuary." *The Endless Frontier.* Vol. 1
  285–99.
Clarke, Arthur C. "Death and the Senator." *Tales of Ten Worlds.* By
  Clarke. New York: Harcourt, 1962. 115–40. Originally published in
  1961.
Clement, Hal (Harry Clement Stubbs). "Answer." *The Best of Hal
  Clement.* Ed. Lester del Rey. New York: Ballantine, 1979. 147–71.
  Originally published in 1947.
Fritch, Charles E. "Many Dreams of Earth." *Orbit Science Fiction* 1
  (Nov./Dec., 1954): 98–107.
Haldeman, Joe. "Tricentennial." *The Endless Frontier.* Vol. 1. 96–121.
  Originally published in *Analog Science Fiction/Science Fact,* 1976.
Hale, Edward Everett. "The Brick Moon." *His Level Best and Other
  Stories.* By Hale. New York: Garrett, 1872. 30–124. Originally
  published in two parts as "The Brick Moon" and "Life on the Brick
  Moon" in *Atlantic Monthly,* 1869 and 1870. The first story about an
  artificial habitation in space.
Hamilton, Edmond. "Space Mirror." *Thrilling Wonder Stories* 10
  (August, 1937): 43–51.
Heinlein, Robert A. "Blowups Happen." *Expanded Universe: The New
  Worlds of Robert A. Heinlein.* New York: Ace, 1980. 35–90.
  Originally published in *Astounding Science-Fiction,* 1940.
———. "Delilah and the Space Rigger." *The Green Hills of Earth.* By
  Heinlein. 1951. New York: Signet, 1952. 13–23. Originally published
  in *Blue Book,* 1949.
———. "Misfit." *Revolt in 2100.* By Heinlein. New York: Signet, 1953.
  170–88. Originally published in *Astounding Science-Fiction,* 1939.
  An early story about converting an asteroid into a space habitat.
———. "Waldo." *Waldo and Magic, Inc.* By Heinlein. 1950. New York:
  Pyramid, 1963. 9–103. Originally published in *Astounding Science-
  Fiction,* 1942.
Ing, Dean. "Down & Out on Ellfive Prime." *The Endless Frontier.*
  Vol. 2. 97–123. Originally published in *Omni,* 1980.
Kingsbury, Donald. "To Bring in the Steel." *The Endless Frontier.*
  Vol. 1. 197–252. Originally published in *Analog Science Fiction/
  Science Fact,* 1978.
Knight, Damon. "Stranger Station." *SF: The Best of the Best.* Ed. Judith

Merril. 1967. New York: Dell, 1968. 143–68. Originally published in 1959. Compelling account of an alien encounter on a space station.

Leinster, Murray. "The Power Planet." *Amazing Stories* 6 (June, 1931): 198–217, 227. The first major depiction of a space station designed to harness solar power and beam it to Earth.

McIntosh, J. T. (James Murdoch MacGregor). "Hallucination Orbit." *Galaxy* 3 (January, 1952): 132–58.

Moore, C. L. "Judgment Night." *Judgment Night.* By Moore. New York: Gnome, 1952. 3–156. Originally published in two parts in *Astounding Science-Fiction*, 1943. Features a beautiful artificial "pleasure world."

Nicholson, Sam (Shirley Nikolaisen). "He Who Fights and Runs Away." *Analog Science Fiction/Science Fact* 102 (1982): 18–50.

Niven, Larry, and Jerry Pournelle. "Spirals." *The Endless Frontier.* Vol. 1. 27–83. Originally published in *Destinies*, 1979.

Oliver, Chad. "Ghost Town." *Cities in Space: The Endless Frontier.* Vol. 3. 163–85. Originally published in *Analog Science Fiction/ Science Fact*, 1983.

———. "Meanwhile, Back on the Reservation." *Analog Science Fiction/Science Fact* 51 (1981): 86–101.

Pollack, Rachel. "Tree House." *Habitats.* 122–41.

Pratt, Fletcher. "Project Excelsior." *Double in Space.* By Pratt. New York: Doubleday, 1951. 9–113. Originally published as "Asylum Satellite" in *Thrilling Wonder Stories*, Nov. 1951.

Rich, H. Thompson. "The Flying City." *Astounding Stories of Super-Science* 3 (August, 1930): 260–78.

Scortia, Thomas N. "Sea Change." *Astounding Science Fiction* 57 (June, 1956): 130–40.

Shaw, Bob. "Small World." *The Penguin World Omnibus of Science Fiction.* Ed. Brian Aldiss and Sam J. Lundwall. Middlesex, England: Penguin, 1986. 63–77. Originally published in 1978.

Sheffield, Charles. "All the Colors of the Vacuum." *Analog Science Fiction/Science Fact* 101 (1981): 60–86.

Smith, Everett C. (plot) and R. F. Starzl (story). "The Metal Moon." *Wonder Stories Quarterly* 3 (Winter, 1932): 246–59.

Tucker, Wilson (Arthur W. Tucker). "Interstellar Way-Station." *Super Science Stories* (May, 1941): 94–101.

Vance, Jack. "Abercrombie Station." *Thrilling Wonder Stories* 39. 3 (February, 1952): 10–47.

Van Vogt, A. E. "Concealment." *Science Fiction Monsters*. By van Vogt. Ed. And with an introduction by Forrest J. Ackerman. New York: Paperback Library, 1967, 1965. 80–92. Originally published in *Astounding Science-Fiction*, 1943.

Williamson, Jack. "Born of the Sun." *Before the Golden Age: A Science Fiction Anthology of the 1930s*. Ed. Isaac Asimov. Garden City, N.Y.: Doubleday, 1974. 461–95. Originally published in 1934.

——. "Crucible of Power." *Astounding Science-Fiction* 22 (February, 1939): 9–32.

——. "Dead Star Station." *The Early Williamson*. Garden City, N.Y.: Doubleday, 1975. 178–99. Originally published in *Astounding Stories*, 1933.

——. "The Prince of Space." *Amazing Stories* 6 (January, 1931): 870–95. The first depiction of a true space habitat in science fiction.

Films and Television Programs

Android. New World/Android Productions, 1982.

"The Ark in Space." *Doctor Who*. London: BBC-TV, 1-25-75 through 2-15-75. Four-part episode.

Babylon 5. Los Angeles: KCOP, 2-25-93. Television movie; pilot for the long-running series of that name featuring a large space station.

Conquest of Space. Paramount Pictures, 1956.

Earth 2. Metro-Goldwyn-Mayer, 1971. Television movie, unsold series pilot.

"Emissary." *Star Trek: Deep Space Nine*. Los Angeles: KCOP, 1-5-93. First episode of long-running series featuring the titular space station.

"For the World Is Hollow and I Have Touched the Sky." *Star Trek*. Los Angeles: NBC, 11-8-68.

Men into Space. New York: CBS, 9-30-59 through 9-7-60. Television series which included the building of a space station.

Prisoners of Gravity. Ontario, Canada: TVOntario, 1990–94. Weekly talk show set on a fictional space station.

Project Moonbase. Galaxy Pictures, 1953. Cowritten by Heinlein, this film probably offers the first space station depicted on film.

Silent Running. Universal/Michael Gruskoff Productions/ Douglas Trumbull Productions, 1971.

The Starlost. Syndicated Canadian television series, 1973–74.

Star Wars. Lucasfilm/Fox, 1977.

2001: A Space Odyssey. Metro-Goldwyn-Mayer, 1968.

"The Wheel in Space." *Doctor Who*. London: BBC-TV, 4-17-68 through 6-1-68. Six-part episode.

Nonfiction

Bernal, J. D. *The World, the Flesh, and the Devil*. New York: Dutton, 1929.

Berry, Adrian. *The Next Ten Thousand Years: A Vision of Man's Future in the Universe*. New York: New American Library, 1974. The possibilities Berry discusses include the construction of Dyson spheres.

Bizony, Piers. *Island in the Sky*. Aurum, 1996.

Bova, Ben. *The High Road*. New York: Pocket, 1983, 1981.

Clarke, Arthur C. *Profiles of the Future*. 1984. New York: Warner, 1985.

Cole, Dandridge M. *Beyond Tomorrow: The Next 50 Years in Space*. Amherst, Wis.: Amherst, 1965.

Cole, Dandridge M., and Donald W. Cox. *Islands in Space: The Challenge of the Planetoids*. Foreword by Willy Ley. Philadelphia: Chilton, 1964.

Dyson, Freeman. *Disturbing the Universe*. New York: Harper, 1979.

Finney, Ben R., and Eric M. Jones. *Interstellar Migration and the Human Experience*. Berkeley: University of California Press, 1985.

Gernsback, Hugo. "Stations in Space." *Air Wonder Stories* 1 (April, 1930): 869.

Gilfillan, Edward S., Jr. *Migration to the Stars: Never Again Enough People*. Washington, D.C.: Luce, 1975.

Harrison, Harry. *Spacecraft in Fact and Fiction*. Baltimore, Md.: Octopus, 1980.

Hartmann, William K., Ron Miller, and Pamela Lee. *Out of the Cradle: Exploring the Frontiers beyond Earth*. New York: Workman, 1984.

Heppenheimer, T. A. *Colonies in Space.* New York: Warner, 1977.

Moskowitz, Sam. "The Real Earth Satellite Story." *Explorers of the Infinite: Shapers of Science Fiction.* Cleveland: World Publishing, 1963, 88–105.

Nicholls, Peter. "Space Habitats." *The Encyclopedia of Science Fiction.* Ed. John Clute and Peter Nicholls. New York: St. Martin's, 1993. 1136–37.

Oberg, James E., and Alcestis R. Oberg. *Pioneering Space: Living on the Next Frontier.* Foreword by Isaac Asimov. New York: McGraw-Hill, 1986.

O'Neill, Gerard. *The High Frontier: Human Colonies in Space.* 1977. New York: Bantam, 1978. A persuasive picture of space habitats that had a strong influence on science fiction.

Savage, Marshall T. *The Millennial Project: Colonizing the Galaxy in Eight Easy Steps.* Introduction by Arthur C. Clarke. Boston: Little, Brown, 1994.

Spinrad, Norman. "Dreams of Space." *Science Fiction in the Real World.* Carbondale, Ill.: Southern Illinois University Press, 1990. 122–35. Originally published in *Isaac Asimov's Science Fiction Magazine*, 1987. Incisive analysis of the philosophy underlying science fiction stories about space habitats.

Stine, G. Harry. *The Space Enterprise.* New York: Ace, 1980.

———. *The Third Industrial Revolution.* New York: Ace, 1975.

Tsiolkovsky, Konstantin. *The Call of the Cosmos.* Moscow: Foreign Languages Publishing House, 1960. Includes several essays and a few pieces of fiction.

Westfahl, Gary. *Islands in the Sky: The Space Station Theme in Science Fiction Literature.* Preface by Gregory Benford. San Bernardino, Calif.: Borgo, 1996.

Zubrin, Robert, and Stanley Schmidt, eds. *Islands in the Sky: Bold New Ideas for Colonizing Space—From the Supersonic Skyhook to the Negative Matter Space Drive.* London: Wiley, 1996.

About the Authors

Isaac Asimov was one of the most popular and beloved writers of science fiction, as well as a prolific writer of books and essays that enlightened countless readers about the sciences. Born in Russia in 1920, he emigrated with his family to the United States in 1923, grew up in New York City, and earned his PhD at Columbia University. Among his honors were several Hugo Awards, the Grand Master Nebula Award, and the American Association of Science/Westinghouse Science Writing Award. His classic science fiction novels and story collections include *The Foundation Trilogy*; *The Caves of Steel*; *The Naked Sun*; *I, Robot*; *The Martian Way and Other Stories*; *The Gods Themselves*; *Nightfall and Other Stories*; *Foundation's Edge*; *The Robots of Dawn*; *Robots and Empire*; and *Forward the Foundation*. He died in 1992, in New York City, where he lived for most of his life.

Stephen Baxter grew up in Liverpool, England, holds a degree in mathematics from Cambridge University and a doctorate from Southampton University, and published his first novel, *Raft*, in 1991. His other novels include *Timelike Infinity, Flux, Anti-Ice, Ring*, and *Voyage*. He is already regarded as one of the finest of the new British writers of science fiction, and was honored with the John W. Campbell Award for his novel *The Time Ships,* a sequel to H. G. Wells's classic *The Time Machine.* Baxter has also been shortlisted for the Arthur C. Clarke Award and has been a Hugo Award finalist.

Greg Bear published his first science fiction story while still in his teens, and established himself as one of the most important of contemporary science fiction writers during the 1980s. Among his most important novels are *Blood Music, Eon, The Forge of God, Eternity, Queen of Angels,* and *Moving Mars.* Some of his best short fiction can be found in his collections *Tangents* and *The Wind from a Burning Woman.* A winner of both the Nebula and Hugo Awards, he lives near Seattle, Washington.

James Blish was one of science fiction's most erudite writers. He earned a degree in microbiology from Rutgers University, published papers on the works of Ezra Pound and James Joyce, edited a scholarly magazine devoted to James Branch Cabell, and pursued interests ranging from music to physics. His *Cities in Flight* sequence, of which "Bindlestiff" is a part, was partly modeled on the historical writings of Oswald Spengler. His books include *Jack of Eagles, Titan's Daughter, The Seedling Stars, Midsummer Century, Doctor Mirabilis, Black Easter,* and *A Case of Conscience,* for which he won a Hugo Award. He emigrated to England in 1969 and died there in 1975.

Ray Bradbury is one of the most visible and critically successful of all science fiction writers, reaching a wide audience with his carefully wrought and humanistic tales. Among his celebrated works are *Fahrenheit 451, The Martian Chronicles, The Illustrated Man, The October Country, Something Wicked This Way Comes,* and *The Golden Apples of the Sun.* Many of his works have been adapted for film and television, and he has been honored with the Grand Master Nebula Award and the Bram Stoker Lifetime Achievement Award. His recent novels include *Death Is a Lonely Business, A Graveyard for Lunatics,* and *Green Shadows, White Whale.* He lives in Los Angeles, California.

David Brin, a graduate of the California Institute of Technology, holds degrees in astronomy and applied physics and published his first novel,

Sundiver, in 1980; he quickly became one of the most popular of the new writers of the 1980s. He has won the Nebula Award, the Hugo Award, and the John W. Campbell Memorial Award. His novels include *Startide Rising, The Postman, The Uplift War, Earth, Glory Season, Brightness Reef,* and *Infinity's Shore,* and he also collaborated with Gregory Benford on *Heart of the Comet.* He makes his home in California.

Sir Arthur C. Clarke became one of the most renowned science fiction writers in the world after the release of *2001: A Space Odyssey,* the Stanley Kubrick film based on Clarke's writings. He is also known as "the father of the communications satellite," and his science fiction is noted for its grounding in reality and genuine possibility. Among his most admired and loved works are *The Sands of Mars, Against the Fall of Night, Childhood's End, Rendezvous with Rama,* and *The Songs of Distant Earth.* He has received many honors for his fiction and nonfiction, among them Nebula Awards, Hugo Awards, the UNESCO Kalinga Prize, the NASA Distinguished Public Service Medal, and the American Institute of Aeronautics and Astronautics Award, and has even been nominated for a Nobel Peace Prize. He lives in Columbo, Sri Lanka.

James Patrick Kelly has had an eclectic writing career: novels, short stories, essays, reviews, poetry, plays, planetarium shows, and, most recently, a column on the Internet for *Asimov's Science Fiction.* His books include *Think like a Dinosaur and Other Stories, Wildlife, Heroines, Look into the Sun, Freedom Beach,* and *Planet of Whispers.* His stories have been translated into eleven languages. In 1996 he won a Hugo Award for his novelette "Think like a Dinosaur." He lives in New Hampshire.

Paul J. McAuley is a critically acclaimed British writer who won the Philip K. Dick Award in 1989 for his first novel, *Four Hundred Billion Stars.* He has a PhD in botany from Bristol University; his training in biology, combined with inventive detail, are on display in his novel *Fairyland,* which received the John W. Campbell Award in 1997. His other novels include *Of the Fall, Eternal Light, Red Dust,* and *Pasquale's Angel.*

Larry Niven published his first story in 1964. By 1971 he had won five Hugo Awards, a Nebula Award, and had established himself as one of the leading writers of hard science fiction with his inventive and ambitious novel *Ringworld*. His other book-length works include *World of Ptavvs, Protector, The Ringworld Engineers, Neutron Star, All the Myriad Ways, The Integral Trees,* and *Tales of Known Space*. With Jerry Pournelle, he is the author of *The Mote in God's Eye, Lucifer's Hammer, Oath of Fealty,* and *Footfall*. Niven's other books include collaborations with David Gerrold, Steven Barnes, Poul Anderson, and Dean Ing. Born in Los Angeles, he makes his home in southern California.

Joan D. Vinge has been honored with two Hugo Awards, one of them for her epic novel *The Snow Queen;* two more novels, *World's End* and *The Summer Queen,* are part of the Snow Queen sequence. Her other books include *The Heaven Chronicles, Eyes of Amber and Other Stories,* and *Phoenix in the Ashes. Psion, Catspaw,* and *Dreamfall* are novels featuring her character Cat. She has a degree in anthropology from San Diego State University, has worked as a salvage archaeologist, and now lives in Madison, Wisconsin.

Gary Westfahl received his BA in mathematics and English from Carleton College and his PhD in English from Claremont Graduate School. He is the author of *Islands in the Sky: The Space Station Theme in Science Fiction Literature* and has published many articles, essays, and reviews. He teaches reading at the Learning Center of the University of California at Riverside and mathematics classes for the University of LaVerne's Educational Programs in Corrections.

Don Wilcox was the pseudonym of Cleo Eldon Knox, a writer who also taught creative writing at Northwestern University. His first short story came out in 1939; much of his work appeared in *Fantastic Adventures* and *Amazing Stories* during the 1940s. "The Voyage That Lasted Six Hundred Years" was first published in 1940.

About the Artists

Chesley Bonestell, born in 1888, was trained as an architect and later became one of the film industry's most successful matte and special effects artists, working on such movies as *Citizen Kane, Destination Moon, When Worlds Collide,* and *Forbidden Planet.* His space paintings, noted for their realism and careful attention to scale and perspective, always conformed to the science of the day. Portfolios of his work appeared in *Life,* in the popular 1950s weekly *Colliers,* and on the covers of the science fiction magazines *Astounding* and *Fantasy and Science Fiction.* His paintings inspired many scientists, writers, and other artists fascinated by the exploration of space, and he lived to see manned space flight himself, dying in 1986 at the age of ninety-eight. Regarded today as a major American painter, he has been described as our solar system's prophetic regionalist.

Don Davis, a painter and animator born in 1952, has no formal art training but was influenced and advised by Chesley Bonestell. His first published work, a painting of the *Apollo 11* landing, was published by the

San Francisco Chronicle while he was still in high school and also working for the United States Geological Survey as a scientific illustrator. He did paintings for NASA, working on the *Viking* project and space colonization. Since then, his work has appeared in Carl Sagan's books *Cosmos, Pale Blue Dot,* and *The Dragons of Eden,* and in numerous issues of the magazines *Parade* and *Sky and Telescope.* He won an Emmy for his work on the PBS television series *Cosmos,* later worked for the Hansen Planetarium and on visual effects for various PBS television programs, and now creates art and animations for television and for video projection planetarium facilities.

Bob Eggleton was born in 1960. Among the influences he cites are *2001: A Space Odyssey, Star Trek, Godzilla,* and dinosaurs. He is a science fiction, fantasy, and horror artist who does cover paintings for books and magazines. He has also worked on comic books. He has received eight Chesley Awards, four Hugo Awards, and the Skylark Award, and has been a finalist for the World Fantasy Award. Two art books of his work, *Alien Horizons* and *The Book of Sea Monsters,* were published by Paper Tiger; a third book, *Greetings from Earth,* will be out in 2000.

Frank R. Paul was born in Austria in 1884. He was trained as an architect, studying in Vienna, Paris, and New York. He was closely associated with legendary science fiction editor Hugo Gernsback, who discovered him in 1914. Paul was the primary illustrator for Gernsback's pulp magazine *Amazing Stories.* His cover illustrations and interior artwork also appeared in *Science Wonder Stories, Air Wonder Stories, Science Fiction Plus,* and many other magazines. The bright and strong primary colors he used greatly influenced the style of other pulp artists, and he was guest of honor at the first World Science Fiction Convention in 1939. He died in 1963.

Alex Schomburg, born in 1905 in Puerto Rico, moved to New York City after World War I, setting up a studio there with his three brothers. This self-taught artist's first magazine cover was done for Hugo Gernsback's magazine *Science and Invention,* and he continued to do magazine covers into the 1980s, with his work appearing on the covers of *Amazing Stories, Fantasy and Science Fiction, Fantastic,* and *Isaac Asimov's Science*

Fiction Magazine. He has also painted book covers; was a comics artist and illustrator, where he helped develop Captain America; and also worked on Stanley Kubrick's *2001: A Space Odyssey.* Among Schomburg's honors are the Lensman Award, the Frank R. Paul Award, and a Special Hugo Award for Lifetime Achievement in Science Fiction Art.

Solonevich is a mysterious figure among science-fiction painters. Scant biographical information seems to be available. He is eighty-four and reportedly still painting. His credits include illustrations for the 1959 children's books *Planets, The Golden Book of Atomic Energy, The Golden Book of Space Travel,* and *The Moon,* all by Otto O. Binder. He did advertising work in both Europe and the United States. The painting for James Blish's novel in this book appears to be the only one Solonevich ever did in the science fiction genre, but this work has been singled out several times, when many more prolific artists are neglected. John W. Campbell, the editor of *Analog,* published good art wherever he could, and this illustration was the only one he ever accepted from Solonevich. We are fortunate to have this very beautiful rendering of James Blish's idea of the spindizzy field, which lofts an entire city into space while protecting it with its gauzy field.

About the Editors

Gregory Benford was born in Mobile, Alabama, and earned his PhD in physics from the University of California at San Diego. He is a professor of physics at the University of California at Irvine and has published well over a hundred papers. He is a Woodrow Wilson Fellow, a visiting professor at Cambridge University, and has served as an advisor to the Department of Energy, NASA, and the White House Council on Space Policy. He is also a critically acclaimed author of science fiction. Among his best-known novels are *Timescape*, which won the Nebula Award and the John W. Campbell Memorial Award, and the Galactic Center series, which includes *In the Ocean of Night*, *Across the Sea of Suns*, *Great Sky River*, *Tides of Light*, *Furious Gulf*, and *Sailing Bright Eternity*. His short-story collections include *In Alien Flesh* and *Matter's End*, and he has edited several anthologies. He lives in Laguna Beach, California.

George Zebrowski was born in Villach, Austria, and grew up in England, Italy, Miami, and New York City. He holds a degree in philosophy from the State University of New York at Binghamton, where he taught one of the first full-credit course in science fiction. Among his novels are

The Omega Point Trilogy, Macrolife, The Sunspacers Trilogy, and *Stranger Suns,* which was a New York Times Notable Book of the Year for 1991. With scientist-author Charles Pellegrino, Zebrowski collaborated on the highly praised novel *The Killing Star.* His short fiction, collected in *The Monadic Universe,* has been nominated for the Nebula Award and the Theodore Sturgeon Memorial Award. *Brute Orbits,* a novel about the future of the penal system, received the John W. Campbell Memorial Award for Best Science Fiction Novel of 1998. His new novel is *Cave of Stars,* a companion to *Macrolife.* He is also a noted editor and anthologist; among his anthologies are the *Synergy* series: *Faster than Light* (edited with Jack Dann), *Human-Machines* (edited with Thomas N. Scortia), and *Creations* (edited with Isaac Asimov and Martin H. Greenberg). He lives near Albany, New York.

Permissions
Acknowledgments

Artwork Permissions Acknowledgments